HOLY SMOKE

HELLBOUND BOOK ONE

GIN GRIFFITH

harbor lane books

ISBN: 979-8-9890320-2-0

Cover design: Clarissa Kezen ckbookcoverdesigns.com

Published in the United States of America by Harbor Lane Books, LLC.

www.harborlanebooks.com

Hey, you.

Yeah, you. Reading this.
You know that dream you have? The one you've been putting off?
The one you've been telling yourself you can't do?

Go fucking do it.

I did—you're holding it in your hands.

Thank you.

Now go grab a beverage, settle in, and enjoy the ride!

- Gin

CHAPTER 1

This little firebug was pissing him off.

Nash Rogan narrowed his eyes at the pink-haired pyromage sitting across from him. She quirked a brow and crossed her legs, revealing a whole lot of sleek, pale thigh. A black combat boot bounced irritably.

"What is your name?" Rogan repeated.

"Who wants to know?" Her voice was high, clear. Cartoonish. It should not have been sexy.

She blew an enormous bubble with her purple chewing gum. It popped. A fake grape scent drifted across the desk. She smiled.

Rogan ground his molars. "As I said, my name is Agent Rogan. But we're talking about you. And how you just set someone on fire."

Pale blue eyes flashed. She leaned forward and stabbed a finger at him. "That asshole put his hands on me. I told him to back off, and he didn't." She hesitated. "But I am sorry." She relaxed deliberately back in her chair. The lines of her body softened, melting into a series of lush curves. She caught her lower lip briefly between her teeth. Lashes fanned high cheekbones. "It won't happen again."

She was good.

"I'm sure." Rogan studied her. Luminous skin, sharp, dainty features, all that bubblegum pink hair falling to a small waist. Nobody looked good under these harsh overhead lights, but this little mage shone like a damn pearl. "Look, I saw what happened. It was self-defense." Lucky for her, he'd been walking past that alley at precisely the right moment. He'd heard her protests, saw the guy's meaty frame cornering her against the brick wall. Right before she'd lit him up like a bonfire. "And you didn't kill him. He's badly burned, but he'll live."

"Great. So, can I go?"

Full of remorse, wasn't she? Rogan looked pointedly at her left wrist. "Where's your trackband?"

She folded her arms.

Right. Rogan came around the desk and gently grasped her elbow. Ignoring her spluttered protests and the fact that her skin felt like heated silk beneath his fingers, he steered her firmly out of the interrogation room.

Magical Law Enforcement was a hive of activity, even at this hour. Agents bustled back and forth, their royal blue uniforms vivid against the bright white corridor. The glowing blue threads of Vortech security wires ran the length of the walls, pulsing gently. MLE headquarters was famous for its marriage of magic and human tech.

Rogan led his little captive past the holding cells, ignoring the catcalls of the junkies and drunks. "You'll be fitted with a standard-issue MLE trackband registered to your name. If you refuse to provide one, you'll be registered as Jane Doe." It had been a while since he'd brought in an unregistered mage, but the script flowed effortlessly. "Should you perform aggressive magic, your trackband will alert authorities, at which time MLE agents will arrive on scene. You will be charged in accordance with the severity of the offense." He nodded at another agent, who leaped aside as they passed.

Near the end of the hall, a glass door labeled Registration came into view. The pyromage spotted it and planted her boots on the shiny white tile, causing Rogan to bump into her tight little backside. He jerked his hips back, gritted his teeth, and pushed her through the door.

A harried female agent glanced up from a monitor. "Agent Rogan." She hurried to stand, smoothing her uniform, her hair. "What can I do for you, sir?"

"Unregistered magical female." Rogan flicked a glance at the pyromage. "Are you a shapeshifter?" Shifter-mage hybrids were rare, but not unheard of.

"No," she snapped. "I—"

"Fire abilities," Rogan continued to the clerical agent. "Level...five." He raised his brows at the pyromage. "Name? Last chance." He watched her gaze dart wildly around the room, looking for an escape. He gripped her arm tighter. "Name refused."

"Jane Doe 0130, registered magical female, pyromage, level five." The clerical agent smacked a button on her keyboard. A tiny chute opened in the wall beside her desk, and a narrow silver cuff tumbled out. The agent ran it under a scanner, waited for a beep, then handed it over.

Before she could protest, he slid the trackband around the pyromage's slender wrist and watched its ends meld together. When a tiny green light appeared in the metal, Rogan released her arm.

She stared at her wrist in shock. "*Fuck*," she whispered.

She was obviously into some shit. Criminals...Blitz deal-ers, maybe. Hell, with those looks and that body, she could be one of the top-dollar escorts down at the Pyramid casino. Whatever she was mixed up in, she'd managed to avoid a trackband this long. That didn't surprise him half as much as the flash of panic in her eyes.

She wasn't just pissed. She was scared.

Rogan gave himself a mental shake. Not his problem.

Mage, trackband—that's how it worked. And someone like her, with blow torches built into her palms, needed to have some accountability.

He guided the pyromage back into the corridor and down the hall toward the main entrance. His presence on the floor caused a lot of raised brows and hushed whispers, and his captive's presence caused a lot of goddamn unprofessional gawking. He almost told a couple of the rookies to put their tongues back in their mouths.

Rogan held the door for her when they reached the lobby. Her scent washed over him as she shoved past—sweet, warm, with a hint of fire. Torched sugar. Cotton candy and a match.

Something stirred inside him, something primal and male and very inconvenient. He smothered it.

"Ms. Doe," he called out as she hit the bustling Friday night sidewalk.

She whirled, pink hair flying. The dark street was alive with flickering billboards, neon signs, and glowing green trackband dots. Somehow, she outshone it all, standing there with her fists clenched while the crowd parted around her.

"Don't try to remove it. Don't try to destroy it. These trackbands have built-in security measures. You *will* regret it."

Her eyes glinted like shards of glass. She flipped him off with both hands, stuck her tongue out, and stalked into the night.

A vibration on his wrist made him tear his gaze from her flouncing skirt. A text from his squad mate had come through on his watch. *Heading to Fifth and Vine. Feeling frisky tonight.*

If Wolf was 'feeling frisky', patrol was going to be a bloodbath. *On my way. Be professional.*

Wolf's professional response included two icons, an eggplant and a splash.

Glowering, Rogan took off at a swift clip.

CHAPTER 2

Jovi was fucked.

She kicked a soda can and scowled at her new jewelry, cold and heavy on her wrist.

And she'd thought she was in a world of shit before.

Stupid asshole frat boy, cornering her in that alley. Stupid MLE with their stupid trackbands. Stupid Agent Observant coming along at the worst effing time.

Well, maybe not the absolute worst time. At least this way, he thought she was just some pyromage. If he'd stumbled across her earlier that night, he might've caught her torching that demon in the alley. Not that he would've known what she was barbequing—these topsiders couldn't see the demons that popped up all over their city.

Except her, of course. They saw her just fine. Apparently, succubi were different.

Usually, that worked in her favor, but Agent Rogan was evidently immune to her charms. She should've tried harder. Lifted her skirt higher, pulled her neckline lower, rubbed up against him a little. She might've even enjoyed it—the man was stupid hot. All that tight muscle poured into black clothes, that closely cropped dark hair, that granite jaw. And those lips…ridiculously full, beautifully shaped, almost better looking than hers. Too bad he was such a stick in the mud.

Jovi kicked at another piece of trash and felt a sting on her thigh. She twisted around and cursed. Blood oozed from the cut she'd gotten earlier, when that demon had taken a slice out of her. He'd been a big one, with four beefy arms, major body odor, and a pair of tusks he shouldn't have been able to talk around.

But he had.

"She'll be so happy to have you home."

Jovi chewed her lip as she walked, insides squirming. There could only be one *she*.

Her mother.

And apparently, Mommy Dearest didn't just want her amulet back, she wanted Jovi, too.

Her combat boots hurried over the neon-lit sidewalk. She needed to get back to her apartment, lay eyes on the amulet, make sure it was still safe. And then, she could curl up under a blanket with a bottle of vodka and a loaded bazooka.

If anyone tried to drag her back to hell, she'd blow their face off.

The city streets went suddenly fuzzy. Jovi blinked them back into focus, shaking her head. She needed to eat. Torching that drunk idiot had really taken it out of her. Her stamina was shit up here—one blast of her hellfire and she went weak as a kitten. So annoying. It was maybe the one thing she missed about hell. Down in the pit, she could throw flames for hours without tiring.

And she had. Whether she wanted to or not.

She followed her nose to the row of food trucks at the curb, waited until the doughnut vendor wasn't looking, and snagged a cinnamon churro from his counter before strolling off. He didn't notice. They rarely did.

The crispy treat practically melted on her tongue. Jovi moaned, weaving through the crowded sidewalk, licking sugar from her lips. The Blender district was smack in the middle of downtown, and busy as always on a Friday night. Magic supply shops were crammed next to tech boutiques, a twenty-four-hour shapeshifter diner that advertised prime cuts of raw meat, and the Sip n' Spell Café on the corner that offered enchanted lattes. An apothecary window flashed with tiny, silent fireworks. She stopped to watch, munching her churro, and caught her eyes in the reflection.

Big, uptilted, and a clear, pale blue. The rest of her might look like Mommy Dearest, but not her eyes. Those, she liked to hope, were from her father.

"Noble, valiant Alistor, wandering the city like a vagrant." It was her mother's favorite amusement, mocking the man Jovi had never known. Even now, she could hear the smirk in Inara's low voice, could see her sitting on that bone throne, perfect feet propped on the amulet's glass case, sipping dark wine while the screams of the damned echoed off the walls. While Jovi stood nearby, wanting nothing more than to rip her dad's amulet from that bitch's sadistic claws.

So she could prove that she was his. Not if, but *when* she found him.

Noble, valiant Alistor. Who was he? What was he? Something…nice? Something good? Maybe that would explain why she'd always hated what went down in her mother's den.

Mommy Dearest must have absolutely lost her mind when she realized the amulet was gone. She loved that thing. What she didn't love was the disappointing daughter with a shitload of power and no stomach for torture. So, why would she want Jovi back? Why not just have her minions grab the amulet and GTFO—unless she wanted to haul Jovi back to hell purely for punishment?

She could try. But Jovi was never going back.

Hot, reassuring tingles rushed to her fingertips, and she took a breath. She could handle hellspawn. Thanks to

Mommy Dearest, she'd had a whole childhood of practice. She glanced down at her hands, slim and pale and capable of incinerating a city block. Or, as she'd found out, a lineup of souls who may or may not deserve it. Or a bunch of demons selected for her to practice on, who always came back for revenge afterward.

Jovi fluffed her hair. So she had hellspawn on her tail. Big whoop. She'd handle them, like always.

The tiny green light from her trackband glinted in the reflection, ready to alert the authorities the second she dealt any aggressive magic. She was willing to bet hellfire fell into that category.

Fuck.

CHAPTER 3

Rogan hit the pavement with a curse. Something cuffed the back of his head as he went down, and he grunted, shooting a murderous glare at the giant white wolf sailing over him.

Wolf skidded to the asphalt on four massive paws. His animal form shone silvery white in the dark alley, a stark contrast to the two hostiles that had appeared seconds before.

Demons. Ugly, snarling, stinking of rotten eggs, and spoiling for a fight.

Happy to oblige.

Now, if Wolf would just keep his shit together, they might actually dispatch these targets like professionals.

Shapeshifters' lenses took a few seconds to relink after they shifted, so Rogan called out the target's position. "Nine o'clock!"

As Wolf launched himself in that direction, Rogan rose to face the other aggressor. Mid-sized humanoid, huge dripping horns, boar-like tusks. Rogan's lens, fitted for his left eye, scrolled with text he didn't need to read.

Species: Demon. Category: Humanoid. Eliminate.

The demon bellowed and charged, swinging a meaty fist at Rogan's head. Rogan ducked, stepped in close, and hammered an uppercut to the thing's jaw, squeezing the activator in his glove. A jolt of electricity shot from his knuckles, zapping the fleshy underside of the demon's chin. It seized up, knees buckling, and one of its tusks gouged Rogan's ribs. He cursed, pivoted, and let the thing fall face forward onto the pavement. His anointed iron throwing knife split its skull a second later.

Something warm and wet slapped the back of his neck. He spun and saw that Wolf had the other demon against the wall, shredding it like a tree in a woodchipper. Rogan approached at a swift crouch, craning to get a visual for his lens.

TARGET UNKNOWN. CAPTURE.

"Wolf! It's a retrieval! *Wolf!*"

Wolf ignored him. Rogan hit the whistler on his belt, and an ear-splitting shriek echoed through the alley. Like a true goddamned dog, Wolf dropped the demon and whirled toward the noise. His animal form was enormous, his canine head level with Rogan's waist. Predator eyes glowed gold in the night, muzzle glinting with black blood. He bared his teeth.

Rogan pointed at the demon. "That's a lab capture. Is there anything fucking left?"

Wolf shook out his fur, backing away as Rogan crouched beside the target and activated the illuminator on his belt, lighting up what was left of the enemy. The thing wasn't much more than a puddle.

He rose to face his squad mate. "Is your lens working?"

Wolf gave a very dog-like sneeze, then stretched his front paws forward, butt in the air and bushy white tail waving.

Idiot. Rogan tapped the comm embedded in the collar of his fitted black shirt. The puncture wound near his ribs burned. "John, you copy? I need a cleanup for lab transport."

John's calm voice came through. "On my way."

Seconds later, Agent John Youngbear appeared in the alley, surrounded by a shimmering veil that disappeared as he solidified. Most people called it teleportation—John called it spirit walking, and when he said the two things were different, Rogan wasn't going to argue. His sheet of black hair hung loose to his shoulders, where his crow familiar, Tika, was perched, as usual. He strode toward them, leather moccasins silent on the asphalt, slowing when he spotted the pile of demon flesh on the ground. He arched a brow at Wolf, who wagged his tail.

John shot Rogan a look before squatting beside the ruined corpse. He lifted long-fingered hands and took a deep, steadying breath as he focused intently, his dark eyes glowing pure white in the gloom.

Rogan smothered the familiar pang of jealousy as he watched the demon's skin knit back together, forming the shape of something like an iguana. Aethromages, or spirit-summoners, made excellent healers. They also made formidable fighters, though Rogan had yet to talk John into a combat role. The man followed The Way, and The Way was peaceful. So, instead of putting his off-the-charts power to use in combat, John served as a medic, teleporter, and researcher. For now.

John rose, flicking his fingers as if to shake off the excess magic. The glow faded from his eyes as he and Rogan stared down at the pathetic sack of skin. At least it wouldn't leak on the way to the lab.

"Your turn." John nodded at Rogan's torso, where the tusk wound throbbed like he'd been nailed by a giant wasp. "That feels nasty."

"You should feel it on my end," Rogan muttered, though he wasn't sure he'd like to feel what John described as *spirit rot*, either. Impatient to get back to patrol, Rogan lifted his arm to expose the jagged hole in his side. John made a displeased noise and propped Rogan's arm against his shoulder, supporting it while he pressed his palms to the injury. His eyes came alive again, and Rogan fought the urge to squirm as the wound prickled vigorously. "Fuck, that itches."

He saw the edge of John's smile beneath his arm. "Cells stitching back together." After a few moments, he nodded and pulled away.

Rogan twisted his torso to test the repair, feeling nothing but a lingering tightness over the injury. He returned John's nod, then glanced at his watch. He cursed. Shift was over, and patrol had been painfully slow—only two hostiles the entire night. Christ, the little pyromage from earlier had been more interesting.

Abruptly, his vision filled with pink hair and flashing blue eyes. Where did she go after flipping him off and stalking into the night? Home, to a boyfriend?

It would take one hell of a man to handle a firecracker like her.

Rogan shook himself, snapping on a pair of disposable gloves before scooping the floppy corpse into one of the biohazard bags he kept in his pockets. The body had started to steam, the smell of sulfur rising like a noxious fog. He tied the bag quickly. "Thanks, John. See you at home."

John touched two fingers to his heart before he and the crow vanished into the ether.

Rogan turned to Wolf. "Go on, shift's over. And we *will* talk about ignoring your lens. The Magistrate won't be happy."

Wolf huffed, then turned and trotted from the alley, no doubt to hunt down some junk food.

Setting the disposal bag gingerly on the ground, Rogan turned to his own kill, put his boot on its skull, and yanked out his throwing knife. Black blood poured. He wiped off the blade and slipped it into its sheath, then pulled a gleaming white marble from his other pocket and dropped it into the black puddle.

He backed swiftly away as the marble began to vibrate. Seconds later, it emitted a short, high-pitched whine before bursting open in an explosion of light. Rogan squinted, holding his breath as the demon's body began to steam in earnest. The light from the marble grew brighter, the steam grew thicker, until abruptly, the corpse poofed into a mist and evaporated into nothing.

He had to give the tech department props—these new vaporizers packed a hell of a punch. Retrieving the marble, he swept the scene for any remaining evidence before picking up the disposal bag. It bulged with trapped steam, and he held it away from his body as he headed for the sidewalk.

The neon flash of billboards and storefront signs cast a turquoise and purple glow over Concordia's city streets. Vortech security grates were pulled over the shops that could afford them, while older, lower quality knock-offs were padlocked over the rest. Hovercars lined the curbs, some with glowing parking tickets stamped on their windshields. Rogan headed for the closest Magical Law Enforcement cyberbike corral, pleased to see a glossy white bike waiting there.

He was less pleased to see the bird shit splattered all over the seat.

Two blue pigeons, named for their iridescent indigo feathers, glowered at him from the corral's posts. They trilled ominously as he approached, beady eyes glinting, pudgy bodies shifting on skinny feet.

He shooed them away. "Fuck off."

The pigeons glared insolently and made low muttering sounds. Rogan glared back and wiped the seat with his sleeve, imagining how satisfying it would be to blast the birds off their perch and watch the feathers fly. Unfortunately, as of last year, they were protected by city sanction. Animages and their endless lobbying.

He swiped his watch over the bike's scanner to unlock it, popped open the storage compartment on the back, and eased the swollen bag inside. Swinging a leg over the seat, he clipped on the attached helmet, scanned his watch over the ignition sensor, and felt the hum of power beneath him as the bike fired up. A cool voice floated through the helmet's built-in earpiece. "Welcome, Agent Rogan."

He pulled onto the empty street, ignoring the flap of the pigeons' wings as they chased him off. The quiet whir of the engine floated up to fill his ears, the blue glow of the bike's underbody lights reflecting off the pavement. He leaned into the handlebars, scanning the horizon as he passed all-night vape shops and diners with animated signs. The Aerial public transit system roared overhead, sweeping people to their destinations like a giant silver snake.

This in-between time made him twitchy as hell. Not quite night, not quite day, streets quiet and shift firmly over. He rounded a corner, engine humming, and felt the familiar tug of pride in his belly as MLE headquarters came into view. It rose like a beacon in the night, a towering column of smooth white and luminous blue, windows reflecting the endlessly blinking billboards.

The Eclipsa Flexphone 10. Go ahead, flex.

Purlessa Glamor Cosmetics. Leave them spellbound.

Primal Steakhouse. Feed the beast.

MLE vehicles glided in and out of headquarters. Narcotics and beat patrols, bringing in Blitz users, petty criminals, drunks…he didn't miss those early days of his career. The scabbed, twitching faces of the Blitz users hit too close to a home he'd rather forget.

He headed around the back to the restricted-access garage, then took the elevator to the top floor, holding the bulging bag carefully at his side. The doors parted silently. More glowing blue filaments pulsed in white walls, the smell of cleaning products and chlorine tickled his nose, and spotless tile gleamed beneath his boots as he passed the fitness center. The few agents sweating on weight machines paused mid-rep when they spotted him. Laughter died, and sharp eyes followed him. His hand tightened on the bag.

Mages, all of them. Except him.

A couple of them nodded respectfully as he passed.

The shooting range was empty. No surprise—most agents relied on their magical abilities and close-range stunners to subdue threats. Beyond the range was the overflow armory and its rows of automated lockboxes, housing thousands of standard-issue stunners, tranquilizers, and phasers.

Rogan stopped in front of the unmarked door in the back of the armory. He scanned his watch, then his right eye, and waited as the heavy door slid sideways into the wall, revealing a small vestibule. He stepped inside. The first door whispered shut, closing him inside a concrete box with more glowing blue lights. This time, another watch and retina scan, a full facial recognition scan, and a voice clearance.

"Agent Nash Rogan," he said clearly into the speaker. "Archetype." His personal passcode. A door at the rear of the vestibule, plastered with *Restricted Access* and *Maximum Security Clearance Required* warnings, slid smoothly aside.

Squinting against the blast of bright light and formaldehyde, he threaded through gleaming stainless steel workbenches, stepped over floor drains, and strode past the huge cylindrical holding tanks that stood sentinel along one wall, their contents floating in ominous silence.

His boots were quiet on the concrete as he made for the far end of the lab, where a slight figure in a white hazmat suit sat hunched over a microscope. He stopped behind her and cleared his throat.

Nothing.

"Tally." He spoke quietly, trying not to startle her.

Tallia Monroe practically leaped out of her chair. "Oh, God!" she shrieked, fumbling the glass slide she was examining. It slipped onto the concrete floor and shattered. Her shoulders slumped inside the hazmat suit. She pushed back her hood, blew a breath upward to clear the fog from her glasses, and looked at Rogan miserably, her blonde braid disheveled over one shoulder. "That's the second one this week." Her eyes landed on the bag at his side, and she gasped. "Is that the reptilian?" She reached gingerly for it. "I saw it come through the monitor; I couldn't wait."

She flitted around, setting up surgical tools and pulling up a holo-monitor. Her fingers danced over the glowing keys. Tallia was an Anomaly, born to mage parents, but without any magical ability herself. Lucky for her, she had the brains to make up for it, a fact that had not escaped the Magistrate's notice. He'd recruited her from one of the top human tech institutes several years back. They still weren't happy about it.

Rogan checked the time. "Are you good here? I'm past my cutoff."

"Yeah, yeah. See you later." Tally waved absently, and Rogan tossed his gloves in a biohazard bin on his way out.

Ten minutes later, he scanned his watch at the secured door to the Bunker. Stepping into the mud room, he shucked his boots and placed them precisely in the boot tray at the bottom of his locker. His was the first in the row of six lining the mudroom wall, each matte black and neatly labeled. *Rogan, Cyrus, Juno, Killian, John, Wolf.*

He followed the lingering smell of southern cooking to the dining room. Handsome walnut paneling mingled with state-of-the-art tech, a large screen mounted to the wall showed a live map of the city, and at the end of the big table, a burly lion shapeshifter shoveled roast beef into his mouth.

Like most lion shifters, Killian Diallo's human form was tall and heavily muscled, but he was even bigger than most.

His hair was a wild, golden tangle around his tattooed shoulders, his beard slightly darker. He glanced up as Rogan entered. "Get into something messy?"

"Lab capture. Wolf shredded it."

Killian grunted, shook his head.

"I'm going to shower."

He grunted again and forked up another mouthful, chatty as usual.

Rogan headed for the atrium, the octagonal hub with glass ceilings at the heart of the compound. A metal staircase curved to the second level, where each agent had their own wing. He opened the bedroom door at the end of his. Sparse, gray, and clean—everything in its place, nothing out of order. A desk in the corner held a lamp, his tablet, and two framed pictures: His dad receiving his medal of commendation, and Rogan on the day of his own commission, the Magistrate by his side.

Brushing past the tactical pants, shirts, and boots lining his closet, he opened the weapons cabinet at the back and disarmed, inventorying as he wiped everything down. His hand slowed as he polished his dad's phaser. The old Model B gleamed, and as always, he left the single remaining cartridge loaded.

After a scalding shower in which he scrubbed every inch of his skin with industrial hand soap, he set his watch on the charging dock by the bed and carefully removed his lens, dropping it into its receptacle on the nightstand. Off duty meant the lens came out, whether you were in research, tech, or the field squad. DE mandate, straight from the Magistrate himself.

Rogan liked rules. Rules made things clear. He followed rules. Usually.

He slid his spare lens into his left eye, blinking it into place. The familiar coolness was soothing in more ways than one.

"Lights." Rogan slid into bed, letting darkness envelop him. He closed his eyes.

And promptly saw a pink-haired pyromage sticking her tongue out at him.

He flipped over, punching his pillow into shape.

CHAPTER 4

Jovi flung open the apartment door with a bang.

Nora, her roommate, jumped in her chair and spun around from the wall of computer monitors. "Jesus! What the—"

Holding up her wrist, she watched Nora's brows pop at the sight of her trackband. She stalked to the refrigerator, grabbed a bottle of sweet sparkling wine, and popped the cork viciously. It shot across the room and knocked over a lamp.

"*Shit.*" Nora crept forward like Jovi had a grenade on her arm. "What happened?"

Jovi took a massive swig from the bottle. The sweet fizz did nothing to improve her mood as she told Nora the story.

Her roommate's dark eyes narrowed beneath heavy black bangs. "Fuck." She tossed Jovi a snack cake from the cupboard and folded her arms, toned and tattooed and bared as usual by a black tank top. She'd been wearing one of those the first time they met.

Busting out of a hellmouth had hurt. A lot. But Jovi had done it, the stolen amulet heavy around her neck as she clawed her way up, up, up. Her skin felt like it was being stripped from her bones as she forced herself through the portal, but she kept quiet, kept going, kept pushing, teeth bared in a silent scream, until she collapsed in a crumpled, naked heap on a cold cave floor.

She'd been so busy hauling ass out of there, looking over her shoulder, that she'd smacked straight into a set of dangling legs. Nora, rappelling down the bluff in a black tank top and a rock-climbing harness, had taken one look at Jovi and assumed she was escaping some sort of human trafficking situation. Jovi didn't correct her.

Nora gave her food, clothes, a place to stay, and a lot of alcohol. Which is how Jovi ended up getting wasted one night and telling Nora the whole story. What she really was, where she really came from, and what she was looking for—a dad she'd never met, who might be a total jerk, clueless about her existence, or dead.

Stupid. She knew better. Demons didn't do trust.

She'd spent the better part of a year waiting for the other shoe to drop. But so far, Nora hadn't stabbed her in the back.

"Fuck," Jovi agreed. She took a huge bite of the sweet, waxy snack cake and slid down the wall to the floor, cheeks bulging. "I can't have MLE on my ass every time I blast a demon." She stomped her heel petulantly. A wicked silver dagger shot out of the toe of her boot, glinting in the light. Nora had gotten her the boots a while back, and they'd come in handy more than once. Like when she totally blew her wad on a demon, ran out of hellfire, and had to kick it in the throat.

"Especially now," Jovi continued, as the snack cake turned to rock in her gut. "She's looking for me."

"Who?"

She told Nora what the demon had said tonight, and what she thought it meant. Mommy Dearest wanted more than the amulet—she wanted her minions to drag Jovi back to hell, too.

Nora frowned. "Why?"

She tossed her hands. "I have no idea. We aren't exactly besties." Far from it. "She wants a nasty little lieutenant to help take over the midrealm, and I'm not it." The kitchen went out of focus as she took a sojourn down Terrible Memory Lane. "I'm a disappointment."

"Midrealm. Like, here?" Nora pointed to the floor.

"Like, *all* of here." Jovi spread her hands wide. "I guess ruling an entire section of hell isn't good enough."

"And she wants your help with this."

Jovi shook her head, at a loss. "I thought she'd be happy to get rid of me."

Apparently, that little dream was too good to be true.

Nora cursed. "I wish I could see these guys. You know I'd fight with you."

Jovi nodded glumly. Nora might be a naughty little tech genius who made her money hacking into databases or whatever, but she was also a total badass who trained in mixed martial arts. Sure would be nice to have someone like that on her side.

But, as usual, she was on her own.

Nora swore again. "Let's go get a drink."

They headed for the nearest bar. The Blender district was still hopping, the sidewalks flooded with happy, stumbling people. Jovi had never seen so many trackbands—or maybe she'd just never cared enough to notice. Now, she saw them everywhere, flashes of silver and winking green lights. Her own trackband felt like a boat anchor on her wrist as Nora dragged her down the block.

The Wicked Wench was all black inside, lit with green and purple lights. Waitresses in slutty witch costumes strutted around with trays of smoking shots, the stripes on their thigh-high stockings vivid enough to make patrons' eyes water. They made a beeline for the bar.

"I'll have a Sea Witch, pronto," Jovi called to one of the bartenders.

He looked up at her, grinning. "You got it, Pink."

Nora leaned a hip against the bar. "Make it two."

The bartender raised two fingers in acknowledgment. Dark electronica pulsed throughout the club. Lasers swung around in time to the music, and trackband lights shone like vivid green stars on the dance floor. The bartender's own trackband glinted as he worked. "Straight up or enchanted?"

"Whaddya got?" Jovi asked.

"Luck, silver tongue, or glamor."

"Luck," they answered in unison, exchanging a dark look.

"You got it." The bartender snagged an apothecary bottle and added three shimmering drops to each glass. He grabbed a glow stick from a jar, cracked the thing so it lit up, and stirred, murmuring under his breath. When he breathed across the surface of the drink, the green liquid glowed momentarily brighter.

"Blessed be, pretty ladies." He tossed the glow sticks into the glasses with a flourish.

They sat at a table in the corner. Jovi scanned the club, sipping her Sea Witch. Frothy, tart, refreshing. She tossed back another gulp and moaned at the coolness sliding down her throat, the explosion of flavor. These topsiders really knew their way around food and drink.

There was a sudden ruckus on the dance floor, a couple guys shoving each other like gorillas. One had a mohawk, the other a bright white sports cap. Mohawk threw a punch, and White Cap fell to the floor. People shouted.

White Cap stumbled to his feet, shaking off the people who crowded around to help. He wiped his bloody nose with the back of his hand, the silver of his trackband catching the light, and thrust his palms toward Mohawk with a foreign shout.

A rippling blast hit Mohawk square in the chest, sending him flying backward into the surrounding crowd.

A shrill whistle split the air like a furious tea kettle. Red light erupted from the trackband on White Cap's wrist, swiveling around until the beam of the crimson spotlight lit his face.

Mohawk went back for more. The two collided and grappled, shoving each other into the circle of onlookers. Some of them tried to stumble off the dance floor, while others drunkenly rooted them on.

The door swung open, and two uniformed MLE agents strode inside. They located the red spotlight and forced their way toward White Cap. Both agents grabbed him by the elbows.

"Hey, he hit *me!* He assaulted me!" White Cap's face contorted in the red light.

"He hit me with a force field or some shit!" Mohawk bellowed, pointing. His wrist was bare.

White Cap struggled against the agents. One of them cuffed his hands behind his back, then swiped his watch over the guy's trackband, silencing the ear-splitting alarm. A second later, the red spotlight was extinguished, and the agents pulled White Cap toward the door.

"Hey! What are you—let me go! He punched me in the fucking face!" White Cap struggled harder, panicking.

The agents apparently decided that shit was about to escalate. One of them pulled a glowing blue device from his belt, and the crowd surged backward. The agent pressed it to White Cap's neck.

White Cap gave a shout of pain, then sagged. The agents dragged him out the door.

The music continued to pulse. The crowd slowly went back to dancing.

"Fuck." Jovi tossed back her Sea Witch.

"That is one thing that makes me glad to be human." Nora

eyed Jovi's trackband, then cursed. "I might know a guy who can help."

———

Half an hour later, Jovi wrinkled her nose against the smell of dead fish. The docks were nasty enough during the day—after sunset, the shadows stretched, the sour smells intensified, and the drug deals went unchecked. No flashy billboards here, just a whole lot of busted windows and unmarked buildings, mottled and weathered by salty spray. A big stone wharf stretched into the sea, crusted with barnacles and algae, with a towering lighthouse rising from the end like a giant middle finger. Nice girls didn't hang out at the docks, but hookers and Blitz dealers did.

Jovi scanned the shadowy corners as she and Nora walked. No demons, but plenty of reptile shapeshifters with baggy clothes and hard eyes. They loitered in groups, calling out pervy "pink" comments that were actually pretty creative.

It was close to one in the morning when they reached a rundown corner convenience store. Decades-old vape ads yellowed in the few windows that weren't boarded up. A bum sat on the steps, picking at a scab on his elbow. Brown scales crept up his forearms and onto his neck, glinting dully in the streetlight.

A bell tinkled feebly as they pushed open the door. The place looked abandoned, with a grimy linoleum floor, barren shelves, and dust motes floating in the weak light. A few yellow fluorescent bulbs buzzed overhead, but the majority were burned out, leaving most of the shop in shadow.

"Who's there?" a heavily accented voice called from the rear of the shop.

Nora cleared her throat. "We want to see Dimitri."

No way. She couldn't mean *the* Dimitri.

An old Asian man shuffled out from a back room. "Who?"

"Dimitri," Nora repeated loudly.

"No Dimitri here."

Nora rolled her eyes. "Chang. It's Nora."

The old man leaned closer to peer at her, eyes bulging. Gills fluttered on his neck. "Who's your friend?"

"Just tell him I'm here."

The old man smacked his lips, then turned and shuffled off, disappearing into the back room.

"*The* Dimitri?" Jovi squeaked, whacking Nora's hip.

Dimitri Zmey was the alpha of the reptile clan. Reptiles were known for being cold, cunning, and absolute geniuses when it came to crafting high-end weapons. The fancy knives in their retail armories were apparently nothing compared to the illegal shit they sold on the black market, and reptiles with the right genetics could make a shit-ton of money selling their own bodily fluids. Reptile venom—V—supposedly gave the user super strength, incredible speed, and a better high than the best Blitz on the market. Dimitri Zmey was in charge of it all, and people whispered about him like he was a god.

"Is this where you got my boots?" If her boots were made by the legendary Dimitri Zmey, Jovi was going to fangirl out.

"Shh."

"How do you know him?"

"*Shh.*"

The door to the back room flew open. It banged against the wall, revealing a glimpse of the smoky room beyond. An enormously tall, broad-shouldered silhouette stood silently in the frame. The air thrummed with power, radiating from the doorway like an electric current. Jovi's fingertips tingled in response.

The man started toward them, moving silkily, shoulders taking up all the space between the shelves. He eased to a stop a few feet away, a shaft of light slanting across his face.

Well, well. Apparently, this was her night for hunky man

meat. Black hair was raked back from a face that looked carved from solid rock, the planes of his cheekbones casting shadows over a sharp jaw and short, black goatee. He wore a crisp white shirt and leather leggings tucked into expensive-looking boots. Classy and refined, he looked like a big, muscled swashbuckler, incredibly out of place and yet perfectly at ease in this shithole of a store. Jovi's gaze traveled up the blade of his nose and stopped at his eyes.

She almost retreated. Framed by black lashes, his luminous orange gaze was unblinking, with a wide vertical pupil surrounded by a vibrant flash of yellow. It was like staring into a blazing fire.

Holy shit. Maybe the rumors were true, and his animal form really was a dragon.

If dragons looked like that, she wouldn't mind riding one.

"Dimitri," Nora said.

"*Sirena*." His voice was smooth, elegant, and inhumanly deep. He didn't smile.

"How've you been?"

He stared at her with those fiery eyes.

Nora huffed out a sigh. "This is my friend, Jovi. Jovi, meet Dimitri Zmey."

His gaze shifted to her. Jovi twirled her hair and smiled, waving her pinky at him. Dimitri glanced down at her legs. "Is this the one who needed the boots?" When Nora nodded, he quirked a brow. "This friend of yours needs a lot of help."

"Hey!" Jovi released the twist of hair between her fingertips.

"Can we go somewhere private?" Nora gritted out.

Dimitri stared for another long moment, then turned his head slightly and directed a loud, sharp whistle over his shoulder. A cacophony of scraping chairs and scuttling feet sounded from the rear of the shop. He turned, and they followed him through the rows of dusty shelves into the back.

Dark and warm, the concrete room had a few bare bulbs

hanging from the ceiling. Heavy duty workbenches lined the walls, littered with scraps of leather, while three fancy-looking metalworking forges took up an entire corner in the back. Away from the forges, several small tables sat beneath a lingering cloud of vape. The whole place smelled like hot iron, vanilla, and sweat.

Dimitri pulled a bottle of reddish liquid from a shelf. He gestured for them to sit at one of the tables before lowering himself into his own chair. He poured three small glasses and distributed them.

Nora gestured toward Jovi. "She needs her trackband off."

Dimitri leveled his fiery gaze at Jovi. She held it. It wasn't easy. Power radiated from him, and it wasn't just from the muscles on his huge frame. His voice, his presence, the way he took up space made him absolutely huge. He reminded her of some of the high demons in hell, the ones on par with her mother, the old ones. The terrifying ones.

Dimitri leaned back in his chair and took a sip from his glass before pointing at her trackband. "When did you get it?"

"Like, two hours ago." Jovi scowled at it.

Dimitri's soft laugh practically rumbled the floor. He shook his head. "I can't help you."

Jovi's heart sank. Nora started to protest, but he held up a palm. "As much as it pains me to admit that I can't complete a simple task for you," he cast a meaningful glance at Nora, who looked away, "these new trackbands are stronger. Smarter." He tapped his temple. A gold ring gleamed on his long forefinger.

"Don't you have a key or something? I've seen you take tons of these things off," Nora protested.

"The old ones, yes. Not these new ones. I could break it, but…" He glanced up at Jovi, made an exploding motion. "Boom." He smiled.

Jovi swallowed. "How do you know that?"

"Luka lost a hand." He shrugged, took another sip before setting his glass back on the table. "What are you?" he said without preamble.

She ignored the jolt in her belly. "Pyromage."

Dimitri looked at her from beneath his lashes. "Please, give me a little more credit. You're something else. I can sense it." He inhaled deeply. "Smell it."

Fucking shapeshifters and their freakish sense of smell. "Uh, rude. I can smell you, too, but I wasn't going to mention it." She took a swig from her glass. Smooth, with a sneaky burn at the end. Kind of like the man sitting across from her.

Dimitri laughed, low and silky. There was something almost hypnotic about him like a big, sexy cobra lulling its victim before the strike. "Fine. Keep your secrets. But if you are just a mage, it's simple. Go home, be a good little witch." He lifted his hands. "No bad magic, no problem."

"Yeah, that's not really an option for Jovi," Nora muttered.

"Oh?" He considered Jovi again, long fingers brushing his lips. "You're a fighter, then. Interesting."

Nora folded her arms. "Do you have *anything* that could help?"

Dimitri leaned back in his chair, a sprawling king in his concrete kingdom. "I sell a lot of things. A potion that prevents your magic from being tracked."

"Really?" Jovi clunked her glass down on the table.

"Does it work?" Nora interjected dryly.

"No," Dimitri said easily. A gold chain glinted beneath his collar. "I also sell a trackband cover. It muffles the alarm and covers the red light."

They both waited.

"It doesn't work, either."

Jovi felt her nostrils flare. "Look, buddy, I'm not interested in the bogus crap you sell to chumps. I need something that actually works."

Dimitri's eyes flashed. "I sell men. Protection. Your track-band goes off, MLE shows up…" He waved a hand. "My men take care of them."

"Oh, yeah, great. I'm sure murdering a bunch of MLE agents wouldn't come back to bite me in the ass." Jovi shoved out of her chair and paced, flapping her hands hard, trying to shake off the tingles rushing to her fingertips. She kicked a heavy metal bucket on the floor and felt her big toe pop. "*Motherfucker!*" Heat built in her belly, seeping out of her skin. Sparks shimmered on her shoulders, traveling down her arms like ominous red and orange glitter.

"You have trouble controlling your magic, little pyro-mage?" Dimitri's eyes tracked the sparks. "Why?"

Jovi glared at him. "Because I'm super duper powerful, okay? Besides, I *need* to use it."

Dimitri just stared at her. Surprise, surprise. He was becoming less sexy and more irritating by the minute. "I understand. But there is nothing I can do for you. And so…" He stood slowly, uncoiling to his full height. "You're welcome here because you're a friend of Nora Alvarez. But you must keep your shit together. If you lose control here and your trackband attracts MLE attention…" He shook his head slowly, eyes burning into hers.

"Got it, Stare Bear." Jovi gave him a wide-eyed, mocking stare of her own. "Thanks for nothing." She whirled, stalking from the room. A second later, she strode back in, downed the last of her liquor, and marched back out.

Nora caught up to her on the sidewalk, where the crisp night air was doing nothing to cool her down. "We'll figure something out."

Jovi scowled. "How do you know him, anyway?"

Nora sighed. "He pulled my drunk ass out of the wharf." A little smile played around her mouth. "*Sirena* means mermaid."

"So, you guys were…"

Nora slid her a glance. "Yeah." She rolled her eyes at Jovi's dramatic gasp. "It was good—really good—for a while. But he got too intense. Overprotective." She shrugged. "He's an alpha. And with the business he's in, it makes sense, but…" She shook her head again. "I can't live like that." She looked at Jovi, black hair swinging around her collarbone, light glinting off of the little hoop that pierced her nostril. "Look, I'm sorry he couldn't help, but just don't piss him off, okay? He's the kind of guy you want on your side."

For some reason, Agent Annoyingly-Hot Rogan popped into Jovi's head. He seemed like the kind of guy someone would want on their side, too—calm, efficient, unflappable. Muscled. She snarled at the thought, and promptly ran her thigh into a fire hydrant.

"Ow!" An angry little fireball shot out of her fingertips, and they both glanced nervously at her trackband. "I gotta get this fucking thing off," Jovi muttered.

CHAPTER 5

ingers around his neck. Mom's latest boyfriend, stinking of Blitz, sitting on his twelve-year-old chest, crushing his lungs, cutting off his air…

The ping of an email jolted Rogan awake. He surged upright, sucking in a harsh breath. His heart thumped. The sheets were damp in his grip, his bare chest sticky with sweat. He scrubbed his face.

Mom, sluggish from her own high, fumbling to pull her boyfriend off of him…

His phone pinged again. He snatched it like a lifeline, squinting at the bright screen.

From: Magistrate Thackeray White
To: Demon Eradication Field Unit
Subject: ARC Meeting Request

Agents,
ARC has requested a meeting. Please clear your schedules and

accept the calendar invitation. A reminder that, as always, animal forms are not permitted inside MLE facilities.

Magistrate Thackeray White

Holy shit. The Archangel Regiment in Command never talked to anyone but the Magistrate. This could not be good.

He checked the calendar invite. Five hours until the meeting.

Rogan dressed quickly and headed for the dining room. He wasn't the first to arrive. Killian leaned against a wall, huge arms folded, hair loose around his massive shoulders. John, Cyrus, and Juno were already seated at the table.

"Could be a new weapon," Cyrus was saying, running a palm over his shaved head. He'd obviously been out all night. There were shadows under his eyes and his dress shirt was half unbuttoned, revealing a smudge of lipstick in the hollow of his neck. The hot pink was shocking against his dark skin. It was all too easy to picture the woman he'd left behind—dazed, sated, with only a fuzzy recollection of the man who'd rocked her world all night. Rogan almost felt sorry for her. Cerebromages with the ability to smudge memories were dangerous enough, and one as handsome as Cyrus needed a damn warning label. But it was better than having a trail of desperate women track him to the Bunker.

Cyrus gave Rogan a sly grin, his blue eyes following him to the coffee bar in the corner. The espresso cup shot into the air before he could lay a finger on it, hovering mockingly at eye level. Rogan snatched the thing and flipped the bird over his shoulder. Cyrus chuckled, and Rogan kept a firm grip on the cup while pulling a shot of espresso, fingers tapping his hip as the scent of salvation filled the air.

"So, what do you think?" Cyrus asked him.

His eye twitched. "I don't know."

Wolf sauntered into the room, wearing rubber ducky pajama pants and nothing else. "Like I'd waltz into the Magistrate's office in fucking wolf form. I do have some self-control." He sidled up to the coffee bar and knocked Rogan's shoulder with his own. Rogan grunted, trying not to spill his espresso. Wolf reached across him to snag his favorite mug, a glossy black monstrosity with *PIMP* spelled out in rhinestones. He poured it half full of coffee from the pot and loaded the rest with fake-flavored garbage.

Rogan took a sip. "Tell that to the reptilian you shredded last night."

John made a noise of agreement into his steaming herbal tea.

"I am the epitome of restraint." Wolf's giant mug glittered like a drag queen as he downed his coffee in one gulp, neck muscles bulging. Unlike most wolves, whose tattoos skewed toward Viking runes, Wolf's bicep sported a frosted cupcake.

Their housekeeper, Gloria, burst through the kitchen door balancing two huge plates of cinnamon rolls. The apron she wore, dusted with flour, barely covered her ample bosom, and sweat shone on her round face. The scent of cinnamon and homemade bread made Rogan's mouth water. They all sat, passing platters and big serving bowls amongst themselves. Rogan loaded up with scrambled eggs, bypassed the cinnamon rolls, and eyeballed one cup of fresh berries, spooning it onto his plate. "Any greens, Gloria?" he asked as she squeezed behind his chair.

"Not today, baby." She stroked his cheek with a knuckle. "And I don't want to see you counting no calories." She whacked him upside the head as she passed. Rogan ignored the snorts of laughter as Gloria made her way around the table, brushing a warm hand over each of them. Even Killian, for a split second, leaned into her touch. "Passing up my great granny's homemade cinnamon rolls…"

"Not all of us have shapeshifter metabolisms." Rogan knocked back the rest of his espresso.

The Demon Eradication Field Unit didn't always have a housekeeper. A few years back, Rogan had convinced the Magistrate that the squad needed someone to handle the cooking, cleaning, laundry, and shopping so they could focus on their jobs. And it was true. But more than that, though none of them would admit it, every single one of them needed a mother.

And Gloria needed a family because the enemy had slaughtered hers.

Rogan had been on rotation that night. He'd seen the demon, a gigantic gargoyle sonofabitch, speeding toward the family gathered around a late-night campfire in their tiny backyard. He hadn't been fast enough. Thanks to his lens, Rogan saw it all in excruciating detail. Gloria only saw her husband and teenage son being shredded in an invisible blender.

The DE's oath of silence was necessary. Rogan understood that—hell, he'd helped write the thing. Most times, keeping that silence didn't bother him.

Most times.

He couldn't tell Gloria what had destroyed her family, but he had done his damnedest to give her a new life, a new home, and a new family to be a part of.

Beside him, Wolf grabbed a cinnamon roll and took a massive bite, gazing up at Gloria with frosting on his face. She laughed and planted a smacking kiss on his cheek, thumbing the white dribble off his chin.

"I heard you brought in an unregistered mage last night." Juno's dark hair was uncharacteristically loose around sculpted shoulders, her strong, tawny legs revealed by cotton boxers. Her worn sweatshirt read *MLE CLASS OF 2093*.

His belly gave a jerk at the mention of the little firebug,

and he frowned, nodding. "Female pyro, blasted some drunk idiot in an alley."

"Strong?"

"Gave her a level five, but I thought about going higher." Rogan cleared his throat and popped his neck, trying not to remember how silky her skin had felt beneath his fingers. He attempted to spear a blackberry with his fork, missed, and stabbed it again.

Wolf cocked his head. His hair, mahogany streaked with the shocking white of his wolf, flopped wildly. "What'd she look like, Rogan?"

He slid him a glance. "Why?"

"Because you're all shifty."

"No, I'm not." Rogan nailed another berry with his fork. "She's small, definitely got something else going on. Fae, maybe? Long, pink hair." He moved his hands around his head and shoulders, picturing the masses of bubblegum strands. "Short skirt, combat boots. Big eyes, sort of tilted upward. Really light blue." Like pale, glittering crystal.

He glanced up from his plate to find them all staring at him.

Wolf's grin was pure evil. "Sounds like one of those sexy anime girls. You know, those slutty little cartoons?" He wiggled his brows at Juno's disgusted look. "Short skirt, big titties…" He ran his tongue over his teeth, and Juno swatted him.

"That's offensive to the entire anime community." Cyrus sipped his coffee. "Although, I did see some very interesting adult anime the other day…"

Thankfully, the conversation turned to slutty animated characters before shifting to speculations about the upcoming meeting. Silverware clattered as they ate, nervous energy buzzing between them. Rogan picked at his eggs, glanced at his watch, and drummed the table. Wasn't the Magistrate going to give him some sort of clue?

When his phone vibrated, he snatched it so fast the others stopped to stare. But it wasn't about the meeting. It was Israel, asking if anyone wanted to train.

He'd never been so glad for a distraction. "Anyone want to play with Israel this morning?" As enthusiastic affirmatives echoed around the table, Rogan raised a brow at Cyrus. "I'm guessing you need to get some sleep."

Cyrus smirked. "Well earned." Anyone else would have missed the flicker of regret in his eyes, but Rogan knew the wham-bam-memory-wipe routine bothered him more than he admitted.

"Want me to scan you for STDs?" John smiled into his tea, then uttered a foreign curse when, at the jerk of Cyrus's chin, his mug dumped itself all over his face. Tika's affronted caws chased the rest of them out of the dining room and down to the gym.

The Bunker's underground training center was designed to look like the streets above—fake building facades, dumpsters, a cyberbike corral, a hover car, and a military-grade weather simulator with a special upgrade. The DE Tech Department had added hyper-realistic demon holographs to the simulator, complete with combat programming and kill sensors. That feature would stay off today.

Rogan and the three shifters had begun to stretch in the center of the gym when the beep of Israel's security badge announced his arrival. The doors whooshed open, fluttering the black waves that framed his striking Middle Eastern bone structure. Heavy-lidded eyes twinkled as Israel chucked his duffle into the corner, kicked off his shoes, and bowed. Then, he sprang into a somersault and chucked a throwing star at them.

It was on.

Israel Stroud was a legend in the combat world. He'd worked with militaries, private security firms, film and television, had won countless MMA fights, and had been featured in more publications than he cared to remember. Now, he taught combat at a boarding school for magical orphans. And occasionally, he came to "play" with the DE.

Rogan blocked the throwing star with a forearm, glad he'd had the forethought to strap the steel guards over his shirt. Juno sprinted for a pillar, Wolf skidded behind a dumpster, and Killian roared, the sound deafening as it echoed off the concrete. He launched himself at Israel, clothes shredding as he burst into full lion form.

Israel laughed with unbridled delight.

Killian's massive golden body sailed through the air. His watch glinted on his foreleg, the band having expanded to fit his animal form. It would shrink to fit his human wrist when he shifted back. Israel dodged an enormous paw and nailed a thunder kick into Killian's side, knocking him off balance. The lion stumbled to the floor, spun, and went for Israel like a clawed, fanged tank.

Israel leaped straight into the air, tucked his feet, and morphed into a blue pigeon.

Asshole. He knew Rogan hated those damn birds.

Israel was the only malleabis Rogan knew to exist. A shapeshifter in the truest, most fluid sense, he could assume the form of any human, any animal—anything with a heartbeat and a brain. Most people considered malleabi the stuff of legends. Others wanted to own them. Israel revealed his true nature to only a select few—his colleagues at the boarding school, and after many years, the members of the DE.

The squad had talked many times about whether to tell Israel what they really did, but it always came back to the same thing; they had sworn an oath. And so, even now, years after Israel had trusted the squad with his innermost secret, they didn't return the favor. To Israel, like the rest of the world, they were simply MLE's most elite field team.

The blue pigeon hooted, flapped its way to a rafter, and shat on Killian's head.

The lion's roar made Rogan's eardrums throb.

A black shape shot past. Juno's jaguar form launched at the wall and pushed off, springing toward the ceiling in a blur of glossy fur. She caught the rafter and swung up like some sort of feline gymnast, landing gracefully atop the steel beam. Her green eyes glowed.

The pigeon squawked, diving from the beam as Juno's teeth snapped at its tail feathers. It hit the ground, morphing into a fuzzy white ferret. The bird streaked across the concrete while Juno leaped from rafter to rafter high above, a swift and silent shadow.

Rogan watched from behind the hover car. It was pointless for a human to try to match an animal's strength or speed, so he waited until the furry white bullet drew close.

Wait for it…

As the ferret zoomed toward him, Rogan yanked a sonic stunner from his belt, pulled the pin with his teeth, and chucked it directly into the ferret's path before plugging his ears.

The sonic boom that exploded from the stunner still made his ears ring. The blast blew the ferret off its paws, its long body flipping through the air like a wet noodle.

Rogan was on it the second it hit the floor, his dagger inches from the rodent's neck. "Dead."

The ferret squeaked and morphed into a laughing Israel, who lay panting on the cement, clutching his head. "Those sonic booms, my friend. Ouch!" He let Rogan haul him to his feet, then threw a vicious right hook that rang Rogan's bell. Payback.

They sparred, pulling back just enough to avoid truly wounding each other. Rogan landed a roundhouse that made Israel stagger, then took him to the ground with a leg sweep. They grappled, and Israel flipped him, gaining the top position.

With his head buried somewhere beneath Israel's armpit, he heard Wolf yell, "Boring!" and felt a tug on his belt.

A thrill of panic coursed through him. "Not the Model B!"

"I didn't touch your daddy's gun. Relax," Wolf said from overhead. "Earthquake!" There was a heavy metallic *thunk*, a scuttling sound, and then the crack and groan of concrete splitting beneath them.

Rogan cursed. Israel whooped and rolled away as a huge gap appeared in the floor between them, spreading rapidly toward a cyberbike corral. Rogan lunged for the tiny fissure-bot, still burrowing its way through the cement. He yanked the thing out and ran for cover, knowing Israel wouldn't give him any reprieve. Ducking behind a pillar, he disabled the bot, keeping his head on a swivel.

Silence.

He glanced around the column. Wolf was facing off with Israel, circling, watching his prey with unblinking focus. He rolled his shoulders and inhaled deeply, preparing to take animal form.

"No shifting," Israel snapped.

Wolf's blue eyes flashed gold, but he bared his teeth in a fierce grin. "Easy."

The kid could fight. He favored fast, short strikes, which made sense for a wolf. They liked to dart in, tire their prey with quick bites, bleeding them until they weakened.

"You've just shifted back from animal form," Israel murmured, his accented voice soft. "Your clothes are shredded. And something's wrong—you can't shift back. You're in human form, naked and unarmed. What are you going to do?"

Wolf growled and dived at him.

Rogan eased out of his ready stance. This would take a while, but it was why they trained with Israel. He spotted chinks in the armor. And when Israel Stroud told you to work on your hand to hand, you listened.

While the two of them sparred, Rogan took it all in: The state-of-the-art training center, the legendary fighter he called a friend, the incredible warriors who called him their leader. He'd done this—built the DE field squad from the ground up. He alone had found the most powerful mages and the fiercest shapeshifters in the city, and he'd convinced them to leave their old lives behind to follow him, an orphan with a chip on his shoulder.

Hell of an accomplishment for the only human in MLE.

But now, the archangels wanted a meeting with the squad, and the Magistrate wasn't giving him any sort of clue as to why. The scrambled eggs churned in his stomach.

Nearby, Juno made a swipe at Killian's tufted tail. He spun, growling menacingly. His animal form was twice the size of Juno's, the shining gold of his pelt a stark contrast to the sleek black of hers. She hissed at him, crouching. Play.

Killian curled his lip, showing his fangs, and turned his back to her. Juno's green eyes flashed. She padded over to settle beside Rogan. Though she cleaned one paw nonchalantly, her thick black tail continued to swish irritably across the concrete floor.

Rogan's watch vibrated with an incoming phone call. His heart leapt, but once again, it wasn't the Magistrate. The name of Israel's colleague, Theo, flashed across the screen. He frowned, swiping to answer. "Hey."

Theodora Donnovan exhaled into the mouthpiece. Rogan could almost smell her black cherry vape wafting through the speaker. "Hey. You got time to come over? Alarm's acting weird."

Rogan eyed Israel and Wolf, who were locked together like wrestlers. It didn't look like he was going to do much more training this morning. "Yeah, I'll head over."

The others barely spared him a glance when he told them he was leaving, but Juno shot him a jaguar glare when he reminded them not to be late to the meeting with ARC.

There was a nip in the air as he left the Bunker and walked the few short blocks to the school he'd helped get off the ground. His original idea had been simple—a boarding school for any kid who needed it. A bed, a roof, a basic education…a place Rogan could've used when he was thirteen, orphaned, and alone. The Magistrate liked the idea so much he offered to fund it himself, with a few qualifications for admission.

The Light House Boarding School for Magical Youth wasn't much to look at. The former factory had been converted into dormitory-style bedrooms, a series of classrooms, a gym, and a dining hall. The kids there learned gen-ed, magic, and combat—perfect prerequisites for the Magical Law Enforcement academy. And, for those who showed exceptional promise, for the Demon Eradication team.

Light House's executive director stood on the broad front steps, her scarlet hair raked into a loose braid and massive coffee mug steaming in one hand. Theo wore her usual fitted tee tucked into wide flowing pants, and the scent of black cherry greeted Rogan as he mounted the steps to stand beside her.

They stood in silence. She offered him her vape pen, track-band glinting on her wrist. He declined. She took another drag, then offered him her coffee mug. The smell of dark roast wafted under his nose, but he shook his head again.

"It's got a cheering charm in it."

Damn it, she knew he was a sucker. Rogan grabbed it, taking a long sip. Practically every Sip n' Spell in the city knew his order—a triple espresso with a double shot of luck. Theo had been behind him in line one afternoon, lips twitching at what must have been the caught-red-handed look on his face when he'd turned around.

They passed the mug back and forth, watching the early morning streets. The old recycling plant across the block was being gutted. Work crews were already swarming the place, electromages welding steel together with arcs of light crack-ling from their hands while telekinetics hefted I-beams from yards away. The sign in the yard read *Pride Construction*. So, the lions had already reworked the framing and would come back to do the finish carpentry when the time came. It would be a beautiful building—Pride work always was. Nine-to-fivers hurried to work, noses in their phones, earbuds stuffed in their ears. Shifters might be twitchy around tech, but humans and mages happily buried them-selves in everything the Trident manufactured. Rogan's pockets were loaded with tech that civilians couldn't dream of.

"Hairstyles these days." Theo frowned, nodding toward a half-green, half-black ponytail that was sculpted into a stiff figure eight. Rogan agreed. They passed the mug some more. When it was nearly empty, he felt her eyes slide over to him. "You feeling the itch?"

There were times, few and far between, when they found comfort in each other's bodies. No strings, no expectations. Just mutual trust, mutual release, and mutual discretion. The arrangement was perfect. Didn't leave him feeling empty at all.

The things Rogan saw, the things he did, weren't pillow talk material. Long term wasn't in the cards. Hell, short term wasn't, either, and that was fine. He had the squad, he had the job…he had higher goddamn priorities.

A pair of crystal blue eyes flashed across his mind, and he shoved the image away abruptly. What the hell?

He smiled tightly at Theo, shaking his head. "You?"

Unoffended, she mirrored his gesture and took a sip of coffee before passing it back to him. "You're tense."

Just an impending archangel ass-chewing, no big deal. And a spitfire he couldn't seem to get out of his mind. "What's going on with the alarm?"

She gave him a look that said she knew he was evading.

"Keeps going off at weird times, and there's nothing there. And just a…weird feeling, sometimes. Creepy."

His instincts lit up. Not only was Theo tough as nails, she was also a powerful aquamage with the ability to manipulate water in all its forms. She could turn every drop of moisture in his body to ice with the flick of her finger, and she wasn't easily spooked. "I'll take a look."

"Thanks. Then go see a movie or something, for fuck's sake. You need to get away from the job." She took a long drag of vape.

"Pot, kettle."

"Yeah, why do you think I can spot it?" Theo replied thickly through a cherry-scented fog. She pointed her vape pen at him. "I've been telling you for years that you need a hobby. Or to get laid more often." When he shot her a look, she just lifted her scarlet brows. "All work and no play makes Rogan a damn cyborg."

Rogan squinted at a tiny pygmy fae crouched on a limb of a nearby walnut tree, who was giggling while chucking nuts at people walking below.

"Do you even remember how to have fun?" Theo pressed.

Rogan nodded toward the fae in the tree. "Like that?" They watched as she nailed another morning commuter hurrying to work. The guy hollered and rubbed his head while she dissolved into tinny cackles. Fuming, the guy started flinging the nuts back up at her.

Theo snickered. "Well, it doesn't *have* to be malicious or childish, but both can be fun." Her silver eyes glinted.

Rogan shook his head. "You would think being malicious is fun."

She laughed, patting his cheek. "Oh, everyone's got a little devil in them. Doesn't make them a demon."

Rogan felt a jolt at her words, but he kept his face blank.

When she headed inside, Rogan popped a piece of gum into his mouth and began a sweep of the perimeter. Light

House kids ran gleefully to his side while he worked. A redheaded seven-year-old named Franklin showed him the shield charm he'd learned last week. Nero, a solemn girl with eyes much older than her ten years, demonstrated a fierce jab-cross combo at Rogan's ribs. Rogan blocked and tapped her chin with a gentle uppercut, making her smile. The sweep took twice as long as it should have.

He found nothing. No claw marks, no charred spots, no whiffs of sulfur. The security fence and alarm system were all in working order.

He didn't like it.

It was a Vortech security fence. A few years old, but still one of the best on the market. If the alarm went off, something was there. Which meant something invisible lurked around the school.

He made another sweep, then a third, checking his watch so frequently his elbow started to creak. Still nothing from the Magistrate.

Headquarters was only a twenty-minute walk from Light House, but he headed downtown with an hour to spare. When archangels requested a meeting, a smart man showed up early.

CHAPTER 6

The Magistrate's office was on the ninth floor of headquarters. Sleek and modern, it was dominated by white furniture, framed awards, and floor-to-ceiling windows with a spectacular view of downtown.

Magistrate Thackeray White stood beside his massive desk, hands clasped behind his back. Blond hair swept over one side of his head in an artful wave, accentuating a handsome, sharp-featured face. The other half of his head was completely hairless, mottled pink, and scarred. The damaged flesh trailed over his temple to end in a jagged ribbon across his right cheekbone. The public story was that he'd been badly burned in a house fire. The real story was a vicious demon attack in his early adulthood.

The Magistrate was born with the ability to see demons, so he'd witnessed his parents' slaughter with brutal clarity. His plans to develop the DE began shortly thereafter.

Now, he adjusted his wire-framed glasses and rocked back on his heels with a benign smile, one hand absently brushing over the medallion that hung from a long chain around his neck. Arcs of electricity danced in glass domes on the shelves behind him—fitting decor for the most powerful electromage the city had ever known.

Seconds ticked by. Rogan stood by the bust of some long-dead philosopher and watched the Aerial whiz past the wall of windows like a monstrous silver eel. Behind him, the squad practically vibrated with tension. He rolled his shoulders, flexed his hands, and tried not to scratch. The Magistrate was powerful enough on his own; add Cyrus and John to the mix, and the amount of magic in the room was enough to make anyone's blood buzz. Rogan tilted his head to pop his neck.

A blinding flash of light lit the room. Rogan jerked with his head mid-tilt, sending pain zinging up his throat. He straightened, blinking rapidly. Behind him, Wolf whispered, "Holy shit."

Four towering angels stood before them, draped in luminous white linen, their heads almost brushing the ceiling. Enormous silver and gold longswords gleamed at their waists, matching the medallions that hung from their necks. Massive wings were tucked gracefully behind their backs, their feathered tips sweeping the floor.

Rogan's eyes trailed upward. He wasn't a small man, and he'd been told he wasn't bad looking, but staring up into those frighteningly beautiful faces, he felt ugly, miniscule…pointless.

His dad's Model B was a comforting weight on his belt. He took a steadying breath.

"These are the warriors?" one of the angels said. Dark brows knit over diamond white eyes. It was like being sighted by a ten-foot hawk.

The Magistrate stepped forward and made introductions, gesturing to each agent in turn. "Agent John Youngbear, aethromage and teleporter." He smiled fondly at John. "Cyrus Aurelian, telekinetic cerebromage. Killian Diallo and Juno DeSilva, lion and jaguar shapeshifters, respectively. Wolf

Fennimore, wolf shifter. And our longest tenured agent and squad leader, Nash Rogan."

"A human?"

"Best fucking one there is," Wolf snapped from the back of the squad.

Rogan felt his eyes nearly bulge out of his head.

"Agent Rogan is the founder of our field team. His loyalty to the cause is unmatched," the Magistrate cut in smoothly. "He is also an exceptional sharpshooter, extremely adept with technology, and arguably the best hand-to-hand combatant in all of Magical Law Enforcement."

Arguably?

The archangels leveled their matching stares at Rogan. He pinned his gaze to the wall and tried not to squirm, mentally flipping through the MLE roster for an agent who could take him at hand-to-hand.

Tell Wolf to keep his goddamn mouth shut, he thought at Cyrus, never so glad that they could communicate in silence. Few cerebromages had the ability, but Cyrus was far from average. Those long nights in their dorm had honed the skill even further, to the point that Cyrus sometimes picked up on Rogan's thoughts when he didn't want him to.

Yeah, no shit. Cyrus's voice cut through his head. *And nobody can take you at hand-to-hand, man, forget about it.*

Rogan shoved Cyrus out of his head and fought to refocus.

"The number of hellspawn in the city is growing," another angel said.

Fuck. "We patrol and eradicate every night...sir." Shit, he had no clue how to address an angel. Your Grace? Your Majesty? Your Holy Hugeness?

"And yet, you have found zero hellmouths."

"None yet, sir." Admitting it was like swallowing a handful of razor blades.

The angel grunted, clearly unimpressed. Rogan opened his mouth, a series of explanations on the tip of his tongue—

"We have another mission for you."

Rogan snapped his jaws shut.

"Our brother has Fallen."

The word dropped like a glacier in the middle of the room. The archangels all made a strange sign over their chests, bowing their heads.

Silence rang.

What the hell did one say to that? "I'm sorry for your loss."

The tallest angel, unbelievably beautiful, with shining blond hair that brushed his massive shoulders, stepped forward. The power radiating from him was immense. "I am Michael."

The angel gave the words a chance to sink in. Someone swallowed audibly. Rogan considered dropping to his knees, and he wasn't even a churchgoer.

Michael gazed around at them. His brilliant white eyes hardened. "Our brother succumbed to the succubus, Inara."

The angels hissed, their perfect faces turning fierce and animalistic. A thrill of fear shot through Rogan. He felt the shifters behind him stiffen in response, and a low growl rumbled from Killian's chest. Rogan knocked his squad mate's boot with his own.

"Alistor was the best of us," Michael continued. "The kindest. A healer. Inara exploited that. She seduced him, and he Fell." The angels made the strange sign over their chests again. "We think he is here in Concordia."

Another lingering silence.

"Why do you think that?" Rogan asked finally. One would think a giant, winged supermodel stalking around the city would be hard to miss.

"We feel him. Here." Michael touched the medallion hanging from his neck. It was the size of an old silver dollar and carved with symbols that caught the light, same as the one the Magistrate wore. "As you know, the time we can spend in the midrealm is limited. We require your aid."

Rogan's chin lifted, his chest swelling despite himself.

"How long has he been missing?" John's voice rang out from behind him.

"Twenty-five years."

Well, shit. "Tell us everything you know."

CHAPTER 7

The path through Unity Park was a nice, leafy shortcut to the docks. Jovi's skin hummed where her father's amulet rested against it, tucked beneath the neckline of her hot pink dress. She'd unearthed it from the shoebox at the bottom of her closet and looped it reluctantly over her head before leaving the apartment. The silvery gold disc buzzed with silent power, making it feel like her sternum was plugged into a light socket.

It was uncomfortable AF, but she would need it to back up her story when she found her dad. Which might happen, like, today.

Dimitri Zmey might have been totally useless, but at least Jovi had gotten some good news last night. Back at the apartment, Nora had logged onto the Darkforum and discovered a message waiting for her. Someone had responded to the post she'd made six months ago, asking for any information related to someone named Alistor.

VladGuy706 had apparently heard the name last week, down at the docks.

Jovi's nerves jangled. They'd followed a lot of dead leads in the past few months, and this was probably another one.

But maybe it wasn't.

She walked past a romantic picnic some poor sap had set up on the grass. A basket, a bottle of champagne, and a candle were artfully arranged on a blanket. Its owner was nowhere to be found—probably snuck off to take a piss. Jovi leaned over and swiped the champagne as she strolled by. She could use a belt of liquid courage.

What if this was it, the day she finally met him?

Maybe she really did have his eyes. Maybe he'd been looking for her, too. Maybe he would sweep her into a big, dramatic hug and she would feel safe and right, like she belonged somewhere, to someone.

Maybe he didn't even know she existed. Even worse, maybe he did, and he hated her.

Jovi popped the champagne cork, sending it flying into the bushes. An angry storm of pygmy fae erupted from the foliage, zooming off in every direction. Jovi tilted her head back, took a swig—and spotted the demon crouched in the branches overhead.

Foam cascaded down her chin as the bottle fizzed over. The demon was some nasty bastardization of a dog, gripping a tree limb with spider-thin legs while its fat, pebbly nose sniffed the air. What was this thing doing out in the daylight? Most demons, excluding herself, could hardly stand the sun...

Her trackband clinked against the champagne bottle. Scarlet eyes landed on Jovi, and a second later, the demon launched at her.

Jovi chucked the bottle aside, and spat a mouthful of flaming champagne at it. The blaze caught the dog demon full in the face. It tumbled backward, yelping. Jovi swung her arm overhead and brought a lasso of pure fire down on the fucker's torso, waiting until it wound around the demon's ribs before yanking it hard, sending the dog smashing into a tree trunk. She jerked the flaming rope the other way, hurling the demon across the path into another tree. Again and again, she whipped it back and forth, bashing it into tree trunks while the smell of burnt fur filled the air.

A shrill, ear-splitting whistle cut through the demon's agonized yelps. Jovi blinked, suddenly realizing there was a bright red spotlight blazing from her wrist.

Shit, shit, shit. She extinguished her lasso, and the dog demon crumpled to the ground, whimpering. Jovi banged her trackband against a park bench, desperate to shut the thing up.

The demon staggered up from the pavement, smoke rising from its charred hide. It shook its horrible, blackened head, let out a dissonant two-tone howl, and disappeared just as two MLE agents jogged around the corner.

Mother fucking—

"MLE. Hands behind your back, ma'am." One agent cuffed her hands while the other silenced her shrieking trackband with a swipe of his watch. Without another word, they tugged her toward the nearby street, where a squad car sat parked at the curb.

Oh, shit, this was bad. "Hey, I thought you were supposed to question me!"

"You'll be questioned at the station, ma'am."

Pedestrians ignored her struggles as the agents stuffed her into the car and slammed the door. The ride to MLE head-quarters took all of two seconds, during which time Jovi scraped her wrists raw trying to wriggle out of the handcuffs. The agents hauled her out of the backseat, pushed her through the front door, and dumped her in one of the hard plastic chairs in the lobby. "Wait here, ma'am."

"Quit calling me *ma'am*." She was barely holding back the angry sparks tingling under her skin.

One of the agents raised an amused brow. "Wait here, Jane Doe…" He tapped his watch, consulting the screen. "0130."

Jovi gave him a filthy look. The agent smirked, then

snapped to attention as someone strode by. She followed his gaze and felt a jolt.

It was him. Agent Annoyingly Hot Rogan, the one who'd put a trackband on her and got her into this mess. He did the slightest double-take as he saw her, then pivoted smartly toward them, coming to a stop directly in front of her.

His gaze never wavered. "Report."

"Unity Park, alone, smelled like a pyro. No victim, no witnesses," one of the agents responded promptly.

Rogan nodded once. "I'll handle it from here, agents."

"Sir, you don't have to—"

"I'll handle it."

They scurried off.

Rogan sank to a crouch in front of her. If he got any closer, those muscular pecs would brush her bare knees. "What is your name?" The words were quiet and carried a hint of mint.

"Jane Doe 0130."

He waited.

She tapped her toe irritably.

He quirked a brow.

Ugh. "Jovi," she said. He was so annoying.

"Jovi what?"

Surnames weren't a thing in hell. She blurted out the first thing that came to mind, staring at the tight shirt stretching over his biceps. "Black. Your turn."

"I told you, my name is Agent Rogan."

She waited, raising a brow.

The standoff lasted several seconds before a tiny muscle twitched below his eye. "Nash." He rose and took her by the elbow, pulling her to her feet, his hand cool on her heated skin. "Let's talk."

He led her to an interrogation room and closed the door behind them, cutting off the sounds of the busy station before swiping his watch over her cuffs to release her hands. He walked around the desk, gesturing for Jovi to sit.

She plopped into the chair, glaring at him. Rogan sat across from her, setting the cuffs on the desk. He leveled his gaze with hers. He was way too good looking, she decided. His eyes were beautifully pale, an unusual green, like the color of the sea glass pebbles that washed up from the bay.

"So, Jovi Black." He said her name deliberately like he was adding details to an internal file. "What happened this time?"

"Look, I was just…surprised. I didn't mean to. It won't happen again."

"That's what you said last night."

Jovi tossed up her hands, noticed they were smoldering, and then shoved them between her knees. "I didn't hurt anyone."

"I gathered that. That's why I'm letting you go. Again."

"Fabulous." She pushed herself to her feet. The room spun, and she swayed before catching herself. Shit, she needed food. "Can I go, then?"

The infuriating man just continued to stare, jaw flexing as he worked a piece of gum. Then, he leaned forward. "Did someone hurt *you*, Jovi?"

He had a nice voice, damn it. Low and smooth like melted caramel. She liked how her name sounded when he said it. And now he suddenly cared if she had been hurt?

A voice squawked through the communicator on his shoulder, requesting urgent backup.

Perfect. "Sounds like you're needed elsewhere."

Sea glass eyes narrowed. "You can go. But Ms. Black," he said as she turned to leave, "Stay out of trouble."

She stuck her tongue out at him.

CHAPTER 8

Jovi trudged down the sidewalk, cursing Nash Rogan under her breath. The docks weren't too far from here —at least those MLE assholes had taken her in the right direction when they'd hauled her in.

Fucking trackband. She glared at it. The silver metal glinted, then blurred as her vision went hazy.

Shit, was she really this wiped? Stupid dog demon. Her boots felt like lead. She weaved toward a bus stop and sat heavily on the bench, trying to blink the streets into focus. A homeless guy toppled onto the bench next to her. She wrinkled her nose at his stench. He belched, then barfed spectacularly at her feet.

Seriously? Holding back her own vomit, Jovi scrambled off the bench and stumbled down the street, wiping her brow. Oh, no. She had the sick sweats. Was she going to pass out? She was going to pass out. She was going to drop unconscious on the disgusting concrete with the fast food wrappers and the dirty puddles, and some bum was going to come puke on her.

Pedestrians bumped into her, giving her dirty looks and

telling her to watch it. She swung into an alley just before her knees buckled, sliding down the wall until her ass hit the pavement. She needed a minute. Just a second to catch her breath, then she'd haul herself to the nearest hotdog cart—

A shout echoed from the far end of the alley. Then another. And then, three unmistakable gunshots—and a massive explosion.

Jovi yelped and cringed, then looked to the far end of the corridor. Her jaw dropped. A flaming building was perfectly framed by the alley walls, spewing smoke and glass and a cloud of dust that rolled over the street like a tidal wave. Car alarms wailed, people screamed. There was an ominous rumble, then a roar of sound as half of the building collapsed.

She was so busy staring stupidly that she almost missed the giant ball of electricity rocketing toward her. She flattened herself against the wall as the crackling sphere shot past, illuminating two silhouettes sprinting from the shadows.

One of the figures hurled another crackling ball of energy. It nailed the other in the back of the knees, taking him to the ground. He yelled and spasmed on the pavement, trying to scramble to his feet, but the attacker was on him too fast, flipping him over, straddling his chest.

"You will pay," he growled in a heavy accent. He reached one hand toward the guy's throat and made a sharp grabbing motion above it. The guy on the ground choked. A horrible snap echoed in the dark alley, and the attacker yanked his hand back. Something soft and dripping was clutched tightly in his grip. He laughed, squeezing it over the face of his victim as the guy made wet, gurgling sounds from the concrete. The attacker flung the dripping object away. It smacked into the alley wall an inch from Jovi's head, and she let out a tiny gasp.

The attacker's head snapped in her direction.

Oh, fuck. She was in trouble. Big trouble. She had nothing left, nothing in the tank. Desperate, she hit the heel of her boot against the ground, and the little dagger flicked out of its toe. She tried to struggle to her feet, but her legs weighed a million pounds. A shaft of sunlight illuminated the man's face as he stalked toward her. His skin was sallow, mottled, and riddled with pockmarks. Stringy hair plastered his head, and his eyes glowed eerily green as they fixed her to the wall.

"Kruzchev!" someone bellowed from the other end of the alley.

Pockmarks glanced toward the sound, curling his lip. Backing away, he conjured a humming ball of energy, refocused on Jovi, and drew back his arm like he was going to launch it at her.

Come on, come on! Jovi raised her hands and tried to summon the hellfire, envisioned it boiling up in her veins, erupting from her body...

Nothing happened. She was empty, defenseless, alone.

"Kruzchev!" the voice roared again.

Pockmarks launched the electric orb at her.

Jovi strained, the edges of her vision going dark. A measly sphere of flame, not even enough to set off her trackband, floated out of her outstretched palm and collided with the ball of energy inches before it hit her face. Another sizzling sphere flew toward her, she ducked, and the ball of energy slammed into the brick wall where her head had been, raining debris.

A beam of light zoomed down the alley and nailed Pockmarks in the shoulder. He screamed in pain, slapping a hand to the wound and shooting a murderous look in the direction it had come.

"Fucking Rogan," he growled in that thick accent. Then, with a last snarling look at Jovi, he threw his hand toward the ground at his feet and vanished in a burst of blinding light.

The crumbled brick scraped her hands as she scrambled to all fours. Her palm touched something wet and fibrous—the dead dude's windpipe. Her stomach lurched, and she hauled herself to her feet, staggering toward the sidewalk.

Footsteps pounded toward her. "Stop!"

Stumbling, Jovi glanced wildly over her shoulder.

Sprinting from the shadows, silhouetted by the flames of the burning building behind him, was Agent Nash Rogan.

Relief, of all things, washed over her.

She braced a hand on the alley wall and puked, narrowly missing the little dagger sticking out of her boot. She stomped her heel to retract it before Rogan could catch a glimpse.

He stopped short when he reached her. "Jovi Black?" His shocked expression vanished as he grabbed her arm and led her firmly out of the alley, head on a constant swivel. "We need to get clear."

Jovi struggled to keep up. Rogan frowned at her, but he didn't slow down, practically lifting her feet off the ground as he pulled her along. "Are you hit?"

Jovi shook her head but stumbled again, sagging.

Rogan cursed. "You're cashed." He wrapped a hard arm around her waist, continuing to drag her down the sidewalk. People cast wary glances their way. Rogan ignored them, tapping the comm on his shoulder with his free hand. "Agent Rogan requesting backup. I need an escort, stat." Heat radiated off him as he continued to bark into the communicator. Still hauling her along, he dug into his pocket, pulled something out, and yanked a wrapper off of it with his teeth. Then he tried to shove it in Jovi's mouth.

She struggled instinctively, wrenching her head away.

"Stop," he gritted, pushing her against a building and pinning her there with a body that seemed to be made of solid steel. With ruthless efficiency, he forced her jaw open and popped whatever it was in her mouth. There was a hit of intense peppermint, a rush of sweetness on her tongue…

And then, just over Rogan's shoulder, a rat-sized demon appeared on top of a trash can.

She blacked out.

CHAPTER 9

"Sir, I beg you to reconsider."

The Magistrate sipped his oolong and glanced up from his tablet, giving Rogan a placating smile that made his blood boil. "Nash, you're too valuable."

"I can handle myself."

"Of course you can. But it's not worth the risk. And we need someone to protect the other witness." He looked down at his tablet again. "What did you say she was?"

"Pyro, level five. Assign someone else." Rogan shot a glance at the Magistrate's assistant, who was clutching his own tablet and hovering like a twitchy rabbit. He might manage every aspect of the Magistrate's calendar, but he wasn't privy to the DE's secrets. "I need to be out there." *Looking for a fallen angel.*

"I understand your eagerness to stay in the field." The Magistrate gave him a meaningful look. "But you were identified, Nash. You know how dangerous the Kruzchev family is. Let the agents working the case do their jobs. From what I understand, they're close to pinning some of the big players, so it shouldn't be long." He tilted his head. "You should see the medical team. That cut on your cheek looks deep."

"It's fine." Rogan glanced at the assistant again. "We don't know that I was identified. And our assignment is too important to put on hold, sir."

The Magistrate sighed, rising from his desk. "Tyrell, give us a moment, please."

The assistant scurried away, closing the door silently behind him.

"Nash." The Magistrate circled his desk and put both hands on Rogan's shoulders. "The rest of the team can continue the search while you're gone. You are too important to risk. What if you were captured?"

His scars looked worse up close, raised and bumpy and shining with the salve he smoothed over them. The pungent, herbal scent of it was familiar. Comforting. It made Rogan feel thirteen again. "I would handle it."

The Magistrate gave him an arch look and went back to his chair. Electric filaments surged inside their glass domes as he passed. "Magical interrogation methods are much different than physical, Nash. You know this."

It was the one thing he'd struggled with at the academy. Mages could throw up magical blocks, and shifters had natural mental shields, but a human mind was a vulnerable, naked infant in the face of a cerebromage's interrogation. Rogan had withstood more than anyone expected, but he'd still landed himself in the hospital with a brain bleed. Twice.

His nails bit into his palms. "I didn't break. I wouldn't break. Our work is too important to me, sir. You know that."

The Magistrate smiled with something way too close to pity. "My decision stands."

Rogan heard something in his jaw crack. He nodded once and left the room.

CHAPTER 10

Jovi opened her eyes. Ugh, MLE headquarters again. Even flat on her back, there was no mistaking all that blue-threaded glass.

There was also no mistaking Nash Rogan's smooth voice rumbling on the other side of it. He was talking to another agent in the next room, their words clipped.

Jovi eased upright, blinking until her head stopped spinning. She was on a rollaway cot in a room by herself. A TV tray held a paper cup of orange juice and two glazed doughnuts on a plate. Her stomach rumbled. She felt the amulet's weight against her sternum and breathed a sigh of relief, patting its hard shape beneath her dress.

On the other side of the glass, Rogan's broad shoulders turned as he glanced around. He slapped his phone onto a table in the other room, then chucked his own paper cup irritably into a trash can before exiting. He came into her room and closed the door just as she took a long, eager gulp of juice. She lowered the cup with a sigh.

He leaned against the door, folding his arms. "Eat."

"Don't boss me," Jovi croaked, then coughed. Her throat

was scratchy and raw. At least now she tasted juice instead of vomit.

He strode over, plucked a doughnut from the plate, and held it an inch from her nose, radiating a whole lot of pissed off vibes. A deep, angry cut streaked across one high cheekbone. Had that been there before, on the street? She hadn't noticed.

"Eat. You need it."

She did need to eat, desperately. Jovi snatched it from him and took a massive bite, felt her eyes roll back in her head at the sweet, soft perfection.

Rogan watched her darkly. He grabbed a napkin from a stack on the tray, wiped his fingers, and turned to stare out the glass walls, every muscle tense. Most mages were either fat or scrawny, made lazy by magic. Not Rogan. Every inch of him looked like a hard, honed weapon. What kind of mage was he?

He finished methodically wiping his fingers, folded the napkin into a neat square, and dropped it into a wastebasket. Dusting off his hands, he brushed an invisible speck of lint from his bicep, used his toe to nudge the wastebasket an inch to the right. Then, he straightened all the fancy tech toys on his belt.

Jovi watched him as she picked up the second doughnut, intrigued. What would Agent Anal Retentive do if she smashed the thing into *his* face? She grinned at the thought.

He turned, about to say something, but stopped when he saw her expression. "What?"

"Nothing. What's up, Nashty Pants?"

"Don't call me that." He scowled, stalking toward her. "You, Jovi Black, are in trouble."

"Hey, I didn't do *anything* this time—"

"You saw something."

That shut her up. The alley rushed back to her—the explosion, the attacker, the burning building as it crumbled. The guy's windpipe as it sailed toward her. The doughnut she'd eaten suddenly threatened to come back up, but she took another huge bite.

"You saw some*one*. And he saw you."

Pockmarks, with his greasy hair and glowing green eyes. "Fuck," Jovi whispered around the mouthful of doughnut. "Who was he?"

"Anton Kruzchev. One of the nastiest thugs in the Slavic crime syndicate, and nephew of its leader. He blew up a building this morning with a couple of his associates, killed three civilians and two rival family members, and assaulted an MLE agent."

The cut on his cheek. "You."

"Me. I'm not convinced *he* knows that—"

"He does." The doughnut had lost its flavor. She set the remainder on the plate. "He said your name."

Rogan stilled. "Are you one hundred percent sure?"

Jovi nodded. "*Fucking Rogan.*"

"Excuse me?"

"That's what he said. I know the feeling," she added out of the corner of her mouth.

Rogan turned away, his hands squeezing into fists.

"So, what now?" Hopefully, he'd let her go. She had been so close to the docks…what time was it? How long had she been out? She craned her neck, looking for a window.

Rogan released a long, controlled breath. "WITPRO." He said the word like he was taking a bite out of it.

She stared at him. "Wit-what?"

"Witness Protection. I was hoping to avoid it. The Magistrate has other ideas. For both of us."

Jovi's brain whirled. "Wait, what do you mean?"

He met her eyes. "You and I are going into hiding together."

CHAPTER 11

"WITPRO? You're kidding," Cyrus said.

Rogan glanced over at his squad mate. He might as well have been on a damn magazine cover, leaning with casual grace against the bedroom door frame, all dark skin and jacked muscle and piercing blue eyes. Someone that good looking shouldn't be so fucking smart. It was irritating. But it was also one of the reasons Cyrus was so good at undercover work, which was also irritating. Everything was irritating.

"Not kidding." Rogan chucked a roll of socks into his duffle.

"Her, I get. But why you?" Cyrus glanced over as Wolf sauntered into view, shirtless and barefoot in a pair of loose sweatpants, loudly crunching a bag of chips.

"The Magistrate doesn't want me in the field until the heat dies down." A surge of frustration bubbled up from his belly. "Apparently, the team working the case is close to pinning him."

"Bullshit," Wolf said around a mouthful of chips. "Bunch of lazy ass desk jockeys."

Cyrus wrinkled his nose. "Man, go take a shower."

"What?" Wolf ran a hand through his mop of hair. It stuck out like he'd poked his finger in a socket. "I just got done working out, man. Give me a break."

"Yeah, you stink."

Wolf snarled at him, an actual animal's growl rumbling up from his throat. Then he turned his gold eyes on Rogan. "What about you? Aren't you going to tell me that potato chips don't have the ideal carb-to-protein ratio for muscle recovery?"

"That's true. You're not doing yourself any favors."

"You're just jealous that you won't get to look for this naughty fallen angel while you're in WITPRO." He popped another chip in his mouth. "Stuck babysitting." He chuckled like a surfer, but wicked intelligence glinted behind his eyes. He knew that being pulled from the mission was killing Rogan and he couldn't pass up the opportunity to rub salt in the wound. He crunched a few times, then stopped short. "Wait, is she hot, though?"

Cotton candy hair, big blue eyes, tight curves…

"Yes." Cyrus grinned.

"She is?" Wolf's eyes grew wide. "Aw, man, now maybe *I'm* jealous! Show me the profile."

"No," Rogan snapped.

Cyrus already had his phone pulled up. He showed it to Wolf, smirking. Wolf took one look and howled, chin to the ceiling.

"Aw, man, is that the anime girl? That pyromage you were talking about? Now I'm definitely jealous! How are you going to handle that? WITPRO is no-touchy, right?"

Rogan zipped his duffle sharply. "I'm a professional, that's how." He headed for the bathroom to pack his toiletries.

"*I'm a professional, that's how,*" Wolf mimicked under his breath. Rogan heard muffled sniggering, then a scuffle like the dumbasses were shoving each other around in his doorway. He packed his razor, shaving cream, toothbrush, toothpaste, and floss. It was probably unnecessary—he was sure the safe house was fully stocked. He glanced up at the mirror.

Without warning, an image of Jovi Black flashed across his mind. Her taut little body was perched cross-legged on his bathroom sink while she twirled a lock of pink hair around her finger, inching her ruffled miniskirt higher and higher up a silken thigh.

Rogan yanked his thoughts back to the present and stalked back to the bedroom, ready to pop in more ways than one. "I need you all to keep me updated. I can still help with the search."

"From the safe house?" Cyrus arched a brow.

Rogan cracked his neck. He needed coffee. "Yes. I'm bringing my tablet. I can research, call our usual informants…" *Be a part of it. Lead. Complete the mission, impress the archangels, prove myself. Prove my worth. Make my dad proud, make the Magistrate proud…*

Cyrus blinked rapidly, shook his head. Their gazes met, and Rogan knew that Cyrus had heard those thoughts. Fuck.

"We'll keep you posted. But you have a new priority mission now, Nash." Cyrus stabbed a finger at him. "Keep your ass, and this anime girl, alive until they get these Slav assholes."

"This needs to be over *fast*." Putting the archangel mission on hold pissed him off, and being pulled from the field made him twitchy as hell. But the idea of holing up alone with Jovi Black set off warning bells in his brain.

And that's what disturbed him the most.

CHAPTER 12

The car was too goddamn small.

Rogan's hands tightened on the steering wheel. They were still fifty miles from the safe house, and he was damn near suffocating himself, trying not to breathe through his nose.

The scent of her was killing him. Sweetness and heat, smoke and sugar. It curled around him, drifting over the console, filling the tight space. It should've been sickly, but underneath the sweetness was something else, something darker, edgier. The combination was intoxicating.

He watched her in his peripheral vision. She was stunning, almost otherworldly with that pale pink hair and those big, uptilted eyes. He couldn't shake the feeling that she was more than a mage. Fae, maybe? There were different classes of fae; some were human-sized. He needed a look at her teeth. "Let me see your teeth."

Jovi looked at him like he'd sprouted horns. "Excuse you?"

"Your teeth. Let me see them."

"Fuck off."

Rogan scowled at the road.

"Why do you want to see my teeth?" Jovi demanded. She swept a strand of hair out of her face, and he caught a glimpse of her scraped palm, evidence of the scuffle in the alley just hours before. His gut clenched as he saw her there again, exhausted and terrified, scrambling over broken brick and gravel. He felt a rush of satisfaction that he had been the one to haul her out of there.

"Are you fae?"

"Fae?" She appeared to think. "I don't know."

"You don't know?"

A brief silence. "I don't know who my dad is." She looked out the window. "I've been trying to find him."

Something tightened in his chest. He knew that dark, bottomless void, and he knew what it was like trying to constantly fill it. At least he had memories of his dad. Apparently, Jovi Black didn't even have those to cling to. "You think he's somewhere in the city?"

Jovi shrugged. "I have a lead or two. Mostly dead ends."

That was familiar, too. Rogan's brows knit together. He and this little flamethrower had more in common than he'd thought, and he wasn't sure he liked it.

He watched out of the corner of his eye while she drummed her fingers, tapped her feet, and fluttered her lips with exaggerated sighs. She propped one boot up on the dash, displaying a lot more leg than was damn well necessary, and tightened her laces before dropping her foot again and leaving a dusty boot print on the glove box. Rogan glowered at it.

"Watch out!" she shrieked suddenly, pointing, and Rogan jerked his gaze back to the road just in time to avoid flattening the squirrel that was darting across the highway. The car swerved wildly, but he centered it before they went into the ditch. Jovi let out a relieved breath.

Rogan glared at her. "Was that really necessary?" His heart thumped.

"You were going to hit it!"

"A squirrel."

"Yeah, a squirrel! What, you just go around mowing down animals?" She shot him a look. "Sick fuck."

"I don't go around *mowing down animals.*" Frankly, he was surprised she cared. Jovi Black: Sets men on fire without remorse, but brakes for squirrels.

The woman was baffling. Maybe that was why she didn't appear to have many friends.

Before they left, MLE had taken their phones and asked for a list of close friends and relatives, anyone who could be used against them. Jovi's list had one name—her roommate, Nora Alvarez. No parents, no family, no coworkers. No significant other.

Seeing that last one blank, Rogan had felt a jolt of satisfaction in his belly that had nothing to do with the job. That pissed him off, too.

"So, how long are we going to be stuck in this safe house, anyway?" Jovi asked. "I've got stuff to do."

"Don't we all." The steering wheel creaked under his grip. "I gave them four weeks. I can handle Kruzchev." He glared at the painted lines whizzing under the car. "I need to be out there."

"Why?"

He stayed silent.

"You do something different, huh?"

He glanced over in surprise, and she rolled her eyes. "Oh, come on, I see the way those other agents cream themselves when you're around. Agent Nash Rogan must be pretty hot stuff." She wiggled her brows. "You obviously do something important."

He stared at her. She was searching for family, she

swerved for squirrels, and she was smarter than he'd given her credit for.

Rogan felt a muscle twitch beneath his eye. "Yes, I am." He slid on a pair of sunglasses. "And yes, I do."

CHAPTER 13

Yes, I am, and yes, I do. Pompous ass. Too bad the words, in that low, velvety voice, had sent a thrill through her.

Nash fucking Rogan.

Jovi fiddled with her trackband. The little black dot, barely larger than a poppy seed, was almost invisible on the inside of the cuff. A tiny GPS tracker, courtesy of a naughty little hacker named Nora Alvarez.

Just in case, she'd said.

It was nice knowing someone gave a shit where she was. It was also nice knowing Nash Rogan had no idea about it.

She smirked over at him. He took turn after random turn, doubled back once or twice, and glanced constantly in the rearview mirror.

"Are we being followed?" Jovi asked finally.

"I don't think so."

"So, can we just get to the place, then? I've got to pee, and my lady bits are getting sweaty on this leather seat." She shifted delicately.

He shot her a dry glance from behind his shades, but less than ten minutes later, they rounded a new corner, and Jovi gasped. The steel blue of the ocean sparkled in the setting sun, a vast expanse of...nothingness. Quiet, shimmering water in a smooth bay. No smelly docks littered with bums and trash. No gray, choppy water or banged-up boats. Just sparkly, serene blue.

They drove alongside the water until finally, Rogan hit the brakes and whipped into a nearly invisible gravel drive tucked among some wild-looking bushes, driving down a long lane until they reached a small cottage.

Rogan pulled to a stop. Jovi turned to unbuckle her seatbelt and found herself pinned by a set of very serious green eyes. They had tiny flecks of gold in them.

"Stay here." The faintest dusting of freckles sprinkled his nose.

Jovi made a face at his intensity, but she stayed put as he got out and closed the door behind him, his head on a swivel. He pulled a phaser from his waistband and began stalking around the outside of the cottage.

The second he disappeared around the back of the house, she hopped out of the car and inhaled deeply. The freshness of the air seemed to buoy her lungs, filling them fuller than they ever had been in the city. She darted up the front steps.

The door was locked. She jiggled the handle. Damn.

Rogan came around the corner. He froze when he saw her, then glanced at the car's passenger door, still hanging open. He looked back at her.

Jovi gave him a winning smile.

He stalked over, swiping his watch over the scanner at the door. The lock clicked. Jovi reached for the handle, but his big hand snapped over hers, trapping it. The metal was cool against her palm. Nash Rogan's hand was warm on top of hers. She glanced up at him. He glared down at her.

"I need to clear the house." Mint wafted over her. "Stay *here*."

"I can't take you seriously with those adorable freckles." She booped the bridge of his nose.

His green eyes went murderous.

She followed him inside. The cottage smelled delicious, like a mix of old wood and wool blankets and fresh sea air. While Rogan made a quick sweep of the place, she found a powder room and ducked in to do her business. Emerging refreshed, she walked around, taking it all in. Simply furnished and obviously rarely used, everything was cream, white, or tan. Small kitchen, living area, large windows revealing a huge back deck that overlooked a sandy path to the beach…

"Holy shitballs," Jovi exclaimed as Rogan appeared behind her with their luggage. "This place is awesome. How often does it get used?"

"Not often. There's two bedrooms and a bathroom upstairs, and a cellar with an escape tunnel downstairs."

She whipped around. "Escape what?"

"Escape tunnel. It leads to the main street in town. A ten-minute jog."

"Nice." Always good to have multiple exits. She'd been like a rat in the sewers down in hell, knew all the corridors, all the hiding places—not that they always worked. As Rogan headed up the stairs, she ventured into the little galley kitchen and yanked open the fridge. It was fully stocked with fruit, vegetables, and pristine cuts of meat. She rooted around for something sugary but came up with nothing.

"I'll show you the tunnel later," Rogan said, reappearing out of nowhere and making her jump. "You need to know how to get to it. Your bedroom is at the end of the hall." He nodded at the ceiling. "Are you hungry?"

"Always."

She could practically see him noting it in his mental file. *Jovi Black, registered magical female, pyromage level five, always hungry.* "MLE stocked the place for us. You're not a vegetarian, are you?"

Jovi snorted.

He pulled out ingredients, washed his hands like a surgeon scrubbing in, and began shaping hamburger patties with practiced efficiency.

"I'm surprised you'd get your hands dirty," Jovi teased. She hopped up onto the counter next to him, admiring the way his forearms flexed as he worked. Her plaid skirt was short—the marble countertop was cold against her butt.

"I'm not afraid to get dirty."

A tingle shot through her. She smiled, crossing her legs. He frowned at them, and she grinned. "Don't like me sitting up here, do you?"

"Your ass does not belong where I'm preparing food, no." He shook some seasoning onto the patties, then went to the sink to wash his hands again.

Jovi smirked. Looking past him into the living area, she spotted an old school liquor cabinet near the sliding patio door. She squealed and darted over, rifling through the bottles. "What's your pleasure?"

"Nothing."

"Oh, come on. You're not technically on duty, are you?" Tequila, triple sec, a cheap whisky, and a decent vodka.

"I'm always on duty."

Jovi rolled her eyes.

"And I'm here for your protection."

"Uh, excuse you. You're here for *your* protection. That mafia dude saw you, too. Besides, I can handle myself."

His jaw flexed. "Like you did in that alley?"

Dick. "Hey, I was empty, okay? If your stupid agents hadn't dragged me in, I would've gotten some food and been fine. Now, do you want one or not?" She wiggled the tequila bottle.

"No." He whipped a towel over one shoulder and headed for the deck.

She rolled her eyes and danced into the kitchen, pouring triple shots into two glasses, anyway. She idly wondered what it would take to get Nash Rogan tipsy.

Even better...what would he do if he let loose?

She finished the drinks and carried them out to the deck. "Tequila Sunrise." She set them on the simple wooden picnic bench, then sat just as a plate of four perfectly shaped, perfectly charred burgers appeared before her. They smelled incredible. Her stomach gave an audible growl.

Rogan sat opposite her, ignored the drink she'd made for him, and set down a glass of water instead.

She stuffed a burger into her mouth and moaned. Flavorful, juicy, and cooked to perfection. She took another huge bite. Across from her, Rogan removed his bun, set it aside, and cut his burger into even portions. He ate methodically, with a fork. Probably counted how many times he chewed.

The tequila went down easy. Really easy. She finished hers. Seeing Rogan's still sitting there untouched, she nudged it toward him. He gave a short shake of his head.

"Just try it. What are you, scared?"

He pegged her with a hard look and a long silence. She wiggled her brows at him. Finally, he reached for the glass, took a tiny sip, and put the drink back down in front of her.

She rolled her eyes, snatched the glass, and drank deeply.

"Do you bartend?"

"Nah, I just really like alcohol, so I play around, see what I can do with it." She smacked her lips.

He stilled, then pointed to the glass. "Did you enchant that?"

She giggled. "Why, are you feeling...floopy?" She was.

His eyes bored into hers. "Did you?"

Grinning, she let the suspense hang for a second before finally conceding, waving her hand. "No, I can't do that shit."

He frowned. "Can't do what?"

"You know, cheering charms, glamors…" She trailed off. He was watching her way too closely. Why was he watching her so closely?

Shit. Right. She was supposed to be a mage. Any mage could do that kind of basic magic. "Just never been my bag," she finished breezily. "Never been good at it."

"What are you good at?"

She leaned forward and whispered, "Lighting shit on fire."

He gave her a dry look. "I noticed."

Jovi threw her head back and laughed.

CHAPTER 14

She was ludicrous. And beautiful. And definitely hiding something.

Rogan forced himself to look away, but not before he saw the slender arch of her neck as she laughed, the curve of her breasts as she leaned back, and the strands of bubblegum hair teasing her delicate collarbone. His groin tightened.

This was ridiculous. He was better than this. He stood abruptly. "I'm going to clean up. Why don't you enjoy the view?"

"Of you cleaning up?" She winked. "No problem."

Damn it. "Of the ocean," he bit out, gathering their plates. "There's a fire ring down on the beach. I can light it for you."

She was already hopping off the bench. "Will I set this thing off if I light it?" She held up her trackband.

Right. She was a powerful pyromage, she didn't need some human to light a damn match for her. "If it's nonaggressive, it shouldn't."

She jumped off the deck and sauntered toward the beach, skirt flouncing, boots kicking up little tufts of sand.

Rogan made quick work of the cleanup, though Jovi's

bartending had left a sticky mess on the counter. He wiped the sink, the stove, the faucet, the refrigerator handle, then inventoried the fridge, the cupboards, the pantry…the fridge again.

He glanced out the windows toward the beach, where a thin stream of smoke curled into the sky like a beckoning finger.

Coffee, stat. He stuffed a little pod into the single-serving machine in the kitchen. While waiting for it to spew the weak breakfast roast that made his lip curl, he drummed his fingers on the counter, argued with himself, then took out his burner phone and called Cyrus.

"Hey, man. How's the safe house?"

"I have a problem." The smell of coffee didn't calm him like it usually did.

Cyrus's tone sharpened. "What's up?"

Shit, he shouldn't have said anything. "Never mind. Any word on the Slavs?"

"No. Now, what's the problem?"

Rogan sighed, slugging back some of the scalding brew. It burned his tongue. "I'm attracted to her." He felt like an idiot.

A pause. Then, a short laugh. "Say what?"

Rogan scrubbed a hand over his face, leaning against the stove. "You heard me."

Another pause. "Like, how attracted?"

"Very."

Cyrus laughed again. "Well, yeah, she's hot."

"It's a problem."

"Like, you don't think you can handle it?" Cyrus suggested in disbelief.

"Of course I can handle it," he snapped.

"Well, okay then. Just ignore it. You can't hit that, and you know it."

"I know that."

"Wait, you *didn't*—"

"No!" He shoved away from the stove, realized he was pacing, and came to an abrupt halt.

"Okay, good. So, just keep it in your pants until you're done with WITPRO."

"I know that. I just..." What, wanted to whine? "Forget it." His teeth were going to be ground to dust by the end of the conversation.

Cyrus laughed again, the asshole. "This is really messing with you, huh?"

Rogan popped his neck. "It's fine. I'll be fine."

"You want me to take over?"

Jealousy boiled up inside him, the ugly, teeth-baring kind. "No!" he barked, then cringed at himself.

Cyrus gave a low whistle.

Rogan knew he should've kept his damn mouth shut. "Just stay on the other missions."

"Yeah, man, we're on it. Listen, just try to stay away from her. I know you've got to watch her back, but just keep your distance. And for the love of God, don't touch her."

"I got it. Call me with any progress." He hung up, glancing out the window. The trickle of smoke beckoned.

Rogan pulled out his WITPRO-issued tablet, planted his ass firmly at the kitchen table, and started researching archangels.

CHAPTER 15

J ovi slept like shit, despite the glorious king-sized bed.

It started out fine—crisp, cool sheets, mounds of fluffy blankets, room to sprawl. It ended with the dream. The memory. The one with the circle of flames and the bent, broken fingers glowing like coals at the ends of her hands. The shriveled, blackened bodies littering the ground. The stink of burnt flesh and piss. The sobs of the ones watching, waiting their turn.

Her mother's low, silky voice. *"You are pain. You are agony. You are the anguish of desire. You are the flames of retribution. That is what you are. Now come, little one...make them burn for what they did."*

Jovi surged awake, a gasp shredding her throat. Though she peeled her eyes wide, images bombarded her. A charred face. A whipped back. Her mother's black eyes. The view from her secret hiding spot, where she would huddle, knees under her chin, hoping she wouldn't be found...

She stumbled to the window and cracked it open, standing in her pink underwear and nothing else, bracing her hands on the sill as she caught her breath. Her trackband glinted in the moonlight. A trickle of sweat ran down her naked spine.

Her bedroom door flew open, and she jumped, whipping her head around.

Rogan stood in the doorway in nothing but black boxer briefs. His phaser swept the room. "What happened?"

Just a shitload of bad memories, no big deal. She latched on to the sight of him, blinking hard to clear the nasty movie reel from her mind. And, damn, what a pretty distraction he was. Every inch of him was lean, muscled, and defined. Broad shoulders tapered to chiseled abs, disappearing below his waistband in a delicious vee. Dark stubble dusted his jaw. The nightmare faded as she watched his abs clench with each breath.

"Jovi? What happened?"

Oh, right. "A dream."

"Oh." Their eyes locked. She was very aware of the cool night air on her bare breasts, still facing the window. He looked quickly away. "Okay." He started to back out, but stopped and leaned in, keeping his gaze averted. "Are you alright?"

"Fine." Jovi's heart thumped. It wasn't from the nightmare.

He nodded, shutting the door gently behind him. His footsteps padded down the hallway.

So much for sleep.

———

Downstairs later that morning, Jovi found coffee waiting in the pot, a clean mug, a sugar bowl, and an unused spoon standing next to it. She poured herself a cup, dumping in half the sugar bowl and a generous glug of cream. She tested it and coughed. Fucking jet fuel. She added more sugar and turned to root through the cupboards. Scowling at the lack of snack cakes or honey buns or anything remotely good, she settled for a granola bar, biting off a hunk just as Rogan came in from the deck. He was wearing loose sweatpants and a tee, looking sweaty and flushed.

"Hiya. We need Toaster Jellies." She wanted to lick the bead of sweat running down his throat.

"There's plenty of food. Toaster Jellies are garbage."

"Hey, you're garbage!" she shot back. "Toaster Jellies are delicious. And I can't eat this healthy crap for a month, I'll go insane." She hopped up on the counter, crossing her legs. "I want to go shopping."

"No."

"Uh, excuse you? I'm not a prisoner." She folded her arms. "And I want candy."

Rogan eased past her knees to snag a bottle of water from the fridge. He chugged half the thing before lowering the bottle. "Fine. I'll escort you."

"Fine. But no hovering." Candy shopping with Agent Health Nut—how fun. She hopped off the counter. He was a good two heads taller than her, and close enough that she could feel the heat radiating off him. She wondered if he was wearing black boxer briefs under those sweats. "I'm gonna go get dressed."

She dashed upstairs and tossed on a little white skirt and a tee that said, "Show Me Your Kitties". Throwing her hair into a big messy bun on top of her head, she was heading out the door when she stopped, glancing back toward the bed.

The amulet was tucked under the mattress. She couldn't leave it there. Couldn't wear it around her neck, either—the last thing she needed was Agent Observant spotting it and asking questions. Ugh.

She unzipped her boot, dropping the amulet gingerly inside. The metal warmed instantly against her ankle bone. Jovi zipped her boot, tried to ignore the feeling of her blood buzzing in her veins, and left the bedroom.

Rogan stood at the foot of the stairs, scowling. She stopped a few steps from the bottom, waiting for him to move. He just stared at her. Their heads were level, and she could practically see the gears turning. Finally, she raised her eyebrows. "What?"

"I'm going to give you something." He held out a tiny black object and pinned her with a Very Serious Look. "This is an MLE communication device. They are not intended for civilian use. But considering the circumstances, I'm giving you this in case of emergency. I've set up a private channel. Yours will talk to mine." He stepped closer, smelling like coffee and clean sweat. He pulled back the neckline of her tee to attach the comm, and his fingertips brushed against her collarbone.

Electricity shot through her. She glanced automatically at his crotch.

"Just touch it."

Her gaze met his. "Huh?"

"Just tap it once and talk normally."

Oh. A giggle bubbled past her lips, and she looked down at the button-sized disc on her collar. She tapped it. "Come in, Captain Tightpants."

Her voice rang from his wrist. He shot her a look, raising his watch to speak into it. "Copy."

His deep voice echoed inches from her ear, giving her goosebumps. "Okay then," she said. "You wanna drop me off, or what?"

CHAPTER 16

Rogan watched Jovi emerge from an old-fashioned candy shop, skirt bouncing and cheeks bulging. She had a bag in one hand and a thick chunk of chocolate fudge between her fingers in the other. The way the woman ate, her sleek little figure was baffling.

His balls tightened. The image of her standing at her window in those pink panties, topless and gleaming in the moonlight, was burned into his goddamn retinas. His dick hadn't forgotten it, either.

He blinked, refocusing on her flouncing down the street. Christ, he needed to get her a wig. And some baggy, frumpy pants. That giant knot of pink hair, that tiny skirt with those black boots—she was attracting attention, to say the least. Men turned for a second and third glimpse, and women gave her the evil eye. Inconspicuous, she was not.

Rogan's stomach squirmed. They shouldn't be here. Too exposed.

Jovi plopped onto a bench, licking her fingers and looking around with interest. White Cove was a tourist trap. The main street was lined with shops, restaurants, and patrons strolling with shopping bags and ice cream cones.

A napkin blew along the pavement. A breeze flirted with the hem of Jovi's skirt, casting a few strands of hair across her face. And across the street, at an outdoor table at the fish and chips place, a man watched her from beneath the lowered brim of a baseball cap.

Rogan frowned from the shadow of a shop entryway. The guy's little fish basket was empty except for its greasy paper lining. He was finished with his meal. But there he sat, focused on the pink-haired stunner in a way that made Rogan's instincts ring.

The shop door beside him swung outward. "Hey, buddy. You gonna come in? Doorways are for customers." The aproned shop owner scowled at him.

"Sorry, just taking a breather." Rogan moved down the sidewalk, maneuvering through the crowd of weekend tourists, keeping his eyeballs glued to the thirty-something white male who watched Jovi from the restaurant patio. He lost sight for a few seconds, shuffling around a throng of female lion shifters, their tall, muscular bodies blocking his view.

Baseball Cap's table was empty.

Rogan whipped his gaze back to Jovi to see the guy easing onto the bench next to her. He was shorter than average, in decent shape, tanned, and wearing a black baseball cap, plain white T-shirt, and khaki shorts. Rogan slipped into another shop doorway, watching the guy lean over and say something. He was smiling.

Jovi returned his smile, responding with a few words and a sweeping gesture toward the bustling street. She popped another piece of fudge into her mouth.

The man leaned forward on his elbows, angling himself toward her, his face shadowed by the cap. Her body stiffened almost imperceptibly. Rogan's hand went to the mini pistol tucked into his waistband. The guy said something else. Jovi replied with a breezy smile. Then, in a move so smooth he might've taught it to her himself, she pretended to scratch her collarbone, and brushed a finger over the comm on her neckline.

He could have kissed her.

"You here by yourself?" The guy's voice came through Rogan's in-ear comm.

"Oh, no, I'm just waiting for my man."

He told himself he did not feel a ludicrous rush of pleasure at those words.

Baseball Cap watched her for a moment. "He shouldn't leave you alone."

A jolt of adrenaline flooded Rogan's system.

Jovi laughed, playing it off. "Nah, he'll be back any minute. I told him I'd wait here while he finished shopping." She smiled, glanced around casually. Looking for him.

The man was quiet for a few moments. Then, he leaned in further. "Nash Rogan knows better than that."

Rogan pulled his piece from his waistband and sprinted straight for them.

The man reached for Jovi's wrist. "I'll tell you what. You come with me—"

The second his fingers touched her skin, she nailed him. Twin streams of fire exploded from her palms, strong enough to send her flying backward off the bench. Baseball Cap bellowed as flames hit him square in the face, his screams mixing with the shriek of Jovi's trackband and the startled cries of pedestrians. The guy disappeared in a swirl of dark shadow, his hands covering his blackened face.

Rogan skidded to a halt next to Jovi, who was sprawled on the pavement, her fingertips sparking. Her eyes blazed crimson in the trackband's spotlight, and in that split second, she looked feral, demonic, like something he would eradicate in a dark alley.

Rogan shook off the thought and grabbed her hand. It was

scalding hot. He cursed. Hauling her to her feet, he silenced the alarm with a swipe of his watch.

"Move. Now." If there was one hostile, there were likely more, and civilians were staring. He tugged her off the main street and toward the end of the block, his head on a constant swivel. People got out of their way. Jovi twisted her wrist, breaking his hold. He snatched her hand again, holding tight to her heated skin, pulling her along. "Are you all right?" He glanced down at her.

"I'm fine." She tried to break his grip again. He clamped his fingers around her arm like a vise.

They reached the end of the block, where things were shady and quiet, and houses lined the street instead of shops. They rounded a corner and came to a small, unkempt blue cottage. Rogan led Jovi to the cellar behind the house. He scanned his watch over the keypad and heaved open one heavy door. Jovi hauled open the other, and they leaped in.

He pulled the doors closed behind them and entered a code on the internal keypad. The heavy lock slid home. Cool silence and the smell of dirt engulfed them as blue lights flared to life along the rough dirt walls. The tunnel was barely tall enough for Jovi to stand in. Rogan had to tilt his head as he approached her.

"Are you all right?" He silenced their comms.

"I said I'm fine."

Rogan grabbed her wrists, turning her hands over to look at her palms. They were red, nearly glowing, but no blisters or burns. Her skin was incredibly soft. It was also literally steaming.

She yanked her hands out of his grasp. "He knew who I was. And who you were."

"I heard." He straightened as much as he could, meeting her icy blue eyes. "You did excellent work, hitting your comm like that so I could hear."

Jovi rolled her eyes and took off at a swift clip, her little white skirt bouncing down the dim tunnel. Rogan caught up.

"He was obviously one of the fucking Slavs," Jovi said.

"Most likely. I didn't see his face."

"I did. Kinda cute, actually."

Annoyance flared. "The Slavs are not cute. And what they do to their victims sure isn't, either." He'd seen the crime scene photos.

She snorted, but then slowed to a stop and leaned a hand against the wall.

"Are you injured?" He scanned her for wounds he'd missed.

"I'm fine. Just tired."

He frowned. "That little blast took it out of you?" She was a powerful mage, she shouldn't be that cashed after one shot.

"Little blast? Look, asshole." She jabbed a finger into his chest. "Being almost snatched by some mafia thug, melting his face off, and then sprinting to an underground tunnel kind of takes it out of a girl."

Shit. Right. She wasn't a field agent, she was a civilian—untrained, unconditioned. He wasn't used to civilians. He cleared his throat. "You did good work, incapacitating the enemy like that."

"Oh, really? Because, technically, you should've arrested me for it."

The venom in her tone took him aback. Rogan studied her in the faint blue light—jaw tight, eyes flashing. "I need to debrief MLE," he said finally. "Let's go. The house isn't far."

She shoved off the wall and headed down the tunnel, wisps of steam trailing in her wake.

CHAPTER 17

ovi made a face at Rogan's broad back. He was punching in the code to the door at the other end of the tunnel, but he turned suddenly and pointed at her, then at the ground.

Jovi saluted him sarcastically.

His tight butt disappeared through the door. A few minutes later, his voice floated out from the dark. "We're clear."

Jovi marched past him, through a little laundry area, and up a short flight of steps into the safe house's living room. She headed straight for the liquor cabinet. Rogan strode past, already on his phone, heading out of the room.

Tequila for one it was. Not that she would offer him any, anyway—he was the reason she was in this mess in the first place. She downed a shot. Then another. Her trackband clinked against the bottle. She snarled at it. After the third shot, the butterflies in her gut had calmed slightly, but hunger roared in their place.

Food. Lots of food. Fried food. Chocolate. Where was a hotdog cart when she needed it? She'd dropped her bag of candy when that stupid Slav attacked her. She whimpered, stomping her foot at the thought. She wanted to throw something.

She took the fourth tequila shot to the fridge with her. Nothing but fucking health food in there. Fuming, she wrenched open the freezer. Ice, frozen fruit, and veggies. No ice cream, no frozen pizza, no corn dogs. What the actual fuck.

Her vision swam. She wrenched open a cupboard and found a bag of baked tortilla chips. Better than nothing. Snagging some salsa from the fridge, she tossed the lid on the counter and attempted to tear open the bag of chips. The fucker was apparently cemented shut. She yanked the thing open, sending its contents flying up into her face and skittering across the floor.

She shrieked with rage, little sparks dancing on her fingertips. She grabbed a massive handful of chips and a scoop of salsa, shoving it into her mouth just as Rogan rounded the corner, looking like he'd swallowed something rotten.

He eyed the chip carnage at her feet. "Hungry?"

Jovi crammed another handful into her mouth, chewing insolently. *Wonder what his spotless shirt would look like with a big salsa stain on it...*

He raised his brows, gum snapping irritably between his teeth. She widened her eyes, sucking the salsa off her teeth with her tongue. Silently, they made bug eyes at each other for a while.

"What?" she demanded finally.

"You're mad."

Boy genius over there. "Wonder why."

"Enlighten me."

She gave him the biggest eye roll in the history of mankind. "This!" She shook her trackband at him. Her fingertips tingled. "This fucking thing! I can't even fucking *defend* myself!" She flung the bag of chips away. They landed on the counter with a puff of smoke.

He folded his big, muscled arms. "You obviously defend yourself very well."

"Yeah, and look what I get for it! Fucking alarms, and handcuffs, and going to jail!" Her bottom lip trembled before she wrenched it back under control. Stalking up to him, Jovi stabbed a finger into his chest. "Do you have any idea what that's like? Knowing that some asshole can do whatever he wants to you, and if you defend yourself, you're the one who's fucked? No, you don't." She held her trackband up to his face, flipping him off while she was at it. "Because you MLE assholes don't have to wear one of these." Sparks shot out of her fingers, perilously close to his smooth cheek. "Those guys are after me, and if I light one of them up, this thing is going to draw all the others right to me."

"I'll be there to silence it."

"I don't want you there to silence it. I want it fucking *off*."

Long, long silence ensued, with a hint of mint. "I can't do that."

She felt disgust twist her face. "You *won't* do it." Reaching behind her for the fourth shot of tequila, she tossed it back, then shouldered her way past him.

"I am here to protect you, you know." He watched her head toward the liquor cabinet and pour herself another. "I've got your back."

Oh, yeah, sure. Right. Where had she heard that before? Down in the depths of hell, right before some demon sold her out to her mother once again. "Yeah? So, where were you when that guy was about to grab me? Why didn't you blast him with electricity or whatever it is you do?" She raked her gaze down his hard body. "What kind of mage are you, anyway?"

His eyes hardened. "I'm not."

"Not what?"

"Not a mage."

Her brain was having trouble keeping up. "What are you, then?"

His jaw ticked. "Human."

She blinked, then refocused. "Whatever. I don't need you to protect me, Agent Rogan. The only thing I need you to do is shut this fucking thing off—" She held up her wrist, "—after I take care of myself."

She grabbed the liquor bottle by its neck and stormed out the patio door.

———

Half an hour later, she was pretty drunk.

The beach was blissfully empty. After walking its deserted shoreline, she'd dropped the tequila bottle in the sand and stripped off her shirt. It was gross and sticky with sweat, and it got caught on her nose when she tried to pull it over her head. She flung it aside, approaching the water's edge in her fuchsia bra, thumbs hooked in the waistband of her skirt.

She peered into the water. No demons. Nothing but gentle waves rippling invitingly in the orange glow of the afternoon sun. Jovi sighed happily, bending over to wriggle out of her skirt. Boots came off next, revealing a glimmer of the amulet inside the black leather.

She yanked out her hair tie, letting the mass of pink strands spill down from its messy bun, and splashed ungracefully into the cool water. It felt divine on her still-heated skin. She let herself fall forward up to her neck and turned to float on her back, arms and legs splayed wide.

Fucking Rogan. Not even a mage? How did he get so high up in MLE?

He must be very, very good at other things. Like weapons, or hand-to-hand combat. No wonder he had all those tech toys loaded in his million-pocket pants. Still, she'd never expected that he was human, the way those other agents practically fell all over themselves at the sight of him.

What was so special about stupid Rogan?

Clouds swirled overhead. Jovi shut her eyes, letting the water cool her skin and the sun warm her eyelids. Eventually, her buzz faded, and she got chilled. Lifting her head, she righted herself, her toes finding the sandy floor.

Nash Fucking Rogan was sitting on the shore, watching her.

Jovi glared at him. He stared at her. She ducked her mouth under the surface and blew a few bubbles. It didn't appear to intimidate him.

Fine.

Holding his gaze, she slowly, deliberately stepped out of the water.

She wasn't a succubus for nothing.

CHAPTER 18

God help him.

She rose from the waves like a siren, hair slicked back from that smooth forehead, those wide cheekbones, that slender neck. Pale skin gleamed as water sluiced down, past a sheer pink bra, between plump breasts. The rivulets trailed into the dip of her navel and beyond, to a white lace thong, drenched and clinging to her hips like a second skin.

Those icy blue eyes burned into his like a dare.

She slinked up to him, sand sticking to her wet feet. Her body was stunningly perfect, lush and tight and curved. It pulled at him like a magnet. His torso seemed to lean toward her as if drawn by an invisible, sizzling thread.

She drifted closer until the curve of her hip was mere inches from his face. He could have turned his head and licked the salt from her skin.

As she bent toward him, Rogan's pulse pounded. He clenched his jaw so hard it was a miracle he didn't crack his teeth.

She reached out. Slender fingers stretched toward his lap—

And grabbed her boots from the sand next to him.

While he pretended that his heart wasn't hammering against his sternum, she continued to pass by him, brushing his shoulder with her bare, dripping thigh. It left a wet spot on his shirt, soaking through to his skin.

Jesus H. Chri—

A roaring fire burst to life in the metal ring beside him, making him jump.

She was punishing him. He'd seen the rage blazing in her eyes when she'd laid into him about her trackband. Her anger went deep, and behind it, there was a wild, animalistic fear. *"Some asshole can do whatever he wants to you, and if you defend yourself, you're fucked."*

She had a point.

It had always been simple. If you had magic in you, you wore a trackband. Do good magic, there was nothing to worry about. Do bad magic, bad things happened. Simple. Easy. Self-defense? It would be assessed by MLE agents when they arrived within the required five-minute response time. It wasn't like every holding cell was full of innocent mages acting in self-defense. He knew that.

A sudden disturbance rippled the waves along the shore. He peered at the water and went dead still.

Ten water demons rose from the shoreline, their pale, slimy bodies practically glowing in the dusk. Round, pupil-less eyes stared past Rogan, fixed on the path that led to the cottage.

Text scrolled across his lens. *Species: Demon. Category: Aquatic. Eliminate.*

Easing into position, he pulled his flamethrower pistol from his belt and nailed the bastards. Their shrieks filled the twilight as he kept the stream flowing. Finally, two and three at a time, they evaporated, leaving nothing but a trail of steam rising from the water.

He'd never seen a group of demons like that, so focused

and intent. And they were staring down the path to the cottage, where Jovi had headed, alone.

He sprinted back toward the house. The backyard was clear. The deck was, too. He pulled his phaser and eased through the sliding door. Living room and kitchen stood dark, aside from the light glowing beneath the microwave. An open jar of peanut butter stood on the counter, and a spoon was tossed in the sink, smeared with thick residue.

He made a quick sweep of the upper level. Clear. A light shone under the bathroom door. Leaning his head toward it, he heard the shower running, accompanied by low, feminine singing.

He released a breath. She was safe.

In his room, he stripped off his shirt and dropped onto the bed, grabbing a protein bar from his stash in the nightstand. He pulled the phone from his pocket and set it on the charging dock, a bitter reminder of the call he'd made earlier.

Reprimanded. He'd been reprimanded for the incident in town. He knew better than to expose them both—a fucking shopping trip, for Christ's sake. The Magistrate's scolding burned like acid in his gut. Nash Rogan did not screw up. Did not break protocol. Did not get rebuked by his superior. Two days with this sailor-mouthed hellion and she was already fucking with his head.

MLE was sending undercover support agents. They would stay at a motel, monitor the town and surrounding area, and sniff out any Slavs. Rogan was to stay at the safe house, and Jovi was to remain with him at all times.

An image of her delicate pink bra, dripping and transparent as she rose from the water, flashed across his mind. The image of ten water demons lining the shore, staring after her, came next. Why the hell were they watching her?

Shaking his head, he forced himself to finish his protein bar before stripping out of his boots and holster, unsticking the lens from his cornea, and blinking a fresh one into place. He eased back against the pillows with his tablet, his fingers pulling up the encrypted file all on their own.

His dad's homicide had been cold from the start. After seventeen years, it was damn near forgotten. Rogan flipped through the familiar case files, the crime scene reports, everything Human Law Enforcement had at the time. His eyes lost focus, but he had it all memorized, anyway.

He stopped scrolling when he hit the obituary, his stomach clenching at the image of his dad's face, handsome and wide-jawed, smiling in his dress blues. The black patch covering his left eye was new, then—the field injury had happened shortly before. The caption read, *Lieutenant Jim Rogan received a posthumous Purple Heart and Medal of Valor for his service in the line of duty.*

Below the obit was an image of the stocky chief of police next to a newly elected Magistrate Thackeray White. The Magistrate was handing two beribboned medals to a waif-thin brunette, while a small, dark-haired boy stood rigidly at her side. *Crysta Rogan and ten-year-old son Nash accept Lieutenant Rogan's decorations. Due to his involvement in the fatal event, Magical Law Enforcement's Magistrate Thackeray White requested the honor of presenting the awards to Lieutenant Rogan's family.*

His mother had still been pretty then.

Rogan scrubbed a hand over his face, tossed his tablet aside and hit the lights, throwing an arm over his eyes and trying not to think.

CHAPTER 19

Jovi woke near dawn with her bladder close to bursting. Stumbling out of bed, she hurried groggily to the bathroom, sighing in relief when she plopped onto the toilet. She was starving. The peanut butter had hardly made a dent all those hours ago.

Business done, she tiptoed to the top of the stairs, heading for the kitchen. A muffled groan made her halt outside of Rogan's bedroom door. She padded over to it and pushed her ear against the wood, hearing faint muttering and pained grunts. Frowning, she cracked open the door. In the dim light from his window, Rogan twisted and turned on the bed, naked to the waist, looking like a sculpted, tortured god. He was mumbling, his dark head whipping back and forth on his pillow.

Nightmare, huh? Good. Let him suffer.

He groaned, his breath hitching. Over tightly closed eyes, his brows knit, and his hands gripped the sheets.

Damn it. Jovi tiptoed to the bed, chewing her lip. She nudged the mattress. "Hey."

More urgent muttering, a jerk of his head. Eyes still squeezed shut.

She shook his shoulder. "Dude—"

The next second, she was flat on her back with a half-naked, crazy-eyed Nash Rogan pressing her into the comforter, his big hands wrapped around her windpipe.

Jovi clawed at his rock-hard forearms, but it didn't seem to register. She beat against his shoulders. Nothing. So, she planted her hands on his chest and blasted him with fire.

He flew off of her, slammed into the wall, and crumpled to the floor.

And, of course, her fucking trackband went off.

Rolling onto her side and coughing into the blanket, she tried to block out the red light and the screeching alarm. There was a cool hand on her wrist, then silence rang through the room. She lifted her head.

Rogan stood before her, breathing heavily, two angry red handprints shining on his muscular chest. They stared at each other in the soft gray light.

His mouth gaped as he searched for words. "I'm—I'm sorry."

"What the fuck?" Her voice came out as a croak, and she sat up, bringing her eye level with his six-pack.

"I'm sorry." He shook his head. "I'm sorry."

Jovi swallowed painfully. He had a strong fucking grip. "Nightmare?"

"I'm sorry. I would never—"

"I know." She waved him off, avoiding his anguished gaze. It didn't make her as happy as she thought it would. "I have one, too. A nightmare. As you know." She eyed his chest, watching blisters form on his really nice-looking pecs.

Ugh.

"Sit down." She nodded toward his burns. "I'll fix that."

Rogan looked down at himself. He frowned, touched one shiny red burn, and sucked in a breath.

Jovi slapped the bed. "Sit."

Shockingly, he obeyed. Jovi swallowed and sank to her knees in front of him, her heart racing. Mommy Dearest forbade this. And when Jovi disobeyed, those punishments were the very, very worst.

A long finger stroked down her bruised neck, soft as a butterfly's wing. Tingles followed its path.

Jovi curled her hand around his wrist, feeling his pulse hammer there, and waited until his eyes flipped to hers.

"I'm fine." She patted his cheek briskly, stubble grazing her palm. "I know you didn't mean to."

A deep groove appeared between his brows. "It's my job to protect you."

The guilt that radiated off him made her stomach turn. She'd seen this more times than she could count, but it never got easier. Shame, despair, hopelessness. A strong man with his head bowed, waiting for whatever punishment came next.

"I keep telling you, I can take care of myself. See?" She nodded pointedly to his second-degree burns. "Now, let me fix this."

Ignoring the nervous squirm of her belly, she closed her eyes and pictured light. Beautiful, white, healing light. A rush of energy cascaded down her arms, filling her palms, and she placed her hands on Rogan's hard chest, focusing all that healing light through her fingers and into him. She didn't know how long she knelt there with her hands on his skin, but slowly, she felt the blisters recede under her palms. She smiled, sighed, and opened her eyes.

Nash Rogan was staring at her like the sun shone out of her ass.

He glanced down at her hands on his healed chest, then back to her. Blazing sea glass eyes leveled on her mouth.

All the air left the room.

He cupped her face in his hands, ducked his head, and captured her mouth with his.

Absolute fucking fireworks.

Those plump, delicious lips moved against hers, strong and insistent, lighting up every cell of her body. Hypnotized, dizzy, she rose up like a wave to meet him, kneeling between his thighs as he bent over her, angling her face so he could go deeper. Everything disappeared but the swirling, pulsing electricity inside her, stoked higher and higher with the glide of his tongue against hers. Head spinning, Jovi edged closer, her bare knees shuffling on the hard wooden floor. His skin was warm and smooth, his shoulders strong, the column of his neck thick and firm beneath her hands. He licked at her, speared his fingers through her hair, tugging her head back. She breathed hot against his mouth, straining to get closer. *Yes, yes, yes.* A tiny moan escaped her lips.

He stilled at the sound. His mouth lifted, and then, on a harsh inhale, he pulled back. "Shit, I can't do this. We can't do this." He grabbed her wrists, pulling her hands away. "Shit."

"What?" Jovi blinked, trying to clear her head. Her entire body was throbbing, flushed with heat.

"I can't do this. It's against protocol. It's against...every-thing." He wiped a hand over his mouth, looking around desperately for his shirt.

She knelt in front of him as he sat, half-naked and stupidly hot, on the rumpled bed. "You're fucking serious."

"It's one of the number one rules."

"Whose rules?" She was still tingling, but it was the dangerous kind now, traveling down into her hands. "And who cares?"

"The Magistrate's, WITPRO, MLE. You name it." He yanked his shirt over his head. "And I care. I can't afford to break any rules."

Her blood boiled. She did not throw herself at men. Men threw themselves at her feet, and they begged for more.

"Fine." She stood, sparks sizzling at her fingertips. "I'm not into choking, anyway."

The guilt that flashed in his eyes gave her immense satis-faction. She spun and marched from the room, giving him a spectacular view of her ass.

CHAPTER 20

He needed to get away from her.

He needed to get far, far away from her.

Reprimands from the Magistrate? Putting the mission in jeopardy? Breaking basic and very goddamn important rules? Unacceptable. Dangerous. Fucking humiliating.

But Christ, her mouth…it was no wonder flames erupted from her skin. She'd been like fire in his hands, against his lips, scorching and consuming. He'd been utterly lost in her, senseless and mindless.

Senseless and mindless could get him killed.

Senseless and mindless could cost him everything.

Rogan grimaced, digging the heel of his hand into the massive erection straining against his zipper. He rubbed his other palm absently over his chest, then looked down to see two small handprints there, still slightly pink. The sight of them, evidence of her hands on his body, made his pulse pound.

A flamethrower and a healer. He hadn't seen that coming. Yet another way he'd underestimated her.

He'd been on the receiving end of John's healing hands

thousands of times, and it had never felt anything like that. There was no prickly sensation of cells stitching back together —Jovi's healing was warm and smooth, like liquid sunshine washing every trace of darkness from his body. The sensation had been damn near euphoric, and judging from the complete and utter joy on her face when she did it, Jovi felt the same. She had literally glowed from within, luminous and golden in the gray light of dawn.

He pressed his palms into his eyeballs. All he could see was her kneeling in front of him, the shape of her breasts clear beneath her thin cotton tank, the little triangle of pink satin peeking out below. Those slanted blue eyes, ice pale yet anything but cold, looking up at him from beneath long lashes, heartbeat fluttering in her slender neck.

He'd almost throttled the life out of it.

His erection deflated instantly. Rogan scrubbed his head, sick to his stomach. The nightmare was coming more frequently.

Coffee. He needed coffee.

He surged to his feet, shucked his tacticals, and dressed in sweats. Coffee, then a workout. No tech, no weapons, just a good old-fashioned balls-to-the-wall sweat session, that's what he needed. A sprint down the beach, maybe, so he could get some distance. Get some perspective.

Except he was supposed to remain with Jovi at all times.

He swore. This WITPRO shit needed to end ASAP. Being away from the job was throwing him off. He needed to get back to the field, back to his team, back to what was important.

This shit could cost him everything, and Jovi Black wasn't…worth it.

He frowned at the stutter in his own thoughts and reached for his shoes.

CHAPTER 21

For not being a morning person, she sure was wide fucking awake at the crack of dawn.

Jovi had heard Rogan running the water in the bathroom, and imagined him brushing his teeth and washing his face. Every tiny sound sent a jolt through her. Her fingertips tingled, and she flexed them.

Fine. He wanted to lay a big, sexy wet one on her and then shove her away? Idiot fucking man. See if he ever got that chance again. He'd *wish* he had the chance by the time she was done with him.

She smirked, letting off little puffballs of fire from her fingers, examining them from every angle. Nash Rogan would look pretty good on his knees, begging.

"Go on, little one. Make them burn for what they did."

Guilt fluttered in her belly, but she shook it off. This was nothing like those practice sessions down in the pit. She wasn't going to actually *hurt* the man. She was just going to torture him a little bit, until he realized how stupid he was to shove her away.

She glanced over at the knock on her door. Lying on the bed in her tank and undies, one leg bent at the knee, she fluffed her hair and put her arms behind her head. "Come in."

The door cracked open. Rogan leaned his head in, keeping his eyes averted. "I'm going down to the deck to work out. MLE has us under strict orders to remain here at the cottage." He paused. "Do not go anywhere."

Hmm. "Can I join you?" She put a smile into the words.

He looked up in surprise, and his eyes lasered in on her puckered nipples. He ripped his gaze to the ceiling. She smirked.

"You want to work out?"

"Don't sound so shocked." She sat up fluidly, making sure her hair spilled over her shoulders. "I like to work up a good sweat."

He cleared his throat, and she bit back a grin. Sometimes it was too easy.

"Fine. Put on something...easy to move in. Meet me on the deck." He whipped out of the room like it was on fire.

This was going to be fun.

————

It was not fun.

Nash Rogan was an animal. She'd planned to do a little light jogging in place, making sure he saw her tits bounce, maybe adding in some slow, deep squats. Agent Hardbody had other plans. Jump rope, pushups, sit-ups, jumping jacks.

And she'd thought she was familiar with all forms of torture.

She never really had to work out—genetics gave her fabulous agility and a gorgeous body. But apparently, vaulting around demons and blasting them with fire was one thing, and jumping lunges for a full sixty seconds was another. Plus, the amulet was in her boot again, and it was digging into her ankle.

After fifteen minutes with Drill Sergeant Rogan, she was drenched in sweat and panting like a dog in the desert. He hadn't even started to glisten. She collapsed onto the deck in her ruffled purple booty shorts and thin white tank top. Her tits hurt. They'd definitely done some bouncing. Maybe she should've worn a bra, after all.

He loomed over her. "That was just the warm-up."

Fuck. "Bring it on, baby. I've got stamina for days."

Rogan gave her a look. "This is serious. You've got bad things—people—after you. And you seem to get tired easily when you use magic. You need to be able to defend yourself without it. Basic self-defense." He placed his hands on his hips. "Top priority, understood?"

She saluted him from the deck. "Aye, aye, Agent Hot Lips."

Heat flared in his eyes, sending a flash straight to her core. "Recover." He pointed toward the table, where two water bottles waited next to his cellphone and phaser. She hauled herself over and plunked down, feeling the rough bench planks scrape her nearly bare ass. Rogan continued his workout, busting out ridiculous superhero moves, big muscles pumping and swelling. He finished a series of one-handed pushups and hopped to his feet, chest heaving. Sweat rolled down the dips and valleys of his arms.

"So." Her mouth watered even as she reminded herself that she was pissed at him. "Basic self-defense?"

He leaned over and grabbed his water bottle. He chugged it, his Adam's apple bobbing with each swallow. He used the hem of his shirt to mop the sweat from his face, revealing his chiseled stomach inches from her nose. "You need better footwear." He nodded to her boots.

"I fight in these," Jovi said without thinking, watching his abs clench with each breath.

He went still. "What do you mean, you fight?"

Shit. She blinked him back into focus. "Nothing. I mean,

they're all I've got, so if I ever do have to fight, I'll be wearing these, anyway."

His eyes narrowed. He really was an inconveniently smart bastard. She needed to be more careful.

"That's a good point," he admitted. "I usually don't train in anything I wouldn't wear in the field." He frowned briefly at his sweatpants and tennis shoes.

Keep him talking. "Where do you train?"

"We have a home gym."

"We?" Did he have a wife? A girlfriend?

Steam shot from her fingertips. She shoved her hands under the table with an inward curse. Apparently, her lady bits didn't remember that they were mad at him, either.

His brow furrowed. "My squadmates. We live together."

"Oh. All male agents?"

A hard mask slid over his face. "Enough. Wear your boots, then." He gestured for her to get up. "Let's start with a choke hold—" He cut himself off abruptly.

Snickering, Jovi hopped up, grabbed his big hands, and wrapped them loosely around her throat, making sure to lean her hips close to his. "I think we both know I can get out of this one. But go ahead, show me your way."

His eyes met hers, shadowed with regret.

"Knee to the balls, then?" She aimed a vicious knee at his junk.

Quick as a snake, he twisted to the side and swept her foot out from under her. Her ass hit the deck boards, sending a sharp pain zinging up her tailbone.

He reached down and hauled her to her feet. "Okay?"

"Peachy." She rubbed her ass.

"A knee strike is good. But if you miss, or you're trapped and can't get your knee up, you're screwed." He took her hands in his, placing them around the corded column of his sweaty throat. "I'm going to break your thumbs—" He demonstrated wrenching them backward. "—and then go for your eyes." Lightning fast, he stabbed his fingers toward her eyes, pulling back just before he nailed her. "And then, I'm going to shove your nasal plate into your brain." One hand grasped her shoulder while the heel of his other drove upward toward her nose. He demonstrated the sequence again, rapidly, before releasing her. "Then, you run. Or go for the balls," he amended, and something glinted in his eyes.

Was that a twinkle? Did Nash Rogan just twinkle at her?

Jovi felt a shit-eating grin spread across her face. Breaking thumbs? Gouging eyeballs? This might be fun after all.

CHAPTER 22

She was unexpectedly good. Surprisingly strong and quick, with impressive agility, like she had springs in those boots of hers. It reminded Rogan of Juno's jaguar gymnastics, but he believed Jovi when she said she wasn't a shifter. There'd been no flashes of animal eyes, no claws slicing out in anger.

And she wasn't a soldier, either, that much was obvious. She was wild, erratic, lacking in focus, and easily distracted. They would need to work on that. When WITPRO was over and they went their separate ways, he would sleep easier knowing she could defend herself out there.

He ignored the unexpected twinge he felt at the thought, choosing to focus on her black boots instead. *I fight in these.* It was a slip, but he'd let it slide, adding it to the list of Jovi Black's mysteries.

"I need a break." She waved him off.

He checked his watch, surprised that it had been an hour. "Good first session. We'll hit it again tomorrow." He pointed at the deck. "Stretch. I'll make protein shakes." God knew he didn't need to watch her bend over, stretching that pert little ass in those ridiculously tiny shorts. It had taken everything in him to ignore the bounce of her breasts, loose under her tank, for the entirety of their session. Juno would have rolled her eyes clear out of her head at the idea of a woman training without a bra—she strapped hers down with what looked like half a straitjacket.

He slid the patio door open, stepping inside. A shadow moved in the kitchen.

Rogan hit the floor just as a beam of light whizzed over his head and exploded in the wall behind him.

His weapon was on the deck. He rolled behind a chair and caught a glimpse of his assailants. Swarthy, dark-featured identical twins.

Slavs.

They sent another blast his way. He kicked the chair toward them. Feeling the mini-bar at his back, he reached over his head, grabbed a liquor bottle, and chucked it at one aggressor, then followed up with another. Glass shattered, and harsh voices rang out.

He rushed at them, taking them both down at once, hitting the floor on top of them. He managed to get his hands on one of their necks and pinch the nerve that would send him into la-la land. The guy slumped to the floorboards, unconscious. It wouldn't last long. The second Slav roared, grabbed Rogan by the hair, and smashed their foreheads together in a brutal headbutt. Pain exploded in Rogan's brain, momentarily stunning him. It gave the Slav just enough leeway to gain the top position, plant his palms on Rogan's face, and send a bolt of electricity through his skull.

"*Motherfucker!*" Jovi's voice shrieked in Rogan's shorted-out ears, and suddenly, the heavy weight was off him, and he smelled burnt hair. He shook his head once, sharply, and surged upright. Jovi was darting toward him, her hands smoldering.

The guy in the corner groaned. Jovi whirled and sent another blast of fire at him. The shot went wide, hit the liquor cabinet, and the whole thing blew like a bomb. Alcohol bottles exploded, raining glass, catching the Slav in the inferno. He writhed and screamed, slapping frantically at himself as his clothes burst into flames. Panicking, he tried to stand, bashed his temple on the corner of the blazing liquor cabinet, and dropped to the floor like a stone. A scarlet puddle formed beneath his head.

Rogan shoved himself off the ground and ducked onto the deck to snag his phaser from the picnic table. When he stepped back in, Jovi stood over the blackened corpse of the other twin, fingers glowing red and trackband wailing. Holding his breath against the smell of charred flesh, Rogan silenced the alarm, yanked her behind his back, and tucked her fingers into his waistband. "Stay behind me."

Glass crunched beneath their feet as they hauled ass up the stairs, his phaser leading the way. The hallway was clear. He kicked open the bathroom door, then his bedroom door. Both were clear.

He whipped Jovi inside and shut the door behind them, stripping out of his sweatpants and sneakers in record time. This was exactly why he didn't train in different clothes. What the fuck was the matter with him? He pulled on his tactical pants, long-sleeve shirt, and boots in a matter of seconds, then clipped on his belt and holster. He snagged a watch battery from the charging dock and slipped it into a pocket. "Ready?"

Jovi nodded. He raked his gaze over her and cursed—those ridiculous little shorts barely covered her ass, and that tank top was paper thin.

"Get behind me." He tucked her behind him again, pulling his piece before sidling up to the door and cracking it open a millimeter.

A gunshot whizzed past his ear, splintering the door frame. Rogan power-kicked the door with the sole of his boot, sending it flying off its hinges. It landed on top of someone.

Rogan pointed his gun straight down and shot through the wood panel. There was a howl of pain. Down the hall, behind Jovi's bedroom door, he heard a scrambling of limbs.

Fuck. They were out of options.

He grabbed Jovi's hand and tore down the steps, swinging his phaser at the bottom. Nothing around but the unconscious twins, lying blackened in broken glass and liquor. Flames licked at the floorboards. The stench of burnt flesh and alcohol fumes made his eyes water as they ran for the front door.

He threw her into the car, then whipped behind the wheel and tore out of there like a bat out of hell, glancing in the rearview mirror the whole way.

CHAPTER 23

She really needed to eat.

They'd been driving for hours, with Rogan constantly checking the mirrors and making random turns. Dusk was falling over the interstate. Jovi's head felt fuzzy, her limbs heavy, and her legs cold.

"I really gotta eat," she said. For, like, the millionth time.

Rogan kept his eyes on the road. "We need to get further away."

She heaved a sigh, then rolled her head against the head-rest to grin at him. "So, you're welcome for saving your ass in that living room."

"I was handling it."

"Bullshit."

He glared at her. "You're welcome for saving *your* ass up in the bedroom."

She grinned wider. "I saw you almost naked. Again."

He pretended to ignore her, but an adorable pink flush crept up his neck.

"You look really good almost naked."

The flush deepened. "Stop."

"Man, you're no fun. Where are we going, anyway?"

"Away from White Cove. I don't know how they found us. I need to report to MLE, and I left my fucking phone." He banged one hand violently against the steering wheel, the rest of him remaining stony.

Sighing, Jovi reached into her boot and pulled out the phone she'd snagged from the picnic table, waving it casually across his line of sight.

His eyes bulged. "When did you—" He snatched it from her.

She grinned again. Waited a beat. "So, you're welcome for saving your phone, too."

He glared at the road.

They found an energy station with a rapid car charger, giving Jovi just enough time to haul an armload of delicious snack foods to the counter. She peeked out the windows and saw Rogan pacing around, holding the phone up to the sky and scowling like he couldn't catch a signal. It wasn't much of a surprise. They were out in the boonies.

She got herself a massive chocolate milkshake from the self-serve machine and a large black coffee per Rogan's request, then paid for everything with the credits Rogan had given her.

He was stewing behind the steering wheel when she slid back into the passenger seat. He hardly looked at her when she handed him the coffee, just downed it in two gulps, hissing as it undoubtedly scalded his throat. He tossed the empty cup out the window into a trash can, pulled a pack of mints from his pocket, and popped one in his mouth. "Buckle up."

As soon as she obeyed, he zoomed out of the parking lot. She waited until they were back on the interstate before unsnapping her seatbelt and unloading her horde onto the dash. A little baggie of chips, a couple juice pouches, a pack of powdered mini doughnuts, a bag of cheese crackers, a few candy bars, and a bag of gummy bears.

"*That's* what you bought?"

She dropped a boring sugar-free protein bar into his lap.

He blinked. "You got that for me?"

Suddenly self-conscious, she shrugged and tore into the chips. "Can't have you hogging all the gummy bears." She probably imagined it, but out of the corner of her eye, it almost looked like his lips twitched. "Where exactly are we going?"

"My squad mate's private cabin. As long as we're not being tailed, there should be no way for anyone to find us there." He raked his gaze over her. "None of the Slavs touched you, did they? The one in town?" Jovi shook her head, and he relaxed a bit. "Good. No tracker, then."

"Cool." She ripped open the mini doughnuts and shoved one in her mouth, moaning at the delicious sweetness.

He shook his head. "You're not even the slightest bit afraid of them, are you?"

"Of those idiots?" Jovi mumbled, spewing powdered sugar onto the console. She wiped her lips with the back of her hand. "Trust me, I've seen way worse."

"Explain."

Yeah, right. She popped another doughnut into her mouth instead.

When he continued to stare in her direction, returning his gaze to the road at regular intervals, she tossed her hands up, spraying more white powder onto the dashboard. A bit landed on his black sleeve. Rogan flicked it off, frowning. "I just grew up around a lot of shitty stuff, okay? I've seen a lot of shitty things." *A torture rack. An airless suffocation chamber. A black, soundless pit. Streams of writhing demons, scalded bodies, screams, the smell of burnt skin and musky sex and coppery blood, and her mother's low, satisfied laugh...*

"Abuse?" Rogan's quiet words brought her back to the present.

Jovi snorted humorlessly, brushing powdered sugar off her bare thigh. It smeared, leaving a white streak.

"Me, too."

She looked over in surprise, her cheeks bulging. The glow of passing headlights illuminated his hard profile. She'd seen a lot of strong men crumble in hell, but it was hard to imagine Nash Rogan being broken. Must've been a kid when it happened. She wondered if he was such a stick in the mud back then—

Something smashed into Rogan's door with the force of a freight train.

Glass shattered as the car flew sideways. Jovi floated out of her seat, her head slamming into the roof. Pain exploded through her skull. The world spun as they flipped—once, twice—and landed with a bone-jarring impact.

What the…

Alarms wailed. Her neck throbbed. She blinked the world into focus and found herself crumpled in a heap on the car's ceiling, which was now below her. She licked her lips, tasting a sickening mix of sugar and blood.

Dazed, she pushed herself up to all fours, glass crunching beneath her knees. Rogan was suspended upside down beside her, arms hanging by his ears, his seatbelt keeping him strapped in. He was out cold, blood oozing from a nasty gash near his temple. She shook his shoulder. Nothing.

"What the *fuck*." Her lip stung—she'd bitten a chunk out of it. Her milkshake had exploded all over, lending a chocolatey top note to the smell of burnt wiring and melted electronics. Shrill alarms and beeps blared from everywhere, adding to her sudden pounding headache.

Footsteps approached.

Jovi peered out of the busted passenger window as a pair of grubby sneakers came into view, shortly followed by a dark-featured face and the muzzle of a gun.

She shot a stream of fire through the window. The dude

stumbled backward, screaming, then tripped and fell on his ass. Thick green tentacles burst from his shoulder blades, unfurling into heavy vines spiked with wickedly sharp thorns.

Great, a phytomage.

Glass cut into her knees as she scrambled out of the window and staggered toward the guy, who was still rolling around on the grass, cradling his face. The vines growing from his back whipped toward her. She ducked, and a vine missed her by inches. Another tentacle swiped at her ankles. She leaped over it but didn't see the other one swing at her from the opposite side. Vicious thorns raked her shoulder, making her gasp, and angry welts appeared on her skin as a burning pain streaked down her arm.

Enough of this shit.

Jovi planted her feet, slapped her hands together, and pulled them apart. A ribbon of flame stretched between her palms. Well, what do you know? She could make vines, too—except hers were made of fire.

She whirled her flaming whips around her head in graceful arcs, then snapped them down. They tangled with the thorny vines, igniting them in a blaze of orange and yellow. A smell like steamed broccoli rose into the air, making her gag, but she held on to her fiery reins, pumping power into them as the plants shrieked and hissed and shrunk back toward their master.

Finally, when they hung like shriveled black shoelaces from the mage's blistered shoulder blades, Jovi shook her hands to extinguish them. She stalked toward him, but stopped short as pain seared through her ankle.

She unzipped her boot and pulled out the amulet, which burned white-hot against her skin. It swayed, shining silver in the moonlight. When it cooled, she looped the chain over her neck, tucking it under her shirt. Having it so close to her heart felt like she'd injected hard liquor straight into her veins, but her poor ankle needed a break.

The plant mage was curled up in a ball, moaning into the dirt. Bits of his shiny tracksuit had melted onto his spine. A black truck hissed and steamed nearby, its front bumper smashed, headlights blazing at awkward angles. Jovi stomped her heel, released the dagger in her boot, and kicked the dude in the kidney. He made a choking, guttural sound.

"Who the fuck are you?" she roared. The welts on her shoulder felt like they were on fire, but a sinister numbness was trickling down her arm. The mage whimpered, rocking. The shriveled vines swayed with his movements, rolling like sunbaked worms across his back.

She kicked him again. "You're one of the Slavs, aren't you?" How did they keep finding them? Was there a tracker on their car or something?

The mage moaned. "You and Rogan will pay for this, bitch."

"That's no way to talk to a fucking lady." She sent him up in flames, feeling immense satisfaction as she watched his flesh melt into a pile of soot.

She didn't like causing pain for no reason. But when someone deserved it, they deserved it.

The wail of her trackband brought her back to reality. She spat on the dude's charred remains and scooped up his discarded gun on the way back to their totaled car. Rogan was still hanging upside down, arms dangling over his head. She squatted by his busted window, grabbed his wrist, and bent it awkwardly to swipe his watch over her trackband. The thing silenced immediately, leaving just the fading, dissonant beeps from the car's melting electronics.

She could leave.

Holy shit, she could *leave*. She could get out of there, ditch Rogan, ditch WITPRO, and get back to searching for her father.

Relief flooded her. Eagerly, she unclasped Rogan's watch and slipped it onto her own wrist. Even on the smallest setting, it practically fell off her hand, but at least now she could deactivate her own damn trackband. She gathered what was left of the snacks, found a jacket crumpled in the back, and slid it on. It was ridiculously huge on her, and under the whiff of chocolate milkshake, it smelled like him.

So annoying.

Irritated, she rolled up the sleeves so they didn't hang so far past her fingertips and shoved the provisions into its pockets. Then, she took every weapon she could find. Rogan's belt was heavy with them—a pistol, an old-school phaser, a newer one, and one of those stunners MLE agents loved so much. She pocketed them all.

As she backed out of the window, buzzing with excitement and whirling with plans, her gaze snagged on Rogan's face, inches from hers. She froze.

He was ridiculously beautiful, even all busted and unconscious and hanging upside down.

Images flashed across her mind: Nash Rogan shoving her behind his back to keep her safe, teaching her self-defense, sitting shirtless on his bed, staring at her like she was something wonderful.

She swallowed, glancing over her shoulder. The long stretch of interstate, and the thick patch of woods beyond it, were dark and quiet. By the time he woke up, she'd be long gone. He'd never find her.

A trickle of blood oozed down his forehead.

"Motherfucker." She reached in and unbuckled his seatbelt.

He crumpled onto the roof, glass crunching beneath his dead weight. She grabbed his armpits and heaved, dragging him out of the window inch by inch, cursing fluidly. He weighed a million pounds. Or maybe that was her exhaustion —she was fading fast.

She kept pulling. His boots trailed in the grass, scraping mud. Finally, several yards from the car, she lost her grip, and he flopped heavily to the ground. She fell to her ass next to him, panting. The welts on her shoulder blazed with pain. She raised a hand to touch them, then thought better of it.

She glanced over at Rogan's beautiful, bleeding face. He was still out cold. She nudged his leg with her foot. Nothing. She leaned over and shook him. Still nothing. He had a pulse, but the gash in his forehead was still leaking blood, and he was starting to look pale.

She'd gotten him away from the car. That was good enough, right? She could still totally blow this place. He'd be fine.

The freckles on his nose stood out in the moonlight.

Ugh. "You've got to be kidding me." She rose to her knees beside him, ignoring her throbbing shoulder and the numbness seeping toward her wrist, wishing her healing abilities worked on herself. Closing her eyes, she called up the light, letting it build inside her. Then, she put her hands on Rogan's head and poured it into his wound.

It took forever. The energy felt thick and sluggish, like she was trying to shove peanut butter through a straw. But she kept going, kept pushing, until she swayed on her sliced-up knees, mumbled, "Fuck," and collapsed on top of him.

CHAPTER 24

S he'd saved his ass. Again.

Rogan stared at Jovi in the flickering firelight. He'd woken under the night sky with her sprawled on his chest, smelling like campfire and chocolate, and had kept still, assessing the situation. Forehead sticky with dried blood, a whiff of burnt flesh and melted electronics in the air, a strange truck smoking nearby, and Jovi passed out on top of him, dwarfed by his jacket and wearing his watch.

So, they'd been in a collision, he'd been knocked unconscious, she'd crawled out of the smashed vehicle and torched a perpetrator, then stolen his watch and almost left him for dead.

Almost.

Twin trails of dirt cut through the grass, leading from the heels of his boots to their totaled car. She'd dragged his ass out, then apparently healed him of some sort of head injury, draining her own strength until she passed out.

The charred body on the other side of the car, and the unfamiliar gun tucked into Jovi's shorts, had filled in more blanks. It would've been helpful to see who the hell the perpetrator had been, but maybe she got a look at his face before melting it off.

She didn't wake, even when he swept the car for salvageable supplies, gathered her in his arms, and trudged the three and a half miles to John's cabin. The hike through the woods hadn't phased him. In fact, whatever she'd done to him made him feel like a god. Or maybe that was just because he'd been holding her body so close to his.

Rogan tried to shake the thought. It was difficult with her lying there on the old couch in front of the fire he'd lit. John's tiny cabin was deliberately primitive. He said it was important to unplug, and there was nothing here—no electricity, no central heat, no cell towers.

And no fucking coffee.

Jovi was pale. She needed to eat. He should wake her, try to get something into her system. But he was stalling.

He liked looking at her like this, when she couldn't look back, when he didn't have to hide it. When she was wearing his jacket, barely clothed underneath.

She'd loaded the pockets with his weapons. He'd felt a jolt of fear when he realized the Model B was missing from his belt, then sighed in relief when he pulled it from the jacket she wore. He'd emptied the pockets but left his jacket on her.

His phone had been smashed in the wreck. He could use his watch to contact MLE once they got within signal range, but it was the middle of the night, and Jovi needed to recover before they could leave.

Rogan stuck the little straw into one of the juice pouches that had survived the crash. Kneeling in front of her, he steeled himself and slid the straw between her pink lips. He gave the silvery juice pouch a little squeeze, and a trickle of red juice leaked out of the corner of her mouth. He caught the liquid with the tip of his finger.

Jovi's hand shot out and grabbed his wrist. Her blue eyes

snapped open. Rogan held back the automatic instinct to break her hold, waiting for her to get her bearings.

Those slanted eyes blinked at him. A pulse jumped rapidly in her slender neck. Slowly, she released his wrist, but not his gaze. He held up the juice pouch so she could see it, placed the straw back in her mouth, and gave a gentle squeeze. Her eyes widened as she got a taste, and soon she was sucking eagerly on the straw, cheeks hollowing. His cock strained against his zipper.

Jovi drained the pouch until the foil collapsed in on itself with a little crunch. She pushed upright, pink waves tumbling around her shoulders. She had a smudge of soot on her cheek, a piece of grass in her hair, and cuts on her knees. His jacket dwarfed her.

"Yummy," she said. Then she dove at him.

His back hit the floorboards, his breath whooshing out of him as her tight little body landed on top of his, legs straddling his hips. Then her mouth was on his, scorching hot, her tongue sliding like silk, her nails raking his scalp. Suddenly, his arms were locked around her, his hands sweeping up to tangle in her hair. She rocked herself against his erection, gripping his head and pressing her breasts firmly into his chest, surging against him in a sinuous, delicious rhythm. His mind went on a little field trip, his hands moving on their own, stroking her back, her arms, smoothing down her waist to grip her thighs while her tongue built a volcano inside him.

He was so lost in her, he almost didn't feel it. But finally, his cockstruck brain registered the hard metal disc pressing into his chest. Rogan pulled his mouth from hers—she'd been sucking his bottom lip and released it with a pop that made his cock jump.

"What's under your shirt?" He hardly recognized his own voice, all breath and gravel.

She grinned wickedly. "Play your cards right and I'll show you."

Jesus Christ. He almost gave in, but his instincts were ringing like a distant but insistent bell. "No, this." He prodded the metal disc beneath the thin fabric of her tank top.

Jovi went very still. "That? Just a necklace." She hopped to her booted feet, and just before she pulled his jacket closed, Rogan saw the outline of something underneath. Something flat, round, and the size of a silver dollar.

The bell got louder. He rose to stand. "Show me."

"My necklace?" She laughed airily.

She was a good actress, but he saw the split second of apprehension in her eyes. He stepped closer, reaching for the whisper-thin chain around her neck. Quick as a cobra, she blocked him. He tried again. She blocked again.

"Don't touch it," she snapped, her voice suddenly harsh.

As that internal bell morphed into a full-blown siren, Rogan backed her toward the wall, careful not to hurt her. She did not return the favor. She landed a few body shots, making him grunt, but luckily, she hadn't recovered enough to burn his ass to a crisp. He finally managed to pin her against the wall. He pulled the chain out of her shirt and froze.

He was staring at a silvery gold medallion. The same medallion he'd seen around the necks of four towering archangels.

He stepped back abruptly, his pulse skyrocketing. The medallion thunked heavily against her chest. "Where did you get that?"

Scowling furiously, Jovi tucked the medallion back into her tank top, wrapped his jacket around her torso, and tossed her hair. "Why do you care? It's just a necklace."

He needed to talk to the Magistrate. Immediately. He glanced at his watch before remembering there was no signal —damn John and his need to unplug. "Where did you get it, Jovi?"

"I don't know, I picked it up somewhere. Why do you care?" Her cheeks were flushed, her eyes like shards of glass.

"Did you steal it?"

Her jaw set in a hard line. She popped a hip, planting a hand on it. "Maybe."

She had stolen it. From whom? The missing angel? His brain whirled. "We need to get somewhere that has a signal." He stared at her chest like he could see through the jacket to the archangel medallion beneath. "We'll leave as soon as it's light."

CHAPTER 25

He recognized her amulet.

How? Did he know something about her father? She was dying to ask, but after that reaction, she wasn't about to reveal anything.

Something about it freaked Nash Rogan the fuck out. He was trying to mask it now—that, and the fact that he'd almost ripped her clothes off an hour ago. She didn't know which pissed her off more.

A tendril of steam curled from her fingertip. If the man shoved her away from his obviously-hot-for-her body one more time, she might actually lose her shit. Why did she even bother? Oh, right, because he was sexy as fuck, and she'd awoken to him kneeling in front of her, feeding her something sweet. Scowling, she tilted the last crumbs of smashed cheese crackers into her mouth, then tossed the empty bag aside.

Rogan sat in front of the fire, his big body silhouetted by the flames. He'd spread all his weapons and tech toys on the floor, and had spent the last hour silently inspecting them, cleaning them, taking them apart and putting them back together, then lining everything up in neat little rows, probably in alphabetical fucking order. By category.

She crossed her legs. *Wonder where he'd put me in his little lineup…where I would fit.*

Ha. She never really fit anywhere, did she?

Irritated, she flicked a finger at his neat little rows. A tiny fireball shot across the room and hit something small and shiny, which skittered across the floorboards, smacked into the wall, and shattered.

Whoops.

Rogan stared at the broken pieces, then turned his head slowly toward her. Flickering firelight danced over his sculpted jaw, making it look even more carved.

"That," he said quietly, "Was the only spare battery for my watch."

Double whoops.

"It's almost dead. It won't last long enough for us to get within signal. Which means we will be *walking* back to the city." A muscle ticked in his jaw.

Shit. Shifting uncomfortably, she uncrossed her legs, and the heel of her boot hit the floor. The shiny little dagger flicked out with an audible *shhhick*. She retracted it quickly, but his eagle eyes had already latched onto it.

Silence rang, broken only by the crackle of the fire behind him.

"Why do you have a knife in your boot, Jovi?"

Her heart thumped. "Protection."

"Protection from what?"

"Uh, sleazebags? It's not exactly safe for a hot girl to walk around downtown."

His eyes glittered. "So, you go around kicking sleazebags with a dagger in your boot?"

He was too effing smart for his own good. "If they ask for it."

His backlit shoulders looked enormous. The stillness in him was taut and dangerous, but when he spoke, his voice was soft. "I know you're not telling me the truth. There's something else going on with you, Jovi Black, and I will find out what it is." He picked up one of his guns, sliding a cartridge into it with a click. "I don't like mysteries."

CHAPTER 26

"There's a cave here."

They'd been walking since the ass crack of dawn. The amulet was tucked in her boot again, warm against her ankle. Rogan hadn't mentioned it. Hadn't mentioned jack shit, actually. Stony and silent all day, he'd marched through the woods like a dog on a scent. It bugged her more than it should.

Now, the light was fading, the temperature was falling, she was starving, and her feet were killing her. She followed Rogan's gaze to a small entrance carved into a stone bluff. Her stomach dropped. A year ago, she'd clawed her way out of a hellmouth and into a cave that looked a lot like that. "I'm not a fan."

Rogan pinned her with a hard look. He was infuriatingly sexy, all stubbled and roughed up, glimpses of golden skin peeking through his torn clothes. "And I'm not a fan of sleeping in an exposed area. We're going in."

"You can go in. I'll stay out here."

"We're both going in."

Jovi chewed her lip. A cold wind whistled through the trees, scattering leaves and whipping a strand of hair into her eye. Goosebumps erupted on her arms and legs, and she looked up just in time for a big, fat raindrop to splatter onto her nose.

Shit. She really didn't want to go in there.

She could feel Rogan's eyes on her. "I'll be there with you." The sharp edges of his voice had softened. Barely.

Jovi swallowed. Another raindrop landed on top of her head, trickling icy cold down her scalp. "Fine. But not too far."

He tilted his head, studying her. "Not too far."

Dry leaves scuttled around their feet as they ducked inside the cave entrance. Jovi swiped hair out of her face, her heart already pounding. They were in a cavern, shallow but large enough to stand inside. Twigs, pine needles, and crunchy leaves littered the ground. A gaping hole yawned on one side.

Great, a tunnel. Jovi sniffed the air. No sulfur, just musty old cave. But the tunnel made her really fucking nervous.

"I need to clear that tunnel," Rogan said, as if reading her mind. He pulled his phaser and started toward it.

Jovi made a noise of trepidation.

Rogan raised a brow. "If there's an animal in there, I need to know about it. I'll be right back." He scowled. "Try not to destroy anything."

Still mad about his busted watch battery, then. "Just wait. I'll go with you." Much as she hated the idea of going deeper into the cave, the thought of him getting slaughtered by invisible hellspawn was worse.

Cool darkness and the smell of damp earth engulfed them as they ventured into the tunnel. Jovi could see just fine, but Rogan hit a switch on his belt, and a beam of light burst from a little device clipped there, illuminating their path. The cave ceiling arched high above them, and rough stone walls flared outward, big as a subway tunnel. Plenty of space to spread out.

Their shoulders brushed frequently as she practically rode his heels.

"You don't like caves." Rogan was clearly adding it to his internal file. *Jovi Black, registered magical female, pyromage level five, always hungry, breaks stuff, doesn't like caves.*

"I don't like what's *in* caves," she hissed, jumping at a distant scuffling sound. She gripped his forearm, holding her breath as a pebble tumbled into view, loosened from the tunnel wall. She let out the breath. Their eyes met, and she released his arm. Nail marks faded slowly from his skin.

She had a very bad feeling about this.

CHAPTER 27

Jovi Black was scared.

Rogan's eyes remained on the path before him, but his mind was on the jumpy little vixen to his left. Though there was ample room to spread out, she inched closer and closer as they moved down the damp tunnel, bumping into him every other step, treading on his heels. Pretty soon, she'd be riding him piggyback.

And she smelled good.

Damn it, he'd wanted to get within signal range today. There was no way his watch would last the night, and bedding down in a cave with her was a very bad idea.

"Sorry about your watch."

He slid her a look.

"I didn't mean to break it. Sometimes I get mad and..." She seemed to struggle for words. "Never mind. I just didn't mean to break it." She shot him a glance before refocusing on the tunnel.

Before he could reply, his watch flashed in the dark, and text scrolled across his field of vision. *EXTREME LOW BATTERY. REPLACE/RECHARGE IMMEDIATELY.*

Shit. If his watch died, his lens died. And if his lens died...

EXTREME LOW BATTERY. REPLACE/RECHARGE IMME-DIATELY.

A familiar scent tickled his nose—one that overrode the hot sugar scent of the woman next to him. Rogan froze. He was imagining things. It wasn't sulfur, just old, dank cave.

He swore.

"What?"

Rogan sliced a hand through the air to silence her. There was no denying it—the smell was getting stronger with each step. Fuck. "Shield charm," he whispered.

"What?"

"Cast a shield. Now."

"I can't do that!"

A powerful mage like her couldn't perform a simple shield charm? He'd dig into that later. Now, he shoved Jovi behind his back. "Stay behind me."

A rasping, scraping sound floated from the depths of the tunnel, raising the hair on the back of his neck. Rogan flipped his phaser to Holy Light as one of the biggest, ugliest demons he'd ever seen slid into view.

Blood-red scales glinted on an enormous serpentine body. Its thick torso curved upward, sprouting four muscular arms ending in bony fingers, and a giant cobra hood that nearly brushed the stony ceiling.

TARGET UNKNOWN. CAPTURE.

Yeah, he'd get right on that.

EXTREME LOW BATTERY. REPLACE/RECHARGE IMME-DIATELY.

Fuck.

Glowing white eyes landed on them. Rogan pulled the trigger, and a beam of Holy Light shot down the tunnel to hit the snake square in the chest. Its enraged shriek ricocheted off the walls, making Rogan's eardrums throb. He fired again. The snake demon darted sideways, and the blast nicked its giant hood. It gave a deafening hiss, mouth gaping wide, displaying yellowed, dripping fangs. A barbed tongue whipped through the air, scenting. Then it charged.

NO BATTERY. SHUTTING DOWN.

Rogan's watch went dark, the demon vanished, and his heart stopped.

Fuc—

Something hard as iron collided with his cheekbone. Stars exploded in his vision, his feet left the floor, and he landed hard on his back, the wind knocked out of him. He crunched up, aiming his phaser—

A tiny, barely clothed, pink-haired lunatic jumped in front of him. She let loose a bellow of rage, launching a swirling ball of fire down the tunnel. A deafening screech echoed all around them. Jovi ducked and rolled, sprang to her feet, and shot another mass of flames, this time aiming at a different spot.

What the—

Rogan's heart threatened to beat out of his chest. He aimed his phaser blindly, but didn't dare fire, not while Jovi darted like quicksilver in the light of his illuminator, shooting flames at something he could no longer see.

But she could.

Rogan leaped up, then promptly hit the dirt again as a massive fireball rocketed toward him. Heat swept the top of his head as it careened past, and he looked over his shoulder just in time to see it hit the ceiling behind him.

The tunnel shuddered. Chunks of stone rained from the cave roof, and he swore, pelting away from the avalanche of rock thundering behind him. When it settled, he held his breath against a cloud of dust, looked back, and found himself staring at a wall of stone.

Trapped.

He spun around just in time to watch Jovi's body slam against the tunnel wall. Her boots dangled, her hands clawed at her throat. The fucking king cobra was choking her.

Rogan darted forward, ready to rip the thing's arms off with his own bare hands. But Jovi was already reaching up, wrenching invisible thumbs away from her neck, then stabbing her fingers forward into invisible eyes. There was an inhuman squeal, and she fell abruptly to her feet before driving the heel of her hand upward into an invisible snout. An enraged hiss ricocheted off the walls, and Jovi's head snapped back. Two puncture marks appeared on her throat, followed by twin trails of bright red blood.

Jovi opened her mouth wide and roared. A firehose of flame erupted from her dainty rosebud lips, and Rogan skidded to a halt as he watched his little WITPRO charge breathe fire like a dragon.

Finally, she stopped belching flame and stomped her boot, releasing that tiny silver dagger. Marching forward, she kicked savagely at the air, over and over, as deafening screeches rebounded off the walls. Then, she conjured an enormous fireball, hefted it high over her head, and heaved it at the floor. It exploded, blowing her hair back and spraying shrapnel in all directions.

Jovi turned to him, her chest heaving. Her trackband whistled in the stunned silence. They stared at each other, the spotlight washing her face in a crimson glow.

He managed to speak. "Are we clear?" He couldn't believe those words were coming out of his mouth.

Jovi swallowed, nodding.

Rogan holstered his phaser, reached into a tiny pocket of his tacticals, and extracted a small silver key. Jovi watched him warily as he stepped closer. He took her wrist in his hand and winced—her skin was damn near scalding. But he held on, meeting her eyes as the alarm wailed.

Rogan inserted the key into the tiny hole of her trackband. The alarm and spotlight cut off abruptly, and the band split apart like it had been sliced by a saw. Slowly, he slid the metal away and pocketed it.

Pure, sweet relief swept over Jovi's features. "Thank you."

His brain whirred. "You could see that?"

Her brows shot skyward. "*You* could see that?"

They stared at each other for a long, tense moment. Rogan looked at the floor, frustrated that he saw nothing but rubble. "Is it dead?"

Jovi scoffed. "Duh." She brought a hand up to her neck, grimacing. She scowled when her fingers came away bloody. "Fucker."

He tilted her chin to examine the damage. Deep, but not critical. Hopefully venom wasn't involved. He reached into his pocket and pulled out a roll of Medimend tape, which was infused with a potent healing charm and good for small, superficial wounds. He tore a strip with his teeth, smoothing it over the twin puncture marks. A tiny pulse fluttered in her neck.

"Do you know what that was?" His murmur ruffled a strand of her hair.

Her throat moved beneath his fingertips as she swallowed. "Demon."

His stomach gave a jolt at the word coming out of her mouth. "Have you always been able to see them?"

She chewed her lip, then nodded. "How can *you* see them?"

Time ground to a halt. Every nerve, every instinct, every fiber of his being screamed at him to keep his mouth shut. But there were hellspawn in this tunnel, his lens was dead…and he was going to need her help.

How the hell did he end up here, standing on the ledge, deciding whether to jump?

He had to force the words. "You know I do something different at MLE."

She nodded.

Staring into those crystal blues, Rogan took a deep breath and started talking.

CHAPTER 28

Demon killer.

Nash Rogan was a demon killer. He killed demons. For a living.

Fuck, fuck, fuck, fuck, *fuck*.

Jovi eyed his broad back while he examined the wall of rocks that had trapped them. It was a relief to be free from his piercing green gaze, from that look on his face as he'd been spewing his secrets like he expected her to keep them. Like something was being built between them.

He could never find out what she was.

As that happy little thought hammered home, something deep inside of her ached.

"It's too solid to break through." Rogan pushed at the pile of stones, muscles stretching against his grubby shirt. "A sonic blast would cave the whole thing in." He turned to face her. "We have to keep going."

"Down there?" Jovi squeaked. "There's probably more of them down there."

"We don't have a choice. I can help if we run into any hostiles. You just have to talk to me, tell me where they are." He huffed out a breath and poked at his eyelid, like he hoped his fancy demon-spotting contact lens could be prodded back to life. "I need you to be my eyes."

This wasn't happening. "Uh, I'll probably be a little too busy to babysit."

A muscle ticked below his eye. "I don't need a babysitter. I'm asking you to communicate with your teammate in the field. I watch your back, you watch mine."

Jovi chewed her lip. *Team* wasn't exactly in her vocabulary. "I don't really know how to do that."

Something soft flickered across his gaze. He contemplated her long enough to make her squirm before saying, "I'll show you. Eat. Then, we should move."

"Eat wha—" She caught the half-eaten bag of gummy bears he tossed at her and gasped. Where had he been hoarding those?

"Don't eat them all. We don't have much."

She nibbled the treat, watching him check his weapons. His forearms flexed as he removed cartridges from each of his guns, blew dust off them, and slammed them back into place.

"What is that, anyway?" She nodded at one of the cartridges. Slender and pill-shaped, it glowed eerily in the gloom.

He hesitated a second. "Holy Light."

She choked on a gummy bear. "Seriously?"

"Yes. We have a relationship with a priest."

Her brain nearly exploded. Add that to the list of things she needed to stay far, far away from…

"And Holy Water." Rogan pulled another cartridge from a different pocket, causing Jovi to reflexively step back. Rogan cocked his head. "Different demons have different weaknesses."

"Cool." *Don't panic. Do not panic.* Jovi mindlessly shoved the last of the gummy bears into her mouth and handed him the wrapper. When he scowled at the empty bag, she tossed her hands up. "Sorry! I eat when I'm nervous."

Something like amusement flashed across his face before he shifted back into serious mode. "Are you ready?"

Hardly. But she gestured gallantly for him to move ahead, cheeks bulging, heart racing.

His jaw flexed. "I need you to go first."

Oh, right. He was demon-blind. Big, bad Nash Rogan needed her to lead the way. She grinned, suddenly feeling strong as an ox.

"Don't worry, handsome." She patted his cheek, which was shadowed with stubble and a nasty purple bruise. "I'll take care of the big bad baddies."

He gripped her wrist, pulling the two of them nose to nose. "No, you will talk to me. You will not engage solo."

She smirked and glanced down at his crotch, latching onto the innuendo like a lifeline. "Don't you ever engage solo?"

"This isn't a joke." He dropped her hand and backed off, looking uncomfortable. "I...need your help."

Man, she could practically hear the rust on those words. Jovi watched his gaze dart around the cave—floor, ceiling, anywhere but in her direction. When his eyes finally landed back on her, her breath caught at what she saw in those glittering green depths. Irritation, shame, embarrassment...and something softer. Something close to trust. The center of her chest gave a tiny pang.

Demon killer. He was a demon killer.

"Okay. Let's go." She moved in front of him.

They walked in tense silence until her eyes ached from peering into the shadows. Rogan was a big, looming wall of heat at her back. "What do you see?" he asked eventually, his voice rumbling in her ear.

"A cave."

"Jovi."

"What? That's what I see."

She could practically hear his teeth grinding. "Tell me about your demon fighting," she said as they crept along.

"No. I need to concentrate."

"No, you don't. I'll tell you if I see anything. Or smell anything," she added. "Can you smell them, too?"

"Yes. Sulfur."

"And those people you live with, they fight demons, too?"

A beat of silence. "Yes. We're a unit."

"How many of you are there?"

"Six."

"And you're friends?"

"Squad. We're family."

Jovi frowned at the twinge in her belly. Family. "How many chicks?"

Rogan stopped her with a hand on her elbow. His fingers on her skin sent a tingle through her. He directed the beam of his illuminator around a corner before allowing her to continue. "One."

Jealousy flared, hot and fast. One chick surrounded by five dudes? She must be a total badass. Probably hot, too. "Is she hot?"

"For Christ's sake."

"What? Is she hot?"

"She's like a sister."

So, she was hot, but he didn't want to bang her. "Are the other dudes as hot as you?"

His frustrated breath puffed against her neck. Then there was a pause. "You think I'm hot?" He sounded genuinely taken aback.

"Are you kidding?" She stopped short, whirling to face him.

He held up a hand. "Don't answer that. For fuck's sake, just walk. And be quiet. I need to listen."

They walked. She kept her mouth zipped as long as possible. "So, do you guys go out *looking* for demons?"

She heard his deep, steadying inhale like he was

marshaling his patience. "Yes. We patrol every night. Take turns."

Her gut started to churn. "How do you find them?"

"How do *you* find them?"

Well, handsome, they find me because my succubus bitch mother is pissed that I escaped hell with her favorite trinket.

"I don't *find* them. I just see them. Shh!" She pretended to hear something in the distance, and he froze. After a beat of silence, he nudged her questioningly.

"False alarm."

They continued.

Stopping to rest after what felt like forever, Jovi plopped down on the hard stone floor, dying to take off her boots and rub her aching feet. The flush from the fight had died down, leaving her skin chilled. She shivered, rubbing her arms vigorously.

Rogan's jacket appeared in front of her.

A different kind of warmth spread through her. She pulled the jacket across her shoulders, and his scent surrounded her, along with a hint of chocolate milkshake. Her stomach growled.

Rogan eased to a seat beside her, aiming his illuminator down the tunnel. He unzipped a pants pocket, reached inside, and wordlessly handed her a peppermint.

She wasn't melting. Demons didn't melt.

Demon hunter.

He popped a piece of gum in his mouth. They leaned against the rough wall, only inches apart. Heat radiated from him. Jovi sucked on the mint and tried not to lean closer.

After a few minutes, Rogan pinched the bridge of his nose and closed his eyes. He looked almost...vulnerable.

"Headache?" It was hard to believe he could suffer something so normal.

He dropped his hand. "Caffeine withdrawal. It's fine."

Jovi's mouth fell open in delight. "Nash Rogan's addicted

to caffeine? And here I was beginning to think you didn't have any vices."

He ignored her, brushing dust from his sleeve.

A comfortable silence fell. Jovi thumped her heel to inspect her boot dagger. It was crusted with snake demon guts and got stuck halfway out of her boot. She smacked her heel again, but the blade didn't budge. She cursed, leaning over to examine it.

"Let me see it." Rogan held out a hand. When she warily handed it over, he scrutinized the sole, the toe, and the mechanism that worked the blade, then pulled a tiny multitool out of a pocket and went to work.

After a while, he murmured, "Tell me about your necklace."

Her stomach flipped. "Seriously? What's with you and the necklace, man? It's nothing special." She swallowed, wishing she had her boot back. The bastard was probably holding it hostage.

Strong fingers moved deftly over the tiny tool. "I've seen one like it before."

She played it cool, despite her heart hammering against her ribcage. "Really?"

He nodded, blew some dirt off the toe of her boot, and glanced over at her. "Who did you take it from?"

She shrugged. "I don't know, it was just laying there."

"Where?"

"For fuck's sake, Rogan!" Her mind spun. Why did he care so much? What did he know? "I don't remember. It wasn't a big deal. Where have you seen one before?"

He peered at the sole of her boot. "I don't remember. It wasn't a big deal."

Asshole.

He smacked her boot against the tunnel floor. The dagger shot out, fully functional and sparkling fucking clean. He banged the heel again, and it retracted smoothly. He handed it over to Jovi.

Irritated, she pulled it on. "Is there anything you're not good at?"

His lips curved ever so slightly. "I like fixing things. My dad taught me." He went abruptly silent.

She zipped the boot up, watching him. "Your dad?"

He bent over and began to re-tie his perfectly knotted laces.

"Was he a handyman or something?"

He inspected a rip in his pants. "Cop."

Her eyes fell on the old-school phaser on his belt, the only weapon he carried that wasn't MLE's latest and greatest. "Is that his?"

"Was. He was killed in action."

She felt another pang in the center of her chest, stronger this time. "How?"

His eyes met hers. The anger in them was old, and colder than the cave floor. "I've been trying to figure that out for seventeen years." He touched the old phaser. "My dad was a hell of a marksman. Someone killed him before he could get off his last shot. It's still loaded. I'm saving it."

Looking into his frigid gaze, she pitied whoever he was saving it for. "How old were you?"

"Ten." He looked away. "Mom died three years later. Got into Blitz, hooked up with some trash." His wide, stubbled jaw clenched. "Lots of trash."

He'd mentioned abuse—that must have been where it came from. "So, where'd you go when she died?"

"The Magistrate was involved in the incident the night my dad died. Dad saved his life. He got me a place to stay, looked out for me." Rogan stared at the wall, into a past she couldn't see. "You don't have to be a mage to go into Magical Law Enforcement, but it's extremely difficult to get in without any magical abilities. The Magistrate made sure I had a shot." He fell quiet, and a distant dripping echoed in the silence.

"And you kicked ass," Jovi finished.

He looked over, and there it was again—the faintest twinkle in his eye. "Yeah."

She smiled, feeling the stirrings of something deep inside her. Pride? Is that what that was? She rolled her eyes, but couldn't seem to wipe the smile from her face. "Of course you did. So, then what?" She wasn't captivated. Demons didn't do captivated.

"The Magistrate was creating the Demon Eradication unit. He needed field agents who could do the job and keep it quiet. I was always good at both of those. He gave me a chance to be something."

An anvil settled in Jovi's gut as she stared at his hard profile. Not only was he a demon hunter with something massive to prove, his replacement father figure was the leader of the magical population. Things just got better and better.

Rogan cleared his throat. "Cyrus and I went through the academy together. Top of our class." He shot her an unexpectedly wicked grin that sent a jolt through her nervous system. "He's a mage, but I beat him at hand-to-hand every time. He doesn't like to mess up his pretty face." The smile vanished. "I shouldn't be telling you this."

"Who am I going to tell?" She nudged his toe.

He rubbed his jaw, his palms scraping over the dark stubble. "Juno was a year behind us. She's a shifter. The academy doesn't get many of those, either." He shook his head ruefully. "She kicked everyone's ass. It made things hard for her."

Jovi frowned. "Why?"

"Because people don't like it when you're better than they are."

"Is that why you don't like me?" She poked him in the ribs.

"I do like you." He shut his mouth so fast she heard his teeth clack together.

Jovi gasped, delighted. Her hands flattened over her chest. "Agent Anal-Retentive likes me? But I'm so…" She gestured vaguely, searching for the right word. "Naughty."

CHAPTER 29

He was such a goddamn idiot.

Naughty. Rogan's cock hardened instantly as that word came out of Jovi's mouth, conjuring all kinds of images. Her, in a black leather miniskirt, thigh-high boots, and nothing else. Her, crawling toward him like a cat, edging her hot little mouth closer and closer to his—

He shifted on the cave floor, trying to covertly adjust himself. He never meant to tell her he liked her. Hell, he never meant to like her at all. But she was beautiful, and fierce, and...funny.

He cleared his throat again. "Anyway, that's how it started, with the three of us. Added a few more over the years." Thankfully, his hard-on deflated as he pictured his squad. Who was on patrol tonight? Had they made any progress with the search? His fingers itched for his tablet. Instead, he was stuck in a cold, damp cave with a lens that was very much dead and a woman that was very much alive.

Jovi peered at him shrewdly. "You're the only human in the squad?"

He nodded shortly, shriveling ever so slightly inside his

skin. He waited for the questions about how he compensated, the assumptions about the others picking up his slack...

"So, obviously you're, like, really good."

He blinked, looking over at her sharply.

Jovi shrugged. "If you can keep up with the best shapeshifters and mages, obviously you're one hell of a fighter."

It shouldn't have hit him as hard as it did. He barely knew her. His teammates, his MLE subordinates, even the Magistrate himself had told him as much over the course of his career. But when those blunt-as-a-hammer words came out of Jovi Black's mouth, something loosened deep inside.

"And I bet you don't just keep up with them," Jovi muttered. "Knowing you, I bet you lead." She stomped the heel of her boot, bending over to test the sharpness of the blade. Her fingernail tinged against the metal. "You're probably really good at that, too."

He stared at her delicate profile. "What makes you say that?"

"Because you're so..." She waved a hand. "Big and strong, and, like, laser-focused." She gestured to the pockets lining his tacticals. "Probably have extras of everything just in case someone needs something." Her tone was teasing, but there was something behind it, something almost yearning. "And you talk about your team like you actually give a shit about them. Give a lot of shits." Her brows knit together. "They're lucky."

His hand reached out all on its own, touched her chin, and turned her face toward his. Their eyes met. The distant dripping, the earthy scent of the rocks, the damp chill...it all melted away, until all he heard was the thump of his heartbeat in his ears, and all he felt was the heat of her skin beneath his fingertips.

"Thank you." He couldn't keep his gaze from drifting to

her mouth. Cyrus's words floated back to him. *For the love of God, don't touch her.*

But he had touched her. And he wanted to touch her again, all the time. Christ, it was like she had magnets under that luminous skin of hers, and he was made of all kinds of metal. He'd been attracted to women before, but he'd never had a problem ignoring it. The relentless pull toward her was different. It was like she had him under a spell.

The thought struck home, ugly and sharp. "Are you enchanting me?"

A slow smile stretched across her lips. "You tell me."

"I'm serious." His fingers tightened ever so slightly on her chin. "Are you using magic on me? Fucking with my head?"

Jovi grew still. Then, her brows slashed down, and she nailed him with a brutal kick to the calf. He grunted in pain and jerked away, scowling at her.

"Why, because that's the only reason you could like me?" She stood, his jacket drowning her. It did nothing to cover the hard, wounded look in her eyes. She shrugged out of the jacket and chucked it at him, marching off in those ridiculous purple shorts. "Forget it. Let's get out of here."

Rogan bit back a curse, got to his feet, and took off after her, scrambling to tie the jacket around his hips.

She was silent as they crept through the tunnel for what felt like hours. Rogan tried to stay close enough to protect her without actually touching her. Dangerous heat radiated from her pearly skin. She was pissed.

His calf throbbed, and his stomach twisted. He would not feel guilty. He would not apologize. She was a mage, or at least claimed to be one. She very well could be enchanting him. It was a legitimate question.

The stench of rotten eggs snapped him to attention just as Jovi stopped short in front of him.

"What is it?" he whispered.

She shushed him sharply, shaking out her hands. "Just stay back and don't shoot me."

She crept into the darkness. He wanted to snatch her back, shove her behind him, and dispatch the target himself, brutally, while she watched. Cut off its head and plant his boot on it while she smiled in approval. Instead, he stood frozen, blind, useless…a goddamn liability.

All the things he fought not to be every day of his life.

Jovi ducked suddenly, thrusting her palms forward. Nothing happened. She tried again.

Nothing. No fire, no sparks, no steam.

Jovi looked at her hands, then shot a terrified glance back at Rogan. The panic in those blue eyes sent a volt of pure, electric fear through him.

The next instant, she was on the ground. Bright red slashes appeared on her white tank top. She gasped, thrashed, kicked—then her limbs froze. She was pinned, spread-eagled on the floor.

Something was on top of her.

Rogan planted his feet, aimed his phaser a foot above her body, and fired. A streak of light flashed through the tunnel. Jovi gasped again, her arms and legs still grounded. More slashes of red appeared on her torso, and Rogan felt each one as if it were his own flesh.

"Higher!" Jovi managed to scream.

Rogan aimed higher, and a chorus of inhuman shrieks echoed off the walls. He was hitting it, whatever it was. He bore down on the trigger while his hair stood on end and panic pounded against his sternum. *Die, you piece of shit! She's hurt, she needs me.*

Finally, Jovi waved a feeble hand. Rogan released the trigger and rushed forward at a crouch. "Clear?" he demanded. "Clear?"

Jovi pushed at the air above her body like she was shoving something off her. There was a heavy thump, then her arms flopped back to the floor. She nodded, panting. Nose filling with the scent of sulfur and iron, Rogan holstered his phaser, dropping to his knees beside her. His heart stopped.

She was shredded. Her beautiful pearly skin was torn to ribbons from knee to neck. Bright red blood soaked her white tank top, her little purple shorts, the ends of her hair. Rogan's stomach leaped into his throat. He whipped off his shirt, pressing it to the worst of the wounds, a gaping six-inch slash over her right ribcage. Exposed muscle shone pink, bits of bone flashed white. Jovi gasped at the pressure, her face colorless.

"You're fine. You'll be fine." His mind raced through his field medic training, but *BAD, VERY BAD* kept blazing to the forefront. Medimend tape was no match for this. "Can you heal yourself like you healed me?"

She shook her head weakly. "Time."

Fuck. He needed John. He needed something. He needed her to be okay. "What was it?"

"Spider thing. Razors…" Her breathing was shallow and fast. She made a little clawing motion. "I didn't have any juice."

Rogan brushed a strand of pink hair from her face. "You did good."

"Got my…ass kicked." Her eyes squeezed shut, and blood pulsed from her wounds, coating his fingers.

"You'll be fine." He wasn't so fucking sure. "We need to stop the bleeding. We'll stay here a while. Hey." He gave her shoulder a little shake when she seemed to pass out. "You have to stay awake. I need your eyes."

And for some reason, he couldn't handle the thought of her going to sleep and never waking up again.

They stayed like that for a long time. His legs went numb, his knees howled, his back ached from hunching over her, but he ignored his discomfort. He had to nudge her awake every few minutes, and it fucking killed him to do it. She needed rest, and he couldn't give it to her. He needed her to be his eyes.

The bleeding eventually slowed. He kept his shirt pressed to her, their bare arms touching. Her skin was clammy. He scowled at her next-to-nothing shorts like it was their fault.

She started to shiver.

"Come here." He slid his free arm beneath her and scooted them backward until he could lean against the tunnel wall, ignoring the shocking cold of the rock against his naked back. He carefully pulled Jovi's little body between his legs, easing her against him while keeping his shirt pressed to her wound. He wrapped his other arm around her.

Despite the fact that she was mortally wounded, it felt good. Really good.

He tossed his jacket over her legs, pointing his phaser and illuminator down the tunnel. Jovi's head lolled against his collarbone. Her hair pressed against his cheek, tangled and sticky with sweat, the ends stiff with blood. But beneath the salty sweat and coppery blood and fading sulfur, he could still smell it…hot sugar.

He looked down at her face, only inches from his. Her skin was paler than usual and smudged with dirt and soot. Black lashes fanned her cheekbones. He moved his shoulder to nudge her awake, and her eyes fluttered open. "I'm sorry." He meant it for more than just waking her.

"Warm," she murmured, nestling against his bare chest.

Heat shot straight to his crotch. Christ, what was he, an animal? He gave his dick a stern reprimand and looked around for something to talk about. "How did you learn to fight?"

She shifted against him slightly, winced, and settled. "Taught myself."

"You taught yourself close combat?"

"Tough neighborhood."

Interesting. "You move like a shifter sometimes." Fierce and wild, with an innate, casual grace.

She shook her head, rolling it on his collarbone. "I wish I was. I'd be a tiger. *Rawr*." She was loopy, sluggish from blood loss, possibly a concussion. She'd hit the cave floor pretty hard.

"Tiger, huh?" He jostled his shoulder again. "You're not too far off."

She grinned, her lashes fluttering down. Rogan squeezed her until she grunted and forced her eyes open again.

"Stay awake," he whispered in her ear. Reaching into one of his pockets, he managed to pull out a pack of mints. It was all they had left. "Eat this." He slid the mint into her mouth, fingertips brushing her pale lips. She made a small sound of pleasure as the mint hit her tongue, and despite the talking-to, his dick responded instantly, crowding his zipper like a dog desperate for attention. Jovi would feel it against her ass any minute.

Redirect, immediately. "What about your fire magic, who taught you that?"

"Mmm. Mommy...Dearest." She made sucking sounds around the mint, and his groin throbbed. "Made me burn stuff." Her head sagged.

Alarmed, he reached a hand around to her cheek, gently turning her face toward him. Their noses nearly touched. "Jovi," he said. "Jovi." She blinked awake. She needed a task. "Do you see anything?"

She scanned the rocky tunnel. "No."

"Good. I need you to keep watch. Understood?"

"Aye, aye, captain." She shook her head sluggishly, trying to clear the cobwebs. "I'll watch out for you."

Jesus, that was sweet. As his heart clenched, Rogan popped another mint between her lips. The tip of her pink tongue snaked out to bring it into her mouth, and he swallowed hard. "So, what did your mom have you practice on?"

Her gaze sharpened. "What?" Peppermint wafted under his nose. His stomach growled, but he ignored it. She could have them all.

"You said your mom made you burn things."

"Oh." She frowned. "Yeah. Are there gummy bears?"

"No, you ate them all. What did she make you burn?" *Keep her talking.* Because of her concussion, not because she fascinated him.

"Anything that could...hurt."

That was fucking disturbing. "How did you learn to heal?"

She shrugged. "I don't know, just did it. She didn't like it. Got in trouble."

A chill went through him. He pictured a tiny child Jovi, all tangled pink hair and big blue eyes, being forced to hurt things. Being punished for healing them later. His fist clenched around the shirt wadded against her ribs. What kind of sick mother did she have? His mom might have turned to men and drugs in her own grief, but right up to the end, she never had an evil bone in her body.

"Can I sleep now?" Jovi mumbled.

"No. I need you." He jostled her gently. "We're a squad, got it? You're on lookout."

"Squad." A tiny smile curved across her mouth, then her head lolled on his shoulder.

The mints weren't enough. She needed real food. Rogan pulled his shirt away from her wound. He caught a whiff of copper, but the blood looked dull, no longer wet and shiny. He breathed a sigh of relief—she was healing. But he still needed her eyes.

"Jovi." He shook her. Her head rolled, hair falling in front of her face. He brushed it over her shoulder, and his hand landed on the curve of her neck. Her skin was so soft, like satin under his fingers. He couldn't keep his thumb from stroking the dip where her neck met her shoulder. So soft. He wanted to lick that spot. Would she taste like torched sugar there?

Her mouth was so close. And her eyes were still closed, and he had to keep her awake, any way he could.

It was a pathetic excuse. Still, he slid his hand up the slender column of her neck, cupped her head, and touched his mouth to hers.

Her lips were parched. He couldn't help but wet them with his tongue. She woke with a slight jerk, then a little moan as she began to respond. His body came alive, humming with electricity as he held her against his bare chest and kissed her, soft and slow. She tasted like mint and something else, something dark and sweet at the same time. He couldn't get enough. He deepened the kiss, his fingers threading through her hair, the damp cave fading away until all he knew was her mouth and skin and the silky slide of her hot little tongue against his.

A shudder racked the tunnel. They broke apart, and Jovi's eyes swept their surroundings. After a few tense seconds, she looked back to him and shook her head. They were alone.

Jesus Christ, what the hell was he doing? She was wounded, and he was going to get them both killed. "You have to stay awake."

She nodded, the gleam of wetness on her lips doing nothing to discourage the massive erection tenting his pants. He shifted uncomfortably, and her eyes flared as the bulge ground into her hip. It took everything he had to keep himself from hauling her mouth back to his.

"I'm going to teach you clock positions." He sounded strangled.

"Whatever position you want." Her voice was weak, but a bit of the old spark was back. And it was already killing him.

He cleared his throat. "Clock positions. So we can give each other directions. If you see a hostile, you need to tell me where it is, quickly." He explained a clock face, something that had long ago become obsolete to civilians. She caught on easily. They practiced for a while, and she grew stronger, the cuts on her legs scabbing over before his eyes.

"Let me see," he said finally, easing her out of the warm cradle of his body. Chilled air hit his bare torso as he took his wadded shirt away from her ribs to inspect the wound. It was starting to scab. He prodded the skin around it.

"Ow!" Jovi batted at his hand, craning her neck to inspect the cut herself. She made a small noise of satisfaction at its progress.

"Can you stand?" he asked. He helped her to her feet. She was white as a sheet, with dark circles beneath her eyes. Her hair was a tangled pink mess around her shoulders, her skin was smudged with dirt and soot, and her white tank top was filthy, torn to shreds and stained brown with dried blood.

She was the most tempting thing he'd ever seen.

They moved slowly down the corridor. Rogan stayed on her like a dog on a goddamn bone. He wanted her loaded with weapons, strapped into MLE's best tactical armor, and tucked safely behind him while he took the lead.

He also, he realized, wanted her fighting beside him. Wild and unpredictable as she was, Jovi was also extremely effective. "What do you see?" he murmured.

"Tunnel."

"What's at three o'clock?"

"A fucking tunnel."

The corner of his mouth lifted. She was feeling better.

"What's on your six?"

Her hand snapped backward, her palm suddenly gripping his crotch. He froze, his eyes practically popping out of his head.

"That," Jovi smirked.

Really feeling better.

She squeezed his instant hard-on and hummed with low satisfaction. Jesus Christ. He snatched her wrist. "Jovi."

She tossed him a wink, releasing him. They continued, though Rogan adjusted his pants about every five minutes. They crept along the catacombs until suddenly, Jovi stopped and lowered into a ready stance. Rogan mimicked her, palming his phaser.

"Ten, twelve, and one," Jovi whispered, glancing up. "Ceiling."

He had an idea. "On your shoulder." Rogan brought his forearms up to rest on her slim shoulder. She nestled perfectly beneath his armpit, and his phaser extended a foot beyond her face. She saw the weapon and ducked away with a muffled squeal.

"What the fuck! Get that thing away from my face!"

He shushed her sharply. "You're too weak to use your fire."

"Then let *me* shoot the thing!" Her eyes darted around the tunnel, apparently eyeing the hostiles that were watching their hissing match.

"It's tied to my fingerprints. You can't use it. So get under here…" He forced her against his body, resting his forearms on her shoulder again, "And aim."

She muttered a string of curses, grasped his forearms, and adjusted them slightly. "Now."

Rogan squeezed the trigger and lit up the tunnel. Something shrieked—a hit. Triumph surged through him. It just might work.

Jovi turned to the right, trying to drag his arms with her. They slipped from her shoulders and she cursed, then grabbed his arms again, trying to aim. But Rogan's senses were alive, and he whirled toward a noise in the opposite direction. They fumbled, stumbling apart. Jovi ducked, and when something flapped past Rogan's ear, he ducked, too. Jovi swore in pain, wrapped one arm around her torso, and brought a palm forward, ready to send off a fireball.

"No!" Christ, she was practically dead on her feet as it was. "Where?"

She ducked again and staggered, looking almost bloodless in the light of the illuminator. "Nine!"

Rogan spun and fired. He heard a shrill squeak and a thud next to him.

"Three. No wait, two. Twelve! Eleven!"

Rogan fired in rapid succession. Nothing shrieked, nothing thudded to the ground. Something streaked past his face, and he felt a sting across his temple.

"Ten!" Jovi shouted, but no—it sounded like seven. He whirled and fired at seven o'clock, twitching as something flapped next to his face. Something else whizzed past his shoulder. He spun, blind and furious.

A shriek close to his ear made him jerk his head, but he wasn't fast enough. Twin needles sank into his neck. He shouted, slapping a hand to the piercing pain. Something leathery and furry writhed under his palm, sending a thrill of revulsion through him. He slammed whatever it was to the ground and stomped as hard as he could, over and over, feeling bones snap and guts squish beneath his boot.

Jovi's cry of pain made his head snap up. She had her back braced against the rocky wall, batting furiously at the air. "Mother*fuckers*!" she screamed, and lit the tunnel up with a billowing curtain of flame.

The blast of heat knocked Rogan back a step. Shit, she wasn't strong enough. He charged forward, ready to shove her behind his back, shield her from these flying fucks any way he could.

"Stay the fuck back!" Jovi shouted at him, flames pouring from her hands like blow torches.

The hell he would. He darted toward her at a crouch, ignoring the flap of wings behind him. Jovi did a double-take as he approached. Her eyes went wide, the flames vanished, and she lunged toward him. Before he could react, she grabbed a throwing knife from his belt and chucked it, staggering off balance.

The blade sliced deep into his thigh and stuck. Rogan saw stars.

Jovi cursed. She yanked another knife from his holster, shoved him aside, and threw the blade past him this time, sloppily but with vicious force. A fiendish scream sounded behind him, followed by a thud and a cloud of dust.

She turned, her eyes blazing. "You stupid sonofabitch." She collapsed against the tunnel wall and slid to the floor. Her head flopped back against the rock, eyes closed, chest pumping. Her hands smoldered, and her tank top shone with fresh blood.

"Are we clear?" It was all he could do to get the words out.

When she nodded, Rogan hobbled to the opposite wall, wrapped his palm around the knife handle, and sucked in a breath. He ripped the blade from his flesh with a guttural grunt. White-hot pain blinded him, and he slid down the wall to land ungracefully on his ass. When his vision cleared, he inspected the cut and was relieved to see that it was deep, but there wasn't any arterial damage. He'd live.

Rogan put pressure on the throbbing wound and raised his eyes. "You threw a knife in my leg."

"You got in my fucking way!" She glared at him from across the tunnel.

"I was coming to assist."

"I didn't ask you to assist, I told you to stay the fuck back!" She closed her eyes again, wincing.

"If you would've aimed the phaser—"

"You kept pulling it in different directions."

"If you would've given me clock positions—"

"I did! They were fucking—" She flapped her arms. "Bat things, Rogan. They were *flying*. And you kept ignoring me and doing whatever you wanted, anyway!"

Rogan glowered through the raw, pulsing pain in his thigh, trying to ignore the niggling feeling that she had a point.

She jabbed a finger at him. "You just can't stand not being in control. You've got this giant chip on your shoulder like you have to prove yourself every second of every day." She tossed her hands. "You've obviously already proved yourself. You lead this team of elite soldiers, right? The fucking Magistrate put *you* in charge. Is anyone trying to kick you out?" When he didn't answer, she shook her head. "You're obviously good enough, dude. Seems like you're the only one who thinks you still need to prove it."

Well, didn't that just strip him to the bone.

He stared at her, stunned, wondering how this near stranger had managed to flay him alive.

CHAPTER 30

Rogan was silent as he knelt over Jovi to inspect her reopened wound. His pants were wet from blood, and he was limping. She ignored the twinge in her belly. Demons didn't do guilt, either.

He pulled a roll of Medimend tape from his pocket, tore off a strip with his teeth, and very carefully applied it over her wound. The brush of his fingers left goosebumps in their wake. He was still annoyingly, mouthwateringly shirtless—he'd used his shirt to mop up all her blood when she'd been ripped to shreds, and now the filthy thing was tied around his hips, stiff and crumpled. Shadows danced over his flexing muscles. She wanted to lick him. She also kind of wanted to stab him again.

Stupid ass. She'd been scared shitless when he came charging toward her during that fight. Those giant vampire bats had been nicely distracted by her fire until he made himself a big, fat target. The sight of the enormous, fanged beast swooping behind him, ready to rip out his throat, had stopped her heart. And that freaked her out.

Demon killer.

Sure, he'd held her in his arms and snuggled her back to

health after the spider shredded her. And he'd spilled his deepest, darkest secrets. And kissed her with intoxicating, delicious tenderness, like she was something precious. But none of that changed what he was. And it sure as shit didn't change what she was.

Rogan finished with the tape and limped across the tunnel, easing to a seat against the opposite wall. He checked his weapons, blew dust off his cartridges, and bandaged his own wound. Even grimy, streaked with blood, and brooding, he still managed to look maddeningly sexy.

After several long, silent minutes, she glanced at his wounded leg. Okay, fine, maybe demons did do a little guilt. Sometimes. "Want me to take care of that?"

"No. Recover." It was a terse command.

"Yes, sir," she grumbled. Then, because she couldn't help it, she asked, "Does your team call you sir?"

His eyes flitted to hers at the mention of his squad. He was probably pissed about all the shit she'd said a few minutes ago, but he just shook his head.

"What do they call you?"

"Rogan. Cyrus calls me Nash sometimes."

"You don't make them call you Captain or something?" Mommy Dearest insisted that her minions call her *mistress*. Her belly twisted at the thought.

"It's not like that."

When he didn't elaborate, she raised a brow. "What is it like?"

He was quiet long enough that she thought he wasn't going to answer. "Family."

Something ached behind her ribcage, and it wasn't her battle wounds. "What's *that* like?" The words slipped out, and she instantly wished she could suck them back in. She cast a glance across the tunnel and found him watching her. Some of the hardness had evaporated from his gaze.

"Like we have each other's back."

She chewed her lip and nodded, pretending to be really interested in the laces of her boots. Her throat hurt.

"We live together, train together, fight together. And we eat together."

She picked at the stains on her filthy shorts. "Sounds nice." A thought occurred to her. "Do you ever have food fights?"

He blinked. "Food fights?"

"Yeah, you know, flinging potatoes and stuff across the table? Getting all messy?" She saw it in a movie Nora had shown her. Everyone was laughing and shrieking and ducking for cover, and not in a way that made her skin crawl. In a nice way. At least, she thought it looked nice. But Rogan's brows were riding his hairline and his lips were twitching. She folded her arms. "Never mind."

"I don't believe we've ever had a food fight." Across the cave tunnel, she could've sworn she saw a twinkle. "Sometimes, Cyrus uses his telekinesis to fuck with our dishes. And we all *want* to throw something at Wolf pretty much every meal."

"*You* want to throw something?"

"At Wolf? Yes. Very much so."

She didn't know this Wolf, but he sounded like her kind of fun. She grinned, and Rogan's lips curved in response.

"I take it you don't have much of a family?"

Her tentative good mood vanished. She shook her head, picked at her shorts, and watched the flakes of dried blood fall to the cave floor.

"Just you and your mom?"

And a shitload of hellspawn. "Yep."

"You guys get along?"

Anger boiled up inside of her at the thought. "No, we don't get along."

"Why?"

"Because she's an evil bitch who loves to torture people,"

she snapped without thinking. "And I'm not. Or at least, I don't want to be. I try not to be." Shit, the words were flying out of her mouth, and she couldn't seem to rein them in. The way he was looking at her made her feel naked. "Unless they deserve it." She lifted her chin. "Sometimes they deserve it."

He stared at her. "I agree."

Her heart pounded furiously in the silence. She needed to change the subject, like, *now*—

"And you never knew your dad."

She shook her head, trying to think of anything else to talk about.

"And you want to find him because you hope he's different from her. Because if he's different, maybe that will explain why you are, too."

What was he, a psychic? Her throat burned, and tears pricked her eyes. She brushed grime from her arms, examined her shredded tank top—anything to avoid looking at him.

When he spoke, his voice was barely above a whisper. "Everyone in the squad is...different. None of us ever really fit where we were supposed to. But we fit together."

Oh, great, now she really was going to cry. Because she wanted that. Wanted it really, really fucking bad. She swallowed hard, bending over to tighten her boots and hide from his too-smart eyes. If he dug for any more details, she'd have to lie. And for some reason, the thought of lying to him made her stomach hurt. So, as she painstakingly tied her laces into perfect fucking bows, she nodded and hoped he would drop it.

There was a long, long pause.

"You'd love our housekeeper. She bakes a lot of sweets."

She looked up in time to catch his crooked smile, and gave him one in return. The vise around her chest eased a little. "I like sweets."

"I noticed that," he replied drily. "Your perfect body

makes no sense." He looked like he wanted to suck back his words, too. When her smile broadened, he shook his head like he couldn't believe his own audacity. "Rest. We'll move when you've recovered."

She nodded and leaned back against the wall, relieved. It all felt too close, like she'd swerved and barely avoided a collision. He was too smart and observant, and she was tired and hungry and off her game. She had to be more careful.

Silence stretched, broken only by the distant *drip*, *drip*, *drip*…

Her eyelids drooped.

Sometime later, a new sound snapped her awake.

Hisssss…

Her eyes shot open, and her stomach lurched. Centipedes. Huge, gleaming, and red. A mass of wriggling legs and flailing antennae moved like a scarlet wave over the cave floor. Pincers snapped, adding a chattering cacophony to the sinister, endless hiss. They scuttled over Rogan's outstretched legs like a blanket, thousands of thin legs squirming against his bare chest. Their shining, flexible bodies molded to the curves of his muscles, curling around the column of his neck. One was plastered over his mouth and nose. Swollen, inflamed bite marks dotted his skin, and his head hung limply to one side.

Jovi scrambled to her feet, thrust her palms forward, and shot a burst of flame at the mass of crawling bodies. The centipedes screeched and curled, tumbling off of him. She blasted them again, gagging as the smell of fried insects rose like smoke from a campfire. Patches of his skin were charred and blistered, making Jovi cringe. Burns, she could heal. She'd seen these creepy crawlies before, and they were nothing to fuck with. Their toxic venom would paralyze him, and then they would eat him alive.

She torched the fuckers. Chased them up the walls, along the rough ceiling, off of Rogan's lifeless body, until their blackened skeletons crunched under her boots. Finally, holding her breath against the stench, she tore the last centipede off Rogan's beautiful lips with a shriek of revulsion. Flinging the thing against the stone wall, she followed up with a final stream of fire, pinning it there until it trickled to the ground in ashes.

Rogan slumped against the cave wall, unmoving. Jovi straddled him, bringing his head upright and wincing at the burned patches of blistered skin and the angry red bites, still swelling and oozing blood. She laid a hand on his chest. His heart thumped steadily.

Relief consumed her, and she pressed her lips to his without a thought. His eyes opened, focusing fuzzily on her.

"Bugs," Jovi whispered. "I took care of them."

He blinked hard. "Stings. Venom?" He frowned down at himself.

"And burns. I'll heal you."

He shook his head, trying to push her off his lap. "You need your strength."

She was already calling up the healing light, closing her eyes to focus. He was right—it would probably drain her. But when that happened, he would take care of her. He'd already proven that.

Her stomach twisted. Relying on anyone was a slippery fucking slope. Relying on a demon hunter was downright certifiable.

"I need yours, too." She poured the healing light into his chest.

He was quiet while she worked. "Thank you."

She cracked open an eye. His skin was once again smooth and healthy beneath her palms, and he looked deeply relaxed, like he'd just come back from the damn spa.

And she, Jovi realized, was glowing.

Her jaw dropped as she examined her hands, arms, and torso. She was frickin' radiant from head to toe, her skin lighting up the tunnel even more than the illuminator, bathing everything in a warm, golden light. It was awesome.

She grinned, turning to take in the sight of Rogan's face. His expression stopped her short. He looked furious. "What?"

"You amaze me." He scowled darkly.

She snorted, but pleasure curled in her belly. She relaxed, fatigue setting in. "Don't sound so thrilled about it."

"I don't get amazed."

"Well, obviously you're hanging around the wrong kind of woman."

"Pretty sure you're one of a kind," he muttered.

"Back at you." It slipped out. She was all drowsy, and he was so warm and firm and gorgeous beneath her, saying sweet things and being adorably irritable about it. Instinctively, she wanted to say something flippant, to pass it off as a joke. But those sea glass eyes flared, holding her hostage.

His abdomen rose and fell beneath her hands. "Why do you say that?"

Her throat was suddenly dry. She should get up, get away from his penetrating stare, try to get her head straight. "You're this big, tough, super serious soldier guy. But you're…sweet."

His dark eyebrows lifted.

Now, she felt stupid. "You are. Not, like, fake sugary sweet. Like, I'll put myself on the line for you sweet. Take care of you and not expect anything in return sweet. Say really nice stuff sweet. Even if you are pissy about it." She made a little face, and was rewarded with an answering twinkle.

"I don't think anyone's ever called me sweet before."

She dropped her gaze to his delicious chest, thick with muscle and sprinkled with hair. "Maybe they've never seen the side of you that I have." She chewed her lip in the silence that followed, ready to bolt. It was ridiculous, saying all those dumb, soft things…

His hand came up to slowly tuck a strand of hair behind her ear.

Jovi released a breath as her eyes drifted shut. It felt too good—his hand, his words, his body beneath hers. She really needed to remember something. What was it? Oh, yeah, that he was a hellspawn-hunting control freak with a gun full of Holy Light. But she was tired, drained from the fight and the healing, and delicious tingles were following along the trail of his fingertips…

"Your ears are pointed."

Her eyes snapped open.

He was laser-focused on her ear. "Are you sure you're not fae?"

She shook her hair loose, shoving down the panic. Lots of things had pointed ears. Lots of non-demon things. "I told you, I don't know. Maybe." She pushed off of him and got to her feet. "Let's get out of here, these bugs stink."

He didn't press the subject, but she knew it was added to his damn mental file. *Jovi Black, registered magical female, pyromage level five, always hungry, breaks stuff, doesn't like caves, has pointed ears.*

They walked, and walked, and walked some more, until her legs trembled, and she had to brace herself on the damp stone wall. She was exhausted, and her stomach burned with hunger. She wanted a churro. She wanted a snack cake. She wanted a Sea Witch.

She wanted Nash Rogan. And it wasn't about payback anymore—it was about him, and who he was, and the things he did to her insides.

She was in really, really fucking big trouble.

She caught the toe of her boot, stumbling. Rogan grabbed her elbow like he had dozens of times in the past hour.

"Stop. You need to recover." He patted his pockets. "We're out of food, out of mints, everything. You need time—" He broke off, sniffing. Jovi smelled it, too.

Sulfur.

The next thing she knew, big hands wrapped around her waist, her feet left the ground, and she found herself planted firmly in front of Rogan's warm, bare torso. She heard him load a fresh cartridge into the phaser, and then his hard arms came around either side of her body. He pointed the phaser in front of her, flicking the safety off with his thumb. "Hands on mine." His low voice rumbled in her ear.

"Are you going to listen to me this—"

"*Hands.*"

She obeyed, sliding her hands over his. He was so much taller than her, she fit into the shell of his body like a glove. He was a wall of warm, solid stone behind her, surrounding her, supporting her.

"Put your finger on top of mine. I won't fight you. You point, I shoot. Understood?"

She swallowed and nodded just as a monstrous, skeletal demon came into view. Loose skin hung over long bones, eyes were fathomless black holes, and a lipless mouth gaped, showing off row after row of needled teeth. The beast was a sickening flesh color like a hairless cat, and it staggered blindly along the tunnel on long, clawed feet. Enormous hands dragged across the cave floor, scraping thin fingernails against the rocks.

The hair on Jovi's arms stood up. She felt goosebumps rise on Rogan's skin, too, but his fingers were firm beneath hers, his bare chest was solid behind her, and his arms were strong around her waist. Against her back, she felt the steady beating of his heart. She was exhausted, out of juice, and face to face with a nightmare she had no strength to fight.

And yet, she had never felt so safe. She didn't know which part was more terrifying.

The demon stilled. It raised its horrific head and took a long, slow sniff. Its sightless eyes pointed toward them, and a hair-raising clicking sound rattled from its throat. Then, it rushed them.

Jovi squeezed her finger over Rogan's. A blast of white light hit the creature's shoulder. It screeched, righted itself, and took another deep inhale. Its head swiveled toward them, and it crouched, freakishly long-limbed and loose-jointed, before springing onto the ceiling.

The demon clung there, upside down, constantly clicking. Folds of skin hung from its skeletal frame as it gripped the overhead rocks, the wound smoking on its shoulder. Its head tilted from side to side. "Youuuu smell familiarrrrrrrr," it hissed, and launched at them.

CHAPTER 31

The rasping, disembodied voice was Rogan's only warning. His instinct was to fire in the direction of the source, but in that split second, as he felt Jovi's lithe little body twist to the left, he made a choice.

If they were going to survive this, he had to let go.

Jovi pivoted, and he followed. She was the target. She was the focus. They were melded at the torso, her back to his chest. Her finger squeezed his, and another horrific shriek echoed through the tunnel.

She turned again. Rogan let his limbs soften, blocking out the damp chill of the cave, the inhuman sounds, the smell of rotten eggs and charred skin. Everything but her body—*their* body—moving as one. Jovi crouched, and Rogan crouched with her. She stood, leaning to the side, and he knew she was about to send off a kick. He leaned and kicked with her. Muscle memory at work. Something else at work. Their boots connected with something solid—a hit.

It became a dance. His body anticipated her movements with the tensing of her muscles, the bending of her knees. She swung their joined hands, and he let her. She squeezed his finger, and he let her. Holy Light flashed, and wet, clicking shrieks ricocheted off the walls.

"Duck!" Jovi shouted, and he did, shielding her in the cocoon of his body. She hit the floor and rolled. He rolled with her, his bare back scraping the floor. He landed face-up with her on top of him, blinded by a curtain of pink. Jovi pointed their joined hands straight up and pulled the trigger. There was a blast of light and a spray of debris. Rogan squinted, holding his breath against whatever was raining down on them.

She let their hands drop, lying breathless on top of him, damp with sweat. His heart hammered in the sudden silence.

"Are we clear?" he asked from behind her hair.

She nodded but made no move to get off him. "That…was awesome."

Rogan felt a full-fledged smile stretch across his face. He laughed, making Jovi bounce on his chest. "Yeah, it was."

She wriggled around to look at him. Something flared in her eyes. "Fuck, you're gorgeous when you smile."

He grinned wider.

Jovi shook her head, taking in every detail. "You let go."

His smile faded. She was right, he had. He'd let go completely, and it had been terrifying. And beautiful. He'd never felt so in tune with a partner during combat, not even with Cyrus.

There was something about her, this vixen who pushed him to the limits of his control and then demanded he let it all go, who challenged him like nothing or no one ever had, who cut straight to the heart of him with a few razor-sharp words. She made him forget things. Want things.

She called him sweet.

He lifted his hand, hesitated, then stroked a knuckle down her dirt-smudged cheek.

An unreadable emotion flashed across her face. "I am in such fucking trouble."

He was beginning to feel the same. "Why?"

"Because this girl is a team of one." She paused like she was debating whether to continue. "But I liked that. A lot."

He could've sworn those crystal blue eyes of hers were saying they liked *him* a lot.

"Would I make the cut? To be on your super special squad?" She was teasing now, though there was something serious behind it.

He pretended to consider it, then gave her a stern look. "You'd need to work on your stamina."

She laughed in mock outrage, slapping at his chest. He caught her wrist and held it, grinning, feeling lighter than he had in—well, he couldn't remember the last time he felt this way.

Her eyes flared. "Big fucking trouble." She rolled off him, clambering laboriously to her feet. "Come on, I hear water."

They made their way toward it. If they were lucky, it would be drinkable—dehydration could become a problem soon. But right that minute, Rogan was more concerned with the way Jovi was dragging those boots like she was about to hit the dirt. When she stumbled, he wrapped an arm around her waist. And when her knees gave out, he scooped her up and walked the rest of the way with her in his arms, feeling like a damn king.

She sighed, her breath tickling his neck. "See?"

"What?"

"Sweet."

Something in his chest fluttered. His arms clenched around her, an unconscious squeeze. He caught her smile out of the corner of his eye. His own lips curved in response.

The tunnel opened into a vast underground cavern. Stalactites stretched from the ceiling like bony icicles, dripping with condensation. Steam rose from a natural pool in the center of the cavern, and across from that was another tunnel leading further into the cave. Moisture trickled down the rocky walls, and all around, tiny bioluminescent plants glowed like soft blue stars. He didn't detect any sulfur, just the humid, mineral scent of the cave and the torched sugar of the woman in his arms. He glanced down at her, cursing his dead lens.

"Anything?" He hated having to ask.

She glanced around, shaking her head. "Clear." Then, she straightened with a gasp. "Is that a hot spring?"

"Looks like it, but we don't know what—"

She was out of his arms and hobbling toward the pool before he could finish. He reached for her, but she evaded him, making her way to the edge of the water. She stripped.

Rogan nearly swallowed his tongue. The blood-stained tank top was tossed carelessly aside, revealing a lean, shapely back. The ruffled purple shorts were next. They were stretchy, made of some flimsy material, and they slid easily down the length of her legs. She bent over to wriggle out of them, pointing her firm, round ass in his direction. His cock shot forward as she unzipped her boots, placed them carefully on the edge of the pool, then lowered herself in without hesitation. She sucked in a breath as she hit the steaming water, groaning as she sank in up to her neck. Her hair floated around her, darker pink in the dim light. Her head suddenly slipped under the surface.

Rogan jolted forward, but she popped up almost instantly, slicking her hair back in a move so sensual it stopped him in his tracks. She floated to the side of the pool and settled herself against the stone, resting her head against the edge with an emphatic sigh.

Abruptly, he realized he was staring at her like a shifter at a steakhouse. He shook himself and turned away to monitor the area, fighting the urge to glance over his shoulder every two seconds.

A long time passed. Water trickled, steam billowed, plants glowed. Imagination ran wild.

"Hey, Agent Hardbody."

He turned to see Jovi facing him, hair slicked and eyes round. The water played around her bare shoulders. She crooked her finger through the steam.

Rogan swallowed, shaking his head.

"These kinds of hot springs have healing powers." She lowered herself in the water, blew bubbles, and kept those luminous blue eyes locked on his. "You look pretty banged-up."

Bad idea. Very bad idea.

But, then again, she was right. Hot baths did help with muscle recovery. And his muscles were very, very tense.

Slowly, like someone else piloted his body, Rogan walked toward the edge of the pool. His brain chugged inside his skull, sluggish and stupid.

For the love of God, don't touch her.

With a superhuman effort, he forced himself to a stop. "I can't."

She stared at him. They both knew he was talking about more than a dip in a pool.

"It's against regulations." It sounded lame, even to his own ears.

She held his gaze for an endless moment. Then, she glided backward through the steam, settled against the edge of the pool, and closed her eyes. "Just get in and hose off, for fuck's sake."

Rogan felt like he'd simultaneously passed and failed a very important test. He took a breath, steadying his racing pulse. Then, her choice of words registered.

It occurred to him that he might stink.

His cheeks heated. His skin felt suddenly filthy, stiff with dirt, sweat, blood, and demon guts he couldn't see. He shucked his boots and tacticals in record time, placing his phaser carefully on the edge of the pool before glancing at Jovi. Her eyes were still closed.

His fingers hooked into the waistband of his boxer briefs,

but apparently, he had at least one brain cell left, because he thought better of it. He left them on, easing into the water. It was deliciously hot, and he barely stifled a groan as he submerged up to his chest. The stone floor was rough beneath his bare feet as he circled around Jovi to the opposite side of the pool, where he found a slight ledge jutting out beneath the surface. He sat on it, trying not to imagine what could be lurking near his toes. Testing the distance to his phaser, he confirmed it was within easy reach and proceeded to scan the cavern continuously, though it wasn't like he could see anything but rock walls and glowing plants. Damn his dead lens.

"You think too much."

His eyes landed on her. Sitting there in the steaming pool with her eyes closed, she looked ethereal like a serene goddess surrounded by softly glowing stars.

He shifted on the stone ledge. "It's my job."

"To think?'

"To observe. And eliminate the threat."

"There's no threat here. Not right now, anyway." She opened her eyes. "I'll tell you if any uglies show up. You can relax."

He prodded at his lens. "I don't really know how to do that."

She snorted. "You don't say." When he shot her a glare, she grinned, then chewed her lip the way she did when she was stewing about something. When she spoke, the teasing quality had left her voice. "I can show you. Like you're showing me how to be a team." Her cheeks flushed pink, and she focused on her own fingers trailing across the surface of the water, avoiding his eyes.

Warmth bloomed behind his ribcage, and as he watched her, one of his few remaining brain cells evaporated. "Where would you suggest we start?"

Her gaze lifted to his, and a wicked smile curled her lips.

"Fun." The mischief in her voice floated across the misty space between them. Her naked curves were blurred beneath the water's steaming surface, but his mind had no problem filling in all the blanks.

He cleared his throat. "Fun?"

Her lips twitched. "Yes, Rogan, fun. Ever heard of it?"

Only a few days ago, Theo had hassled him about the exact same thing. He scowled. "I have fun."

"Oh, yeah? What do you do?"

She was healing before his eyes, the cuts and bruises fading, her radiant glow returning. Hot springs really did have healing abilities. He lifted an arm out of the water before remembering that his own cuts had already scabbed over thanks to Jovi's healing infusions—the reason she was so exhausted in the first place.

Guilt flooded through him. They would stay here until she was strong as a bull.

"I spar, train, target practice," he replied.

"Anything *not* job-related?"

He opened his mouth, but nothing came out. Damn it.

She grinned. "That is so sad. You need to live a little, son."

What was so wrong with doing his goddamn job? "And what do you do for fun?"

"Swim in the ocean," she said dreamily, a little smile playing on her mouth. "Try all the food trucks. Go to the fights in the Arena, go out dancing, get really drunk and make out with cute guys…"

Jealousy slammed into him like a battering ram. He could just see it, Jovi all tarted up and looking like sex on a stick, tossing back shots and grinding on delighted men of all races. He heard something in his jaw crack.

She grinned, closing her eyes again as she leaned her head against the edge of the pool, her slender throat arching.

The idea of any other man touching her soft, sensitive skin made him want to punch a wall.

She sighed, breathy and content. His cock twitched in answer.

Right, he was in here to hose off. He scrubbed his shoulders, neck, and behind his ears. His hair felt crusty. Grimacing, he took a breath, ducked under, and rubbed his head vigorously. As water rushed into his ears, he tried not to picture Jovi in a barely-there skirt, running her hands all over some asshole in a sleazy bar. Temper flaring hotter than the hot spring, he broke the surface and opened his eyes.

Jovi was gone.

He whipped around in the water, scanning the cavern, seeing nothing but dots of glowing light and stalactites spearing from the vast ceiling. Water sloshed as he spun. "Jovi?" His voice echoed back at him, urgent and sharp.

A giggle sounded from somewhere to his left. He whirled. "Jovi?"

A snort, then a girlish snicker.

The little minx was hiding from him.

Disbelief warred with amusement—and some deep, primal thrill. *Chase.*

"Jovi." He waded to the edge of the pool and heaved himself out, trying to stay as silent as possible. He stood stock-still, dripping, his boxer briefs plastered to his hips and steam rising from his skin as he waited for another hint of sound. "Do you really think this is the time?"

"Lesson one: Life's short." Jovi's voice bounced off the rocky walls, and he turned his head sharply, trying to pinpoint its source. "And it's fucked, most of the time. Gotta have fun when you can."

A pebble rolled across the cave floor. He whipped toward it, just as another came flying from the darkness to ping him in the forehead.

A snarl rumbled from his throat, answered by another snicker from the depths of the cavern. Lowering to a crouch, he stalked toward the sound on silent feet, leaving wet footprints behind. There was a flash of white behind a large, craggy stalactite, and another pebble sailed toward him. He dodged it and darted forward, making a swipe around the stalactite as a shriek rebounded off the walls and Jovi bolted from cover, stunningly naked, hair hanging in long, wet ribbons down her back. Rogan lunged for her, but she evaded him with a delighted scream, using her feet to spring off the stone wall and rapidly change course. His fingers grazed her bare hip, but she twisted away, leaving him swiping at air. Laughing, she ran backward as he pelted toward her, his pulse racing from exhilaration and the sight of her, naked and smiling and bouncing…

She glanced over her shoulder, saw the steaming pool behind her, and jumped for it with a whoop, tucking her feet and grasping her knees to land in a massive cannonball. Water sprayed like a geyser, catching him full in the face as he skidded to a stop at the edge of the pool.

He thought about it for a split second, then cannonballed in after her.

Her shriek echoed off the cavern walls, muffled only by the torrent of bubbles that filled his ears when he went under. He broke the surface, shook the water from his face, and opened his eyes to find Jovi inches away, her chest heaving beneath the waterline, her crystal gaze gleaming.

"I think there's hope for you, after all."

He hauled her against him and slammed his lips to hers.

Heat erupted between them. The game, the danger they were in, his goddamn sanity—all of it vanished, incinerated by the inferno of her mouth. Her tongue slid against his, her arms winding around his neck as she brought her body flush with his beneath the water. Their naked thighs brushed, her bare breasts pressed against his chest, and his brain short-circuited. His hands were everywhere, stroking her curves, gripping her hair. He spun to press her back against the rock. Water sloshed. She gasped, her fingernails tightening in his hair as she wrapped her legs around his hips.

He pushed against her, unable to help himself, his soaked boxer briefs the only thing separating his cock from her core. A rough sound escaped him, somewhere between a growl and a groan. She tasted like heaven and hell, sweetness and sin, and he wanted more, more, more. Water slapped against the rocks, loud enough to cut through his haze, and he jerked his lips from hers, scanning the perimeter on instinct.

Jovi wrenched his face back toward her. "Me," she hissed, and descended on his mouth again.

Yes. Her. Just her, only her. He lifted her out of the water, groaning at the sight of her glistening wet breasts before capturing one in his mouth and laving the taut bud with his tongue. He dragged his lips up her throat to snag her earlobe between his teeth, breathing in the scent of her. Sweet, with that hot, wild edge. It drove him insane.

She made a desperate noise, pushing against his shoulders. For a split second, he thought she was saying no. He loosened his hold immediately, but she didn't shove him away. Instead, she pushed herself up onto the edge of the pool, lay back on the steam-warmed rock, and opened her legs to him.

His eyes nearly rolled back in his head. She was stunning, all creamy limbs and lush pink petals, a dewy, exotic flower blooming before his eyes. Dazed, he stroked his hands up the silk of her inner thighs, gripping her hips to pull himself closer until he was nestled between her legs. His head spun. A little mewling sound escaped her. He looked up to find her propped on her elbows, biting her bottom lip, watching him. Slowly, breathing hot on her glistening pink flesh, Rogan lowered his mouth and took the first long, slow lick.

Her cry echoed around the cavern. She collapsed back onto the rock, her hands gripping his hair.

"Fuck, yes." Her heels dug into his back, hips rising to

push harder against his mouth. He licked again, flicking his tongue over her swollen nub, and she gasped, shuddering.

Something in his brain snapped.

The cave, the woods beyond it, the entire world receded into that one point, that tiny pearl of flesh that swelled and pulsed beneath his tongue. He forgot that he was MLE, forgot they were on the run, forgot he should be looking for a fallen angel. All he knew was that there was a goddess beneath him, and he had her trembling.

He swirled and stroked, savoring every rise and fall of her hips, every moan that rang into the humid air. He used the thumb of one hand to pull on her flesh, exposing the sensitive nub even further, and circled it again with his tongue. She cried out, her nails raking his scalp, pinpricks of delicious pain.

He kept working his tongue over her, rocking his erection against the rock wall of the pool. Her bud swelled beneath his mouth, and he couldn't resist suckling. Jovi made a strangled sound, and he did it again, trailing his free hand up her thigh until he reached her shining wet center.

He slid one finger inside her. She was so silky soft, so impossibly smooth, it stole his breath. She groaned deeply, and he glanced up. Christ, the sight of her splayed before him, taut belly quivering, pink-tipped breasts heaving—it nearly drove him senseless. Hell, he was senseless. Her scent, the silken glide of her core, the steam rising around them…

He was in a fog, a haze made of her, and nothing else existed.

He slid another finger inside and this time, his eyes did roll back in his head. He stroked her, deep and firm, until her groan told him he'd found her spot. He bent to swirl his tongue around her tight little nub again, circling faster and faster while pumping against her sweet spot. She cried out wildly as he drove her up, his tongue moving faster, his fingers sliding deeper, until finally, he closed his lips around her swollen wet clit and sucked hard.

She came in a firestorm, her harsh cry echoing off the cavern walls, bucking against his mouth as he kept sucking, kept stroking his fingers deep inside. Power surged through him, a rush of primal male satisfaction. He was doing this to her. No magic, no shapeshifter strength, no tech. Just him.

When she collapsed against the rock, he heaved himself out of the water to crawl up her panting body. She glowed like a lantern, lit up from the inside like she did when she'd healed him. He'd done that. He stamped hot, wet kisses over her quivering skin, loving the feel of her, the way she lay sprawled beneath him, beads of water rolling down her curves as he dripped all over her.

Her eyes blazed into his, holding him captive as she slid her hand between them, slipped it beneath the waistband of his boxers, and closed her fingers deliberately around his length. She ran the tip of her pink tongue over her lips. He almost exploded then and there.

A loud sucking noise sounded behind them.

Rogan whipped his head around. The hot spring was draining like an enormous bathtub, water whirlpooling in the center and disappearing rapidly, inches at a time.

"What the—" Jovi craned around him to look.

Cursing, he jumped up and hauled her to her feet, keeping one eye on the draining pool while he yanked his pants over his straining cock and shoved his phaser into its holster. He tossed her filthy shorts and tank top at her, and she pulled them on quickly.

He shoved his feet into his boots as Jovi zipped up her own. He could still smell her, all over his nose, his lips, his chin. He hastily wiped a palm over his mouth. Jesus Christ, what the fuck was he thinking? He'd lost his goddamn mind, burying his face between a woman's legs in the middle of enemy territory...

Jovi grabbed his hand as she ran past, yanking him along with her. "Move, move, move!"

A deep, ominous sucking sound rose behind them. He glanced over his shoulder and felt his eyes widen. The water from the pool was soaring over the edge in one giant wave, roaring toward them like a tsunami. They sprinted for the tunnel exit.

Too late.

The massive wave overtook them. Jovi's slim fingers crunched under his grip as they went under, and it was all he could do to keep hold of her hand as the water tumbled them, bashing them against the floor, the walls, the ceiling—

Jovi's body rammed against his, and he managed to get his arms around her, locking his wrists together behind her back, trying to shield her as best he could. Suddenly, they were zooming backward. Bubbles whizzed past his face, pink hair floated in his vision, and he heard Jovi's muffled cry, warped under the water. There was a sharp slice of pain across his back as the water pulled them down, down, spinning, tumbling. His lungs screamed, his sinuses burned, and something sledgehammered into his temple.

Everything went dark.

CHAPTER 32

"Smells weird."

Rogan awoke with an inner snap. He remained still, keeping his eyes closed and his ears open. Softness beneath him, salt in the air, the sound of waves. A beach?

"Human. Armed," a deep voice said from somewhere overhead. Footsteps moved further away. There was a deep inhale. "She does smell weird."

"Smoking hot, though."

Rogan's eyes flew open. A stunning orange sunset painted the sky overhead, and gentle waves lapped at coarse black sand.

Black Beach? It couldn't be. How the hell had they washed up in lion territory?

Rogan turned his head, feeling like a rusted machine in desperate need of oil. Several yards away, the heads of three lion shapeshifters snapped toward him. Two males, one female, all with big, brawny human forms in various shades of bronze. As the two males strolled closer, Rogan caught a glimpse of what lay behind them.

Two pale, booted legs stuck out from behind a huge chunk of driftwood.

He struggled to sit up. White-hot pain seared through his right side, and he hitched a breath. A broken rib, maybe more. He propped himself up on one hand, forbidding himself to vomit.

"Touch your weapons and die," one of the lions said casually, looming over him.

"Is she alive?" he croaked.

The lions were silent. The female stood beside the driftwood, her arms folded. Several daggers glinted from her thigh holster.

"Is she alive?" Rogan repeated.

"Who are you?" the male closest to him asked.

"Concordia Magical Law Enforcement. Undercover. She's my charge. Is she alive?" He felt a flutter of panic in his gut. Her boots hadn't moved.

The males glanced back toward the female. She nodded shortly, and Rogan nearly sagged.

"How did you get here?" A long chestnut braid flowed to the female's waist, ending in a tuft that very much resembled a lioness's tail. Her feet were braced, her eyes sharply trained on him.

Rogan leaned over, trying to get a better look at Jovi. The males mirrored his movement, blocking his view. Rogan leaned further. His ribs screamed. He forced himself to back off, his breath catching in his throat. Black sand stuck to his bare torso and wet pants. Sand was the enemy of speed, as were broken goddamn ribs. If he tried to jump to his feet, he would fail. If he aggressed, they would take him down.

"I don't know," he said finally. "We were in a cave system near the eastern coast. There was an underground hot spring. It drained, sucked us down. What part of Pride lands is this?"

Their hard stares revealed nothing.

Jovi's boots still hadn't moved. Rogan licked his parched

lips, his waterlogged brain whirling. It was highly unlikely that the Pride was involved with the Slavs. And they needed aid. He took a breath. "My name is Agent Nash Rogan. Killian Diallo is my squad mate."

The lions went predator still.

Rogan locked eyes with the female. "I request an audience with Alpha Diallo."

CHAPTER 33

Jovi jerked awake when her head almost bounced off her neck. Blinking groggily, she realized she was in some sort of open vehicle, staring up at an orange sky streaked with the purple of approaching dusk. It was hot. The backs of her thighs were sweaty, stuck to the hard seat. She felt the amulet against her ankle bone and let out a breath.

The backs of three unfamiliar heads bounced in the seats in front of her. As she blinked, a fourth head spun around from the passenger seat, one she was very familiar with.

Rogan's eyes found hers, and she watched a shitload of relief flash across his face. His jaw, though, stayed clenched tight. Nasty cuts, scrapes, and bruises slashed his bare back, his shoulder blades, and across his eyebrow. His nose was pink with sunburn. But he was alive. They were both alive.

She eased upright, clutching her head when it threatened to explode. Her sinuses hummed, scrubbed raw from snorting a tidal wave up her nose.

In unison, the strangers turned to peer at her. All were various shades of tan and bronze, with blade-like bone structure, wide-bridged noses, and predatory stares. Lions?

Jovi raised her brows, still clutching her head. "The fuck

are we?" Scrubby foothills and vast sand dunes flew past, hot air whipping her hair into a frenzy.

"Pride lands," Rogan said grimly over the rumble of the dune buggy. "We washed up on Black Beach. We're going to see the alpha." He gave her a Very Meaningful Look. In other words, *Keep your mouth shut.* She nodded, rubbing her temple.

"Are you okay?"

She nodded again, though her head pounded. Screwing up her face against the pain, she squinted at the ugly cuts and bruises on Rogan's muscled back. "You?"

"Fine." He swept a glance over her body, and something flickered in his eyes before he turned around. Suddenly, she remembered what they'd been doing before they were so rudely interrupted.

Nash Rogan had a very talented tongue.

One of the blond males twisted to face her. He looked her up and down, lifted his chin, his nostrils flaring. "What are you?"

She was so not in the mood. "Excuse you?"

"You smell weird. What are you?"

"*You* smell weird, asshole. Ever think about that?"

Rogan tried to hide a smile as the other male shouted with laughter. The blond shoved him, but he looked back toward Jovi, harsh speculation in his eyes.

She braced herself on the seat as the buggy bounced along. "Look, buddy, we've been attacked by Slav gangsters, hit by a truck, trapped in a cave, and sucked down a giant watery sphincter. Pardon me if I'm a little less than fresh."

Their eyes gleamed with interest. The female in the driver's seat glanced curiously at her in the rearview mirror. Rogan pinched the bridge of his nose.

"Slavs?" the female questioned. "As in, the Slavic mafia?"

Whoops. They were still in WITPRO—probably shouldn't be spilling their secrets to furry strangers with big teeth.

"We can't share that." Rogan tossed Jovi a warning look.

The female's eyes glinted in the mirror.

The landscape changed as they bounced along the dunes. Scrubby brush and odd-shaped trees began to stud the dry desert. They crested a hill, and Jovi gasped.

Red River really was red. Winding lazily through brick-colored bluffs, the river sparkled in the setting sun like a huge scarlet snake. It looked nothing like the dirty, foam-flecked water that cut through the city. Here, the waves took on a reddish-orange glow like richly colored glass.

Trees flourished the closer they got to the river, growing thick and dense until finally, they neared the edge of a lush jungle. The buggy ambled through the foliage, flushing jewel-hued birds from their perches. Jurassic ferns swayed lazily in a warm breeze. They passed bright neon flowers, fat hanging fruits, and insects as big as her hand. Jovi was so busy gawking that she almost missed the treehouses.

Her jaw dropped. They were everywhere. Beautiful six-sided wooden huts tucked high up in the canopy, all wrapped with wide platform decks. Lights glowed in the windows, flickering to life before her eyes as the forest sank into twilight. Pink faebugs pulsed lazily, floating like rosy stars in the humid jungle air.

They rumbled to a stop at the base of an enormous tree. Its huge limbs twisted and curved, sprawling outward before reaching up toward the canopy. Four deep claw marks slashed the dark trunk. An enormous treehouse nestled high in the foliage, barely visible beyond its surrounding deck.

The female lion powered off the vehicle. "Wait here. Do not move." She leaped lithely from the buggy, her long braid swinging as she glanced up at the platform. A soft whistle came from between her teeth.

A burly sentry appeared on the platform. Yellow eyes glinted down at her, then surveyed the buggy.

The female murmured something. The sentry's lips moved. Shit, was their hearing really that good?

The sentry disappeared. A few long seconds passed. Rogan turned stiffly in his seat. Jovi frowned. Was he hurt?

"Let me do the talking," Rogan murmured, ignoring the shifters who sat between them. "The alpha and I are acquainted." He gave her another Meaningful Look.

Jovi nodded absently, scanning him for whatever injury he was trying to hide.

A trap door opened in the treehouse's platform. A bundle tumbled out, and a set of handsome rope-and-wood stairs sailed down the trunk, unfurling with a flourish. Heavy iron stakes dangled from the bottom step. The female stomped them into the forest floor with practiced ease, securing the staircase.

"Alpha will see you now."

Jovi climbed out of the back. Her muscles screamed, stiff and sore from being battered in a gigantic drainpipe and then jostled in the buggy of doom. Rogan slid rigidly from the passenger seat, his knuckles white against the doorframe.

He *was* hurt.

Jovi caught up with him and couldn't hold back her gasp. Beneath his stiffly held arm, the entire right side of his torso was black. He shook his head sharply at her, focusing intently on the thousand-foot staircase before them. His jaw clenched, but he started forward. She hurried to follow.

The rope ladder vibrated with each step. Jovi stayed close behind Rogan's broad, bare back, ready to catch him if he toppled backward. A nasty foot-long cut raked his shoulder blades, crusted with dried blood and black sand. He kept his arm glued to his side.

A watery vision flashed before her eyes. Rogan, fighting to get his arms around her beneath the raging water, clutching her tight as they were battered against the sharp rocks. He'd wrapped her in his arms to take the brunt of the beating. Her heart gave a pang.

Her leg muscles burned as they reached the trap door and

stepped onto the platform. The treehouse was beautifully built, natural wood planks stacked artfully on top of each other and delicately charred, emphasizing the grain. Golden light flooded the wraparound deck, pouring out of a huge double door flanked by two robust guards.

"Let them in," a deep voice rumbled from within the hut.

The guards motioned them forward, their eyes tracking them as they passed.

Inside, the alpha hut was all warm wood and cozy tapestries, throw blankets in rich colors, squashy pillows, and windows letting in the humid air and dwindling light. A table stood in one corner, displaying an enormous platter piled high with roasted meat. And at the back, a huge, heavily muscled man lounged shirtless on a plush armchair.

Auburn waves fell loosely around a wild, rawboned face and outrageously wide shoulders. Shadows danced over bronzed ropes of muscle. One long leg dangled over the arm of the chair, while a thick arm draped across the back. Pale golden eyes glinted as they approached.

A tall blonde female stood silently behind the alpha. She looked Jovi up and down in that special bitchy way some women had. Jovi ignored her, focusing on the tall hunk of man meat sprawled on his throne.

"Alpha Diallo," Rogan said, coming to a halt.

"Rogan."

"This is Jovi Black. She's my ward in the Witness Protection program."

Alpha Diallo barely spared her a glance. Maybe she was losing her touch. Frankly, she didn't care. The smell of roasted meat was making her mouth water, and her stomach gave a ridiculously loud growl.

Rogan's eyes slid over to hers.

"Sorry." She shrugged. "I'm fucking starving."

The blonde behind the alpha scowled. But the big, rangy lion turned his head to face her. "Jovi Black, you said?" His pale yellow eyes roved over her. "And what landed you in WITPRO?"

"Sorry, I can't answer that. It's kind of supposed to be a secret." She winked at him.

The blonde looked like she was about to have a conniption fit, and Rogan tensed even more beside her, but Alpha Diallo tilted his head and smiled. He had a wide mouth full of large, straight teeth. Jovi had no trouble imagining them elongating into some serious fangs.

"Is that so?" His gaze traveled over her battered body, bloodstained clothes, and hair that no doubt resembled a pink rat's nest. His smile broadened.

Rogan shifted ever so slightly closer.

Jovi stifled her own smile. "So, what's your name?"

The blonde sucked in an outraged breath. Rogan's hand was suddenly crushing hers. Jovi yanked it free, scowling up at him. "What? I'm sure he's got an actual name." She rolled her eyes back toward the alpha. "People are so weird about this stuff."

The alpha grinned openly. "Cullen," he purred. "Cullen Diallo."

"See?" Jovi patted Rogan's biceps. "Nice to meet you, Cullen. Thanks for inviting us up in your treehouse. Now, are you going to eat all that? Because we haven't eaten in, like, three days."

CHAPTER 34

Lions definitely knew how to char some meat.

Cullen sat across from them at the table in the alpha hut while Jovi scarfed down strips of succulent meat and Rogan ate in slow, measured bites. The alpha watched them, sipping purple wine. Nobody spoke, which was fine. At first. Then it just got awkward.

"So," Jovi gestured between them with her fork. "How do you guys know each other?"

The tension skyrocketed. Rogan raised his eyes to Cullen's, fingers tightening on his silverware.

"Agent Rogan recruited my brother," Cullen replied evenly.

The staring continued. Jovi glanced between the two of them, kind of hoping she was about to see some half-naked wrestling. "Okay?"

"Alpha Diallo believes Killian should be in the Pride business instead of working with MLE," Rogan explained.

"Alpha Diallo does believe that," Cullen growled.

More charged silence. Jovi chewed thoughtfully. "Is your brother a grown ass man?"

Rogan kicked her sharply under the table.

"Ow!" She kicked him back. His eye twitched.

Cullen stared at her, his eyes flashing an animalistic orange. His face was carved, the bone structure wild-looking even in human form. "Killian is eleven months younger than I am."

"So, he's a grown ass man. Let him do what he wants. Pretty sure Rogan didn't kidnap him—it's not his style."

Silence. Jovi shrugged, taking a large sip of wine.

"Why are you here, Rogan?" Cullen asked quietly.

Rogan took a breath. His bare shoulder brushed against Jovi, warm and smooth. "We were attacked at our safe house, then again in our car on the freeway. We ended up on foot and sheltered in a cave system. It caved in. We were making our way through and came to an underground hot spring…" He paused, searching for the right words.

"And got sucked out," Jovi finished around a mouthful of meat. She made a swooshing motion with her hands. "Right outta there. I guess we washed up on your beach?" She looked at Rogan for confirmation. He nodded. "We're trying to get back to the city, but stuff keeps trying to kill us."

Cullen studied her. His chin lifted slightly, nostrils flaring. "You're different."

Fucking shifters. "Thank you."

"Alpha Diallo," Rogan interjected. "Thank you for your hospitality. We would be grateful for a ride back to the city at your convenience."

Cullen leveled his predatory gaze on Rogan. "My brother won't come pick up his precious comrade?"

Rogan's jaw was granite. "My comms are all dead. If I could use a phone—"

"No need." A very feline smile stretched across the alpha's lips. "I'll take you myself. At my convenience." He rapped his knuckles twice on the table, and a guard appeared in the doorway. "We have guests tonight." Cullen looked Jovi up and down. "Would you like one room, or two?"

"One," Rogan snapped.

Cullen's smile didn't slip. "Fine. But I'd like to visit with Miss Jovi Black first." He snapped his fingers. "Show Agent Rogan to the guest house."

Rogan didn't move. Cullen arched an auburn brow, slowly pushing up from the table to rise to his full, impressive height. Rogan mirrored him, albeit more stiffly.

Jovi swept her tongue over her teeth. Maybe she'd get to see some half-naked wrestling, after all.

"I'm under direct orders from Magistrate White to stay with Miss Black at all times."

Cullen blinked lazily. "Magistrate White has no authority in Pride lands."

Uh oh. Rogan was going to implode. Or explode. Or throw a grenade and burn the place to the ground.

Jovi stood, patting him on his big, tense shoulder. "Go ahead. The kitty has some questions. I can handle them."

The silence that loomed was thick. Finally, Rogan tore his gaze from the alpha and looked down at her. "Call out if you need me." A muscle ticked rapidly in his jaw. Jovi wanted to bite it. "Understood?"

"Yep. Got it."

Rogan shot a look of pure ice toward the alpha. He turned and strode rigidly out the double doors, disappearing into the dark jungle. Even when he was moving like he had a stick up his ass, he made those ripped pants look damn good.

"He likes you," Cullen smirked at her through lowered lids. "He didn't want to leave you alone with me."

Jovi waved off the comment and the pleasure it brought. "Nah, I drive him bat-shit crazy. He just takes his job *really* seriously." She moved away from the table toward the center of the room, pretending to look at the billions of rugs, tapestries, and fluffy pillows. Really, she needed to get out of that corner. The lion was eyeing her like a snack.

"Mmm. I don't think that's it."

She gestured to the open windows. "Don't you guys have screens?"

He gave an amused snort. "Bugs avoid us, not the other way around."

Cocky, wasn't he? "You sure do have a lot of blankies."

Cullen shrugged those muscular shoulders and padded closer. Even his feet were golden tan. Did he ever wear shoes? "I'm a cat. I like soft, warm things." His yellow eyes traveled appreciatively over her body.

Any sane female would have dropped her panties right then and there, but all Jovi could think about was Rogan and his obviously broken ribs. She squared off with the lion. "So, Mr. Alpha Cat, what can I do for you? Because honestly, I've been through the fucking ringer, and I'm really ready to go to bed."

His eyes gleamed. Shit, she shouldn't have mentioned a bed. He moved forward slowly, and she stepped back. Was she really being stalked by a lion? She was.

"I want you to tell me—" he replied smoothly, "—what you are. Because you're very unusual, Jovi Black. And while I find that intriguing, you smell...strange." He stroked one long finger down her cheek, scenting the air. "And I don't like strange things sneaking around my people."

Jovi stepped back with a snort, though her pulse jumped a few notches. "Trust me, buddy, if I was trying to sneak around, you wouldn't have a clue I was here."

Wrong thing to say. The alpha's eyes flashed orange. "What are you?"

Mayday, mayday. "A mage," she said, exasperated. "Just a mage."

He grabbed her wrist. "If you're a mage, where's your trackband?"

Jovi twisted swiftly out of his grip. He looked mildly surprised that she'd succeeded. "They took it off for WITPRO.

I'm supposed to be someone else, remember? A trackband would be a dead giveaway."

Cullen leaned closer. The shadow of his lion flickered under his skin, a big cat's face illuminating under human bones. The hair on Jovi's arms stood up.

"Bullshit."

"Well, sorry. I'm a mage." A stroke of brilliance hit her. "A pyromage, in fact. Wanna see me play with fire?" She glanced significantly around his pretty wooden treehouse filled with soft, flammable fabrics.

Cullen's lip curled.

Smiling, she brought her hand up, blowing a tiny ball of fire into her palm. "See?"

The lion stepped back, pointing at her. "There's something else." He studied her for another long moment. Then, he snapped his thick fingers, the sound like a bullet, and a guard materialized at the door. Cullen jerked his head toward it. "Go on, then, firebug."

Asshole. Jovi closed her hand with a flourish, extinguishing the fireball. She gave His Royal Rudeness a withering curtsy and sauntered out of the treehouse.

CHAPTER 35

The guest hut turned out to be a small, basic treehouse on the outskirts of the compound. A guard drove her there on a four-wheeler.

"Don't wander around the jungle at night," he warned shortly, and left her standing at the base of the tree in the dark.

Weren't they just a courteous bunch in lion territory? Jovi scowled, looking up at the platform surrounding the tree-house. Just as she opened her mouth to call out, a rough trap door flung open, and a square of golden light illuminated a very familiar phaser, pointed directly at her.

"Uh, can I come up, or are you going to shoot me?"

The silhouette of a dark head emerged in the doorway. It disappeared, replaced by a rough rope ladder that came tumbling down the trunk. Jovi grumbled and began to climb.

The second her head breached the trap door, big hands grabbed her shoulders and hauled her the rest of the way up. A pained curse followed. Rogan kicked the door closed, then hustled her inside the guest house. It wasn't much more than a hexagonal wooden room with a tiny kitchenette, a bath-room, a tall wardrobe, and a bed and nightstand in the corner.

"Did he touch you?"

She turned to face him. The little treehouse was barely illuminated by a single lamp on the nightstand. Shadows played over Rogan's features, making his stubble look darker, his features sharper. He must've found a change of clothes—he was wearing a soft green T-shirt that looked incredible with his eyes, but apparently, he didn't want to change out of his ripped tactical pants. He looked downright edible.

"What?" Jovi said, distracted.

"Did he touch you?"

She pictured Cullen's long, tanned finger tracing her cheek, his hand gripping her wrist. "I mean, technically, I guess, but—"

"Did he hurt you?"

Jovi cocked her head. Besides looking edible, Rogan seemed spring-loaded. Ready to snap. "No."

"Did he try to…" He cut himself off. "Did you…" His hands flexed at his sides.

He was jealous.

Cullen was right. Nash Rogan was a mess, practically vibrating with rage, because she'd been alone with the big, sexy, half-naked alpha.

"No." Jovi felt a shit-eating grin stretch across her face.

"No?"

She shook her head, feeling radiant. "He totally wanted to, though."

"I bet he did," Rogan said darkly.

Delighted, Jovi stepped toward him. His chest rose and fell with deep, measured breaths. She looked up at him, ready to tease, but she was totally and completely blindsided by what she saw in his eyes.

Raw, animal desire.

She was up against him the next instant, his mouth crushing hers, those plump lips devouring and demanding. His entire body hummed, aggression held tightly in check. It was for her, all for her. Jovi slid her hands over his chest, stroking firmly around his torso to clutch his back, loving the feel of him against her.

He jerked, hissing in a breath. Jovi wrenched her lips from his. "Shit, your ribs—"

He grabbed her face and held her in place while he kissed her, hot and angry. Dizzy, she lost focus. He was so warm, so chiseled, so deliciously hard under her fingers…

He jerked again.

Jovi pulled back. "For fuck's sake." She backed him toward the wall. He grunted as his back hit the wood planks. She pulled up the hem of his shirt and swore.

His entire right side was black and purple, tinged with a sickly green. He was basically one giant, ugly contusion. He had to be in a shit-ton of pain. She laid her palm gingerly against his swollen, puffy ribcage and closed her eyes, but his hand snapped around her wrist. She looked up into his eyes.

"No. Don't waste it on me."

"You're not a waste," she retorted.

He grabbed her other wrist. His back was against the wall, he had both of her hands in an iron grip, and their bellies pressed against each other. His cock was rock hard between them. She rolled her pelvis against it, and they both groaned.

"You need to save your strength," he bit out.

"You'll take care of me after." She knew it, trusted it.

Trusted him.

There it was—that slippery slope. And there she went, sliding all the way to the fucking bottom.

Something like tenderness softened his features. Slowly, he released her hands. His breaths were short and shallow. Jovi slid her hands beneath his shirt and poured the healing light into him, sending that beautiful energy into his body, giving him her strength.

At some point, she thought she felt his lips on her forehead. She was getting tired. Leaning into him, she let him hold her up while she kept flooding his injury with light. He was recovering, his strength building. She could feel it. She could also practically hear his brain whirring.

"You're thinking too much again," she murmured, eyes closed.

He made a low noise, the sound rumbling in his chest. "How do you know?"

"I can tell."

He was quiet for a moment. "Can you hear thoughts?"

She made a face. "Ugh, no. That would suck."

"Why?"

"Are you kidding? People say enough asshole shit as it is. I'd hate to hear what they're actually thinking."

"You're probably right." There was a pause. "One of my squadmates can do it."

"Hear thoughts?"

"Sometimes. It doesn't work with everybody."

"Is it Cullen's brother?"

"Killian? No, he's a shifter. Incredibly strong, exceptional at hand-to-hand."

"Better than you?"

A snort ruffled her hair. "In brute strength, maybe. And there's something to be said for pure rage."

Jovi tried to picture Rogan sparring with someone who resembled Cullen. She'd never actually seen Rogan fight on his own—he would be quick, focused, ruthlessly efficient. Beautiful. "So, who's the mind reader? Is it the chick?" Another rush of scalding jealousy.

Silence.

She lifted her head. He was staring across the room, his jaw tight. Jovi nudged him. "Hey."

Nothing.

Jovi pulled away. His ribs were healed, the bruise barely visible now, and her limbs were heavy with fatigue. "Hey, Statue Man." When he still refused to meet her gaze, she snapped her fingers in front of his nose. His eyes whipped to hers, the pale green depths hard as stone. "What's the deal?"

He stared at her for a long moment. This close, she could see every freckle on his nose, every inch of dark stubble on his cheeks. He looked sexier than ever. Colder than ever.

"I can't tell you these things," he said shortly. His fingers circled her wrists and deliberately removed her hands from his body.

Something started to burn in her belly. She tugged free, watching a mask of hardness slide over his features.

"I can't do this." He gestured between them, then shook his head, pissed. "I *don't* do this."

"Don't do what?" Jovi took a step back. A single spark traveled down her arm.

"This." He gestured between them again. "I don't get distracted. I don't compromise the mission. I don't talk about the team, and I don't disclose confidential information. I sure as shit don't play naked hide-and-seek in enemy fucking territory." He wiped a palm over his face. "You make me reckless, and I can't afford that. We're going back to the city soon." He touched his phaser like he was reassuring himself that it was still there. "Jesus, I don't even know what the hell you really are."

The words hit Jovi like a blow to the chest.

You are pain. You are agony. You are the anguish of desire. You are the flames of retribution. That is what you are.

With him, she'd started to feel like more than that.

Something ugly flared to life deep within her, like he'd shoved a blade through her sternum and awakened something dangerous. A wild beast, wounded and cornered and ready to lash out.

That soft heart is going to make you suffer one day.

She hated it when Mommy Dearest was right.

Her eyes burned, but fuck if she would cry in front of him. Instead, she took another step away. "Fine."

Regret flashed across his face before he was able to mask it. Jovi turned away, her chest aching. She was such a fucking moron. She glanced around the room, but it was all a blur. "Is there food?"

"No."

Of course there wasn't. She stalked to the wardrobe and wrenched it open to find stacks of clean clothes inside. It made sense that shapeshifters would stock them everywhere. Hoping he was watching, she stripped, tossing her filthy tank top and purple shorts to the floor, bending deliberately over to unzip and step out of her boots. Her feet sang in relief. Her heart did not.

Bare assed, she reached for one of the folded T-shirts in the wardrobe, then stopped. Why make it easy on him? She strolled naked to the bed and whipped back the covers. White linens. Ugh. She felt grimy, sticky with dried sweat, and had sand in too many of her crevices. She'd kill for a hot bath.

The last bath she'd had in the hot spring flashed before her eyes—the one where she'd ended up with Agent Hot-And-Cold's head between her legs. And despite the howling ache in the center of her chest, she went wet at the memory.

Adding sexual frustration to the inferno of anger in her gut, she climbed naked into the bed. Leaving the sheets off her torso, she stretched like a cat, sinuous and slow, torturing him with the sight of her gorgeous tits.

He wanted to know what she was? She was pain. She was agony. She was the anguish of desire. Hell hath no fury like a woman scorned. Mommy Dearest had taught her that lesson very well.

The lamp on the nightstand was an old fashioned one with a pull cord. She yanked the chain clean off and chucked it at the wall as the room went dark.

CHAPTER 36

A roar below the treehouse jolted her awake.

Her eyes popped open. It was still dark, but Jovi could see Rogan clearly in a shaft of moonlight, fully dressed, standing with his back against the wall and his head angled to look out the open window. His beloved phaser glinted in his hands.

His eyes met hers, glistening in the dark. He held a finger to his lips.

Jovi slid out of bed and moved silently to the wardrobe. She pulled a T-shirt over her head and slid into a pair of sweats. Ugh. Muddy green was not her color, and the lions were all a million feet taller than her. The fabric bagged around her body, sweatpants puddling around her toes. Scowling, she grabbed the hem of the shirt and tied it in a knot at her waist. Better.

More growls sounded below. Jovi snatched one of Rogan's knives from his belt, stabbed a hole in the sweats, and ripped the fabric, creating a pair of ragged cutoff shorts. Much better.

He watched her. She tossed the knife carelessly in his general direction, kind of hoping it would land in his leg again. Rogan snatched it out of the air like he knew what she was thinking.

She pulled on her boots. The amulet was hard against the bottom of her heel. With a flash, she realized he could have stolen it while she slept. Stupid. She had to be more careful.

The climb back up the slippery slope was going to be fucking brutal.

She mirrored Rogan's stance on the other side of the window, but she could barely see over the frame. She stood on tiptoes, craning her neck to try and peer out. Stupid giant cats. "What's going on?" she whispered.

He shook his head, frowning intensely out the window. Jovi stomped her foot in frustration. The dagger shot out of her boot with a little *shhhick*. Rogan glared at her, turned back toward the window—and then dove at her.

She hit the floor with an unladylike grunt as his body landed on top of hers. Beyond his broad shoulders, she glimpsed a dark shadow sailing through the window. It crashed to the floor. She shoved at Rogan, and they leaped up just as the dark shape sprang up on two bowed legs. A long tail unfurled.

"A *monkey*?" Jovi squeaked.

The thing bared a mouth full of fangs, gave a screeching cry, and launched itself at them.

Rogan blocked it with his forearm, grunting as its fangs sank into his flesh. He tried to fling it off, but it clung, claws scrabbling bare skin. Rogan pointed his phaser and blasted the thing in the head. It thunked to the floorboards.

A deafening roar sounded in the distance. Several more echoed it, coming from all sides. The lions were sending up the alarm.

The treehouse's trap door burst open. A flood of dark, fuzzy bodies swarmed through the opening, their fangs glinting in the moonlight.

"Go!" Rogan shouted.

He didn't have to tell her twice. Jovi took a running leap and vaulted out of the open window. Leaves smacked her face. Her chest landed hard against a tree limb, and she scrambled wildly to hang on. Rogan hit the limb a moment later. It swayed under his weight, and she almost lost her grip. Cursing, she hooked one leg over and heaved herself up.

Rogan was already straddling it, cool as a cucumber. He pulled something from one of his pockets, yanked at it with his teeth, and chucked it through the treehouse window.

"Cover your ears." He plugged his own.

She should've listened. A deafening sonic boom exploded from inside the treehouse. Her eardrums howled. Too late, she clapped her hands to her ears, unable to hear her own curses.

Rogan, on the other hand, was scanning the ground below like nothing had happened. He whistled sharply through his teeth.

A growl reverberated up the trunk. Jovi peered down, working her jaw to ease her blasted eardrums. Golden eyes glinted from the base of the tree. In one smooth, fluid movement, the lioness shifted into human form and rose naked from the ground. She was tall and leanly muscled, with the long braid that seemed to be the female lions' trademark. A tribal tattoo coiled around her neck. She looked like she was accustomed to killing.

"We're under attack," she advised in a low voice, glancing around.

"Monkeys?" Rogan asked.

She shook her head. "The monkeys are running from it. Try not to kill them." She frowned up at the treehouse, now emitting a faint, eerie blue light, and swiped at the blood trickling from her ear. She shot Rogan a hard look. "And keep your fucking tech out of it. Can you handle yourselves?"

Rogan nodded. "What is it?"

"Don't know. Can't get eyes on it." She melted back into her lioness form and disappeared into the jungle.

Great, an invisible enemy. Wonder what it could be?

Rogan slapped a cartridge into his phaser. "Are you good to go?"

She shot him a withering look and jumped to the ground. It was further than she thought. The impact jarred her feet, shooting a stab of pain up her shins. She bit back a curse and wobbled to a stand just as a big, dumb, muscular action hero landed next to her. Rogan rose slowly to tower over her, his eyes scanning the dark jungle. Every inch of him was hard, focused. Strong.

I don't even know what the hell you really are.

Her heart panged. Stupid thing. Served it right.

He slid the safety off his phaser. "Let's go."

"I'll lead the way, shall I?" Jovi said. She felt a rush of satisfaction at his answering glower.

They moved slowly through the dark. Faebugs pulsed like tiny, luminous hot air balloons in the night. Glowing fungi and ferns dotted the undergrowth—plenty of light for her to see by, but she'd bet Rogan was having trouble. She smirked.

Sure enough, his illuminator clicked on, and a wide swath of light burst from his belt. Bugs scurried into the shadows.

"Turn that off," Jovi snapped. He ignored her.

They both whirled at a rustling nearby. A pair of amber eyes gleamed at them from the undergrowth, reflecting the light of the illuminator. With a low growl, the male lion slunk away.

A monkey's wild scream tore through the night. Jovi jumped, and Rogan's hard arm brushed hers. Another scream sounded, then a roar. Everything sounded both miles away and inches behind them, the dense foliage muffling and magnifying at the same time.

They kept going, brushing past enormous plants, some big enough for Jovi to walk beneath. She pushed aside a curtain of vines and came to an abrupt halt. A hot spring steamed in a small clearing, phosphorescent plant life illuminating its rocky floor.

Tension flared between them. Jovi spun away. *Do not think about his tongue between your legs.*

An eerie giggle sounded in the dark.

She froze.

Another giggle, to the right. Then, a chilling whoop from the bushes straight ahead. The hair on her neck stood on end. There was a beat of silence.

A hyena exploded out of the leaves, its sharp fangs glinting from a red, gaping jaw. It leaped toward her.

Rogan's shoulder knocked her aside as he caught the hyena in a bear hug, the impact throwing him onto his back. He rolled, straddled the hyena as it struggled wildly, bucking and thrashing and howling in broken, high-pitched yelps. He yanked a knife from his belt and slashed the hyena's throat in one fluid movement. The manic yipping became a wet gurgle. He rose swiftly as the hyena flopped limply, bleeding out.

There was an ominous rustle in the undergrowth, a rush of sound that grew steadily louder, coming at them like a wave. A flurry of dark shapes rushed over their feet—rodents. Something flapped by Jovi's head. She ducked, then ducked again. Bats?

The cacophony of sound sped toward them, roars and animal cries and pounding paws, boiling up from the depths of the foliage and rushing toward them like a hurricane.

Rogan's hand closed around hers, and they ran.

They pelted over roots, hurtled boulders, and ducked under low-hanging vines. Tiny animals scurried over their boots, faster than they were. They leaped over fallen limbs, swatted at thorny brambles. Jovi caught a glimpse of Rogan's face in the dark—stony and focused.

They burst into a clearing and separated, both falling into

a ready position. Jovi shook out her hands, tingles zooming to her fingertips.

Their eyes met for a split second. Then, the foliage opened up, and a wall of animals exploded from the jungle. Shrieking monkeys, screeching birds, squeaking rodents. And behind them, a wave of cackling, wild-eyed hyenas, leaping from the undergrowth like rabid dogs. They thudded to the ground, skidding and scrambling to regain balance, whooping to each other. A dozen at least, maybe more.

"We don't want trouble," Rogan announced to the grinning hyenas.

"Are those *shifters*?" She'd never heard of hyena shifters, and the ones before her looked feral.

A dozen sets of teeth snapped at them. Even if they were shifters, apparently they weren't open to diplomacy. Rogan pulled a short metal stick from his belt loop and flicked it in a move so casual it was sexy. The stick glowed blue and expanded rapidly, section after section, locking into itself. In seconds, Rogan was holding a glowing six-foot staff with a wicked blade glinting at the end. He sank backward into a combat stance, his eyes sweeping the moonlit clearing. "I've got six to twelve, you've got twelve to six. Copy?"

Jovi focused on her side of the clock. Shifters or not, these fuckers were eyeing her like a takeout meal. "Yeah, I copy."

Ding, ding. Like the starting bell had been rung, two of them charged at her, leaping high into the air. Jovi ducked, and as they sailed overhead, she blew a flaming kiss at their underbellies. Their spotted fur caught fire instantly. They yelped in pain, tumbled to the ground, and scurried wildly around the clearing, yipping. Wherever they ran, the jungle erupted in flames.

Uh oh.

Pockets of fire roared to life, merging and growing until, in what seemed like seconds, a ring of fire encircled the clearing. Smoke rose into the night as flames crackled and hyenas yipped.

And then, the lions arrived.

Huge golden bodies vaulted into the clearing, knocking over the clustered hyenas like bowling pins. Some of the cats singed their tails or bellies in the flames. Roars split the night. The smell of burnt fur filled the air.

Shit. Maybe fire wasn't the best idea in the middle of a jungle. She needed a weapon; something more useful than her boot dagger. One of those knives on Rogan's belt, maybe.

She pelted toward him. He swung the staff in wide, graceful arcs, keeping the hyenas six feet away, slicing them only if they got too close. He was rhythmic, laser-focused, stunning.

Jovi yelled his name as she ran toward him, and he took a split second to glance over. She saw his eyes register the growing inferno, but he didn't break his rhythm. Keeping the staff swinging, he pulled another gun from his belt and opened his arms wide, falling into a spinning crouch as he pulled the trigger.

A cannon blast of water shot from the muzzle. Rogan spun on the spot, staff in one hand, gun in the other, looking like such a fucking badass that Jovi skidded to a halt, her jaw dropping. The gun shot a steady stream of water a good twenty feet, extinguishing the ring of flames even as the stupid hyenas continued to run their hides off.

Shaking herself, Jovi bolted to intercept one of them. She tackled it and rolled, trying to put out the fire and subdue the thing at the same time. Flames licked at her skin like a warm ray of sunshine. The hyena's claws did not feel as pleasant.

As searing pain ripped through her stomach, she rolled on top of the flailing, furry body, shoving it facedown in the dirt, somehow managing to smother the flames before it finally bucked her off. She landed hard on her tailbone. The hyena spun and lunged for her, and she leaned back, aiming a kick at the side of its head. Her boot dagger sank into its jaw and stuck. It yelped and jerked back, dragging Jovi with it. In its panic, it tugged and scrambled backward, yanking Jovi along the jungle floor in a series of staccato bursts.

"Fuck's...*sake*!" The slice in her belly ripped further, the pain momentarily blinding her. She managed to yank her dagger out of the hyena's jaw, and the animal scurried away, tail tucked. Jovi rolled to all fours, clutching her bleeding abdomen. *Do not puke.*

An ear-splitting roar tore through the night. Jovi looked up to see a monstrous lion with a majestic red mane land in the center of the clearing. The ground shuddered beneath his weight. The majority of the remaining hyenas scattered, disappearing into the steaming jungle.

The massive lion melted into a very big, very naked, and very angry Alpha Cullen Diallo. A bloody gash gaped across his wide chest, stark red against his golden skin. He stalked toward a pair of lionesses who had two hyenas pinned to the ground.

"*Shift!*" he roared. The lion was still in his voice, and Jovi flinched at his command.

Across the clearing, Rogan pushed a button on his glowing staff. The thing retracted in sections, folding itself up into the short stick that he returned to his belt loop. He walked toward the group while Jovi lagged behind, her arm still wrapped tightly around her bleeding stomach.

The two pinned hyenas shifted into a pair of lean, wheezing women. The lionesses stayed in animal form, their paws pinning the women to the ground.

"Who sent you?" Cullen's growl was more animal than man.

"Renatta," one of the hyena women panted. She bled badly from a leg wound. The other woman looked barely conscious.

"Why?"

"Broke the truce." The last word came out as a squeak as the lioness's paw pressed on her throat. Cullen flicked a glance at her, and she eased up. The hyena gasped for breath.

"We didn't break the truce."

The hyena gave a rasping laugh. "Killed three of us."

"Where? When?"

"Two days ago, near the border."

Cullen's hands clenched. He looked at the faces of the lions who had shifted to human form, all standing stock-still, burly, and naked in the moonlight. Each one of them shook their heads. Cullen returned his gaze to the hyena. "It wasn't us."

"Only one thing makes claw marks that big—a lion." She spat blood on the ground. Her comrade had passed out beside her.

Jovi's eyes met Rogan's. They could both think of other things that could make some big, nasty claw marks.

Cullen looked swiftly around the clearing, at the steaming brush, now wet from Rogan's water pistol, at the hyena bodies littering the ground. He jerked his chin at the lioness who still pinned the hyena in place, and she stepped back. The hyena woman pushed herself upright on shaking fore-arms, her dark skin bloody and smudged with soot.

"Can you walk?" Cullen asked.

The hyena avoided his gaze. Her partner lay limp on the ground.

"We'll drive you back. I need a meeting with Renatta tomorrow." Cullen snapped his fingers and two males moved forward. Without another word, they scooped the women into their arms and strode away toward the village. With another snap and gesture, two more males scooped up the dead hyenas and disappeared into the night.

"Now," Cullen rumbled, turning slowly to face Rogan and Jovi. "Who the fuck set my jungle on fire?"

CHAPTER 37

Rogan was well and truly fucked.

His watch and lens were dead. The magical mafia was on his tail. He had been reprimanded by the Magistrate, was actively failing a mission for archangels, and was currently at the mercy of an extremely pissed-off alpha who already had reason to hate him.

And despite all of that, he couldn't seem to tear his thoughts away from her.

She baffled him. Aroused him. Amused him. Naked hide-and-seek, for Christ's sake. She told him he didn't need to prove anything, that his team was lucky to have him, that he was sweet. Then, she fought like a dragon and exhausted herself tending to his wounds, trusting him to look out for her afterward.

She was healing them all.

After Cullen had roared at her for almost burning down the jungle, she'd simply placed her palms on the alpha's naked chest, said, "Shut up and let me fix it," and started to glow from within.

It had taken every ounce of restraint to stand back and watch. Rogan wanted nothing more than to knock her hands off Cullen Diallo's bare chest and punch him in his too-handsome face, but she was making a point that desperately needed to be made.

Jovi, friend. Jovi, good. Jovi could actually help, and not just mouth off and set the jungle on fire.

The other injured males couldn't line up fast enough. Thankfully, one of them had run to the nearest outpost and brought back a stack of sweatpants. Rogan wasn't sure how he would've handled her touching a dozen naked men. She was mouthwatering in her knotted T-shirt and little ripped-off shorts, even with the nasty cut on her belly. She'd insisted the injury was nothing, and told him in no uncertain terms to fuck off, but he still watched her like a hawk. Which meant he saw every lingering glance, every speculative gaze traveling up and down her curves.

"You like her."

Cullen appeared next to him. The gash across his chest was nearly gone. Rogan ground his molars and chose not to respond. Cullen smirked in the silence and folded his arms, mirroring Rogan's stance. His head tilted as he watched Jovi tend to the wounded, glowing like a faebug. "What is she?"

Mine. Rogan squashed the thought with a sharp shake of his head. "A mage. At least."

"You think there's something else, too." When Rogan remained silent again, Cullen slid him a glance. "She's extraordinary, whatever she is. Fire and light."

Something vicious snarled to life inside him, a dog guarding its bone. His nails bit into his palms.

Cullen grinned, but it faded quickly. "We didn't take out those hyenas."

Rogan met his eyes, soldier to soldier. "You sure?"

"My people don't kill without my order."

Rogan was inclined to believe him.

"There's been some weird shit in the jungle lately."

A nasty tingle went through him. "What do you mean?"

"Smells, sounds. Animals killed and not eaten."

The nasty tingle grew stronger. "What kind of smells?"

Cullen's nose wrinkled in disgust. "Sulfur." He glanced over, his yellow eyes glinting with sharp intelligence. "Why do you ask?"

Shit, forget the spat with hyenas. If demons were infiltrating Pride lands, the problem just got a hell of a lot bigger.

He needed coffee.

Rogan took a breath. "You need to call your brother. I need my team here. Or my supplies, at least."

"My brother made it very clear he doesn't give a shit about Pride lands," Cullen snapped, a hint of lion in his voice. "What supplies?"

But Rogan wasn't listening. Jovi had just stumbled. She wiped a hand across her brow, dark circles shadowing her eyes. He left the alpha in the dust, stalking across the clearing to shoulder aside the next shifter waiting to be healed.

"She's done." He scooped her into his arms, ignoring her spluttered protests. "We need food. And rest." He didn't wait for a response.

Jovi's weight barely registered as he marched into the jungle. He was one of the few uninjured from the fight, and he suspected he was still riding the high from the last healing session she'd given him—right before he'd poured the cold water of reality over them both.

The pain on her face had shocked him, and the sick feeling in his gut had yet to disappear. But no matter how much she stirred something inside him, he was right to put a stop to this thing flaring between them. It couldn't go anywhere, couldn't be anything.

Even if he was starting to wonder how, of all the women in the world, he'd ended up in WITPRO with the one who could see demons and carried an archangel's medallion.

Meant to be.

Jesus Christ. He swatted the thought away and refocused.

She obviously knew the medallion was something special. He hadn't seen a glimpse of it since the night at John's cabin.

He looked down at her, cradled in his arms. Even tight-lipped and fuming, her face was stunningly beautiful, luminous, almost angelic in the moonlight.

Angelic.

He froze mid-stride, his boot crunching over a twig. What if she hadn't stolen the amulet? What if it was hers?

Jovi shoved at him. "Put me down."

Rogan obeyed, his thoughts spinning.

"Where the fuck is the goddamn treehouse?"

Right. Stupid thought. If angels talked like that, heaven was a truck stop. "I was heading for the hot spring. For your wound," Rogan added quickly, as awareness snapped to life between them.

Her eyes flashed. For a minute, he thought that she would refuse out of pure spite. "Fine."

The hot spring steamed quietly in its little clearing, faintly illuminated by bioluminescent plants at the bottom. Jovi hardly stopped to strip, and Rogan barely managed to rip his gaze away. He got real interested in a floating pink faebug, but the slight splashing sounds behind him still made his dick hard. After several moments, a tired sigh made him glance over his shoulder. Jovi had dunked her entire body into the steaming water, her wet hair slicked back from her face, revealing those dainty pointed ears. He'd almost forgotten about them.

Her head leaned back against the edge of the pool as she rested. Her eyes were closed, her face drained of color. He kept his phaser at the ready and an eye on the surrounding jungle.

A male shifter appeared silently at his side, and in the next instant, Rogan's safety was off and his phaser was pointed at the man's temple.

The lion raised a brow, holding up a basket. "Alpha sent food." He studied Jovi with undisguised appreciation.

Rogan stepped in front of him, blocking his view. A menacing growl rumbled in the shifter's throat, and Rogan felt his own lip curl. "Give Alpha Diallo our thanks," he snarled through gritted teeth. The shifter handed over the basket and retreated into the jungle.

How many goddamn cats were lurking out there, hoping for a glimpse? Rogan felt a muscle tick under his eye. He set the basket on the ground, scanning the darkness with renewed suspicion.

Several long, silent minutes passed. He usually liked silence. As usual, with her, things were different. "Is it healed?" He glanced back.

Crystal blue eyes flipped open, luminous and sharp. "Let's see." She stood. Water cascaded down her naked curves, making everything gleam. Rogan pinned his gaze to the sky while his dick crowded his zipper.

"It's better." More splashing. He risked another glance, catching sight of her as she climbed out of the pool, stunningly naked and completely unconcerned.

He was beside her in a split second, yanking the knotted shirt over her head. "For fuck's sake," he growled, struggling to get the thing on the right way.

"Hey!" Jovi's muffled cry came from the depths of the fabric.

"There are goddamn lions everywhere out here." He got the shirt over her head, then hurried to hold her little cutoff shorts open at her feet so she could step into them. Her ass and graceful little slit were inches away from his hands, and his cock surged, swelling painfully in his tacticals.

"So?"

"So they can see you."

"So?"

"So I don't like it!" He hiked up the shorts and picked up

one of her boots. A metallic flash inside the leather barely registered. He grabbed one of her legs and slid the boot onto her foot, knocking her off balance. Jovi squeaked and grabbed at his shoulders, sending a ridiculous thrill of satisfaction through him. The other boot slid on more easily. He zipped them both, grabbed her hand, and stalked away from the hot spring toward the treehouse.

She twisted and pulled, attempting to wrench out of his grip, but Rogan was expecting it, and just gripped her tighter. They would have to work on her predictability during combat.

Jovi shrieked with rage, and she nailed him in the thigh with one hell of a side kick.

Pain exploded in his leg. He let out a guttural grunt, gritted his teeth, and marched onward. Here and there, glowing eyes dotted the dark landscape, alight with curiosity.

He stopped short. Shit. The basket. He gathered himself before spinning and pointing over Jovi's shoulder. "We left the food."

"*You* left the food, you fucking maniac. Let me go."

"No." He felt slightly unhinged.

Leaves rustled nearby, and a female shifter appeared from the darkness. "What's going on?"

"Nothing," Rogan said.

Jovi's eyes flashed. Her chin lifted. "He's manhandling me, is what." Her wet hair left dark patches on the T-shirt, puckering her nipples. Her skin grew steadily warmer beneath his fingertips. A spark flickered across her collarbone.

"Jovi," he warned.

She looked directly into his eyes. "I want to see the alpha."

Rage erupted inside him, a scarlet beast uncoiling rapidly from his gut, pounding against his skull, glaring out of his eyes. He wouldn't be surprised if they were blazing red.

The female glanced between them. "All right."

"No." The word shot out of his mouth like a bullet.

"Why? Is that against your rules, too?"

The world disappeared, the way it so often did with her. The entire world, gone—sucked into a black hole, leaving nothing but the icy fire of her eyes and the inferno in his chest. Rogan wanted to throw her over his shoulder, haul her back to the guest house, feed her, make sure she was healed, and keep her far, far away from the perpetually half-naked Cullen fucking Diallo.

Jovi focused on the female shifter. "Take me."

"All right." She jerked her head toward the dark jungle.

Jovi wrenched her wrist out of Rogan's grip, giving him one last blazing look before disappearing into the night.

Fine. Good. This was better. Simpler, even. She wasn't his, couldn't be his. She had every right to sleep with Cullen Diallo. In fact, she should. It would make things a hell of a lot clearer, and his life a hell of a lot easier.

Blood pounding in his head, he turned and stalked blindly back to the guest house, where he vaulted up the rope ladder and proceeded to methodically, systematically, lose his mind.

CHAPTER 38

Cullen sure knew the way to a woman's heart.

He offered Jovi food the second she entered the alpha hut. Gesturing gallantly toward the table, he cast one lazy glance at the guards standing just outside his double doors. They melted away, closing the doors silently behind them.

The table was piled with tropical fruit and charred meat on skewers. Jovi grabbed a skewer and ripped a hunk of meat off with her teeth. She was starving. Setting the jungle on fire, getting gutted by a rabid hyena, then playing doctor to a dozen shapeshifting lions tended to do that to a woman. Not to mention the blinding rage.

Nash Rogan could suck her dick. All those burning looks, those hot kisses, those moments in the cave where they'd become an actual team. All those times she'd saved his ass. Healed him. That mind-blowing orgasm he'd given her in that underground hot spring. All those times he took care of her, made her feel things. Want things. Let her guard down. Trust him.

All thrown back in her face.

He'd made it very fucking clear that his precious MLE

meant way more to him than she did. He'd put a stop to this whole thing between them, and now he had the nerve to act possessive? Fucking gorilla. Jovi plucked a fat purple fruit from the table and bit into it. Tart and juicy, it dribbled down her chin. She swiped at the sticky juice.

"You have a gift for healing," Cullen murmured in her ear.

She jumped, spinning to face him. When had he gotten so close?

"I'm forced to thank you, even after you almost destroyed my jungle."

Jovi rolled her eyes. "Oh, please, that little campfire? I bet you've had more fiery shits."

Cullen's wide mouth stretched into a grin. He really was a handsome cuss, so wild-looking with those cheekbones for days. She waited for the tingle in her nether regions.

Nothing. Fucking Rogan.

"Maybe. But no more fire in the jungle. Understood?" Cullen took his time selecting a ripe red berry from the pile before moving it toward her lips.

Jovi batted it away. "Look, bud, if some psycho hyena attacks me, I'm gonna use whatever I've got."

Cullen's brows knit together. He tossed the berry back onto the table and shook his head, waves of auburn hair brushing his broad shoulders. The man apparently didn't own a shirt. She was pleased to see that the gash across his muscled chest had healed completely. "We've had a truce for the past decade. Renatta knows we wouldn't break it."

"Is that the hyena alpha?"

Cullen nodded absently. He paced, his bare feet padding over the layers of plush rugs. "She knows we have nothing to gain from a raid." He ran a hand through his hair, tousling it even more. "Claw marks…"

Jovi chewed her lip. Claw marks, indeed. "None of your people would go rogue?"

"I would know."

"How?"

"Alpha," he said, like that explained everything.

"What about jaguars?"

"They avoid the area. Nothing for them to gain, either. Hyena land is damn near barren aside from the river; they're scavengers. Not always the smartest, but Renatta's no fool." He shook his head. "Something's going on. That weird smell —" He pinned her with a stare. "You know anything about that?"

"A weird smell? No."

"Your man knows what it is."

"He's not my man," she snapped.

Cullen laughed softly. "Then what is he doing at the bottom of my tree?"

Jovi's belly leaped into her throat. "His precious job, no doubt."

Cullen leaned in. "And what are you doing here in my hut?"

The question dangled in the air like one of his tempting tropical fruits, ripe and ready to pluck. This was her chance. Punish Rogan and get some well-deserved sexual relief at the same time. Why shouldn't she? Cullen was here, he was sexy as hell, and all she had to do was reach out and take a big, juicy bite.

Fine.

She stepped closer to Cullen's hard body and slid a hand up his warm, smooth chest. He was suede over steel, coiled power and heat. She rose on tiptoes, aiming for that softly smiling mouth…

She stopped, her lips a breath away from his. Seconds ticked by. He didn't move a muscle.

Son of a bitch-sucking, motherfucking cunt…

She couldn't do it.

Jovi opened her eyes. Amusement gleamed back at her.

Cursing, she lowered to her feet and huffed out a frustrated breath that ruffled a lock of his hair.

Fucking Rogan. She wanted to kick something. She wanted to cry.

Cullen tilted her chin upward. "Lions play these games, too. Want to give him a reason to roar?" He eased closer, his big hands sliding over her shoulders to cup her elbows.

"Diallo!" Rogan's voice floated up from outside, making her heart flutter. "We need to talk."

Cullen winked at Jovi. "Go away, Rogan," he called loudly.

"We need to talk now."

Cullen signaled for Jovi to wait, then he sauntered to the door, sinking his thumbs into the waistband of his sweatpants and pulling them deliberately lower on his hips. He stood in the glow of the porch light, leaning a shoulder against the frame. "What?"

"Where's Jovi?"

"Here."

A pause. "Is she all right?"

Cullen snarled. "What the fuck are you implying?"

"She needs to eat. Healing takes it out of her."

"I fed her."

The silence turned razor-sharp. "You fed her?"

Cullen examined his fingernails. Jovi frowned.

"Did you claim her?"

Claim me? What the fuck? Jovi stomped a foot to get Cullen's attention. He waved her off with a hand behind his back. She marched over to the door, squeezing past him to the platform. "What does he mean, claim me?" she demanded. When he only smirked, Jovi peered over the edge. "What do you mean?"

Rogan stood at the base of the tree, feet braced and fists clenched, staring at Cullen like he was imagining snapping his neck with his bare hands. The sight of him did stupid things to her stomach. "Did you eat from his hand?"

"No. Why?"

"That's how a male shapeshifter claims a female as his."

A vision of Cullen offering her a juicy red fruit flashed before her eyes. Outraged, Jovi smacked the alpha's huge shoulder, then shook her stinging hand. "You tried to feed me that berry, you dick!"

Cullen only smiled.

"Jovi," Rogan said from below. "Come with me."

She folded her arms, staring down at him.

He held out a hand. "Please."

Her belly did that little flip again. *Fine.* She could give him a piece of her mind. Jovi glared at Cullen and headed for the trap door. He blew her a silent, suggestive kiss, and winked again. Jovi descended the rope ladder, muttering the whole way. She turned to face Rogan, who was staring up at the platform with murder in his eyes.

The alpha's low chuckle drifted down. "You'd better claim her yourself, then, Rogan."

Rogan gripped Jovi's hand and led her into the jungle.

CHAPTER 39

R ogan was silent all the way back to the guest hut, but his fingers were like steel around hers. He practically pushed her up the rope ladder and into the treehouse. The lamp on the nightstand cast a warm glow over the interior—he must have fixed the broken chain, the stupid good-at-everything jerk. Jovi spun on her heel and planted her hands on her hips, watching as he bent to shut the trap door.

She had all kinds of things to say to him. A whole list about keeping the He-Man bullshit to himself and minding his own business about who she fucked or how many lions she decided to heal, or whether or not they saw her naked in a hot spring.

"I didn't want him, anyway," she announced to his back. "He has better hair than I do."

Rogan turned. His sea glass eyes were molten. He started toward her, yanking his shirt over his head and tossing it aside.

Her breath caught. The man was a carved statue come to life. Muscle rippled in the lamplight as he closed in on her.

Jovi got one foot behind her before he caught her.

He crushed her against him, his mouth capturing hers. Fire erupted in her veins. He tasted hot, angry, his tongue demanding. Jovi snaked her arms around his neck, meeting him stroke for stroke, furious at him and ravenous for him and crazed by the taut, quivering tension of his body. That control, that iron grip he held over himself, was close to snapping. She wanted it to snap. Wanted him to lose it completely, to go wild, to show her the Rogan nobody else got to see.

And she was going to get it.

She jumped up, locking her legs around his waist. He caught her and spun toward the nearest wall. The second her back hit the wood planks, he pinned her with his hips and yanked out the knot in her T-shirt. Grabbing the neckline with both hands, he tore it in half, making a primal sound that drove her out of her mind. The humid night air hit her naked breasts, and he ducked his head to lower his mouth to her nipple.

Hot, wet, electric. His tongue circled the taut little bud, flicked it, making her groan. He made another noise, and switched to the other nipple. He laved it, sucked it hard, gave it a tiny nip with those straight white teeth. Jovi yanked his hair.

He spun her away from the wall. She bit his plump lower lip, gripping his torso with her thighs as he stalked across the room and threw her on the bed. As the mattress bounced beneath her, his strong fingers hooked into the waistband of her cutoff shorts and pulled them down her legs. He whipped them off, leaving her bare except for her boots. She sat up, yanked the shredded shirt off her shoulders, and tossed it aside. He was already on his knees between her legs, laser-focused on the apex between her thighs.

His eyes blazed into hers. "*I* do this to you." He pushed her knees apart and dove down, burying his face between her legs.

Her cry rang through the treehouse. Those lips, that

tongue, licking, sucking—pleasure speared through her, and she dug her booted heels into his bare back. The little dagger flipped out with a *shhhick*. Neither of them paid any attention.

She was the succubus. She was supposed to be the one driving him out of his mind with desire, but he was the one bewitching her, stealing her thoughts, making her delirious. He circled and stroked, first with the flat of his tongue, then the tip, teasing and tickling while his strong hands held her legs apart for his feast. Tiny mewls of pleasure escaped her, growing louder and louder in the bare wooden hut as his tongue swirled faster and faster, the pressure building, the heat engulfing her.

She exploded, coming so hard she saw stars. A scream tore out of her, echoing in the jungle beyond the open window. She clutched his head. He sucked her clit harder and slid two fingers inside her soaked core, wrenching another scream from her as she clenched and released around him. He pumped his fingers into her, flicking them against her sweet spot deep inside, and her eyes rolled back in her head as she came again with a deep, strangled cry.

Finally, when she collapsed, he pulled away and rose from his knees, his eyes glittering with wild heat as they roved over her. He shucked his boots, unzipped his pants, and kicked them off.

He was stunning, so powerful and taut, his cock jutting proudly from his hips. She reached out and wrapped her hand around his solid, velvety length. So hard, so smooth. She stroked him from base to tip, and he sucked in a breath, abs clenching, eyes aflame.

He knocked her hand aside and fell on top of her, catching himself with palms on the mattress. Then, he planted a knee on the bed, gripped the back of her neck, and, when their gazes collided, he thrust deeply, deliberately inside.

Her gasp shredded her throat. He was so thick, so hard

inside her, filling her up, stroking that perfect spot as he plunged in and out, in and out. Lightning struck every nerve ending. He was breathtaking above her, sinuous and strong, brows drawn, eyes fierce.

Steam swirled around them. It was her. Mist rose from her overheated skin, surrounding them in a sultry veil until he looked like a golden god emerging from the ether. She hooked a hand around his neck and pulled his mouth to hers, groaning again at those luscious lips, that silky tongue.

Her hands moved desperately over his body, reveling in the feel of him surging over her, around her, inside her. The flex and release of his muscles drove her wild—he was all hard, coiled steel, and she wanted to feel it from every angle. She rolled on top of him. His thighs were strong beneath her, drawing tight as he thrust upward, his hands firm on her hips, her waist, her back. He sat upright, bringing their chests together, fisting her hair, sucking her neck until she whimpered. She finally shoved him back, kept a hand on his chest, and rode him. Hard.

He sucked in a breath and gripped her hips, working her against him, his head thrown back, tendons straining, outrageously beautiful. One strong hand glided up her body to cup her breast. She put her hand on top of his, encouraging him, squeezing. The pleasure was mind-boggling, inside and out, an inferno, a firestorm of tingling heat and delicious, building pressure. Jovi let her head fall back. That same strong hand glided up her throat, brushing her lips, gripping her jaw. She snagged one of his fingers with her mouth, slid her tongue around it, sucked it, released it. He cursed, and she rode him harder as the storm gathered between her legs. Her cries echoed out of the open window, into the dark jungle.

Rogan made an animal sound. His muscles coiled beneath her, and he flipped her smoothly onto her back. Pushing her knee upward, he opened her wider and drove inside, hard and thick, hitting that sweet spot over and over and over, so good it was almost painful. Jovi wrapped her other leg around his pistoning hips and moved with him, raking her nails down his back, viciously alive. He thrust again and again, harder, deeper, until finally, with a fierce shout and a deep, final plunge, he collapsed on top of her.

CHAPTER 40

They lay panting for several minutes. Jovi's limbs flopped lifelessly onto the bed as steam rose from her skin, enveloping them in a heated mist.

"Fuck *me*," she breathed into his shoulder.

Rogan pushed up to look into her face, muscles bulging. His eyes roved over her before he pressed a soft kiss to her mouth, then slid carefully out, wringing a small sound of disappointment from her. He crossed the room, snagging a washcloth from a stack by the wardrobe. The nail marks slashing his back gave her immense satisfaction.

He came back to the bed and gently blotted between her legs, cleaning her up. All she could do was stare. She'd had a lot of sex in her life, but none had ever come close to that. And no dude had ever cleaned her up afterward.

Nash fucking Rogan.

Tossing the cloth into the hamper, Rogan lowered himself onto the bed beside her, propping his head on one hand. She turned to him, her heart still thumping. Their eyes met through the steam.

He smiled. Slowly.

If she'd been wearing panties, they'd have melted. There

were dimples peeking out from his dark stubble. Dimples? *Kill me now.*

"You are…" The grin vanished, and his brows slashed downward. "Incredible."

Despite his glower, something warmer than hellfire bloomed in her chest.

His fierce gaze followed his fingers through her hair. "I can't seem to control myself around you." His gaze locked with hers, hard and hot. "It pisses me off."

She trailed a fingertip across his abs, her lips twitching. "But look what you've been missing."

He made a low, masculine noise that shot straight to her core. One long finger traced the curve of her breast to circle her nipple, slow and deliberate. "Don't you think it's one hell of a coincidence, us ending up in WITPRO together?"

More like someone's idea of a cruel joke. "I don't believe in coincidences."

"Neither do I." His hand moved to cup her neck, and he waited until she met his eyes. They were burning with intensity, gold flecks sparking in the pale green depths. "I meant what I said. I don't do this. I could get in very serious trouble for this."

Some of her buzz faded, replaced by the stirrings of guilt.

His thumb brushed her lower lip. "But the idea of him touching you—of *anyone* else touching you…" He broke off, shook his head. "You do something to me. I don't understand it, and it makes me fucking crazy. But...I don't want to let you go."

He didn't?

Happiness exploded inside her, obliterating every trace of guilt, of caution, of sanity. Rays of golden light burst out of her pores, spearing across the treehouse like she'd swallowed the sun. Rogan squinted against the sudden blaze.

How. Fucking. Embarrassing.

Jovi's mouth fell open. She snapped it shut, feeling a flush creep into her cheeks.

Rogan's face split with a devastating grin. He snagged her chin and planted a hot, silken kiss against her mouth before pulling back. "Are you hungry?"

Her stomach growled.

"Cullen didn't feed you after all?"

"There was a pile of fruit and stuff on the table. I had one bite. He did try to feed me a fucking berry and he didn't say shit about it *claiming* me—"

His mouth was suddenly crushing hers, stealing her breath with a kiss that ended in a punishing little nip. He pulled back and strode across the room to snatch a basket from the floor, his round ass flexing as he moved. Every inch of the man was delectable.

Jovi sat up and scooted against the wall, naked except for her boots. At least the glow had dimmed enough that Rogan didn't have to squint when he came back to the bed, holding a plump red berry between his fingers.

He extended it very deliberately to her lips.

Their eyes met.

Jovi's pulse skyrocketed. "I thought that was just a shapeshifter thing."

"I'm not taking any goddamn chances."

They stared at each other. He didn't waver.

What the fuck was she doing?

I don't want to let you go.

Maybe, just maybe, he meant it.

Jovi opened her mouth. Rogan placed the berry gently inside. She bit into it. Sweet and delicious, but nothing compared to the look in those sea glass eyes. Tingles and flutters, thoughts and fears, swirled in her belly.

He fed her more fruit, forest nuts, salty dried meat. They lounged on the linen bedding as their skin cooled and the sounds of the jungle drifted through the window. She felt like a queen, being fed by her sexy naked pleasure slave.

Her smile died abruptly. She'd seen this kind of scene before—rumpled bedding, flickering candles, naked slaves lounging at Inara's feet, stroking her, feeding her, tending to her every desire, her every demand.

She shook off the image. "Cullen thinks you know what attacked the hyenas."

Rogan scowled. "I told him I need my tech. If I can get a watch battery and a fresh lens, we can look into it." He jabbed at his eye, his dark brows furrowed. "I don't know if he'll do it. He doesn't seem to be in a hurry to get rid of us." He considered her. "Maybe that will change now."

"Why, because I lit his jungle on fire?"

"Because you're no longer available." He gripped her jaw and kissed her, hard.

When he pulled away, a shaft of silvery light cast a glow over his cheekbones. The moon was fat and round and perfectly framed in the window, and Jovi pointed at it over his shoulder, feeling like her chest was filled with something just as luminous, just as full. "Ooh, let's go look."

He glanced backward. "Now?"

She grinned. "Lesson one."

A dimple flashed, and he let her tug him toward the window. He gave her a boost, and she climbed onto the sill, naked but for her boots. There was enough of a handhold to climb onto the gently sloping roof. Rogan's curse drifted up from below as she sat on the smooth wood planks. She heard him grumble something about not waiting to clear the area. Grinning, she watched his head pop up a second later, scanning for threats. In a smooth, fluid motion that made his muscles flex, he pushed himself onto the roof and tested his footing. He'd put his boots on, too, but the rest of him was deliciously bare, moonlight gleaming on the carved planes of his body.

He sat carefully next to her. "If I get a splinter in my ass, you're paying for it."

She laughed and leaned back on her elbows, the warm night air kissing her skin, faebugs pulsing pink in the darkness. Rogan's scent drifted over her. She nodded at the moon. "Isn't it pretty?"

Rogan studied the glowing orb. "Never thought about it."

Jovi shook her head, sighing. "Lesson two: Appreciate." There was no moon in hell, only an endless, blazing, blood-red sun. The first time she saw the moon, hanging like a shimmering crystal ball over the city streets, she stared at it until dawn.

"Appreciate the moon." He said it like he was adding a task to his daily checklist.

"The moon, the stars, fresh air, good food...*good* food," she repeated, knocking his boot with hers. "Not that healthy crap you eat. Life's too short, son."

He snorted. "You sound like Wolf. Eats like a garbage disposal and still beats me in a sprint." He shook his head.

She watched his jaw tick. "I bet he can't do that cool spin move, though."

Rogan arched a questioning brow at her.

"That cool spin move you did with that staff thing."

His mouth curved. "Like that, did you?"

That smile did things to her insides. "Yeah, maybe. You looked like a fucking superhero. I bet none of the others on your squad can do that."

His face hardened ever so slightly. "Yeah, they can just turn into lethal animals. Or move things with their mind."

"Yeah, so? So can, like, a million other shapeshifters and mages, right? I don't see other humans strutting around busting out moves like you do. *You're* one of a kind, like I said."

He shook his head, staring unseeingly at the moon. "I have to work three times as hard just to fucking keep up."

"That's it." She pushed up from her elbows and swung a leg over his naked hips to straddle him, gripping his face and bringing them nearly nose to nose. His green eyes widened in surprise. "Why do you think the Magistrate put you in charge? Because you're the kind of guy who actually *will* work three times as hard. Everyone else would say 'fuck this' and give up, or recruit a bunch of fuckoffs to make themselves look good. Not you." Her fingers tightened on his face. "You're Nash fucking Rogan. You built a team of the best, and you work your delicious ass off to make sure you're one of them. Now stop talking about yourself like you're the runt of the damn litter. It's insulting to my impeccable taste."

He blinked at her in stunned silence. She stared back, daring him to contradict her.

"Where the hell did you come from?" he murmured. Muscle tightened beneath her thighs as he sat forward, cupped her face, and touched his lips to hers. Soft, sweet, tender, the kiss went on for what felt like hours. When he finally pulled away, Rogan shook his head, watching his hand thread through her hair. "Come on. We should get some sleep."

They climbed through the windowsill and back into the guest hut. Rogan whipped back the bed linens, set his boots neatly by the nightstand, and bent to unzip hers.

Her belly gave a little nervous jump, but she let him slide them off her feet. If he noticed the amulet inside her shoe, he didn't mention it. He lined her boots up next to his, then pointed toward the pillows. "Bed."

"Hey, I'm not on your squad, you can't boss me around." But she slid under the sheet and laid her head on the pillow, her heart pattering, some tiny part of her thrilled at the idea of being a member of his team. A member of his family.

There was a faint click, and the room went dark. The mattress dipped. A hard, warm body came against hers, and a strong forearm slid over her ribs to pull her close. Tingles flooded her entire body, like her veins were full of happy butterflies.

What the fuck was she doing? She shouldn't do this. Shouldn't trust this. She knew better.

She fell asleep almost instantly, smiling.

―――――

A sharp whistle jolted her awake. Rogan surged upright, a shaft of midday sun turning his skin the color of gold. His phaser was already pointed at the trap door.

"Rogan!" someone shouted from below.

He slid out of bed and pulled on his pants, striding shirtless to the door. He kicked it open and peered below.

"Alpha wants you both at his hut."

Jovi threw on a fresh pair of massive sweats and a T-shirt. She shuffled over to the door, holding up the pant legs. That badass lioness with the neck tattoo was standing at the base of the tree, hands on her hips.

"Why?" Jovi asked.

The female eyed her. "He's going into hyena territory and wants you with him." She lifted her chin at Rogan. "You killed Renatta's niece."

Rogan swore.

"Yeah. You need to account for it." She jerked her head. "Bring your weapons."

He kicked the trap door shut, heading for the wardrobe. "Fantastic."

"Yeah, killing the alpha's niece probably isn't great." She was mildly distracted by the warm fuzzies building in her belly, watching him pad around in bare feet, getting dressed. Was this what people meant by *homey*? "What does she mean by accounting for it?"

Rogan pulled a fresh T-shirt from the stack. "I need to make it clear that Cullen's people didn't kill her. But you can bet your ass he also wants me there to sniff around for whatever attacked those other shifters." He yanked the shirt over his head. "I can't do it without my tech."

"I can." Jovi grabbed a knife from his belt and made herself a new pair of cutoff shorts, a little shorter this time, for his benefit. She tossed the scraps at his head, wiggling her brows, then used the knife to turn the shirt into a cropped tank. She swiveled and crouched, testing her mobility. She threw out a kick. Good. Feet went into boots, the metal of the amulet reassuring against her heel. "You just worry about making nice with the queen hyena."

She looked up. Hunger glittered in Rogan's eyes. "I really wish you didn't look so damn good."

Jovi gave him a sly smile. Slowly, deliberately, she bent over, taking her sweet time to zip up her boots.

Their departure was delayed by several minutes.

CHAPTER 41

Hyena territory was apparently a million hours away by dune buggy. Cullen eyed them up and down when they arrived at his hut, nostrils flaring. He smirked, and the trio of males next to him did the same, but they didn't comment. The group split into two buggies.

Cullen and Rogan took the middle seat of the first buggy, while Jovi sat in the back with the badass female. Her name was Senna, she had beautiful cinnamon skin, and she looked like she could strangle you with her long braid and enjoy doing it.

The convoy bumped out of the jungle and into the blazing heat. Once out of the lush jungle, there was nothing but dusty foothills as far as the eye could see.

Jovi sweated in her seat. "Did anyone bring snacks?" she called over the rumble of the motor. Nobody answered. She was relieved when the reddish bluffs finally came into view. They headed toward them, catching glimpses of sparkling water as they got closer.

The hyena settlement was a large compound near the river, surrounded by a huge barbed-wire fence. Redrock cottages and flapping canvas shades were visible on the other side. Sentries watched their approach from two rough wooden towers.

"Nobody gets out until I say so," Cullen murmured as the convoy eased to a stop. He unfolded himself from the buggy, his thumbs looped into his waistband. Surprisingly, he was actually wearing a shirt.

The hyena sentries' hands tightened on big black guns as he approached. Jovi saw Rogan's fingers twitch against his thigh.

"I'm here to see Renatta," Cullen called out.

"One guard only," a sentry called back.

Cullen raised a brow at Rogan, who nodded shortly and hopped from the buggy. As they started forward, he shot Jovi a glance over his shoulder.

She waved him on. Showtime.

Climbing out of the backseat, she stretched and began a trek across the cracked earth. There was a thatch of timber a ways from the compound that looked like a promising place to search for evidence of hellspawn.

She wasn't surprised when Senna appeared next to her. "Do you know where the attack happened?"

Senna flicked her long braid. "I can find it." She sized Jovi up. "You wanna sniff around?"

"Yep. You in?"

"Hell, yeah. We're in a world of shit and it wasn't even our fault." She signaled for the other lions to remain with the vehicles, then lifted her chin and took in a long, deep inhale. "That way."

Senna led the way into the thicket. The dappled shade provided little relief from the baking sun, but it was better than nothing. Senna was laser-focused on the scent she tracked, following an invisible path, leaping lithely over rocks and thorny brambles. She stopped to sniff the air every so often.

"Those shifter senses are really something, huh?"

Senna glanced at her, nostrils flaring. "They're useful. You're a mage?"

Jovi nodded, feeling the hard metal of the amulet against her heel.

"Don't smell like a mage. You got something else going on?"

Before Jovi could respond, Senna's head swiveled away as if drawn by a magnet. "There." She frowned, sniffing the air again. "It's fresh blood, though. Couldn't be from three days ago."

They pushed through a scrubby hedge, parted a curtain of prickly vines, and found themselves in a wide clearing full of tall trees, big rocks, and a very familiar odor.

Sulfur, smoke, and the iron tang of blood.

The clearing was torn apart. Broken tree limbs and smashed rocks littered the ground. Dark blood stained the dry dirt, and a trio of massive claw marks gouged the thick trunk of a baobab tree. In the middle of it all was a big, charred circle of earth.

Oh, shit. Jovi stepped nervously toward it. The scorched black circle was the size of one of their dune buggies and radiated a whole lot of get-the-fuck-away.

"What the hell is that?" Senna's eyes flashed amber, and her nostrils flared again. "Burnt. Something else, too. Bad vibe."

You have no idea.

Senna backed away, glancing around the clearing and the scrubby timber beyond. She pulled a wicked-looking knife from her thigh holster.

Jovi swallowed, reached out a hand, and hovered it over the blackened earth. The sensation of a thousand stabbing needles skittered up her arm. She yanked her hand back, her heart pounding. Shit, shit, shit. She backed quickly away.

Senna glanced at her, alarmed. "What is it?"

Jovi shook her head. "I need to talk to Rogan."

"What is it?"

"Bad." Jovi brushed past her. "Really bad."

They picked their way out of the thicket. Jovi fought the urge to run, releasing a breath when they emerged from the scrubby brush. She had to get to Rogan, let him know they had way bigger problems than a dead—

A low giggle drifted up from behind them.

She whirled around, and her heart leaped into her throat, closely followed by her stomach. A monstrous, drooling hyena staggered from the thicket. One eyeball dangled from its socket, swaying grotesquely as the animal lurched toward them. Chunks of spotted fur were missing from its hide, revealing patches of raw, oozing skin. Foam bubbled at the corners of its mouth, and a string of drool stretched toward the dirt.

Senna growled, tossing her knife to her other hand. She pulled a short sword from the sheath strapped between her shoulder blades.

"*She wants you*," the hyena rasped, followed by a long, low whoop.

Jovi's blood went cold.

The hyena charged. As Jovi lifted her hands to blast the thing with fire, Senna stepped in front of it and casually swiped her sword across its throat. The hyena stumbled, lurched upright, and kept coming. Senna spun, slashing its ankles from behind. The hyena flopped to the ground, struggling toward Jovi with manic focus. Black blood poured onto the dusty ground.

Black blood. Demon blood.

A thrill of fear went through her. Possessed. It was possessed.

Mommy Dearest had finally done it.

The hyena dragged itself toward her, crazed, leaving a smear of oily black in its wake. Its dangling eyeball bumped against its nose, rocking with each movement. Jovi raised her hands again, ready to blast the thing off the fucking planet.

"Wait," Senna shouted sharply. "Make sure it's identifiable."

She adjusted her aim and lit up the hyena's torso, trying not to burn its face off. Trying not to panic. Finally, it stopped twitching, its red eye staring lifelessly as smoke rose from its ruined hide.

Senna stared at Jovi. "What the fuck was that?"

"I don't know."

"Bullshit." Senna pointed her dripping sword at the stinking, smoking mess on the ground. "What the fuck is that?"

Jovi turned away, marching blindly back toward the compound. Her mother had always been obsessed with possession. The idea of warping something from within fascinated her. Her experiments down in the pit were sickening. But as far as Jovi knew, Inara had never successfully shoved a demon inside of a mortal creature before.

Looks like Mommy Dearest had been hard at work.

Senna kept stride easily. "It said, *she wants you*. Who wants you?"

Jovi's brain whirled. Inara was hunting her, and using possessed shapeshifters to do it. Her minions in the city hadn't managed to haul her back to hell, so she turned to the world's best trackers. She'd always had it out for shifters, her disdain so vicious that Jovi sometimes wondered if one of them had done something to her. How that could be possible, she had no idea, but she knew Mommy Dearest would relish the idea of corrupting the clans. Was Jovi's escape the final straw, the thing that finally pushed her to capture one? Cullen had said something about hyenas not being very smart. Was that why Inara targeted them?

Jovi felt a flash of true terror. Those incredible senses, that speed and strength, all focused on tracking her down and hauling her back to the pit…

She was beyond screwed. She needed to get as far from the shifter clans as possible—and far, far away from Rogan. Like, now. Before he found out.

Her stupid heart squeezed.

"Who wants you?" Senna repeated.

"I don't know." Sun scorched her shoulders as they crossed the cracked earth, but it was nothing compared to the burning feeling in the pit of her stomach.

"You're lying. I can smell it."

The hyena compound came into view, and the male lions waiting in their dune buggy glanced over. Eyes locked onto Senna's dripping sword. Their blades came out instantly.

"Where's Alpha?" Senna asked.

"Still talking," a muscled blond man replied. "What happened?"

"An attack. Some fucked-up hyena. It looked rabid. But it talked. Said someone wants *her*." Senna pointed her sword at Jovi, and every single head swiveled toward her. "There's a big burnt circle on the ground over there. Nasty vibe, bad smell. She knows something."

They stared her down, a bunch of big, half-naked bullies with gleaming predator eyes.

Fuck. She was fast, but the last she checked, Jovi couldn't outrun a pack of lions. She'd have to bide her time, find the right moment to sneak off. In the meantime, she would warn Rogan about the hellmouth and the possessed hyenas, so he wouldn't be completely blindsided after she was gone.

Her heart squeezed tighter, making it hard to breathe. "I need to talk to Rogan."

"Bower. Kenzo," Senna snapped from behind. "Guard the body, due east. Roman, with me."

Senna and the muscled blond flanked her, like two giant sculpted statues as she marched up to the barbed wire fence, shielding her eyes to look up at the sentry in the watchtower. "Let me in."

He shook his head.

"Well, one of your people is dead out there, so you're gonna want to let me in."

The sentry spoke into an old-fashioned walkie talkie, and another hyena shifter appeared from behind the fence. Young, wiry, heavily freckled—how did he not fry out here? He opened the gate, and Jovi strode through with her lion entourage. A trickle of sweat ran down her spine.

They followed the freckled shifter into the compound. Redstone bungalows lined a winding dirt road with neat triangles of fabric stretching between the roofs, providing wedges of shade in the baking heat. An outrageous amount of plucked birds were strung on lines around a massive fire pit, and darkly tanned people lounged in doorways, their arms folded. Kids scuttled away in groups, eyeing them warily.

The road led them to a large redrock cottage under one of the few shade trees. The broad backs of Cullen and Rogan were visible just inside the open door.

The freckled guide held out a hand for them to stop, and he continued toward the door alone. Jovi rolled her eyes and cleared her throat loudly.

Rogan and Cullen turned their heads at the sound, and Freckle Face shot her a glare.

She spread her hands. "Sorry, buddy, but we don't have time for your fancy introductions." She marched up the path, ignoring the tension that thickened with every step. A bird cawed far overhead. Cullen and Rogan watched her approach, but they didn't budge.

"Are you guys talking about the dead hyenas?" Jovi stood on tiptoes, trying to see over their broad shoulders. "Because you've got another one out there. It just attacked us. Something *seriously* wrong with it." She gave Rogan a Very Important Look, and a tiny muscle ticked under his eye.

"Who is that?" a sharp female voice called from the dark cottage. A pair of fingers snapped.

Rogan and Cullen exchanged a glance, then parted. Jovi stepped between them. It was significantly darker and cooler inside the hut. Windows were covered with thin fabric, dimming the light. Outdated human tech was displayed on tables and shelves like art, and a ceiling fan clicked overhead.

A small, lean woman eyed Jovi from an impressively carved chair. Billowy red pants and a cropped top revealed tawny skin decorated with intricate dotwork tattoos. Beads circled her ankles and wrists, and short, dark cornrows hugged her scalp. Hard eyes swept over Jovi as she approached.

The hyena alpha, Renatta.

Four other hyena shifters stood in human form nearby, ready to slaughter Jovi at a moment's notice.

"Who are you?" Renatta demanded.

"I'm Jovi. The one who lit some of your guys on fire."

Renatta's eyes flashed pure black. A growl rumbled from one of her guards' throats. "And you've just killed another one?" She looked coiled, ready to launch and tear Jovi's throat out.

"I put that guy out of his misery. He was sick. Fur falling off, foaming at the mouth, black blood…" She glanced at Rogan, who watched her like a hawk. "Anyone else like that around here?" *Please say no.*

Silence rang like a gong.

Shit.

"Renatta," Cullen said.

She shot him a fuming look. "A few," she spat. "We don't know why."

"Where are they?" Rogan stepped up to Jovi's side. His hard body brushed against hers. Jovi resisted the urge to lean into it.

They were hunting her, and she was leaving.

"We're keeping them quarantined." Renatta jerked her

head bitterly, stepping away from her throne. Her feet were bare. "This way."

They followed her through a back door into the sweltering heat. She walked quickly, with long strides for someone almost as short as Jovi. "It started a couple weeks ago. Sentries would disappear while on patrol. Some started coming back, but they were..." She shook her head. The other hyenas focused straight ahead. "We had to put down one of our own." Fury bubbled in her voice. "I will not do that again."

Yeah, good luck with that.

They rounded a copse of trees. Several yards away, near the bluffs that dropped into the sparkling river, five rabid-looking hyenas milled about behind a rusted fence. The enclosure was tall enough to sway in the breeze that drifted off the water. Sharpened sticks were secured to the top.

"This holds them?" Rogan said dubiously as they approached. Jovi hung behind him, hoping his big body would block her from view. The last thing she needed was for one of the possessed fuckers to open their mouth and say something about her again.

Renatta leveled her black eyes on him. "That is Vortech security wire. It's red dust, not rust." She picked a rock off the ground and hurled it at the fence. It exploded, spraying them with debris. Renatta didn't blink.

"I see." Rogan brushed a shard of rock from his shirt.

"It's also routinely warded by a professional security mage, as are all of our perimeters."

Rogan inclined his head toward her. "Impressive."

Cullen gave a soft snort.

"I use the best available resources to protect my clan," Renatta snapped.

Cullen folded his brawny arms. His mouth twitched, but he kept it shut.

Jovi peered around Rogan's shoulder. The possessed

hyenas prowled the fence line. Matted fur, oozing wounds, a crazed look in their eyes. They paced, snapping and snarling at each other, sniffing the air.

"Do they speak?" Senna's dark eyes were on Jovi.

Renatta scoffed. "In animal form? Of course not."

"Let's find out," Senna said, and shoved Jovi out from behind Rogan's back.

Jovi stumbled into the open. She froze. Every captive hyena turned its glowing red eyes on her.

"*You*," one of them gurgled.

Another gave a soft, low whoop. "*She wants you.*"

Shit, shit, double shit, fuck.

Rogan's eyes met hers. Then, all hell broke loose.

The demon hyenas charged the fence. An enormous burst of blue light sent them flying backward, but they leaped up, ramming the fence like they hadn't even felt it. Cullen bared his teeth. Senna melted into animal form, her clothes shredding as her body expanded, and Renatta's guards followed suit, shrinking into canid bodies. The air throbbed with animal growls. Rogan whipped his phaser from his belt and fell into a low crouch.

"No!" Renatta yelled.

Jovi ran.

She turned and ran for her life, pelting over the cracked earth, her boots sending up clouds of dust as snarls and shouts rang out behind her. A lion roared, followed by the explosive snaps of the security fence blasting the hyenas back, again and again.

She chanced a glance over her shoulder. The possessed hyenas had gotten smart and climbed on top of each other like a pack of fucking cheerleaders. As she watched with wide eyes, tripping over her own feet, one of them clawed its way to the top of the pyramid, leaped off its brother's back, and soared over the fence. Its belly caught on one of the sharpened sticks lining the top, but it didn't seem to notice. It landed in a cloud of dust outside the enclosure, black blood pouring from its sliced gut, smoke rising from its electrocuted fur. Its eyes found her across the desert.

Horror rooted Jovi to the earth.

"Davi!" Renatta shouted. The hyena twitched but kept its eyes on Jovi, an inky puddle growing beneath its ripped belly. "Davi!"

The hyena who had once been Davi grinned.

Her heart was a jackhammer in her ears, but even from two hundred yards away, Jovi still heard it.

"She wants you back." The hyena crouched, preparing to spring—

The beam from Rogan's phaser hit Demon Davi square in the forehead. The hyena dropped like a stone.

Renatta screamed, a wild animal howl, and she dropped beside the dead Davi. Her sentries whirled on Rogan, and Rogan swung his muzzle toward them. Two lions leaped between them. The air thrummed with snarls, Renatta's wails, the zap of the electric fence, and the whoops of the demon hyenas still behind it. Cullen stepped into the fray, shouting.

Rogan locked eyes with Jovi over the teeming crowd.

She couldn't hear his thoughts like his squad mate back at home, but she knew exactly what was going through his head as he watched her on the verge of fleeing. *Don't you fucking dare.*

"Enough!" Cullen roared, and there was enough lion in his voice to make them all jump. Everyone grew silent. Cullen turned, spotting her halfway across the desert. He pointed one very deliberate finger at her. "You. Come here."

So much for escape.

Jovi avoided Rogan's eyes as she forced herself to walk back to the group. Flanks were heaving, lions and hyenas were panting, and all of them were staring daggers at her. The dead demon hyena lay in a pool of black blood, a tendril of smoke curling from a neat hole in its forehead.

Senna melted into human form, rising from all fours to stare at Jovi. "See?"

Renatta bared her teeth at Rogan. "That's the second member of my extended family you've killed, human." Her voice was rough, warped.

"I'm sorry. But that wasn't whoever it used to be." He looked at Jovi, and there was a hard edge to his stare. "We have a problem."

The urge to run was an electric sizzle in her veins. She wanted to get the fuck away from all of this. Lions and hyenas, questions and suspicious stares, possessed animals tracking her down. She wanted to be back in the city, minding her own business, getting drunk with Nora and looking for her father. She wanted to be back in the little treehouse, tucked safely against Rogan's hard body, with those sea glass eyes looking at her like she was something special.

I don't want to let you go. He wouldn't say that once he found out why they were after her.

"This is bigger than you both," Rogan said to the alphas. "I need my team here."

Senna suddenly pointed toward the enclosure. "Shit."

It was empty. Scraps of bloody fur dangled from the sharpened sticks at the top, and a cloud of dust trailed toward the scrubby timber in the distance.

Jovi glanced at Rogan. "We have a *big* problem."

CHAPTER 42

"No way in hell am I allowing MLE into my territory to destroy my people."

They were back in Renatta's cottage, and she'd called for food. Apparently, even when you were mega pissed and on the verge of an interspecies war, stuffing your face was an absolute necessity. Everyone, Jovi and Rogan included, devoured the roasted birds and fish piled on the table. Senna and Roman had been given spare clothes that should've looked ridiculous on them given the size difference between hyena and lion shifters. Instead, they just looked like a couple of gorgeous, scantily clad fitness models.

Rogan sat stony-faced beside Jovi. "Those aren't your people anymore."

"And I'll ask again. *What are they*?"

Rogan's jaw clenched.

Renatta tossed her hands, disgusted. Her eyes were still that depthless hyena black—no pupils, no whites, just an endless inky pool, eerie as fuck. They reminded Jovi of her mother's gaze, and they were leveled on Rogan like she was sizing up his jugular.

Maybe she couldn't keep him, but she didn't have to sit

here and watch some shifter bitch eye him like a target. Jovi slapped the table, drawing that freaky black stare toward herself. "Look, it's not rocket science. Rogan works for MLE and has classified information about this shit. He can't tell you about it. End of story. But he can *help* you if you let him." She looked around the table at the other hyenas, who were back in human form. "Do you guys have phones?"

They glanced at Renatta, who curled her lip. "There are no towers out here." She glared at Cullen. "Someone won't allow them to be built."

Cullen sucked the meat from a fish's spine.

"Our phones are solar powered. They'll have enough charge by nightfall." Renatta pointed a finger at Rogan. "You call your team. But I want to know what is happening to my people." She pounded the table on the last word. A chicken bone rolled onto the floor.

Rogan leaned forward, holding her gaze. "If I can tell you, I will."

Finally, Renatta gave a terse nod. "You can wait in one of the guest huts until dusk." She looked at Cullen. "Alpha Diallo and I still have things to discuss."

Jovi and Rogan were led to the far edge of the compound, where a small hut stood near the river. "The water is clean. You should wash." Their escort eyed Jovi's black-splattered cutoffs. "Clothes are in the hut. Food is in the cook tent. We'll come get you at dusk." He left without another word.

The hyenas' guest quarters were even more sparse than the lions'. There was a double-size cot set low to the floor, a rough table, and a chair with a stack of spare clothes. The windows were high and small, keeping the place dark and cool. It got even darker when Rogan shut the door behind them.

Silence.

He stared at her in the gloom. She stared back, her pulse pounding in her ears.

"You ran."

She swallowed.

He stepped closer, tilted her chin up, and waited until she finally met his eyes. "What happened in the timber?"

He was too much—too warm and tempting and overwhelming. Jovi stepped away, making a show of looking through the stack of clothes on the chair. It was easier to talk without those sea glass eyes staring into her soul.

She told him about the demon hyena, skipping over the fact that it had talked about her, instead focusing on the burnt circle of earth. "It's a hellmouth," she explained. "Where the demons come through."

"How do you know?"

"I've seen one before." *When I crawled my way out of it.*

The silence was palpable. She finally glanced over. He was staring at her like he was determined to pierce her skull and read the thoughts he'd find there. "Do you know how to close one?"

Jovi shook her head, feeling like she'd swallowed a tiny, fluttering bird.

He stepped closer again, crowding her, giving her no escape. The pad of his thumb traced her lower lip. "It said *she wants you*," he murmured. "Who wants you?"

Lying was easy. Smooth, effortless. Like slipping on a silk robe.

Usually.

"How should I know? It was a crazy possessed demon." If her heart beat any harder, he'd hear it.

His thumb kept brushing her lip, leaving tingles in its wake. "You're a good liar. But I know you, Jovi Black." His other hand came up to frame her face. "You're in trouble, aren't you?"

The tiny, fluttering bird squeezed down her throat and landed in her stomach. She wanted to tell him. Staring up at the chiseled planes of that gorgeous face, the wide jaw shadowed with stubble, the freckles sprinkling his nose, she let herself imagine it for a split second. She could make up a story to explain why a high demon succubus was after her. The two of them could be a team, fighting off Mommy Dearest's minions, figuring out how to close the hellmouths, frolicking through the fucking fields, screwing each other's brains out until the end of time.

As long as he never found out what she was.

Something sharp sliced through her heart, shattering any illusion of the life they might have.

"Tell me."

She was such an idiot. Demons didn't do happily ever after.

"Tell me." It was a command.

"You have things you can't tell me. I have things, too." Like how it was literally his job to destroy her. Jovi stepped away from him. The sharp thing sliced deeper into her stupid heart. "I'm going to go jump in the river."

The door swung shut behind her as she left the hut. She stalked toward the river, swiping at her cheek. She had to let him go before this thing ripped them both apart.

CHAPTER 43

She was trying to push him away.

Rogan had followed her to the river—no way in hell was he going to leave her naked and alone around another bunch of shifters. She'd found a secluded pool where the water was divided from the main channel by a large rocky island, and trees provided some shade and privacy. Rogan inspected the area, then turned to tell Jovi it was safe to get in.

Of course, she had already stripped and was wading belly-deep before he even opened his mouth. The sight of her beautiful bare breasts hovering above the water, pink nipples stiffened, made him forget what he was going to say, anyway.

There was something after her. Someone. Some female. Who was *she*? And why wouldn't Jovi tell him?

Something dark and oily bubbled in Rogan's gut. Maybe she thought he couldn't handle it. Maybe she figured a mage or a shifter would be stronger, more capable. Maybe she hadn't fallen as completely head over heels for him as he had for her.

He watched her paddle around in the water. Her strokes

were short, childlike. She didn't look like she had spent much time swimming. They would have to work on that in the pool back at the Bunker.

And just like that, he saw it—Jovi smiling sleepily, her hair a tumble of pink against his white linen sheets. Jovi sitting cross-legged at the big dining table, devouring Gloria's cooking and giving the boys shit. The two of them sparring in the gym, swimming in the pool, making hot, slow love against his tiled shower wall.

He wanted to keep her. Really, truly keep her.

The realization burst inside him, filling him in a rush. The Magistrate would understand. He would have to. They would all have to. Rogan had given his entire goddamn life to MLE, sacrificed everything for the DE. They would give him this.

It shouldn't be hard to convince them—she was a fighter, a healer, and she could see their enemy without a lens. Hell, it would be stupid not to bring her into the fold.

And he wanted her. Even with her secrets and her baggage, even with someone trying to track her down. Whatever monsters needed slaying, he would fucking slay them. The maddening little minx had torched her way into his heart, and he wasn't letting her go.

He stripped and slipped into the water. It was deliciously cool on his sunbaked skin. He waded slowly toward her, filled with a buzzing determination.

She watched him warily, her wet hair slicked back over those delicate pointed ears. Her eyes had lost their mischievous spark. "Don't."

He planted his feet on the sandy river bottom and pulled her slick, naked body against him. "Do you not want me anymore?"

"That's not it."

"So, you do."

She avoided his gaze. "I can't—"

He wrapped his arms more tightly around her. "Whatever it is, we'll handle it. You and me. You point, I shoot."

Her lips curved in a sad smile.

He put some steel into his voice. "Jovi, you infuriating woman, you drive me up the fucking wall." He tried to catch her eye, but she avoided him. "And it's the most alive I've felt in decades."

She bit her lip, staring into the water.

He gave her a tiny shake. "I don't want to let you go."

She finally looked at him. And just like that, his whole world shifted. The job, the mission, the life he had known before, came second. Like a flashing scoreboard, she had just taken the lead.

Priority mission.

The clarity was a goddamn relief. He released a breath and smiled, letting his gaze devour every inch of her face, his thumbs tracing her features, guiding a drop of water off her delicate brow.

Something desperate and aching flickered in her expression, and she suddenly gripped his head, hard, with both hands. "You see me. Right? You see *me*?"

He felt like he was falling into her, wanted her to fall into him. Cupping her face, he brought their foreheads together until their eyes were inches apart. "I see you. I see your fire, I see your strength, I see your crazy mouth and your good heart. I see you heal everyone else when you're dead on your feet. I see your humor." His lips twitched, then he grew serious. "I see that you're hiding something because you're scared." He held her gaze, watched the crystal blues shimmer with tears. "I see you. And I want you. All of you."

She slowly shook her head, rolling it against his. "We're so fucked," she whispered. "And it is totally your fault." She pulled his mouth to hers.

Triumph roared in his chest as he crushed her to him. She was suddenly wild in his arms, climbing him, slippery and weightless in the water as her legs wrapped his waist. Her kiss was molten, her lips and tongue urgent, devouring him, consuming him. Her thighs squeezed his hips, her body surging against him in an endless wave. He fisted her wet hair, squeezed her ass, ground her against him. Small, hot hands gripped his jaw, tilting his head, opening his mouth wide beneath hers. It was more than a kiss. She poured herself into him, giving him everything, and he took it all, inhaling her, swallowing her essence, wanting her inside of him.

"Nash," she breathed, sending a thrill through his blood-stream. It was the first time she'd called him that. Not many people did. Nash was the man beneath the mission, the boy who yearned for things he lost, the raw beating heart under the tactical shirt.

He parted her with his hands and thrust deep inside, sucking her gasp into his mouth, mindless with the sizzling pleasure of her in his arms, in his lungs, in his veins. Her sheath was hot silk around him, slipping, stroking like fire around his cock, building a volcanic pressure. As he drove deeper, he felt her clench around him, heard her harsh cries, and he let his head drop back, reveling in the bliss of letting go.

CHAPTER 44

The hyena phones were old and outdated. It took him twenty goddamn minutes to get through to Cyrus.

"Hello?" The connection crackled, but Cyrus's smooth, deep voice was unmistakable.

"It's me."

"Jesus, Nash, where the hell are you? We heard about the safe house, you all right?"

"We're fine. We're in hyena territory—"

"*Hyena*—"

"Shut up. I don't know how much time I have. Their phones are shit. Listen." He gave Cyrus the bare-bones rundown of what had happened, leaving out the part about completely losing his head over Jovi. That part was an in-person discussion.

Cyrus listened silently, at one point giving a short, sharp whistle away from the mouthpiece. Rogan wondered how many of the DE were gathered around the phone now. He prodded at his left eye as he talked, feeling his lens stick to his cornea.

"You're on speaker," Cyrus said when Rogan paused for breath.

"I need you all here ASAP. Bring everything. Bring extra. Bring me a goddamn fresh lens and more batteries than you think you'll ever need. We've got a potential hellmouth and demons possessing shapeshifters."

Lots of swearing erupted on the other end of the phone.

"I can flash two, maybe three of us, to your location before I'll need to recover." John's voice crackled through the earpiece.

Rogan stole a glance at Jovi, who was sitting at the hyena's long table, eating roasted crayfish with obvious enjoyment. Cullen sat across from her, lazily licking his fingers and smiling at her exuberant noises of pleasure. Rogan's eye twitched.

"Do it," he said. "Cyrus and Killian first. Bring as much as you can carry. And spare clothes. And coffee, for fuck's sake." Chuckles came through the speaker, but he was watching Jovi pile her hair on top of her head to fan her slender neck. "And candy."

Laughter died. "Candy?" Cyrus asked. Juno's voice rang out in the background, "Is he okay?"

"Candy," Rogan repeated. "Lots of it."

There was another moment of stunned silence. "Give us an hour."

Rogan hung up, heading to the table. He handed the solar phone back to the hyenas, who were tense and twitchy. Cullen was the only one who seemed remotely relaxed. Rogan met his eyes and nodded, then he turned to Renatta, seated at the head of the table. "My team is coming. At least three of them will be here in an hour. The others will get here as soon as they can. We'll wait to engage until the whole squad is here."

"Engage in what, exactly?" Cullen asked.

"I can't disclose that."

Cullen sucked his tongue over his teeth, taking his time to

select a fat crayfish from the pile. "I don't like secrets in my territory, human." His voice had gone dangerously soft.

And I don't like your condescending fucking tone. "This is my job. Let me do it."

A low growl rumbled from the alpha's chest, but he kept his mouth shut. That was the difference between him and his brother—Killian would've flipped the table, popped his fangs, and roared.

Nerves twisted in Rogan's gut. The team would arrive soon, and not only would the brothers meet after a seven-year separation, the squad would see that he and Jovi were something more. He wouldn't hide it. He couldn't. There would be shock and questions. And pushback.

He'd just had her. Christ, it had hardly been an hour since the river. But he couldn't shake the feeling of a massive ticking clock looming over them.

Rogan touched her shoulder. She gazed up at him from the bench, and he tilted his head toward the guest hut. She rose, sucked the meat from a crayfish's head, and chucked the empty skull on the table. When he held out his hand, she slid her fingers into his. They fit together perfectly.

"We'll be back," he said. Two pairs of glowing alpha eyes watched them walk away.

Desperation hummed beneath his skin as he led her to the guest hut and kicked the door shut. Her hands were already on his shirt, yanking it over his head and then smoothing over his chest, making noises of approval. Her mouth was hot against his. She tasted like salt and spices and Jovi. It made his head spin.

He tore the damn shapeshifter clothes off her and backed her toward the cot in nothing but her sexy boots. But before he could lay her down, she spun, tripping him. He bounced onto his back with a breathless grin, loving that she could catch him off guard. The grin vanished as she stripped him of his boots and pants, dropped to her knees, and took his cock into her mouth.

His head nearly exploded. Holy Christ, her mouth, her lips. He slid his hands into her hair, watching her head bob as she sucked, swirled, and slid her lips up and down his length. He swore. She moaned, and it vibrated around his shaft. Rogan's eyes rolled back in his head. Her mouth was scalding hot around him, burning him up from the inside out as she worked him up and down. Her hands glided up his legs to tickle his thighs and cup his balls. She did something with her tongue that nearly had him blowing right there into her mouth. Desperate, he hauled her up his body with a growl.

Jovi straddled him, her eyes glittering and lips glistening in the dim light. She ducked her head to lick at his nipple, sending a jolt of electricity straight to his dick. In a smooth, fluid movement, she sat upright, flipping her hair, and his brain went blank at the sheer beauty of her, the stunning sensuality. She was the sexiest thing he'd ever seen, and he was the luckiest man alive.

Her hand snaked between them to grip his shaft, slick and wet from her mouth, and she impaled herself on him with a cry of pleasure.

Her core was like liquid fire around him, so hot, so wet, so impossibly smooth. He gritted his teeth against the blinding pleasure of it, forcing his eyes open. He had to see her.

She was glorious above him, pearly skin glowing in the gloom, naked curves gleaming beneath a tumble of pink hair. Her eyes were closed, her head thrown back. She rocked against him once, deep and deliberate, and they both groaned. His lips parted as she began to move, her pelvis tilting sinuously, setting a slow, mesmerizing rhythm that drove him out of his mind.

Slender fingers found his wrists, and she brought his hands up over his head, pinning him to the bed. She bent to trace his ear with her tongue, then gave it a naughty bite. His cock nearly exploded. "Fuck, Jovi."

Her low chuckle tickled his ear before she surged upright. With a vixen smile, she planted her feet on the bed so she was crouched over him like some tribal sex goddess, and speared herself on his dick again. As he groaned, she leaned back to brace her hands on his shins. And then she rode him like a wild thing.

Dirty, filthy, primal...her legs were split wide on either side of him, and he could see everything—her swollen pink folds, his wet cock pumping in and out, her breasts bouncing. He'd never seen anything so fucking hot in his entire life.

He gripped her ankles, bracing them both, desperate to give her more, to give her everything. He drove deeper, faster, and words spilled out of his mouth, but he had no clue what they were. She cried out, little yips of pleasure with every thrust, and his eyes peeled wide as he stared at the sheen on her pussy, watching it grow wetter and wetter around his cock. The pleasure was insane, short-circuiting his fucking brain, lighting every nerve ending on fire. But he had to hold back, had to light her up, had to see that steam...

She came with a desperate cry and a frenzied bucking of her hips. Her body lit up, steam seeping from her skin, and he cut the leash, erupting inside her with a burst of volcanic pleasure and a loud, guttural roar. Her muscles clenched around him, sucking at him, taking everything he had to give.

She collapsed on top of him, their hearts pounding against each other like they, too, wanted to touch. He blew her hair away from his mouth, stroking the curve of her spine. *Never letting this go.*

A knock on the door made them both jump. "Your crew is here," a voice called curtly. Footsteps retreated.

Jovi's crystal blue eyes met his.

"It'll be fine," Rogan said firmly, though his gut squirmed.

CHAPTER 45

The sight of Cyrus standing tall and loaded with duffles made Rogan feel like a two-ton weight had been lifted from his shoulders. He returned Cyrus's grin as they clapped each other into a hard hug. The gathered shapeshifters watched, curious.

You good? Cyrus's voice floated into his head.

I think I love her.

They both froze. Cyrus pulled back, his eyebrows raised to the sky. Rogan was just as shocked. He hadn't meant to say it, hadn't meant to think it. He didn't even realize he'd felt it. They blinked at each other, stunned.

"Um," Jovi said from behind him, "Are you going to introduce us, or are you just going to keep it awkward for everybody?"

Cyrus snapped out of it, dropping his duffles and offering his hand. "Agent Aurelien, MLE." He gave her his megawatt smile, making Rogan scowl despite himself. Cyrus took Jovi's pale hand in his dark one. "Cyrus. And you're Miss Jovi Black."

"The one and only." Jovi dropped her hand quickly. She was nervous, and he couldn't blame her.

Cyrus held out a battery to Rogan. Relief flooded him as he swapped it for the dead one in his watch.

LENS ACTIVATED.

The beautiful little green dot appeared at the corner of his left eye. Rogan let out a breath. Was that how Blitz users felt after a long-awaited hit? Speaking of which…

"Coffee?" he asked, hopeful.

Cyrus smiled and nodded, but his pale eyes searched Rogan's face. *What the hell happened, man?*

Later.

The air in front of them shimmered. John and Killian appeared from a misty veil, slowly becoming solid. Every single shapeshifter went still as stone. Killian hitched his three duffles higher on his shoulder. He saw Rogan, jerked his chin in greeting, then scanned the crowd. His eyes landed on Cullen.

A dangerous silence thrummed the air. They stared at each other.

Cullen's lion flashed under his skin, disappearing just as fast. Killian looked away.

John clasped Rogan into a quick embrace. His sheet of dark hair brushed Rogan's cheek, smelling like sweet smoke and herbs, and Tika fluttered to his other shoulder. "Good to see you." The white glow slowly faded from his eyes.

"You, too. We need your expertise on this one." He gestured toward Jovi, who hovered at his side, chewing her lip. "This is Jovi, my WITPRO charge."

John smiled at her, but abruptly, his brows slanted, and the glow surged back into his eyes. He frowned.

What the... "John?"

John blinked, and the glow faded from his eyes. He tore his gaze from Jovi. "Nothing. Sorry, I'm tired." He shook his head. "I've got one left in me. Juno?"

Rogan nodded. He glanced at Jovi, who was staring at the crow on John's shoulder like she expected it to peck out her eyes. John inhaled deeply and faded into the ether. Rogan stared after him. What the hell was that about?

"Where's the base?" Killian asked.

Rogan hefted one of the duffles as John reappeared with Juno, dressed in tacticals and loaded with bags. She spotted Rogan, dropped the gear, and pulled him into a rough hug, cuffing him on the shoulder as she pulled back.

"Dick," she said without heat. "You scared us." She focused on Jovi, and there was a beat of silence. Rogan caught sight of Cyrus's carefully still face, then watched Juno's dark brows rise.

He'd told her.

Rogan met Juno's hard stare. Neither of them could communicate telepathically, but they didn't need to—they'd known each other a long time. Right then, her eyes were saying, *We'll definitely be talking about* this *later.* She nodded shortly at Jovi, her dark ponytail sliding over her shoulder. "Agent DeSilva."

Beside her, John swayed almost imperceptibly. Tika cawed, nibbling his ear.

"You good to get back?" Rogan murmured.

John nodded. "Give me a few hours and I'll be back with Wolf." Rogan clapped him on the back as he faded away.

"Useful skill." Renatta gazed at the ripple of air where John had disappeared. The gleam of speculation in her eyes was pure scavenger. "Rare, isn't it?"

"You said we can set up near your place," Rogan said firmly, ignoring her question. "We'll need some tables." And some goddamn privacy.

CHAPTER 46

The team spread their supplies across several tables near Renatta's hut. Rogan and Juno worked at one, Cyrus and Killian at another. Rogan's breath eased as he scanned the stockpile. Phasers, pistols, Holy Light cartridges, daggers, stunners, vials of Holy Water…

Home sweet home.

Rogan slid a fresh battery into his illuminator, watching Jovi chuck a throwing knife into a tree trunk. Her aim was improving—she hadn't nailed anyone in the leg, at least. The stretchy tactical leggings and shirt she'd borrowed from Juno molded to her curves like a second skin, making her look like a pink-haired ninja. Rogan's lips twitched at the dozen candy necklaces circling her throat.

Juno's gaze bounced between them. "Yeah, about that." She slid a cartridge into a phaser with a satisfying *shhhunk* and checked the aim before setting it aside, her bare shoulders gleaming with sweat in the desert heat.

"Not now."

"She's a mage. You sure it's not a spell of some sort?"

"Just…not now." He needed the Magistrate's approval

first. After that, nobody could argue. They'd learn to like her. Love her, even. Like he did.

Warmth flooded through him, but it was not the time to marvel. Especially not with a disapproving jaguar eyeing him from across the table.

"You're right, there's something off about her," Juno continued. "Like you said the first time you saw her, remember? Something else you couldn't put your finger on?" She watched Jovi for a moment, her eyes flashing jaguar green.

Deflect, ASAP. "How much do you know about Cullen and Killian?"

Juno gave him a look that said she wasn't fooled by the change of subject. "Just what you've told me. Alpha is pissed that his little brother wants nothing to do with the family business." She unrolled a pack of water cartridges with a practiced flick. "It's not like Killian's offering up a lot of details. Not that he would to me, anyway. Do you know anything more about it?"

Rogan shook his head and slugged the remains of his third cup of coffee, wishing it was stronger, especially considering what he was about to ask. He gestured to the scene around them. "Does the Magistrate know about any of this?"

Juno was quiet as she slid cartridges into water pistols. She shook her head shortly.

Relief rushed through him, followed by a hot surge of shame. He could see the writeup very clearly. *Agent Nash Rogan: 1. Blew his cover in WITPRO. 2. Got jacked on the interstate. 3. Killed a high-ranking hyena shifter. 4. Revealed classified information. 5. Performed physically intimate acts with his WITPRO charge.*

He would've fired his own ass so fast it would've made his head spin. And still, his team was protecting him.

"Bastelli nailed some pretty big Slavs at The Pyramid a couple nights ago," Juno explained, giving him a chance to swallow the lump in his throat. "Anton Kruzchev was one of them. I think you could argue for release from WITPRO." She glanced at Jovi. "Not sure about her."

His phone vibrated in his pocket. Juno reached for hers, too. It was a group text from John. *Incoming with Wolf.*

Rogan waved everybody over. The team needed to know what Jovi could do.

As they gathered around the tables, John and Wolf materialized in the clearing. Wolf bounded over, his wild hair flapping. "Son of a bitch, man, I thought we were gonna have to come rescue you. Oh wait—we are." He stuck out his tongue with a maniacal grin and slapped Rogan on the shoulder. "And *whoa*—" He did an exaggerated double-take as Jovi approached. "You're the little WITPRO pop tart." He snatched Jovi's hand and kissed it. "No wonder Rogan was worried about keeping his paws off. Did he manage it?" He leaned in, giving her a roguish wink.

Rogan was going to need more fucking coffee.

CHAPTER 47

Apparently, being beautiful and broody was in the job description.

Jovi glanced around at the Demon Eradication squad. If there was such a thing as *Sexy Secret Soldiers* magazine, these guys would all make the cover. Each one of them was in incredible shape, annoyingly good looking, armed to the teeth, and staring at her like she had a target on her forehead.

Oh, and they were all professional demon hunters.

This might be one of her stupider ideas.

The guy named Wolf was the only one wearing a grin. "Dude, this is awesome. She can *see* these fuckers? Without a lens?" He eyed Jovi like she was a shiny new toy.

"How?" Juno demanded, her bronze arms crossed. Lean, muscled, with insane cheekbones and a thick dark ponytail, she was just as hot and badass as Jovi had feared. She was also kind of a bitch.

Jovi shrugged. "Always have been able to."

Juno glanced at her teammates. "I'm not buying it."

"The Magistrate was born with the ability." Cyrus's pale blue eyes pierced hers, and she looked quickly away. This guy was the one who could hear thoughts. If he caught a whiff of hers, she was screwed.

"Yeah, the Magistrate can!" Wolf echoed. "Plus, you're a pyro? And you can heal? And fight?"

Jovi tossed her hair, feeling a bit better. She nodded.

"She's green," Rogan added, and her mouth dropped open in offense. His lips curved, and his eyes softened infinitesimally. "But good."

There he went, melting her. She wanted to leap up on him and suck that plump bottom lip like a lollipop. Instead, she winked and did her best to ignore the niggling little worm that had been burrowing into her belly ever since the river, when he'd told her again that he didn't want to let her go. When she'd fooled herself into believing they could work.

He saw her. He said he really saw her.

"She gets tired easily," Rogan continued. "Her fire is powerful, but it wipes her out fast." He gestured to the candy necklaces circling her throat. One of them was already half gone. "Sugar helps."

"So she's a liability," Juno said.

"She is an asset. One who doesn't need tech to do the job. None of us can say that." Rogan pegged each one of them with a look.

Killian, who was a blonder, broodier, beardier version of Cullen, shrugged his massive, tattooed shoulders. "She wants to fight, let her. She survives, we'll deal with it then."

Well, if that wasn't a warm welcome, she didn't know what was.

One by one, the others nodded, gathering close while Rogan briefed them about the possessed hyenas. He was detailed, thorough, and completely in his element. This was him. This was what he did. The squad listened carefully, asked short, succinct questions. She chewed the inside of her cheek, waiting for him to tell them that the hyenas had talked about her.

He didn't say a word about it.

Her heart stumbled, tripped all over itself, and fell completely.

He was protecting her.

"And what about the hellmouth?" Cyrus asked.

John cleared his throat. He had a calm, steady presence, and despite the fact that his eyes seemed to glow freaky white when he focused on her, he'd been nice so far. The crow on his shoulder, however, glared at her beadily. That bitch had her number. Good thing familiars couldn't talk.

Jovi jumped as the crow let out a blaring caw.

John stroked the crow's throat. "I've been working with research and Father Scott, and I've got a technique to try to close it. Well, I have a few things to try. Let's hope one of them works."

———

Night fell, and the squad gathered around one of the picnic tables back in the hyena compound. Shifters eyed them suspiciously but gave them space, devouring spit-roasted birds in their own small groups. The DE pretended to ignore them, but six pairs of eyes continuously scanned the scene, casual glances that missed absolutely nothing.

They talked easily, gave each other shit, stole food from each other's plates, radiated power and cool confidence. Jovi sat next to Rogan, trying to ignore the warm fuzzies setting up shop in her chest.

Squad. Team. Family.

Rogan glanced down at her, and a small smile appeared on his lips. Could a heart explode in a good way?

"You kids sure you don't need any help with this secret mission of yours?" Cullen's deep voice rumbled over her shoulder.

Jovi turned. The lion alpha loomed like a mountain in the

flickering firelight, his thumbs looped casually into his waistband. A strip of bronze abs peeked from below his shirt.

"We've got it," Rogan said, firm but polite.

"Do you?"

"Yep."

"Because I hear there's something really nasty in that thicket. I'd like to offer my services." Cullen smiled nastily. "Considering it's on my land."

"Yeah, you wouldn't be any help," Wolf said, stripping meat from a chicken leg with his teeth.

"Really?" Cullen's eyes flashed, and he slashed his hands through the air. Huge, razor-sharp claws shot from between his fingers, the equivalent of dropping his pants to display a gigantic cock. "These wouldn't be any help?" Blood dripped from his hands. "I find that very hard to believe."

"That's because you don't know what you're talking about," Killian muttered, eyes on his plate. His voice was rougher than Cullen's, with a harsher, wilder edge.

Cullen took one long step forward. "Then why don't you *enlighten* me, little brother? Or are you too chicken shit to do that, too?"

Killian shoved up from the table. The rest of the squad did the same.

The clearing went very still. Crickets chirped. Jovi watched from the bench, wishing she had popcorn.

"Boys." Juno glided sinuously between them, placing a hand on each of their broad shoulders. "Not in front of the kids." She gave Killian a hard look and then smiled at Cullen, lifting her empty plate. "I need a refill. Show me?"

The brothers held each other's gaze for a few long seconds. Jovi licked her fingers. Some half-naked wrestling? Finally?

"After you," Cullen rumbled to Juno, gesturing in front of him. They strolled off toward the food tent.

Killian's massive claws split his skin, and his mouth burst

open in a silent roar, fangs erupting from his gums. He watched with blazing yellow eyes as his brother led Juno's sleek, black-clad figure away.

Wolf gave a low whistle. "You wanna go a couple rounds, bud? Unleash some of that rage?"

"Keep it together," Rogan muttered.

Killian spun and marched toward the dark river, flexing his claws. Blood pattered the dirt in his wake.

Jovi fanned her cheeks. "My, my."

"You, too." Rogan scowled at her, and she couldn't help but grin.

CHAPTER 48

Dawn came all too soon, painting the sky in swaths of orange and pink. Fog rose in the thicket and collected on the scrubby trees in millions of sparkling dewdrops. It was pretty. Might almost have been peaceful, if not for the portal to hell smoking in the middle of it.

The amulet hung heavy against Jovi's sternum. Rogan had kissed her this morning and asked her to wear it. "Take it out of your boot," he'd said. "We might need it."

She should've known better than to think he'd forgotten about it. Nash Rogan didn't forget anything. She didn't like the idea of wearing it, but she'd looped it over her neck and tucked it under Juno's borrowed black shirt, out of the way and out of sight. Because he'd asked.

She was so screwed for this dude.

She peered at him across the clearing. He was sexy as fuck in his full tactical gear—black on black, freshly shaven, intensely focused, and loaded with armor and weapons and tech toys she didn't know the names of. She couldn't stop staring.

As if he felt it, his gaze slid to hers. He pointed two fingers at her, then at his own eyes, then at the hellmouth in the center of the clearing. She stuck her tongue out at him. A dimple flashed in his cheek for a split second, sending a jolt to her lady bits. Then, he went back to scanning the thicket.

He said he wanted to keep her. Maybe, just maybe, he could. She was good at lying, good at keeping secrets. When it mattered.

He mattered.

First, she had to get the possessed shifters under control before they ratted her out. Closing this hellmouth was a damn good start. Sure, portals could pop up anywhere, but if she had to spend the rest of her life hunting down hellmouths to keep her mother's minions at bay, so be it. Rogan was worth it.

The hellmouth smoked ominously like a massive, stinking cigarette burn in the center of the clearing. The smell of sulfur, frightening and familiar, triggered all kinds of happy memories. The gut-churning kind.

John stood barefoot in front of the charred circle, palms held toward the earth, eyes closed, face utterly calm. The crow, whose name she'd learned was Tika, stood serenely on his shoulder.

What kind of mage was he, anyway? He could flash to different locations, which was apparently super rare. But other than that, he'd just given off a real spiritual, one-with-the-earth kind of vibe. He'd moved around the hellmouth with bundles of smoking herbs, drew symbols in the dirt, and trailed a stream of salt around the perimeter. Then, he'd closed his eyes, took a deep breath, and stood perfectly still.

For, like, a really long time.

Jovi drummed her fingers, watching a fat beetle waddle over her boot as she flicked dewdrops off a bush. Biting back an impatient sigh, she glanced around at the team, stationed at regular intervals around the clearing.

Anticipation buzzed between them. Wolf flipped a dagger

in the air, over and over, his neck bobbing like he had a song in his head. Further around the clearing, Juno kept her eyes on the hellmouth while she moved through a series of low, fluid stretches. Ground-hugging, primal movements, catlike and mesmerizing. She wore loose athletic shorts and a tank top, her feet bare in the dirt. Several yards away, Killian was practically naked—loose pants rode low on his hips, his tattooed torso on full display. He flexed his hands, loosened his jaw, and rolled his shoulders.

Jovi's eyes traveled upward. Cyrus stood on a tree limb, leaning against the trunk with casual elegance. Dark and sleek in tactical gear similar to Rogan's, he practically melted into the shadows. Jovi watched his pale eyes follow the trajectory of Wolf's flipping dagger. A second later, the blade shot sideways into a nearby tree trunk.

Wolf's head whipped up. He spotted Cyrus, snatched a rock from the ground, and chucked it into the branches. Yanking the dagger out of the tree, he snapped his jaws at his squad mate. Cyrus's grin gleamed, bright white against his dark skin.

Family.

Across the clearing, Rogan snapped his fingers, stabbing a finger toward the hellmouth. Everyone fell silent.

John inhaled a deep breath and opened his eyes, reaching into a leather pouch tied to his belt to pull out a small corked bottle. He held it up to Tika, who plucked the stopper out with her beak. John whispered something, spilling the clear liquid onto the smoking ground.

There was a fierce hiss like a gigantic, angry snake. A long, low groan sounded from deep within the earth, fading into an ominous silence.

John pushed his hands forward, muttering through his teeth, his eyes glowing that creepy pure white. The hair on Jovi's arms stood on end. Shit, what if he did something that affected *her*? Like, banished her, or bound her to the earth or something? That would be a hard one to explain. A hysterical giggle bubbled up in her throat, but it was interrupted by the earth quaking beneath her, sending tiny pebbles dancing around her boots. John planted his bare feet in the dirt, his hands braced against an invisible wall. The squad tensed as his chanting grew louder. Even Wolf was motionless, focused unblinkingly on the hellmouth with eyes gone wolfish gold. The sky darkened abruptly like a thunderstorm rolling in, plunging everything into the shadows.

A great roaring sound rose from beneath them. John's eyes glowed like lanterns in the gloom as he shouted beautifully terrifying words in a language Jovi didn't understand. All the cells of her body were electrified, screaming and singing at the same time, and she wanted to run, and she wanted to laugh, and she wanted to shout at everyone that this was a really, really bad idea.

The portal erupted.

John was blasted off his feet, but Jovi didn't see where he landed. All she saw were the monsters.

They boiled out of the earth in a writhing, slithering mass. Skeletal, fleshless things. Tentacled things. Red eyes, empty sockets. Things with too many legs, things with none at all. Leathery wings, dripping fangs, gleaming claws. Shrieks and screams, warped bellows and wet gurgles. Then, an angry cloud of insects, moving like a school of piranhas in the sulfurous air.

The whir of Rogan's phaser cut through the chaos. Demon after demon dropped to the ground, their foreheads smoking. He pulled something from his belt, chucking it into the fray. There was an explosion, and more demons hit the dirt.

A massive boulder sailed across the clearing, smashing into a swath of demons. From high in his tree, Cyrus's eyes followed the boulder's arc. He jerked his chin, and the boulder flew toward the hellmouth. Shrieks split the air. Demon guts smeared the earth.

Jovi took cover behind a tree, shooting blasts of fire around the trunk. The stench of burnt flesh and rotten eggs made her stomach roll, and from across the thicket, a wild wolf howl raised goosebumps all over her body.

A pair of drooling hellhounds, tall and gaunt with too many teeth, charged toward her. She whirled her arms in fast circles, conjuring a spinning vortex of flame. She threw the fiery tornado at the hounds, who were sucked into its orbit, yelping and making horrible, dissonant cries. They fell to the ground in ashes.

A sudden pain seared her thigh. She looked down, cursing. A gigantic blood-red wasp had its stinger embedded in her tight black leggings. She slapped at it instinctively, and a burning pain flooded her leg, making her suck in a breath. "Mother*fucker*!" She made a gun out of her fingers and sent a flaming bullet at the wasp. It curled to a crisp, leaving a melted hole in her leggings. At least the stinger melted along with it.

A train rammed into her from behind. She flew forward, hit the ground like a bag of bones, and managed to roll to her feet, spitting dirt.

It wasn't a train. It was a gargoyle—a big, chiseled gargoyle with some serious 'roid rage. Huge, ugly, with enormous curling horns and flapping black wings, it roared, strings of spit stretching between gigantic yellow fangs. Its gaping mouth was big enough to swallow her whole.

Jovi planted her feet and roared back.

The gargoyle cocked its horned black head. "It is thou." Its voice was so low, it warped. "She is not happy with thee."

"FUCK *OFF*!" Jovi screamed, heaving a boulder of fire at it. The boulder crashed into its belly, sending it flying backward. It bellowed, smashed into a tree, and went up in flames. The tree caught fire.

Whoops.

Battle sounds battered her eardrums—screeches, growls,

roars, words in foreign languages, the whir of Rogan's phaser, the pops and groans of a tree being uprooted. Jovi ducked as it flew toward the hellmouth, trailing stringy roots and clumps of dirt behind it.

And all the while, more demons poured from the gaping hole in the earth.

John stood on the uprooted tree, riding it like a surfboard while Cyrus guided it back toward the hellmouth. He was going to make another attempt to close it. He didn't have a chance.

It was a swarm. Worse than that—it was an escape. Something big was coming, and all the smaller guys were running from it.

Jovi swore, marching into the clearing. "Everybody clear the fuck out!"

Everyone ignored her.

"Rogan!" she screamed, ducking under a fat, dripping tentacle and lighting it on fire.

He glanced at her, then did some fancy, lightning-fast martial arts moves on three different demons. They dropped. He snapped another demon's neck, slashed a throat—brutally efficient, beautiful, just like she knew he would be. "Clear out!"

The team fought their way away from the hellmouth as Jovi yanked one of the candy necklaces from her throat, sending little pastel discs flying. She dumped the candies into her cheek and tossed the string aside, then shook out her hands, spread her limbs wide, and set herself on fire.

Fire exploded from every pore. She was a human blow torch, a flamethrower, a forest fire. She fed the inferno, pushing and straining until a massive wall of flame stretched across the clearing with her at its center. Demons burned to crisps, shrieking and howling and writhing in agony. Jovi lowered her chin, sucked on the wad of sugar in her cheek, and held on.

"John!" Rogan yelled over the roar of the flames. Jovi glanced over and saw John darting forward, graceful as a fox, maneuvering outside of the wall of fire to the opposite side of the hellmouth. He began his whole chanty-chanty, eye-glowy thing, and Jovi held her flame while the fight raged behind her.

Distantly, she heard Rogan scream, "Clear!" Seconds later, a sonic blast knocked her to her knees. She flailed, her wall of fire swaying wildly before she could cut it off. John shouted in pain. Shit, she'd hit him.

Ears ringing, Jovi pushed herself up from the dirt, shook her head to clear it, and found herself face to face with two rabid hyenas. One of them gave a low, excited whoop.

She scrambled up and ran for her life.

Her boots flew over the earth. Half of the clearing was on fire now, but she ran toward the blazing trees, fear giving her speed.

Something slammed into her back. She hit the ground hard, breath whooshing out of her as her face smashed into a carpet of crispy demon carcasses. Savage claws sliced into her calves. She screamed. The claws sank into her flesh, dragging her backward over the stinking, slippery ground, toward the smoking hellmouth.

True terror shot through her. *Oh, fuck, no. No, no, no…*

She scrabbled and flailed, trying to flip onto her back so she could blast them with fire, nail them with her boot dagger, something, anything. But the claws were too deep, shredding her muscles as she flopped on her belly like a fish. She snatched a dagger from her belt loop and stabbed blindly backward, hitting something soft and hairy. There was a yelp. Jovi stabbed again, wildly, screaming, clawing at the ground with her free hand, ripping her fingernails. But the landscape rushed away from her, the blazing trees receding as the hyena pulled her back, back, back.

Bucking and twisting madly, she willed her entire body to

light up with flame. But it didn't, it wouldn't. She didn't have enough juice, and it was dragging her so fast, back to the pit, back to hell, back to her mother. She couldn't go back. She wanted Rogan. She couldn't go back—

The whiz of a phaser shot past her ear. One of the hyenas tumbled lifelessly to the ground, but the other's claws were still deep in her muscles, dragging her across the dirt.

An ear-splitting roar reverberated through the clearing. There was a blinding pain in her legs, and they were suddenly free. The second hyena sailed through the air, knocked loose by a massive paw. Jovi flipped onto her back just as Killian Diallo, in full lion form, landed overtop of her. His legs straddled her body, bringing her eye level with an impressive lion penis.

She scuttled backward, sliding out from beneath Killian's furry belly, leaving smears of bright blood on the ground. Crispy bugs crunched under her palms like dried leaves. *Away, get away, away from the hole...*

Suddenly, she flew backward through the clearing, zooming into the trees to land on her ass next to Cyrus. His handsome, dark face dripped with sweat. Pale blue eyes darted around the clearing like he was on Blitz, while giant rocks and lifeless bodies flew across the battlefield with every flick of his hand.

He ducked as something sailed over his head, swore, and then sank to one knee beside Jovi. He shoved a palm toward the sky. A shimmering bubble appeared around them, abruptly cutting off all sound.

Her ragged panting was suddenly deafening in her ears. A second later, two dark bodies rammed into the bubble, bouncing off noiselessly.

"Can you heal yourself?" Cyrus gritted between clenched teeth, a hand braced overhead.

Jovi shook her head. "It takes time. Fuck." She heaved herself to a sitting position and gasped at the excruciating pain in her legs. Blood soaked the dirt beneath her. She didn't know if she could walk.

"Shit," Cyrus said, as more bodies collided with the shield. Jovi shoved another candy necklace in her mouth, breathed deeply through her nose, and tried not to pass out while the battle raged silently outside their cocoon. Killian swatted and roared in his massive lion form, a huge white wolf tore into demon flesh with frenzied abandon, and further away, a sleek black jaguar sailed through the air, taking out three demons at once with one flying sweep of her claws. She landed in a somersault, vaulted off a tree, and went back for more.

Rogan's face appeared against the shield. He pounded a silent palm against it, whirled to fire his phaser, then pulled the pin of a grenade with his teeth and lobbed it into the air. He chucked a throwing knife sideways, instantly followed it with another, then pivoted to pummel a pair of goblinish things with a flurry of fists and feet. They dropped to the ground. He shot them each in the head, banging his palm backward against the shield again.

Holy fuck, he was magnificent.

Cyrus groaned savagely, splitting the bubble with one hand until Rogan fell inside. He slammed the force field up again, his face dripping with the exertion.

Rogan's face was grim. "There are too many."

"No shit," Cyrus shot back.

Rogan turned his blazing eyes on Jovi. "I need your medallion." And before she could even open her mouth, he'd reached into the collar of her shirt and pulled the amulet out by its chain.

"Archangel Michael, I summon you!" Rogan bellowed. He slammed both hands around the metal disc.

A blast of white light exploded from between his palms. The protective bubble of the shield charm vanished as they were all blasted apart. Rogan and Cyrus each landed on one knee like a pair of superheroes. Jovi landed on her ass, blinking into the blinding light.

An enormous man stood with his back to her, towering and radiant, almost blinding in the gloom. Trailing between his shoulder blades was a pair of colossal white wings.

Every single fiber of her being lit up in awe, terror…and a deep, primal recognition she couldn't begin to explain.

Angel.

The angel strode across the clearing, the earth shuddering with every step. He drew a gigantic sword, the metal ringing like a bell as he pulled it from its sheath. The sword flashed as he swept through wave after wave of hellspawn, graceful as a dance, parting them like water, obliterating them into nothing. His glimmering white robes billowed behind him, brilliant in the smoky shadows.

He reached the hellmouth and whispered something over the belching pit. It carried across the clearing, cutting through the cacophony of the battle. The language made Jovi's heart clench, made her skin crawl, made the amulet buzz violently against her chest.

A deafening shriek erupted from the portal. The angel raised his sword high over his head and brought it crashing down, slicing deep into the ground. A blast wave radiated outward, undulating the earth, shaking the corpses, knocking everyone off balance. And then, with a final sinister hiss, the gaping hole sealed shut, until only wisps of smoke curled from the charred ground, trailing upward to the slowly lightening sky.

Jovi was so busy staring at the angel that she barely registered the squad as they finished off the few demons that remained. The angel turned, an expression of pure triumph on his perfect, breathtaking face. Diamond white eyes landed on Jovi.

His beautiful face twisted, morphing into something monstrous. "*You!*" He stretched a huge hand toward her, and though he was across the clearing, Jovi felt his fingers close around her neck. Her breath cut off, her ass left the ground, and she was suddenly dangling in midair, clutching her throat while her boots kicked furiously. Her heart threatened to beat out of her chest. The raw fury on the angel's face was more terrifying than anything that had come out of that hellmouth.

"Wait!" Rogan's voice cut through the pounding in her ears. "She's with us!"

"She is with *them*." The angel's fingers tightened, and Jovi felt something in her windpipe pop. Her eyes bulged.

"Please. It's her medallion that summoned you!"

The angel's brows slashed. "Where?"

"It's on her. I'll show you." Rogan held up a hand, panic flashing across his face. "Please."

Jovi flew backward, her back slamming into a tree. Pain exploded up her spine. Her throat was suddenly released from the phantom grip, and she coughed, eyes watering, as the angel's earth-shaking strides brought them face to face.

He glowed with shimmering internal light and smelled like sunshine on skin. Golden hair framed a stunningly beautiful face, but his perfect features were warped in contempt as he studied her. He hooked a finger beneath the chain around her neck, pulling the amulet from beneath her shirt. Shock flooded the angel's face. "Alistor?"

Jovi's heart leaped. "That's my father," she croaked. "Do you know him?"

The angel's eyes flashed up to meet hers. "*Father*?"

Jovi nodded, her mind whirling. Her throat ached, but she talked through the pain. "I'm trying to find him. She said it was his." She could feel blood trickling down her torn calves.

"She?" It was a harsh whisper.

"My mother."

"Your mother." His eyes raked over her, lips curling with disgust. "She is the one known as Inara?"

How did he know that?

Over the angel's massive shoulder, she saw the squad gathered close, battered, bleeding, and stunned. Standing in front of them all, Rogan stared at her with something close to horror.

Jovi tore her eyes away from him, met the angel's savage gaze, and nodded.

CHAPTER 49

No.

No, no, no.

It couldn't be. She couldn't be.

Succubus.

Rogan fought the bile that rose in his throat, the denial trying to burst from his lips. He'd trusted her. Thought he loved her.

Succubus.

His chest was splitting in two, like someone was trying to pry it apart with a crowbar. Voices rose and fell, but he couldn't understand them over the roaring in his head. His team brushed past, approaching the tree where Jovi was pinned, soot-smudged and bleeding, pink hair tangled in the rough bark. Her eyes, the slanted crystal blues he'd lost himself in so many times, burned into his own, glimmering with unshed tears. She shook her head pleadingly.

See me, she mouthed.

As the crowbar pried his chest further apart, Rogan took one step back.

She was an excellent actress. The pain that slashed across

her face, the tears that rolled down her cheeks to pool in the corners of her trembling mouth—it was all very convincing.

He was a goddamn fool.

The roaring in his ears grew louder. Her struggles, her cries, her curses were muffled as the Demon Eradication unit surrounded their target. The archangel waved a hand, and Jovi's chin dropped abruptly to her chest. The angel jerked Alistor's medallion off her neck, taking a few strands of pink along with it. He thumped it fiercely to his chest, then nodded at John.

John stepped forward, ready to teleport the capture back to the lab. Because that was protocol. Because the Magistrate and ARC would absolutely want her.

But John's hand hesitated, hovering over Jovi's arm. He shot a concerned glance toward Rogan. His entire team looked at him. The roaring in his head faded into utter, suffocating silence. And Rogan did something he had never, ever done in the field.

He turned his back on the demon and walked away.

CHAPTER 50

Well, this bitch could hit.

Pain exploded in Jovi's cheek, her head whipping to the side as Juno's fist connected with her jaw. The next instant, claws raked her chest, slicing through her shirt. Scarlet blood splashed into the pool of water at the bottom of the cold white cell.

Holy Water, several inches deep. The bottom of the cell was flooded—she'd woken to find herself shackled to the tile wall, suspended a few inches above the water line. And Juno must've dunked her claws in the shit because the welts in Jovi's chest howled with pain. She blew her hair out of her face. "You're just ruining your own shirt, you know."

"I've got more. Why did you fuck with Rogan?" The jaguar was in her voice.

The gashes in Jovi's chest throbbed. Her stupid heart throbbed, too, at the thought of Rogan somewhere, letting them torture her. But what the fuck did she expect?

That soft heart is going to make you suffer one day.

Stupid, stupid girl.

A booted foot cracked her cheekbone, spraying Holy Water from the leather toe. The droplets stung Jovi's cheek, but they didn't feel like they were burning a hole in her face, so that was a bonus. She spat blood. Her lip hurt. Her heart hurt.

"Why?" Juno repeated.

"What do you mean, why? Are you blind?"

Juno halted, one leg raised in preparation for another roundhouse kick, her shin parallel to the water. She should have looked ridiculous. Instead, she looked like a coiled water snake, dark and deadly and ready to strike. "Excuse me?"

Jovi rolled her eyes. "He's gorgeous. I'm sure you've noticed, even if he does say you're like a sister." She winced as a drop of water ran into her eye. "Maybe I just couldn't keep my paws off him, ever think of that?"

"It was information, wasn't it? That's why you targeted him."

"I didn't fucking *target* anybody. You assholes were the ones who put a trackband on me and threw me in WITPRO with him!"

Juno leaned in. Her eyes glowed green, her pupils eerily vertical. "That man is closed tighter than a steel trap. He *made* this unit. This job was his life. And you got him to break every one of his own fucking rules and reveal top secret information in less than *a week*. What I want to know is what you're planning to do with it."

She was right. Mommy Dearest could do some major damage with intel like this. She'd already figured out how to possess shapeshifters, and if Jovi had to guess, was probably planning to turn the packs against each other, forcing them to slaughter their own people. It was the kind of thing Inara loved—manipulation, mind games. Watching them destroy themselves would give her no end of pleasure.

Juno kicked an arc of Holy Water over her. The cool wetness morphed into an agonizing burn, and Jovi swore. She didn't mean anything to these people. Even after fighting alongside them and healing Rogan's ass more times than she could count, they didn't give a shit who she was. Only what she was.

I don't even know what the hell you really are.

He didn't see her at all.

She hadn't known it was possible to hurt this much, and she'd grown up in hell.

Deep inside, some ugly, vengeful part of her whispered that it would be very satisfying to hurt him back.

She raised her eyes to Juno. The female frowned, then started hissing something in Latin. Apparently, Jovi was immune to Latin—the words didn't do anything. But the split second of fear in those green eyes did.

The jaguar was scared shitless about what Jovi could do to her family.

And just like that, all the fight went out of her. Her head dropped. She was so tired. "He didn't tell me anything."

Juno stilled. "What?"

"He didn't say anything about you guys, okay? He didn't breach confidentiality. He didn't say anything."

"We know he did." Her eyes narrowed. "We were there for a big fucking part of it."

Jovi looked straight into that freaky feline gaze. "He didn't tell me anything. Got it?"

She was such an idiot. After everything, she still fucking loved him.

CHAPTER 51

Rogan jolted at the knock on the door, but his head didn't leave his hands. He waited for whoever it was to fuck off.

No such luck.

The door swung open, and the scent of black cherry wafted in. "Jesus fuck, Rogan." Theo wrinkled her nose as she looked around the room he'd been given at Light House. Clothes and empty bottles littered the tiny drop-leaf table in the corner, while cheap burrito wrappers and soup cartons drew flies in the sink. Rogan sat shirtless and unwashed on the loveseat in the dim light, a bottle of vodka dangling from his fingers. Plasma glass from the shattered television screen littered the carpet across from him.

A coffee mug was thrust under his nose. A bit of steaming liquid sloshed over the rim, splashing onto the crotch of his sweatpants. Rogan jerked back and scowled up at Theo. She glared down at him, mug in one hand and silver vape pen in the other.

"I don't have an espresso machine, princess, it's just coffee. But I did the enchantment myself. Snap-The-Fuck-Out-Of-It spell. Extra strength."

Rogan waved her off. She didn't budge, just shoved the scalding mug against his chest, forcing him to take it. When he did, she marched over to the window and whipped back the curtains.

Rogan squinted. "Get out of here, Theo." His voice was gravel.

"*You* get out of here. You haven't left for a week. Your team keeps calling. People are starting to ask me if you're dead."

He set the coffee mug aside, taking a swig from the vodka bottle instead. It burned going down. If only it would numb him. "They're not my team anymore. Now just…fuck off."

Theo snatched the bottle out of his hands.

Anger was a sudden, animalistic thing inside him. "Theo, I'm warning—"

She slapped him upside the head.

Hot, boiling rage erupted within him, and he was on his feet before he realized he'd moved. A blast of arctic cold knocked him back. Thick ropes of ice appeared from thin air, encircling him, wrapping him tight. Razor-shape ice crystals bit into his skin, and he struggled like a lunatic in a straitjacket.

"Look at yourself." Theo's breath frosted in the air.

The more Rogan fought, the tighter the icy bonds held him. He stopped struggling, let his head drop back, breathing through his nostrils as he stared at the ceiling. His chest pumped. The ropes burned.

"What the hell happened?"

Rogan gazed mutinously at the water-stained ceiling tiles. "I told you. They kicked me out."

"Why?"

"I broke the rules."

"What rules?"

"Confidentiality. Among others." His neck ached. He lowered his head. "Let me go."

She didn't. "Isn't it *your* team?"

"Not anymore." The raw, gaping hole inside his chest throbbed.

She watched him, just stood there watching while he bled out in front of her, while he suffocated, drowning in his own disgrace. "It's more than the job, though, isn't it?" Theo scanned the filthy room. "Is it a woman?"

Rogan closed his eyes.

"Ah, it is." He heard a thunk as she set the vodka bottle down. "What happened? Did she get in the way of the job?"

Rogan swallowed. Hard. He still couldn't manage to clear the lump that had lodged itself in his throat a week ago. "She lied."

A pause. "Okay. How so?"

The burn of her freezing ropes gave him something to focus on. It took his mind off things like humiliation, betrayal, the weight of his weapons being stripped from him while his squad watched…the disappointment in the eyes of the man who had given Rogan everything.

"What did she lie about?" Theo pressed.

"Who she is. What she is." Visions flashed across his memory—her stunning body undulating beneath him, her brilliant smile the first time she'd healed him.

Succubus. Succubus. Succubus. The word had been hammering through his brain for a week, and all the vodka in the world couldn't drown it out.

"I don't get it."

"You don't need to fucking get it. She lied. Made me think I—made me think she…" He bit off the rest. "She lied."

Theo snorted. "And you never lie."

Rogan glared at her.

"Did she—" Theo waved her hands. "—have a good reason to lie?" When he was stubbornly silent, Theo cocked her head. "Huh. Maybe she did."

Christ, she was pissing him off. "Whose side are you on?"

She blew a cloud of vape at him. He screwed up his face against it, struggling against the icy binds. "I'm just calling you on your bullshit, Agent Rogan. Did she apologize?"

He saw Jovi pinned against that tree, her eyes pleading with him.

"Did you even give her the chance?" Theo continued. When he didn't say anything, she laughed humorlessly. "Imagine that."

"You don't know what the hell you're talking about. Let me go." He wrenched against the freezing ropes.

"No. You're fucking unstable. I've never seen you like this." She gestured to the filthy room. "You're day drinking, eating junk? This place is disgusting." She leaned in. "And I think you were about to hit me a minute ago."

He deflated like a pricked balloon. The hole in his chest ached. "Fuck. I'm sorry."

She eyed him beadily. "It's fine. You made a mistake. Even Nash Rogan isn't perfect."

Shame turned to fury in a split second, and he felt his lips curl back from his teeth. Shit, was this how Killian felt? Hairtrigger all the time? He felt a stab of pain at the thought of his now-ex-comrade. "Fuck off."

Theo's silver eyes glinted. "Touched a nerve, huh?" She moved closer, stabbing a finger at him. "Got news for you, buddy. Nobody's perfect. Not even you." She raised her scarlet brows and stepped back before flicking a hand. His limbs were suddenly free. "So, your girl lied. You lie all the time, you fucking hypocrite. I don't even know what you really do, after all these years. I know it's more than you tell me."

He smothered a twinge of guilt.

"Did she do it on purpose? To hurt you?"

Succubus. Succubus. Succubus. The word pounded through his brain, but behind it, deep down, some tiny, truthful part of him whispered, *No.*

Theo sighed. "These kids lie all the time, too." She looked around at the walls like she could see her students through the plaster. "Mostly because they're scared. They finally found some love here and they're afraid to lose it." She cast another look around the trashed room. "Jesus, she really messed you up."

Rogan collapsed onto the sofa and dropped his head into his hands, digging his palms into his eyelids to shut out the light. The darkness was no relief. It was fathomless, endless. Suffocating.

He'd known pain before, when Dad died, when Mom spiraled into Blitz and men and left him an orphan long before her body left the earth. This was a different pain, a different darkness—deeper, blacker. He wasn't sure he could climb out of it. Hell, he wasn't even sure he wanted to.

And where the hell did that leave him?

The words fell out of him in a whisper. "I don't know what to do."

Theo stepped closer. She lifted his chin, forcing him to meet her eyes. "Listen. I know you like everything to fit into a nice little box, but not everything does. *Nothing* in this world is black and white. Not you, not me, not your girl. People make mistakes. People fuck up. People lie. Does that make them bad people? Down to the core?" She snatched the vodka bottle off the end table again. "Everyone's got a little devil in them. Doesn't make them a demon."

The same words she'd uttered two weeks ago hit him like a battering ram. Visions of Jovi bombarded him—sticking her tongue out at him, glowing like a nightlight as she healed an army of lion shapeshifters, passed out on his chest after dragging him from a wrecked car.

Succubus.

Theo cast another glance around the room, shaking her head on her way out the door. "Figure it out. And clean yourself up, for fuck's sake. This is embarrassing."

Succubus...

His phone chimed. Feeling like he'd just been brained by a two-by-four, Rogan dug for his Eclipsa under a pile of junk food wrappers. Chips, processed meat sticks, snack cakes—he'd had a gut ache for a week. It was nothing compared to the rest of him.

The Magistrate's private number blared at him from the screen.

Rogan's heart jolted as he swiped to answer. "Hello?"

"Nash. Are you well?"

He had no words. The Magistrate's cool voice was like a balm to his injured soul. He could picture his gentle smile, could almost smell his distinctive salve, so pungent, so familiar. The scent of a savior, offering an orphan a home, offering a man a purpose.

The Magistrate cleared his throat. "I won't mince words. We have a proposition for you."

"Sir?" Rogan almost tripped over the word.

"I'm sure you've guessed that we have been interrogating the latest capture." He paused. "We have been...unsuccessful."

Rogan's pulse beat like a jackhammer in the silence.

"Based on what it's said, we feel that you may be more effective."

Rogan's heart stopped entirely. "What did she say?"

A small sigh. "The demon claims you never mentioned your work with the DE. That it knew you were an agent assigned to its WITPRO case and nothing more." The slightest throat clearing. "Of course, we know this is a lie."

She was protecting him. He knew it with bone-deep certainty. How many times had he told her he could get in trouble for disclosing this information? And now, she was lying under torture, telling them he hadn't breached confidentiality when his entire squad knew the truth?

As Rogan's heart roared back to life inside his chest, the

Magistrate's voice softened. "The squad is not the same without you, Nash. We want you back. *Need* you back. I can do this for you. Bring you back, full rank restored. But first, you must interrogate the demon that calls itself Jovi."

Every cell in his body lit up in violent, electric rebellion.

"You've always been such an example of loyalty to the cause. All I ask is that you prove your loyalty once again. Interrogate the demon, and then eliminate it. Like any other."

In a sudden, vibrant burst, the word that had been pounding through his brain all week was sledgehammered aside by a new one.

Angel.

Pure, undiluted sunshine exploded within him, and he suddenly found himself on his feet, heart hammering. The Magistrate's questioning voice broke through the buzzing in his ears. "Sir, I would ask you to reconsider."

A slight pause. "To reconsider?"

"Jovi. She can be an asset." The words spilled out and he couldn't stop them, didn't want to stop them. They were the words he'd been choking on for days. "She's more than what she seems. I think—"

"She is a demon, Nash. The spawn of a succubus."

"And an angel."

It rang through him like a bell. In a rush, he was back in the dark cave, feeling the warmth of her healing light. Back in the humid jungle, watching her suffer through her own wound so she could tend to others. Back on the rooftop under a full moon, staring into her blue eyes while she demanded he stop doubting himself.

A shocked silence. "And you think that makes her any less evil?"

"She's not evil." It shot out of him, angry and sharp.

Another stunned silence.

Rogan raked a hand through his hair, his brain whirling. "Sir, she's not perfect, but she's not evil. She's a healer. She's a fighter, too, but she doesn't hurt anyone who doesn't deserve it. And she is extremely effective in combat. She can see demons without a lens—"

"Because she *is* one, Nash." The Magistrate scoffed. "Son, I understand that some things transpired between the two of you, and I'm willing to overlook this lapse in judgment." His tone became deliberate, like he was trying to explain a simple concept to an imbecile. "Because she is a succubus, and that's what those creatures do. But you must admit that's what she is. A *demon*. Nothing more."

But she was more. She was so much more.

She was everything, and he was a fool.

Rogan's hand tightened on his phone. "Sir. Please. I've given my entire life to MLE. I rarely ask for anything. Just give me a chance. Let me show you she's a good person—"

"*Demon*, Nash."

"She's different. Let me prove it to you. Please." His heart thundered into the long, palpable silence.

"I can see there's no reasoning with you," the Magistrate said finally. "This breaks my heart, Nash. I thought what we had meant more to you. I thought you were better."

The line went dead.

Rogan stared at his phone.

One. Two. Thr—

He was getting her out.

CHAPTER 52

Theo glanced up from her tablet as Rogan strode into her cramped office. A scarlet brow arched. "Out of the dungeon?" She looked back to her screen. "You still smell like one."

"I need your help."

Her gaze sharpened on him. "I don't think I've ever heard those words come out of your mouth." She set her tablet on the desk. "What is it?"

"I need to break a prisoner out of MLE."

Stunned silence. "Would this prisoner, by chance, be your girl?"

Pleasure shot through him. *His girl.* "Yes."

"I'll be damned." Hinges creaked as she leaned back in her old office chair. "What'd she do?"

"Nothing." The truth of it rang out of him, buoying his chest, strengthening his resolve.

"Mmm." Silver eyes glinted. "If you say so, I believe you. And you know I'm not MLE's biggest fan." She shook her wrist irritably, her trackband flashing. "Those holding cells are no joke, though."

"It's not a regular cell, it's a special holding cell in the Magistrate's lab."

Her brows shot to her hairline. "Lab?"

"Top secret, highly confidential, heavily secured." His toe tapped inside his boot. "We'll need help."

Theo blinked. "You're serious, aren't you?"

He nodded.

She stared at him for so long, he thought he might burst out of his skin. "Let me see who's up for getting arrested."

Rogan released a breath as Theo reached for her phone and sent a text. "Meet me at the gym in twenty. Kids will be at lunch." She tossed her phone down, stabbing a finger toward him. "Go take a damn shower. And you'd better have a plan."

———

Twenty minutes later, Rogan was showered, caffeinated, and standing in the Light House's vast gymnasium, where students trained in physical fitness, hand-to-hand combat, and offensive and defensive spells. Cracked vinyl mats covered the walls all the way to the ceiling, where long, knotted ropes hung from exposed beams. Racks of balls and training dummies lined the back wall, and in front of Rogan stood four of the most powerful mages in the city—on their school lunch break.

Ulric Ungar, the basic magic instructor, squinted at Rogan with eyes that were sharp despite his advanced age. He stabbed the end of his walking stick into the floor. "What the hell is this about?" His voice was like an old car trying to start.

"Theo said something about breaking into MLE?" Solara York raised a dark brow. A bright scarf held her trademark halo of curls back from her striking, mahogany-skinned face. Half mage, half human, and undisputed genius, Solara was responsible for creating the trackband's first prototype. She left MLE shortly after.

Rogan took a breath. "Yes. They're holding someone prisoner there. I need your help to get her out."

"Why?"

"They're holding her without just cause."

"Are you sure, my friend?" Israel Stroud folded his arms. "MLE is everything to you."

"Was everything," Rogan corrected.

"MLE are a bunch of dicks." Ulric spat on the shining wood floor. He flicked a gnarled hand, and the spit vanished.

"The woman they're holding has done nothing wrong. They're torturing her." Rogan's stomach clenched. He blinked once, hard, to clear the image of Jovi being interrogated by his own team. "Likely until they kill her."

A flicker of momentary shock went through them.

"Bunch of dicks." Another spit.

"I don't want to hurt anyone, but I'm getting her out," Rogan continued. "I need you to trust me. She's...Other. But she's not evil, and she's done nothing wrong. I would owe you."

"Deal," Ulric said instantly. "You had me at *break in to MLE*." He wore a toothy grin. "And Mr. Nash Rogan owing me a favor is nothing to sneeze at."

Rogan nodded and looked over at Solara, whose expression was dark. "Is White behind this?"

"It's his top-secret program, yes."

"But he's the one doing this, right?" Her mouth was tight. "Holding this woman captive, calling the shots?"

Rogan frowned. He'd never seen Solara look so...hard. "Yes."

She folded her arms and returned his nod. "I'm in. But the plan needs to be airtight."

"The children." Israel's dark eyes were intense. "Someone needs to take care of the children if this all goes to shit."

Rogan already had a plan for that. "I'll get backup in place for the kids."

Israel nodded, and gratitude, relief—hope—surged through him.

"This chick better be something pretty fucking special," Theo muttered, as Rogan pulled out his hastily sketched maps.

He allowed himself a tight smile. "You have no idea."

———

Much later, in the dark quiet of his room, Rogan made a phone call.

Cyrus answered on the first ring. "Nash. Jesus, man, are you alive?"

"I need a favor."

He could almost hear Cyrus running a palm over his shaved head, the way he did when he was stressed. "Aw, man, don't do this to me—"

"I need your word that all of you will take over Light House, if necessary."

A sharp silence. "What are you doing, Nash?"

"I need your word. Promise me, Cyrus. It's the last thing I'll ask of any of you."

"What the hell are you doing, Nash?"

"This isn't about me, it's about the kids. Promise me."

"Fine. Yes. We won't leave the kids hanging. Now, what are you—"

"You'll always be my brother." Rogan hung up.

CHAPTER 53

Ulric, out of everyone, was the best at glamor charms. "Hot tamale," the old man muttered, his bony hand hovering inches from Rogan's face. They were in Israel's quarters, an apartment at the back of Light House with an exterior door that would allow them to slip out unnoticed. Exotic rugs and throws covered almost every surface, and trinkets and artifacts from mysterious places crowded the shelves. The entire place smelled faintly of incense. The undercurrent of magic in the air was strong enough to make Rogan's blood buzz.

Theo came into view, rolling her eyes. "You can't make him hot, Ulric. The idea is to blend in." She smoothed her own hand in front of Rogan's face. A tingling sensation followed her palm. "There."

"He doesn't have to be a dog!"

"He's not a dog. He's just not a goddamn supermodel!" Theo flicked her scarlet braid over her shoulder, considering Rogan's face. "Perfectly average. Not pretty, not ugly." She pursed her lips and waved her hand over his chest. "Tits need to be smaller, though."

Rogan ground his molars as his pecs prickled.

"There." Theo stepped back to Ulric's side. Their heads tilted in unison as they admired their work.

Enough. Rogan waved them off, heading for the full-length mirror resting against the wall. An extremely average-looking woman stared back at him. His tacticals bagged shapelessly on his new female frame. Plain brown hair, neutral skin tone, no features of note. Ulric and Theo appeared behind him.

Rogan nodded, and the woman in the mirror did, too. "I'll need a standard-issue uniform shirt."

They all frowned at his deep voice.

"Well, I've got the uniform, but the voice is a different story." Solara closed the door behind her as she entered with a large bag in one hand. "Can't glamor a voice."

The others murmured in agreement. Ulric scratched his whiskered cheek. "Songbird charm?" He waved a hand over Rogan's throat, muttering to himself. "Say something."

"Hellooo," Rogan said. It came out as a resonant, vibrating baritone note, as if he'd sung the word instead of speaking it.

Ulric swore, while Theo snorted with laughter. Shaking his head, Ulric waved his hand over Rogan's throat again. "There."

"Hello." This time, Rogan's voice was soft, higher pitched, and distinctly feminine. "I'm Agent Anderson, I'm new."

"Perfect. Now, go get changed." Solara reached into the bag, threw an MLE uniform shirt at him, and distributed business-casual clothes to the others.

When Rogan reemerged, dressed in a standard-issue shirt but still wearing his own tactical pants, the others were gathered around Israel's small kitchen table. Solara had spread out comms and other tech, fast-acting nutrient gel packs, and a collection of nubby, coin-sized objects Rogan didn't recognize.

"Scramblers." Solara handed one of the knobby discs to him, her expression grim. "Human tech. Still kind of underground."

Rogan examined the scrambler, raising a brow in her direction.

She sighed, untying her bright hair scarf and tossing it on the table. Her tight brown curls exploded around her head. "They mess with shapeshifter physiology, interfere with their ability to shift. At the very least, it will make them very, very uncomfortable." Maple eyes met Rogan's.

Fuck. He pocketed the scrambler and tried not to imagine being forced to fuck with Killian, Juno, and Wolf's shifting abilities. If it all went to plan, none of the squad would even be there. "Where did you get them?"

"I still have connections in the Trident." Solara didn't look thrilled about it.

"Thank you." He felt sick.

She shook her head.

Israel entered, a sheen of sweat shining on his forehead. He carried a tray piled with to-go boxes from the Light House kitchen. "Last class is done. Let me shower. Everybody should eat." He raked a glance over Rogan in his female disguise, grinned, and swept into the bathroom.

Of course Israel would think Rogan's glamor charm was funny—the bastard could change into anything he wanted, any time he wanted, with no spells necessary.

They ate, talking through their planned routes, reviewing alternates. Rogan confirmed what tech he knew to be present throughout headquarters and in the lab. They inventoried their portable charms and other assets. Solara had already talked with the other mages about the best ways to get past the security protocols.

As the others discussed tech-breaking spells, Rogan mechanically lifted his fork, chewed, and swallowed. He hadn't slept, but he was wired, buzzing from cup after cup of Theo's strong coffee. She'd added a luck charm. They were going to need it.

He tried to focus, but his mind kept snapping back to Jovi,

imagining what kind of shape she was in, what might have been done to her, what kind of medical attention she might need. The four mages with him could handle basic healing spells, but it was very possible those wouldn't be enough, that she would be too far gone.

Hold on, baby. I'm coming.

CHAPTER 54

Three o'clock. Shift change.

MLE headquarters was a swarm of activity. Agents came and went, phones rang, trackbands wailed and were silenced. Nobody noticed the four civilians entering with a solitary female agent.

The white and blue of the lobby, the indistinct chatter, the beep of the door scanners, the smell of stale coffee and glass cleaner—so familiar, and yet, somehow, so foreign. Had it really only been two weeks since he'd been there, slapping a trackband on a pink-haired pyromage? It felt like years.

MLE agents bustled about, calling to each other, in a rush to get home or hit one of the cop bars downtown. His stomach took a dive at every familiar face, but he strode purposefully to the back of the lobby, doing his best to project nonchalance.

Sweat beaded on his upper lip. Cyrus and Juno were better at this undercover shit.

He led the others toward the secured corridor at the rear of the lobby. His access code was no doubt red-listed by now, and the bogus barcode on his fake badge wouldn't actually get him anywhere, so he timed his stride to coincide with an agent exiting the corridor. The agent scanned his badge and pushed the door open into the lobby. Rogan snagged the handle and stepped to the side. The agent had his phone to his ear, barely sparing Rogan a glance as he passed. *Guess the smaller tits were a good idea.*

The five of them slipped through and headed down the corridor, lined with offices. Rogan gestured occasionally, making a show for the security cameras. They would see an unremarkable female agent giving a tour to a few important civilians. It wasn't uncommon. Headquarters' impressive union of magic and tech drew a lot of high-status visitors, and the Magistrate liked showing it off.

They rounded a corner at the end of the hall and came to an unmarked door. The rumble of thumping bass vibrated its handle. An ID scanner blinked at them.

Rogan scanned his fake badge for the camera and gave Solara a covert nod. Her mousy blonde glamor was extremely convincing. She murmured something over his shoulder, and he tried the door handle. Nothing.

He shook his head minutely, and Solara muttered something else. Nothing.

Fuck.

As exit routes and redirection scenarios blitzed through his mind, Rogan felt a surge of energy behind him. Solara's hand, pale instead of rich mahogany, snuck around him to press against the door handle. Her urgent whisper tickled the back of his neck, and the door cracked open.

Rogan slipped inside and dropped instantly into a crouch, easing the door shut behind him.

Holomonitors glared in the darkness of the DE tech lab. Techno music pounded his eardrums, the walls practically pulsing with the incessant beat. At a long workstation in the back, Demon Eradication tech engineer, Raj Anand, sat hunched over a keyboard, his back to the door, oblivious.

Rogan scuttled along the wall, obscured by worktables,

heading straight for the shelf that housed the DE phaser cartridges. He didn't know what they might run into in the lab, and they'd stripped his watch and weapons, cutting him loose with nothing but his dad's Model B. It was a reassuring weight in his pocket, but it only had the one shot. And though it might make him the world's biggest fool, he was still saving that.

Raj suddenly jerked upright. Rogan snatched his hand away from the shelf, practically flattening himself to the floor as the man bolted out of his chair, sending it spinning. Rogan watched beneath the worktables as his sneakers raced to the far corner of the room.

He held his breath, heart thumping in time to the techno beat.

Raj's red hightops shuffled back to his workstation, kicking the chair into place. He plunked into it, holding a steaming microwave burrito.

Rogan let out a silent breath. Reaching behind him, he located the cartridges by feel and loaded his pockets until they bulged. Eyes on Raj's hunched shoulders, he crept back toward the door—and stopped short when his eyes caught sight of his MLE watch, perched on a charging dock on one of the shelves, plain as day.

They hadn't bothered to take his lens—it was useless without the watch, which was the first thing they'd confiscated. His lens was still in his eye. He'd never removed it. Habit. Hope.

He snatched the watch from the charging dock and scuttled toward the door.

The song ended. Rogan froze, not daring to move. The engineer stretched at his keyboard, groaning. A new song began to thump over the speakers. Raj rocked back in his chair, fingers laced behind his head, staring at the monitor in front of him. Rogan pried the door open with his fingertips and slipped into the hallway.

The booming bass quieted as he eased the door shut behind him. He rose, nodding at the others, who visibly relaxed. He brushed past them, strapping his watch onto his wrist.

Jesus Christ, he felt like a kid reunited with his damn security blanket. He hit the power button, waited, and nearly whimpered when the little green light flashed across his left eye.

If they ran into any uglies up there, he would be ready.

Moving down the corridor, they tried to look casual. Rogan's pockets clinked faintly with every step. The elevator loomed at the end of the hallway. He prayed it was empty. The doors slid open.

Tallia Monroe smiled brightly, a scorch mark staining her white lab coat.

Rogan's stomach dropped.

Tally shoved her glasses up her nose, hitching up the stack of books in her arms. "Going up? Me, too."

Shit. Rogan forced himself to smile, gesturing for the group to enter the little steel box ahead of him. She wouldn't recognize him. She couldn't. He was a woman.

The doors slid shut as they squeezed inside. "Floor?" Tally said.

"Second, please," Rogan replied in his female voice. Tally would likely be going to the lab, where they should be going. But a tour guide would have no business on the tenth floor. They'd go to the second, to the machining room, where the trackbands were made.

"Taking a tour?" Tally asked pleasantly as the elevator rose.

"Yes, very interesting." Israel was disguised as a middle-aged white male. He covered his accent flawlessly.

The elevator stopped, the doors opened, and they stepped out. "Enjoy!" Tally shoved her glasses up again as the doors slid together, obscuring her from view.

"We'll have to tour this floor now," Rogan muttered. They walked as quickly as they dared, which was torturously slow. Rogan gestured again for the cameras as they came to the large viewing windows outside the machining room. Huge automated bots pumped out dull silver cuffs while a bored-looking agent supervised from his stool. He straightened when they came into view, hurriedly pushing some buttons on his holomonitor and pretending to look busy.

They looped back to the elevator. Rogan made a very conscious effort to not glance up at every security camera along the way.

I'm coming, Jovi. I'm coming.

He refused to consider the idea that he was too late.

The elevator was blessedly empty this time. They watched the indicators light up with each passing floor.

"Last chance," Rogan murmured as they came to a smooth stop, his nose inches from the doors. Behind him, he heard Ulric snort, his gravelly voice odd coming out of a thirty-something Asian male.

The doors parted soundlessly. Steeling himself, Rogan led them past the main armory, the shooting range, the empty swimming pool, and the weight room. He kept his eyes forward, a mildly bored expression on his face. Giving tours of headquarters was a tedious job usually turfed to rookies. Nobody spared them more than a passing glance.

They rounded the corner to the auxiliary armory. He swiped his fake badge for the camera again while Solara whispered behind his back. He heard a click, then a swish as the doors opened. They slipped inside.

Cyrus stepped out of the access door at the rear of the armory.

Fuck.

Cyrus's eyes narrowed. He strode toward them, the vestibule doors sliding shut behind him. He was dressed for duty, and his temples gleamed with sweat. He shouldn't have been there. None of the squad should have been there. It was too early for patrol, too late to be dropping off a specimen from the night before.

Unless they were interrogating Jovi.

"What are you doing here, Agent?" Cyrus flicked a glance at Rogan's fake badge as he approached. He looked drawn, tired. His sculpted face was etched with more lines than Rogan remembered.

His heart clenched. "Tour, sir," he replied.

Cyrus frowned. "We don't tour the aux armory." Sharp blue eyes swept each one of them.

"Sorry," Rogan said quickly. "I'm new. First time." He gestured to the group. "Let's head back down." They turned, heading toward the armory doors. *Goddamn it.*

Nash?

Rogan's stride faltered for a split second. Cyrus's voice in his head—so familiar, so missed, and so not what he needed right now. He pictured a brick wall, trying to blank his thoughts. Jovi was counting on him.

"Hey," Cyrus called out sharply to Rogan's retreating back.

Shit.

"Hey!"

He couldn't believe he was doing this. *I'm sorry.*

Rogan nodded at Theo. She flicked a finger, and there was a strangled sound behind him, followed by the heavy thump of a body hitting the floor. Rogan couldn't bring his chicken-shit self to turn around, but he knew Theo had probably bound and gagged Cyrus with her icy ropes. They wouldn't freeze the most dangerous part of him, though—his mind.

Ulric whispered something, then repeated it more forcefully. "He's out. Tough sonofabitch."

"He probably sent out a telepathic alert." Rogan felt ill. "We need to be fast." He spun, trying not to see Cyrus stiff and unconscious on the fucking floor, and headed for the vestibule doors.

"We can use him." Solara's voice was quiet.

Rogan's heart turned to lead. He clenched his jaw, staring at the doors that would take them to the lab, knowing what it would take to get past the security clearances. Knowing she was right.

It wouldn't hurt Cyrus, but it would make him feel fucking violated.

Rogan turned and met Israel's disturbed gaze, somehow coming out of a white male's face. Israel had known Cyrus for years, sparred with him in the training center like everyone else. "Are you very sure about this?"

Rogan wanted to puke. "Do it."

"You'll explain later." It wasn't a request. Rogan nodded.

Israel bent to lay a gentle hand on Cyrus's cheek, and the average-looking white guy melted into the ebony-skinned male model that Rogan loved like a brother. Israel rose smoothly and rolled his—Cyrus's—wide shoulders. It hurt to look at him.

"*Occulo*," Ulric muttered, and Cyrus's unconscious body disappeared from view.

Jesus. Knocking someone unconscious and then turning their entire body invisible took serious power. It was damn impressive, but Rogan didn't know how long Ulric could hold it. He moved around the armory, handing out weapons, grabbing anything that might be useful.

They stepped around the space where Cyrus's body lay invisible and headed for the vestibule. Rogan's heart threatened to beat out of his ribcage as he made sure everyone was out of range of the scanner. He motioned Israel forward, pointing to his watch. Israel held his wrist up to the scanner. It cleared. Standing to the side, Rogan pointed at his eyes, then at the retinal scanner. Israel stepped forward, and the narrow beam drifted over Cyrus's pale blue eye. The door slid sideways into the wall. They all squeezed inside, jostling each other, grunting, stepping on each other's toes. It might've been funny if he wasn't so close to losing his shit.

He waited until the door whispered shut, then pointed at Cyrus's watch again. Israel swiped it over the second reader. It cleared.

Rogan pushed Israel up to the full facial scanner, sharply motioning for the others to duck out of range. They all sank into a crouch. The blue beam passed over the high, carved cheekbones, the straight nose and full lips, the strong jaw that Rogan had cracked once while sparring.

"Agent Cyrus Aurelian, *periculo pulchritudo*," Rogan whispered to Israel, praying he'd spoken quietly enough. The Latin for *dangerous beauty* was so Cyrus—charming, unexpectedly intelligent, and cocky as hell, which was why Rogan knew his passcode at all. The smug bastard had shared it with him after one too many beers.

Shame coiled in his gut at his own betrayal.

Israel repeated the words in Cyrus's smooth voice. The pronunciation was so perfect it sounded native.

A red light appeared on the scanner. *Fuck.*

He glanced at Rogan, still crouched with the others. "Not so perfect," Rogan whispered.

Israel turned back to the scanner and repeated the phrase, easing up on the accent, sounding a little less like an ancient fucking Roman. The red light turned bright blue, and the door slid into the wall. Rogan squinted against the abrupt surge of light, the smell of disinfectant and formaldehyde both caustic and familiar.

At a nearby surgical table, Tallia Monroe straightened with a scalpel in her hand. Her hazmat hood was pushed back, her blonde hair coming loose from its low knot. The demon on the table looked like some sort of multi-headed vulture. Tally's eyes widened behind her glasses.

"Uh, Agent Aurelian, what are you doing? These people don't have clearance—"

Ulric stepped forward, a small, smiling Asian man holding out placating hands. He muttered something, and Tally winced, bringing a hand to her temple. Ulric repeated the word, and Tally shook her head as if she'd taken a blow. As her soft brown eyes cleared, she focused sharply on Ulric.

Even as his heart panged at the idea of hurting her, Rogan cursed inwardly. Tally might be an accident-prone Anomaly, but she was the furthest thing from stupid. Her exceptional mind had gotten her there, and now, it was proving tough for Ulric to break.

Ulric hissed another word, more harshly this time. "*Tranquilium*."

Tally frowned, blinked, then swayed. Rogan darted forward, catching her by the shoulders. He eased her into one of the chairs near the surgical table. Peering into her familiar face, he saw that her eyes were glazed, but she was conscious.

"I'm sorry," Rogan whispered, making sure she wasn't likely to fall over before releasing her.

Solara and Theo were already waving their hands over the walls, scanning for security spells. Rogan pulled what looked like a hockey puck from his pocket, set the round disc in the center of the room, and hit the tiny switch on its side. A beam of white light burst from the top of it, hit the ceiling, and bloomed into a blade of light that swept over the entire room. Every bit of tech glowed electric blue. His own pants were lit up like a neon sign, all the toys in his pockets shining through the black fabric. He met Solara's eyes, directing her to sweep one side of the lab while he inspected the other.

Most of the tech was standard and benign, but he knew the Magistrate would have beefed up security after he was dismissed. He had to be sure the place wasn't rigged.

Israel had stopped at the surgical table. "What in God's name is this?"

Apparently, everything carried over when Israel assumed Cyrus's form. Clothes, watch—his lens.

Rogan met Israel's eyes and reminded himself he wasn't actually looking at his former squad mate. "Later."

As Israel gazed around the lab, a revolted understanding dawned over Cyrus's familiar features. He took in the surgical tables, the partly autopsied vulture demon, the creatures floating in the enormous tanks along one wall. "What are we rescuing, Rogan?"

"Later." He'd found something he didn't recognize, a tiny device tucked into the corner of the room. He whistled sharply through his teeth. "Got something here."

"Here, too." Solara raised her voice just enough to be heard across the room. She motioned to the others. "Get back." As the others moved away, she raised her palms and made a vast circle with her arms, muttering under her breath.

Nothing happened.

"Shit." Solara shoved back the blonde's sleeves and headed to the nearest corner, repeating the words inches from the device. Nothing. "Theo!"

Theo, disguised as a prudish brunette librarian, strode to her side. They performed the spell in unison, pushing their palms toward the tiny disc on the floor. Rogan's fingers drummed against his hip bones, his gaze drawn like a magnet to the doors that led to the holding cells. There was a pop, then a flash of light as the device burst into pieces.

"Yowch!" Theo shook out her hands. "Zinger."

"Interesting," Solara breathed. "Let's back off a bit. Disable, not destroy." She headed for the device in the next corner and leaned close like she was listening to it. She shook her head in frustration. "It's not talking to me."

Fucking mechmages. "We don't have time for this." His growl didn't have the same effect in the feminine tone.

"Smother charm?" Ulric joined the other two, and the three of them weighed the pros and cons while Rogan crawled out of his skin. He continued to scan the rest of the room, found some simple devices he disabled himself while trying to forget the sight of Cyrus's body lying on the floor of the armory, and Tally's soft brown eyes, glazed and disoriented.

There was a muffled crash behind him. His head whipped around.

Tallia's chair was empty.

Rogan swore, ducking beneath the surgical table. Tally was hunkered there, lethargic and unfocused. Her hand fell to the floor—it had been raised, touching something on the underside of the table.

An alarm button.

"*Shit*," Rogan hissed.

Tally's eyes flickered open, and she managed a smug, "Ha."

Rogan pinched the pressure point on her neck that knocked her unconscious, knowing it wouldn't last long. He slid out from under the table. "We're about to have company. Disable the other devices, *now*." He strode to the rear doors leading to the holding cells, wishing now more than ever that he was in his own body. They were out of time.

Curses sounded behind him. There was a flurry of activity, some hushed muttering, and three rapid pops as the other devices burst. Israel appeared at Rogan's side, quickly joined by the other three. Israel lifted Cyrus's watch, holding it over the scanner.

The doors parted with a whoosh and a blast of cold, sulfurous air. The mages recoiled, wrinkling their noses. Rogan pulled his phaser before swinging around the corner to get a visual.

Clear, thank Christ.

He moved quickly down the chilly corridor, his heart pounding. He squinted against the harsh light. Jovi would be in the most secure cell at the very end, if she was still there at all.

Be here. Be alive.

Israel started murmuring in another language as they continued. Rogan heard the group's footsteps falter as they slowed to read the clipboards mounted by each cell.

"What the fuck…" Theo whispered.

Rogan saw the water first, a six-inch pool flooding the final cell. He approached the bars cautiously, and his heart stopped.

Jovi was chained to the far wall, her arms and legs spread and shackled. She still wore Juno's borrowed black tacticals, but they were practically shredded, bits of fabric hanging in ragged strips. Her head hung limp, tangled pink hair obscuring her face.

Fear surged through him. He holstered his phaser and gripped the bars. "Jovi!"

She stirred, and his heart started to beat again.

"Israel!" he hissed.

Jovi raised her head, her eyelids fluttering. She looked nearly bloodless.

"Israel!" Desperation threatened to make him do something really stupid, like beat at the bars with his fists until he broke every bone in his hands. When Israel appeared at his side, he gestured to the scanner on the cell door. "It's another retinal."

Cyrus's eyes stared into his. "What are we setting free?"

Rogan fought the urge to haul him up to the scanner by his shirt. "She shouldn't be here. Trust me. *Please.*"

Israel stared into him for what felt like an eternity. Then, he stepped forward and allowed the scanner to pass over his eye.

The sound of the bolt sliding back was loud as a gunshot. Snatching the small key that hung from a hook near the clipboard, Rogan heaved the barred door aside, stepped over the iron plates, and splashed into the cell. He reached up and gently, so gently, turned Jovi's face to his.

"Jovi," he whispered. "I'm getting you out of here."

Crystal blue eyes flickered open, narrowing on his face. He stroked her cheek, wanting to press his lips to hers so badly it ached.

"Who the fuck are you?" she mumbled.

Shit. Right. "Ulric, get this goddamn glamor off of me!" He dug in his pockets for the sugar straws he'd stashed, ripped the paper tops off all of them at once, and held them to Jovi's mouth.

She pulled back. "Who are you?"

His skin prickled, his shirt got tight, and he returned to his full height, bringing his gaze even with hers. Jovi's eyes flared.

He touched her cheek, her jaw, and saw that his hands were his own again. He held the sugar straws to her lips. "Eat this." His voice was his own again, too, and he wanted to say a hell of a lot more. "We're getting you out of here."

She stared at him another moment, then opened her mouth. He tilted the sugar onto her tongue, then squeezed a gel nutrient pack into her mouth. She made a face as she swallowed.

"I know." Relief almost buckled his knees. She was here, she was alive, and she was making faces at health food. "They're bad."

He released her feet first, fury in his belly at the red marks circling her delicate ankles. The shackles were pure silver. His idea, all those years ago. The pool he stood in had to be Holy Water—his idea, too. Smothering the guilt, Rogan eased up against her, his entire body humming at being so close to her again. Keeping her pinned against the wall, he released one wrist and draped her cold arm around his shoulders, knowing her joints must be aching, the feeling rushing back to her limbs like a thousand burning needles. He hitched one of her legs around his waist and held her against him while he unlocked the final shackles.

The moment she was free, he swept her up into his arms, holding her tightly against his chest. He allowed himself a split second to turn his face into her hair, squeeze his eyes shut, and inhale her scent. "I'm sorry." His whisper was fierce. He pulled back to look into her eyes. "I *see you*. I love you."

The four disguised mages stared at them from outside the cell. Theo's mousy librarian face was slack with shock.

"Holy shit," she said. "You really do."

CHAPTER 55

He'd come for her.

The fucking bastard had come for her. And had the nerve to tell her he loved her.

And brought her sugar.

Jovi's entire body ached. She was bloody and bruised and freezing cold, and her wrists and ankles stung from the silver shackles. But her stupid heart was soaring from the feel of Rogan's strong, warm arms around her. She'd thought she was hallucinating when the uniformed brunette chick suddenly morphed into the man who had broken her heart. But he was here.

He was here.

He held her tightly as he sloshed out of the cell into the corridor. "Can you stand?"

She didn't have a clue, but she pushed at him, anyway. He lowered her cautiously, keeping one arm around her waist. The tile was icy under her bare feet—those assholes had taken her boots. She took a step, and her knee buckled like a wet noodle. Rogan caught her before she hit the floor. Irritated, she got her balance, shoved his arm away, and then turned to rummage in his pant pockets.

"There's more sugar in the lower right pocket." While she tore into the sugar straws, he pulled a pair of strappy gloves from his belt. "Amplifiers." He slipped them over her hands and cinched them tight. Some sort of techy-looking disc ended up flat against her palms.

"We need to get the hell out of here," the little Asian man snarled.

Rogan tugged her forward, but she eyed the group warily as they started toward the exit. Who were these people? And what the fuck was Cyrus doing here, busting her out? He'd tried to break into her mind a few minutes ago, and that shit hurt. A lot. Like her brain was being stabbed with a million frigid ice picks, then slowly squashed by a semi.

"It's not him."

She glanced up at Rogan. He looked like shit, his face haggard like he hadn't slept in days. "It's a glamor. It's not Cyrus. Whatever he did…we're getting you out." Pain radiated from his every pore. She felt coated with it, suffocated by his regret. "I'm so fucking sorry." He touched her face.

She wanted to jerk away. She wanted to leap into his arms. She wanted to slap him, kiss him, light his ass on fire, throw him to the floor and ride him like a seesaw, rip out his heart and stomp on it, feel it squish beneath her feet…

One thumb brushed her cheekbone, and her dumb heart thawed a bit more.

Nash fucking Rogan.

A loud bang made her jump. The demon in the cell next to them charged the bars, spitting venom. As the others yelled in confusion, Jovi pushed by, heading for the exit. Rogan caught up to her and muscled her aside as the doors parted.

And then, everything went to shit.

Shouts and flashes erupted on the other side of the doors. Rogan pulled something from his belt, chucking it into the other room. A tremendous bang and a burst of light made

Jovi cringe, and the demons in the cells behind them went ballistic—screaming, hissing, battering the bars in a frenzy.

She peered around Rogan's wide shoulders. Whatever he'd thrown into the other room had covered everything in a thick, milky fog. People were shouting, calling Rogan's name. Then, the mist parted, and she saw a sliding door.

Freedom.

Jovi bolted into the fog, narrowly avoiding the swipe of Rogan's hand. *Get out, just get out…*

The door disappeared into the mist again, but she kept running, sprinting blindly forward—until she bashed into something solid and metal, smashing her hip bone, making her gasp as pain exploded in her pelvis. Her hands moved frantically along the cool metal edge, finding her way around it. A table? She was almost grateful for something to hold on to—even with the sugar, she was in shit shape.

An animal snarl rumbled in her ear. Jovi yelped as a hard hand gripped her arm and yanked her around, bringing her face to face with a yellow-eyed Killian.

"Don't make me do this." His lion flickered under his skin, sending a surge of primal fear through her.

Jovi planted her hands on his enormous chest and blasted him.

She was close to exhaustion, but the amplifiers strapped to her palms turned her puny lighter flames into blow torches. Killian's chest hair singed and blackened, his golden skin blistering. He roared and jerked away, barely keeping hold of her arm with claws that bit into her flesh. She bellowed her own rage and tried to twist free. Somewhere in the fog, she heard Rogan's harsh yell. There was a clatter, then a high-pitched whine.

Killian's huge body jerked, spasming like he was in the throes of a seizure. His claws retracted into his skin with a sickening snap, and he staggered to his knees, teeth bared, blood dripping from the webbing between his fingers. More cries of pain sounded around the room.

Another hand gripped her arm—Rogan. He pulled her wordlessly along with him, running at a crouch through the mist, dodging tables and equipment. She was jostled against him as they ran, the phaser on his belt bumping painfully into her ribs. Her bare feet slipped on the tile, but Rogan hauled her upright and kept going, heading for the sliding door across the room.

Holy shit. He really was getting her out.

"*Purifico!*" someone shouted, and the fog vanished.

Rogan yanked her to a halt. The exit door was just a few feet away. And directly in front of it stood Magistrate Thackeray White.

CHAPTER 56

Rogan's stomach dropped.

"I cannot believe you would do this to me." The Magistrate's whisper was as loud as a scream in the sudden, taut silence. Behind his glasses, blue eyes that had always radiated warmth glittered with cold, vicious rage.

A thrill of fear raced through him, like a child who'd been caught by an angry parent. The look on his face...Rogan's fingers tightened protectively on Jovi's arm. "I'm sorry. But I told you, she's different."

The Magistrate shook his head.

Defying the man hurt. It was a visceral, physical pain like a punch to the ribs, stealing his breath. "Please, just let us go. You don't need her."

"We don't set demons *free*." The Magistrate stared at Rogan with something close to pity. "You sound just like your father."

The bottom fell out of the room.

His brain stuttered. "What?"

"He thought some of them deserved to live, too. Although he didn't *fuck* one of them."

The word rang through the room like a slap, jolting his brain into a slow, sluggish churn. "My dad wasn't a part of this..."

"Oh, he very much was. How did he tell you he lost that eye? Injured on duty, for the human police?" He let the question hang between them, then shook his head ruefully. "Those first lenses were problematic. I wasn't as strong an engineer as I thought." He smiled, small and bitter. "And he wasn't as devoted as I thought." *Like father, like son*, his expression added. "That's what got him killed, in the end."

Rogan felt his head shaking in denial, his pulse pounding in his ears. The Magistrate nodded. "Oh, yes. We ran into a couple of verbal humanoids one night, and Jim—he thought he could *reason* with them. He thought they might be..." His cold, blue eyes shifted to Jovi. "Different."

Jovi's skin heated ominously beneath his hand, but Rogan held tighter, his thoughts spinning. Images flashed across his mind—a dark alley, his dad's broad shoulders, a shadowed fight. He could almost hear the distant echo of a deep voice, calling for a ceasefire.

"And they slaughtered him," the Magistrate finished simply. "Because that's what they do."

Pain lanced through his chest, sudden and sharp. Crime scene photos bombarded him—his dad, so strong and solid, sprawled and bloody on the asphalt, his remaining eye staring blankly, one finger still curled around the trigger of his Model B. A young Thackeray White standing behind police tape, giving his statement to human police.

Clarity dawned like a sudden, brutal sun. Rogan stared at the man who'd given him everything, recalling all the times he'd given a kind word, a reassuring smile...

A quiet, comforting lie.

Bitterness coated his tongue. "You lied to me."

"I never lied." Icy eyes glinted. "You assumed. You

assumed that he died in some standard back alley scuffle, and I let you, because I needed you to trust me above all else. *I* needed to be the one who showed you this world. Couldn't have you harboring your father's doubts, could I?" The Magistrate's gaze roamed Rogan's face. "You were so perfect. All of Jim's strength, all of his determination, none of his questions...and all the longing in the world." A sudden sorrow washed over his features. "You were supposed to be better. I *made* you. And I wanted you to be better." His mouth spasmed like a kid about to cry. He looked around at the other DE members, each frozen where they stood. "Get rid of him."

A shocked silence rang out through the lab.

Juno took a step. "Sir—"

The Magistrate stabbed a finger at her, his thin chest pumping. "No. Don't make this harder. You all know the rules. You all swore an oath. He has proven that he can't be trusted." His upper lip shone with sweat, and he swiped at it with the back of his hand, his gaze bouncing between Rogan and Jovi. "That he's beyond saving."

He didn't think there was much of his heart left to break, but now, it shattered. Pain sliced through him, horror and betrayal threatening to take him to the ground.

Silken skin heated beneath his fingers. From the corner of his eye, he saw sparks erupt on Jovi's shoulder, traveling down her arm like dangerous glitter. He tried to ease her behind him, but she refused to budge.

Cyrus started forward, a hand outstretched. "Sir—"

"No." Anger flashed across the Magistrate's face, and he held up another warning finger, bringing Cyrus to a halt. "I gave him everything. I gave him a life, I gave him a position, I gave him my secrets...I let him walk away after this *egregious betrayal*!" Spittle flew from his mouth, and a lock of blond hair fell over one eye. He smoothed it into place.

Killian's low, menacing growl rumbled from across the room.

"I've been too soft." The Magistrate slashed a hand through the air, and a whip of pulsing green light appeared in his grip. The long, sinister length curled and crackled against the tile floor, humming with electricity. "I'll clean my own mess."

CHAPTER 57

Well, this fucker obviously needs to die.

Jovi launched a ball of flame right at the Magistrate's face. The amplifiers made it feel like a cannonball erupting from her hands.

The Magistrate cracked his electric whip, knocked the fireball aside, and the end of the whip caught Jovi's arm.

Agony.

Her muscles seized, her lungs stopped. As her teeth clapped together, she bit out a chunk of her tongue. The coppery taste of blood flooded her mouth. She made a choking sound, and her knees slammed to the floor, pain blossoming in her kneecaps.

Another crack echoed through the room. Shouts rang out, followed by angry cries and animal growls. A heavy weight landed beside her—Rogan, shuddering violently on his own knees, tendons straining in his thick neck.

And then, the ceiling caved in.

A deafening explosion sent Jovi flying sideways. Her back hit something solid, knocking the wind out of her. She staggered to all fours and tried to stand, her muscles quivering with the remnants of the Magistrate's electric shock.

A shaft of warm afternoon sunlight speared through the ceiling, spotlighting the slabs of concrete and the shards of glass that rained from overhead...

And the flood of demons pouring through the jagged hole in the roof.

"Theo, throw a shield!" Rogan shouted, pelting ungracefully toward Jovi. She struggled to her feet just as he snagged her around the waist and hurled her across the room. She landed on her ass several yards away, watching as a steel ceiling beam slammed to the floor where she'd stood only seconds before. Rogan stumbled back just in time.

"What the fuck!" a scarlet-haired woman hollered. She and the three other strangers huddled in a corner beneath the bubble of a shield charm. Rogan's crew, whoever they were, must've dropped their glamors.

Across the room, Wolf roared in pain. "What the fuck, I—can't—*shift*!"

"Solara, the scramblers!" Rogan yelled. "Keep that fucking shield up!"

A beautiful black woman shouted from behind the shield bubble, and something small and knobby flew out of the rubble inches from Jovi's bare foot. A second later, a terrifying series of sounds erupted from around the room—guttural snarls, a wildcat scream, an ear-splitting roar. The sounds of three deadly, pissed-off shapeshifters bursting into their animal forms.

The hair on Jovi's neck stood on end as the frenzy escalated all around her. More demons dropped through the ruined ceiling. How the fuck was this happening? She shot a fireball at one and smashed a side kick into another. The sole of her foot rang with pain. Where did those assholes stash her boots?

Something hit her behind the knees, dropping her back onto the floor. She barely managed to flip onto her back as a huge, nasty crocodile demon bore down on her, snapping its massive jaws. Jovi caught the thing in the belly with a geyser of flame. It shot to the ceiling, riding a column of fire, and crashed into an overhead light, which exploded, raining glass in glittery shards.

These amplifier things were awesome.

Jovi directed the demon over to a wall, where it smashed into the cinder blocks and dropped to the floor. A pure white wolf tore into it a moment later, hunks of scaled flesh flying.

Where was Rogan?

"What the hell is it?" The redhead in the corner bellowed again. "Rogan!"

"Don't you drop that shield!" Rogan shouted from somewhere to her left. "Jovi!"

Jovi took off in the direction of his voice, darting past the huge holding tanks lining the back of the room. She ducked under a flying fist, drove her knee into a demon's balls, and breathed fire into its face, igniting its strings of oily hair. Where was Rogan?

There he was, locked in combat with three uglies, holding them off with his expandable staff and his pure, focused rage. His uniform shirt was tight across his muscular arms and torso, sweat streamed down his face, and an angry red welt encircled his neck. He was covered in dust, splattered with black blood, and so fucking beautiful her heart almost stopped.

A skinless, skull-faced demon appeared before her, blocking her view. She firehosed it, sending it smashing into one of the enormous glass tanks at the back of the room. A big, jagged crack appeared in the tempered glass.

Uh oh.

The crack expanded rapidly.

Uh oh...

The tank exploded, unleashing a tidal wave of splintered glass and rushing water. Something huge and long slithered from the liquid in a blur of milky green.

"No!" the Magistrate's horrified shriek rang out over the cacophony. A sizzling jet of pure white electricity sailed toward the creature attempting to escape the broken tank.

Everything turned to slow motion.

Jovi's gaze followed the arc of the electric bolt to the sleek black jaguar who stood a few feet away, battling a pair of demons on the edge of the growing puddle. The cat snarled and swiped, so fast her limbs were a blur. One black paw was planted in the water.

Jovi launched herself at Juno, colliding with the mass of muscle and fur, sending them both tumbling to the ground. She rolled to her feet just as the shockwave hit the water.

The puddle lit up like lightning.

The jaguar convulsed, her powerful limbs jerking, while bones—Juno's bones—flickered beneath her pelt.

Something bellowed behind her. Jovi whirled to see an enormous gargoyle hurtling toward her, its wicked horns lowered like a charging bull. As she raised her hands to blast it, Rogan appeared from the rubble, sailing toward the demon in some kind of superhero leap. Unsheathing his dagger in midair, he landed on the gargoyle's back, stabbing it in the jugular as he rode it to the floor. Before it quit bouncing, Rogan sliced its head from its body, stepped over the corpse, and offered Jovi a hand.

She was such a fool for him.

She slid her palm into his. Dimples flashed in his cheeks.

And over his shoulder, through the gaping hole in the ceiling, her mother dropped gracefully into the room.

CHAPTER 58

Rogan spun, putting his body between Jovi and whatever had put that kind of unbridled terror into her eyes.

A stunning woman stood in the rubble. Blood-red hair fell down her back like a satin sheet, and a black reptile-skin jumpsuit hugged a tremendously tall, lush body. Her skin was pale as the moon and every bit as luminous, glowing with otherworldly light as she picked her way sinuously across the debris-strewn floor. Black eyes focused unblinkingly on Jovi, and her scarlet lips curved.

"Jovael. I've been looking for you, little one."

Inara.

The air surrounding her pulsed with silken menace as she wound her way toward them, careless of the battle raging around her. Her black eyes were as soulless as a shark's. Every nerve ending in Rogan's body went on high alert, and he tucked Jovi further behind him.

A crimson brow arched. "Oh, found yourself a strapping young man?" The corner of her mouth lifted. "You are your mother's daughter. Pity he's so mortal." She swept her hand casually, as if flicking away a fly, and Rogan went flying.

He braced himself for the crash, tucked himself into a ball, and hit the steel exit door with his shoulder. The metal rang like a gong. Rogan landed in a crouch and charged toward them, leaping over fallen bodies and wreckage, the sound of combat and the smell of charred flesh all around him. He ducked under a spiked mace and hammered his fist into a demon's chest, lighting the thing up with his electroglove. He shoved the body aside and continued, undeterred.

"I'm not coming back." The pure, undiluted fear in Jovi's voice made his heart clench, and gave his feet speed.

Inara's low laugh was the stuff of nightmares. "Oh, yes, you are. We have work to do. I'm *delighted* to see you can survive the midrealm for such an extended period of time. You look well, aside from the torture." She glanced around the lab with thinly veiled fury. "Do you see now, what these mortals are like? They care for nothing but themselves. Greed and blood and disdain for anything but their own kind." Black fire sparked at her fingertips. "You will come back to me. I have plans for you. And I want my amulet."

"It's not yours."

Rogan pulled his staff from his belt, flicked it to expand it to full length, and took out three advancing targets with one sweep. He moved on, holstering his staff and pulling his phaser.

Inara snarled as he drew close. "You again."

"Me." He nailed her with a stream of Holy Light. It hit her in the sternum, sending her stumbling backward. But she was older, stronger, and much more powerful than their usual targets. Even as he squeezed the fucking trigger for all it was worth, he knew it wasn't going to be enough.

Rogan held the trigger down anyway, and charged her.

The chaos around them faded to nothing as he jumped over a body, leaped onto an overturned surgical table, and launched himself at the bitch, unsheathing his anointed iron knife with his free hand.

He almost got her.

She leaned back, just barely enough, and his blade grazed her slender throat, leaving the smallest scratch on her luminous white skin. His body collided with hers, and they hit the ground, his phaser clattering to the floor. His knife followed, skittering out of reach.

Inara had him straddled in a split second. She drew back her hand, her stunning face a mask of animal rage. Sinister black flames crackled in her palm.

"No!"

He heard Jovi scream, but Rogan was already thrusting his hips high, freeing his leg and wrapping it over Inara's reptile-skinned body, wrenching her off of him. Her black fireball shot wide, and as Rogan gained the top position, he reached for her head, ready to twist it right off her pearly neck.

An explosion blasted them apart.

Rogan cursed as he flew across the room, bashing into something bony and soft before rolling swiftly to his feet.

Behind him, the Magistrate scrambled to sit up. "You!" His hair was tangled, wet with sweat, and sticking to the wrong side of his head. "You ruined *everything*!" His eyes were manic, wild, and unhinged, unlike Rogan had never seen.

There was a lot about the man that Rogan had never seen.

He spun back toward Inara and felt a stab of terror. She rose from the rubble in a swirling cloud of smoke, crimson hair floating away from her body as if blown by an invisible wind. Black flames coiled around her body, flickering, growing, alive, propelling her toward Jovi like a billowing black wave. She stretched a hand toward her, teeth bared.

She was too far for a throwing knife. Too powerful for a stunner. His phaser lay halfway across the room. Rogan grabbed the Model B from his belt, flicked off the safety, and fired straight at the bitch's black heart.

She turned at the last second. The blast of pure white light hit her in the shoulder, spinning her off balance.

Holy Light. The Model B's single remaining shot was Holy Light.

Dad really had been fighting demons.

Inara focused those inky eyes on Rogan. "Enough." Her voice rang over the noise of the battle, deep and resonant and filled with enough power to drop a man to his knees.

But Rogan wasn't an average man. He looked that cunt right in the eye and sprinted straight for her.

Her power was the kind of thing a human like him could only dream of. He had no magic, no claws, no weapons…and he didn't give a shit. She had threatened his woman, and she was going fucking down.

He poured every ounce of himself into it, felt every contraction of his muscles, every beat of his heart, every pump of air in his lungs, and he knew without a shred of doubt that he was going to take her out.

A flash of light hit him like a solid wall. Rogan skidded to a halt, throwing up his arms, blinking into the blinding white. Fuck. Where was she? *Fuck!*

The light vanished, sucked abruptly into a single point in the center of the ruined room. In its place, standing directly beneath the gaping hole in the ceiling, stood an enormous figure.

Tall, muscled, with rippling black hair that skimmed the waist of his massive trenchcoat, the man surveyed the room with slanted crystal blue eyes.

Those eyes landed on Inara, and the flash of rage on his hard, beautiful face was terrifying. He descended the pile of rubble in huge, shuddering steps. From beneath his black coat, he unsheathed a mammoth sword.

"You." His voice rumbled, echoing off the walls.

Inara's lips curved. "How the mighty fall, indeed."

The man raised his weapon, lengthening his massive strides toward her. His face twisted.

Another flash of blinding light. Then another. And another. One by one, the archangels appeared, enormous and radiant, towering over the destruction. One of them sucked in a breath when they saw the trenchcoated angel. "Alistor."

Rage flickered in Inara's black eyes. "I see you haven't forgotten *him*," she hissed, and drew her arms wide. A cloud of oily black smoke swirled around her feet, traveling rapidly up her body, enveloping her in seconds.

She was getting away.

As Rogan pelted toward her, Alistor launched his enormous sword through the air.

The blade sliced into Inara's shoulder and stuck. Her eyes widened, her scream tore through the room, and she and the sword vanished in a whirling black haze.

Son of a bitch. He'd had her. He'd fucking *had* her.

The fight was dwindling. Killian and Wolf melted back into human form as Cyrus smashed a ceiling beam into a final group of hostiles. The Light House mages were all in their own skins again, emerging from their shield in the corner, bewildered and disheveled, but alive.

A flash of pink caught his eye. Jovi was darting toward the row of holding tanks. She shouldered an archangel aside, ruffling his immaculate robes as she headed straight for the remnants of an exploded tank and the naked woman who lay motionless beside it.

No. Not Juno.

Rogan sprinted over. Killian was already on his knees, cradling Juno's head in his lap. The shock must've jolted her back into human form. Jovi skidded to a stop, spraying water, and knelt beside them. Killian bared his teeth.

"Let her," Rogan snapped.

Jovi laid her palms on Juno's chest and closed her eyes.
She'll heal her. Jovi will heal her. She'll be all right…

"Kill her," the Magistrate croaked. He was braced against the exit door, clutching his bleeding arm. He pointed at Jovi.

"You will not," Alistor thundered. The walls trembled, raining a smattering of dust.

The other angels stared at him in shock and wonder, sorrow and disbelief. The Archangel Michael stepped forward. "My brother..."

Alistor ignored him. He approached Jovi slowly while the rest of the room watched with bated breath. As he drew closer, Rogan planted himself in front of her, ready to face off with an enormous fallen angel if he had to. He might be Jovi's father, but he might also be an unhinged psychopath. He'd just thrown a sword at someone, and his fists looked like they could hammer through a brick wall. Rogan scanned his towering form for more weapons, but couldn't see anything beneath that trenchcoat.

Alistor peered around him. "She heals," he murmured.

Rogan glanced over his shoulder. Juno's toned torso was glowing with that pure, warm light, and Jovi was lit up like a faebug. Juno stirred, her head twitching on Killian's lap. Dark eyes blinked open, staring up into Killian's face.

Killian's huge shoulders shuddered as he sucked in a breath. He eased Juno's head to the floor and burst to his feet, stalking away with flexing fingers.

Rogan turned back to the fallen angel, relief nearly making him sag. "She does."

"She is a *demon*!" The Magistrate screamed from across the room. He looked around like he was hoping to find someone with a shred of sense. "She's the daughter of that *thing* that nearly killed us all!" He flung a hand across his ruined lab.

Alistor turned, leveling his gaze at the Magistrate. "She is the daughter of an archangel."

Magistrate Thackeray White went pale.

"I may have Fallen, but my sins are not hers."

A small hand slipped into Rogan's. He looked down. An

exhausted Jovi stood at his side, dust-covered and barefoot, splattered with black blood and streaked with soot. She took in Alistor's face, his hair. "I'm yours?" she whispered.

Alistor gazed down at her with eyes that matched her own. "Apparently, you are."

They stared at each other for a long, breathless moment. Then, Jovi frowned. "How am I so short?"

CHAPTER 59

They left through the back stairwells.

They had safe passage. The archangels had ordered that no harm should come to any of them. The fury on the Magistrate's face would no doubt keep him up at night, but Rogan knew the man would never disobey a direct command from ARC.

Somehow, by some miracle, they were free.

The streets buzzed with activity. Cars whirred, cyber bikes glided by, street vendors set up for the evening rush. Pedestrians cast curious glances at their battered group—Rogan, Jovi, the Light House mages, and an edgy Alistor—as they stood squinting on the pavement.

He pulled Jovi tight against him. It was done. She was out. She was with him, and had maybe even started to forgive him. The rest of his world had just crumbled at his feet, but she was here. The feeling of her small body leaning against him for support made him feel a thousand feet tall. He dug the last sugar straw out of his pocket, tore the wrapper with his teeth, and handed it over. Her answering smile made his pulse stutter.

"Are you going to tell us what the hell just happened in there?" Theo said.

He glanced at her over the top of Jovi's head, nodding once. "We need a place to stay."

Her silver eyes narrowed. Theo's hair was a mess, a purple bruise had begun to spread over one cheekbone, and she was missing a shoe. Somehow, she still managed to look intimidating. "Fine. We could use a school nurse." She lifted a brow at Jovi.

Rogan nearly choked, trying to imagine Jovi mopping up tears and mending scraped knees. They'd have to find something else for her—

"Sure, I'll patch the little shits up."

The other mages chuckled, but Theo was watching Rogan. "I think it's time we added a tech-ed class, too."

Rogan nodded, unable to speak. He would have a purpose. He and Jovi would have a place.

Alistor stared down at Jovi. "I will find you there, daughter."

"Wait, I—"

But, with a flash of light, he was gone.

Jovi's shoulders slumped, and Rogan gave her a squeeze. "You'll see him soon." And if the bastard didn't show, he'd track him down himself.

"Got room for a few more?"

Emerging from the back stairwell, bleeding and coated in dust, was the rest of the DE field squad. Wolf, Killian, and Juno were dressed in spare sweats from the locker rooms. Juno was pale, but she walked under her own steam. Each had a duffle looped over their shoulder.

Juno was the first to speak. "We fucked up." Her voice was rough. She reached into her duffle, pulled out a pair of small black combat boots, and handed them wordlessly to Jovi, who took them warily. "I'm sorry."

You know I would never have taken you out. At the familiar voice in his head, Rogan found Cyrus's eyes. They were wet. *I'm sorry. I was a total fucking chicken shit. You're my brother. I'm sorry.*

The lump in Rogan's throat was too damn big to swallow. *I'm sorry, too.*

Killian looked Jovi dead in the eye. "I don't give a fuck what you are or where you came from. You've proven you're squad, as far as I'm concerned." His gaze shifted to Rogan, and there was something wild and pained in the yellow depths. "I'm sorry I didn't stick by you." The words were so rough they were hardly audible.

"We're all sorry." Deep grooves bracketed Cyrus's mouth, and a fierce line appeared between his brows. Self-loathing practically radiated off of him. "To you, too, Jovi."

There was a long, strained silence while Jovi stared at the people who had shackled her, interrogated her, done God knows what to her…

"It's cool. You all hit like little bitches, anyway."

Blinks of surprise, chuffs of laughter, and reluctant grins bounced around the gathered group. Jovi squeezed Rogan's hand.

He'd forgotten how it felt to have his heart beat fully. "Are you all saying you're done?"

"With that guy?" Wolf jerked a thumb over his shoulder. "Hell, yeah. The Magistrate's lost his goddamn mind. You should've seen how ballistic he went after ARC let you leave." His eyes met Rogan's, all traces of humor gone. "I do a lot of stupid shit, but I'd never…" He shook his head. "I didn't sign up for that. You're Pack."

There went his throat, getting all tight again.

"But," Wolf added, "Your boy needs a job, and I'm too dumb to do anything but fight." He glanced around at the Light House mages. "You guys need some muscle? Tradesies for room and board?" He snapped his fingers. "I know, we'll bring a great cook. She makes *insane* cinnamon rolls."

The others chuckled, but Theo frowned. "Is this going to cause problems with him?" She jerked her chin toward headquarters, where the Magistrate undoubtedly stood in the rubble of his ruined lab.

Rogan met her eye and nodded, utterly serious.

Theo sighed deeply. "Fine."

CHAPTER 60

Jovi groaned, rolling beneath the sheets. The sound of laughter and little feet running down the hallway drifted through the door. Did those damn kids always get up so early?

She rolled again and found herself staring into a pair of gorgeous sea glass green eyes. Rogan lay on his side, a sexy slab of muscly man lounging like a bronze god in their bed.

Their bed. In their little place. Where they lived together.

They'd moved in yesterday. The Light House had a bunch of vacant rooms, and they'd given one to each member of the squad. Rogan and Jovi got one of the big ones at the end of the hall.

The squad. She was one of them. They'd said so.

Jovi grinned at Rogan, trailing a finger down his sculpted chest. His eyes twinkled. She knew for a fact that they didn't do that for anyone else. "How can you be all twinkly at this hour?"

He smiled, eased up to her, and kissed her, hot and slow.

Later, after she'd had her wicked, wicked way with him, they showered together, and she tried not to get distracted by the soap bubbles running down his naked body.

"I'm taking Daddio to a Sip n' Spell today." She snorted at the idea of huge, fierce Alistor glowering in line for a sugary coffee drink. She could hardly wait.

She still couldn't believe Nora found him. The whole time Jovi had been running around getting chased by Slavs and pissing off shapeshifters and falling for a demon hunter, her roommate had been following up on the lead on her dad.

When she found him, she pointed him toward the GPS location of Jovi's trackband, which was still in the pocket of Rogan's tacticals when he came to rescue her.

It had taken some convincing, but Alistor had moved into Light House with the rest of them. They were getting to know each other, and she was showing him how to *really* do the midrealm. He'd lived here way longer than her, but the guy was seriously sheltered, and even stuffier than Rogan. She was going to have a blast corrupting him. Last night, she and Wolf had taken him to the Wicked Wench for his first-ever drink. He'd been hit on by men and women of every race, and blushed like a schoolgirl every time.

Rogan eased closer and took her face in his hands, gazing at her intently while water trickled down his freckled nose. "Are you sure you don't need me to come with you?"

He'd made it clear that he didn't like the idea of her going out in public so soon. The Magistrate was pissed, the Slavs might still be looking for her, and although she was probably in rough shape from getting a sword stuck in her shoulder, Mommy Dearest could pop up at any time. Still, Jovi had set Rogan straight the first night in their new place. She wasn't an inmate, she had flamethrowers built into her hands, and she doubted anyone would mess with her when she was flanked by a giant guy in a trenchcoat and a crazy-eyed shifter.

She didn't escape hell to live in fear for the rest of her life.

Plus, she'd told Rogan if he was a good boy and didn't go

all prison warden on her, she just might give him a screaming hot blow job every night.

So far, it had worked.

She shook her head. "I can handle the Sip n' Spell, babe."

"Do you *want* me to come with you?"

Her heart melted, but she shook her head again.

His eyes bored into hers. "Will you bring me a triple espresso with a double shot of luck?"

Jovi bit back a laugh, nodding solemnly. Happiness bubbled up inside her.

Rogan planted his hands on his hips, somehow managing to look completely businesslike while totally naked. "We need to strategize when you get back."

The happy bubbles deflated. "I know. She's going to keep targeting shifters."

Wet palms cupped her face, and she suddenly found herself pinned by a burning green gaze. "And *you*, Jovi. She's going to keep targeting *you*."

Her stomach twisted, but she shrugged, looking away. "What's new?"

He tilted her chin up, forcing her to meet his eyes. "*I'm* new." When she tried to look away again, he gripped her jaw, holding her in place. "And I'm not letting anybody take you away from me again."

She blinked rapidly, caught up in the size, the strength, and the sheer intensity radiating from him as he stared down at her, hard and fierce.

"Everything was dark before you. Dark, and hard, and cold...and I was fine with that." His eyes softened ever so slightly, his gaze dropping to her mouth. "And then you came along, and you *lit me up*."

Her vision went blurry.

"And I let them take you from me." He cupped her face again. "I'm so *fucking* sorry."

Her throat ached. A tear trickled down her cheek, mixing with the steaming water. "Me, too. I'm sorry I lied to you."

His eyes blazed into hers, fingers tightening on her skull. "Never again." It was a promise.

She nodded, grabbing his face. "Never again."

He kissed her, hard and passionately, and she gave it all back to him, pouring all her fear, all her regret, all her hope into it. When they parted, he rested his forehead against hers, and she let her lids drop, breathing in the scent of him, the safety of him.

His low whisper drifted across her face. "I was *broken*, Jovi."

Her breath hitched. "Me, too." Then, because she really didn't want to go back to those memories, and *really* didn't want to start blubbering, she added wryly, "In more ways than one."

He pulled back, horror flooding his face.

Shit, shit, shit. She was trying to lighten the mood, not drag it into a pit of despair. "What I mean is…" She sniffed, slid her hands down his steely forearms to circle his wrists. "You'll have to let me handcuff *you* next time. Even things out."

It took a second. But then, there it was…a twinkle.

His eyes heated, traveling over her naked body. "You just say when."

She felt her lips curve, and he gave her a look like she was killing him, and then her back was against the shower wall and his hard body was against her and his tongue was in her mouth, silky and hot, with a desperate edge. He hitched her legs around his waist, caught her bottom lip between his teeth, and plunged inside, pumping in and out, wrenching a cry from her with every perfect stroke. Her fingers gripped his short hair, her thighs clenched his lean hips, and her core pulsed around his hard shaft, pleasure spreading like fire in her veins.

He came with a guttural grunt and a firm, final stroke, pinning her to the tile while their chests heaved against each other.

"I love you," he breathed into her neck.

She tucked her lips against his ear, eyes squeezed tight. "I love you, too." Her heart fluttered madly against her ribcage.

He pulled back, shoulders flexing from supporting her weight, and gave her a smile as radiant as the sun.

She shook her head, dazzled. "Nash fucking Rogan."

When he lowered her to the tile floor, she had to grab his arms to keep herself upright. He bent to wash her, cleaning her up, running soapy palms over her thighs while water trickled over his lickable abs.

How the hell had she landed a man like him?

Squatting at her feet after carefully washing her soles, Rogan inspected her wrinkled fingertips and peered up at the showerhead. "Jesus, they must have one hell of a water heater."

She snorted, then laughed, stupidly happy.

He winked at her—fuck, the man was hot—then drew himself up with a sigh. "We have another complication." His jaw clenched. "The Magistrate owns Light House."

Shit. She slipped her hands around his waist, blinking water from her lashes. She would never forget the look on Rogan's face when that fucker broke his heart. Even now, her blood boiled with rage, and steam thickened in the shower. She wanted to torch something, starting with the psychotic bastard who'd threatened her man.

Her man. Hers. "Are you really okay?" She'd asked the same question dozens of times since they left the ruined lab, and his answer was always the same.

He met her gaze, smiled softly at whatever he saw, and nodded. "I will be."

She stood on tiptoes to kiss him, then tilted her head to rinse conditioner from her hair. It smelled like cupcakes and had been a gift from Juno, who was obviously trying to buy her forgiveness. It was kind of working.

Each member of the squad had come to her individually, owning what they'd done, asking for forgiveness. Even John, who hadn't done any of the actual torturing, but said he had *felt the light* in her and was ashamed that he hadn't fought harder against her captivity. None of them made any excuses. Jovi understood—when your back was against it, you did what you had to do. It had been the same for her down in the pit. Plus, they kept bringing her candy and stuff.

A fingertip lifted her chin. "I mean it, though. We're going to need your help. Do you know anything about your mom's strategy?"

Her belly squirmed, but she chewed her lip and shrugged. "I can tell you how she thinks."

"Good. We'll get the squad together and talk it over. You tell us how her mind works, we'll put together a plan." Rogan nodded, satisfied.

And even with the threat of her bitch mother looming, even knowing that a big, nasty war was probably on the horizon, Jovi couldn't hold back a smile. "I point, you shoot?"

His dimples flashed, and he kissed her senseless.

ACKNOWLEDGMENTS

First of all, I have no idea where half of this book came from. I didn't set out to write about a saucy succubus and her demon-hunting man...if these guys said or did anything that totally offended you, it is NOT MY FAULT.

Thank you to my agent, Leslie Truex, for seeing something in that initial manuscript and taking a chance (and a lot of time) on an overeager author. I owe you a million candy necklaces.

Thank you to Dawn Dowdle and the entire community at Blue Ridge Literary Agency for the ongoing warmth and support for all its authors.

Thank you to Harbor Lane Books for being so incredibly kind, enthusiastic, and patient with all of my questions, ideas, and exclamations. I'm so excited to keep working with you all.

Thank you to my author heroes for inspiring me, and for showing me that it's okay to write LOTS of f-bombs (looking at you, J.R. Ward).

Thank you to the paranormal romance community for being shamelessly, unapologetically YOU.

Thank you to my friends and family for your astounding love and enthusiasm. I'm so grateful, and so blown away. Special shoutout to those who cheer me on even when you *ahem* don't really read this kind of stuff.

Thank you to my parents for always encouraging and never stifling my writing, for keeping baskets full of my scribbled stories, and for being behind me, cheering, every step of the way.

To everyone I completely ignore on my Dragon Days, thank you for being so kind and understanding about my need to guard my writing time like a ferocious beast.

And finally, thank you to my incredible husband for your unwavering confidence, for putting up with endless hours of chillout music, for plot ideas, for bringing me snacks, and for dancing in the kitchen after every milestone, no matter how small. I'm the luckiest dragon alive.

Writing is a solitary thing, but because of you all, I have never felt alone. *Thank you.*

xoxo,

Gin

ABOUT THE AUTHOR

The real world is boring. Gin prefers the realm of fantasy, where heroes smolder, heroines kick ass, magic is real, and love conquers all.

When she's not writing paranormal romance, she's usually reading it. Otherwise, you can find her singing in her retro band, Vandello, enjoying good food and cocktails, or training to be a superhero in her home gym.

She lives in the midwestern woods with her golden retriever and her husband, who has a sexy beard he's forbidden to shave.

Favorite things include: funky music, tart drinks, strong candles, and big, goofy dogs.

ABOUT THE PUBLISHER

Harbor Lane Books, LLC is a US-based independent digital publisher of commercial fiction, non-fiction, and poetry.

Connect with Harbor Lane Books on their website www.harborlanebooks.com, TikTok, Instagram, Facebook, Twitter, and Pinterest @harborlanebooks.

Milton Keynes UK
Ingram Content Group UK Ltd.
UKHW040316080224
437360UK00004B/156